BLINK

BY

CHRIS CHANDLER

Book One
of the Crystal Spire Saga

Published in Great Britain 2026
by Crystal Spire Publishing
ISBN 978-1-9194121-3-9

BLINK is the first installment in the Crystal Spire saga.
Take your first step into another world:

www.thecrystalspire.com

CHAPTER 1

There was an intruder in Pandora's room. It was well past midnight as she lay facing the window, the bedroom door out of sight behind her. The curtains were open so she could enjoy the glow that lingered above the mountains after sunset, and bask in the rays of the new dawn each morning.

Tonight there was a full moon hanging in the window like a silver lantern, casting a lustrous glow across the bed. Perhaps it was the moon that had awoken her, or some night animal flying past the window, casting a transient shadow over her face. But no, something inside the room had disturbed her. She lay very still and listened, fearful of an unseen presence standing close by. There was silence.

Of course there was no one there. The front door was locked and all the windows were securely closed. Holly was asleep, safe and sound across the hall. There were no pets in the house to prowl around in the silence that remained after the humans had retired to bed. Yet the feeling of some uninvited visitor lingered, giving Pandora a prickling feeling on the back of her neck as if someone was standing directly behind her, just out of sight.

A floorboard creaked and the moon was darkened by a figure standing over the bed. She cried out, instantly upright and reaching for the bedside lamp. A scrape and a thump as the lamp fell from the nightstand to the floor. The fallen lamp shone upwards, illuminating a young woman wearing a nightdress, with blonde curls framing her pretty face.

'Holly?' Pandora breathed a sigh of relief. 'What on earth are you doing out of bed? You gave me the fright of my life. I thought you were a burglar or something.'

Her sister did not reply. Holly had been diagnosed with nonverbal neurodevelopmental disorder at a young age, and she had never spoken a single word in the twenty-nine years of her life. She stood beside the bed, twisting her hair around her fingers anxiously. Pandora rose and placed her hands gently on her sister's shoulders. 'Come on, let's get you back to bed, shall we?'

Across the hall, Holly's room was spacious and airy, adorned with many potted plants Holly delighted in caring for, watering them with prudence and washing their leaves to keep them free from mildew and pests. Pandora led her sister by the hand, but at the door Holly halted and refused to go any further.

'What's the matter? Holly, it's the middle of the night, you should be asleep.'

Holly leaned into the room, flicked on the light, and turned her eyes up to the ceiling. Following the line of her sister's gaze, Pandora saw a fat spider crawling ponderously above the bed.

'Oh Holly, really?' There was a Kleenex box on the nightstand and she pulled out a handful of tissues. 'Y'know, I don't like spiders either. Maybe it's time you learned how to get rid of them yourself?' She held out the tissues and Holly retreated into the hall, wide-eyed with fear.

Abandoned and alone with the monster, Pandora climbed onto the bed and gathered the spider in the tissues. She misjudged her footing on the soft mattress and knocked it off the ceiling. The spider fell between the bed and the wall and disappeared.

'Dammit,' she swore softly and hopped down onto the

floor. She crouched on the carpet and lifted the fitted sheet to peer into the darkness, searching for the spider among the dust bunnies under the bed. She couldn't see anything. Regaining her feet she scanned the room, looking for nooks or crannies where the bug might be hiding in the shadows.

Holly had been terrified of spiders since she was seven years old. The family was having a picnic in Libbey Park when a spider dropped out of a tree into her hair. She panicked and tried to brush the creature away, but it ran inside her clothes and crawled all across her body. Her lifelong silence ended in an instant and she shrieked like a banshee, contorting her body like she was possessed by Pazuzu himself. Since that day Pandora had been routinely tasked with removing eight-legged invaders from the bathtub, the sink, the bedroom, even the backyard if there was an occupied web near Holly's favorite spot in the gazebo by the fish pond.

She peeked behind a pot of coral berries and kicked aside a pile of dirty laundry. The spider was nowhere to be seen. She had no intention of moving furniture around in the middle of the night, and since Holly was still hiding in the hallway she decided a small deception was called for. She opened the window, then slammed it shut.

'There we go,' she called out. 'All safe and spider-free.'

Holly reappeared, beaming with gratitude, and rewarded Pandora with a bear hug and kisses.

'Okay, okay, you're welcome. Now can we go to sleep, please?'

Holly leapt into bed and made herself elaborately comfortable, spreading her limbs to every corner of the mattress in a broad 'X' shape. Pandora went to the door and turned off the light. 'G'night, Hol. Sleep tight.'

Back in her own room, she rescued the stricken lamp from the floor and climbed into bed, letting the comforting glow of the moon lull her to sleep once more.

A loud crash woke her almost at once. Holly was screaming. Pandora leapt out of bed and dashed across the hall. Holly was standing on the bed, shaking her head violently, raking her hands through her hair. Then the room exploded.

A blinding flash burned Pandora's eyes. She cried out in pain and fell backwards into the hall. Something heavy thudded beside her head and it seemed as if the whole house was falling down around her. Then everything was silent and still.

CHAPTER 2

Pandora was blind. She stood and flailed her arms, found the doorway and stumbled inside. Her foot collided with something and she tumbled back onto the carpet. She had fallen over the nightstand, lying overturned beside the bed.

She rubbed her eyes until the dancing colors faded away. The room was in disarray. Holly was nowhere to be seen.

'Holly?' she called out and went into the hall. A vase stand lay broken beside the door. She must have knocked it over when she was thrown out of Holly's room by the explosion.

The explosion? There was no evidence of fire. The walls were not scorched, there was no smell of smoke. The blazing light that had knocked her down was accompanied by no sound and no rush of air. It was only the sudden shock which had caused her to fall and topple the vase stand. The only sound had been Holly's shrieks of terror.

She couldn't understand where her sister had gone. There were no doors except the one she was standing in. The window was still closed.

A movement caught her eye. The missing spider crawled across the carpet and under the dresser.

She crossed the hall and opened the doors to the bathroom and the studio above the garage. There was no sign of Holly. She went downstairs and searched the living room, the dining room, the kitchen. Holly was not in the house.

With growing alarm she broadened her search, returning to the kitchen and opening the connecting door to the garage. Here was the Chevrolet Blazer, a lawnmower, two bicycles, but no Holly. Another door led to the backyard. The tiny barbecue kitchen was empty. So was the gazebo where Holly sat to watch the Koi carp on lazy afternoons.

At the side of the house was a white gate. She pushed past onto the short driveway leading to the street where she halted, peering one way then the other. At this hour there was no traffic. Every house looked peaceful and undisturbed.

She clenched her fists and took a deep breath. Holly had disappeared before. She could sit for hours, unmoving, staring into space, occupied with the contents of her own mind. Then abruptly she would stand up and start walking, pacing around the house or the yard for hours at a time. When she was in one of these moods, Pandora often took her to the park where Holly enjoyed the sights and sounds of nature, reaching out to touch the trees or running barefoot through the grass. Sometimes while Pandora sat on a bench reading, Holly would wander far from her sight only to return later in the day with flowers in her hair and mud on her knees.

Once she went missing for three days. It happened at the downtown supermarket while Pandora was picking up the weekly groceries. Holly was normally content to trail around after her sister in her usual dreamy way, but on that day she was agitated and distracted. She continuously looked over her shoulder as if she feared someone was following her, flinching away from other shoppers, clutching at Pandora's hand. Pandora tried to soothe her with calming words and offers of chocolate mint ice cream, Holly's favorite luxury food. These efforts were in vain, and so she decided to ignore her sister's behavior, suspecting it might be the beginnings of a bad habit of attention-seeking. It was a decision she had regretted ever since.

When Pandora finally pushed her overloaded shopping cart to the checkout, Holly was no longer beside her. At first she was unconcerned. Holly had a strong independent streak and disliked having her younger sister fussing around her at all hours of the day. Her wanderings and meanderings had a kind of orbital velocity to them, and she always ended up back at Pandora's side eventually.

However, by the time she pushed the cart out to the Blazer and loaded the shopping into the cargo area, Holly had still not returned. Pandora was annoyed.

After waiting five minutes she returned to the supermarket and stalked up and down every aisle, mentally rehearsing the angry words she would share with Holly when she found her. Half an hour later she started calling friends. An hour after that she called the police. It was the beginning of a nightmare that did not end for seventy-six hours.

As a vulnerable person, Holly's disappearance was treated with greater urgency than an ordinary missing person's case. Ojai Valley Police Station was commanded by Chief Geoff Brooks, a gray-haired former Marine and an old family friend. He immediately organized an official search, but assured Pandora that Holly had probably just wandered off and gotten lost. Despite these reassurances, Pandora was unable to stop her imagination cycling through endless blood-curdling scenarios in which Holly had been abducted, raped, and murdered. Her sister was a sweet and trusting soul who would have no reason to suspect strangers with bad intentions.

Word quickly spread around the small town of Ojai, where Holly was popular and well-known by many residents By early evening, missing posters were on every lamp post and volunteer groups were patrolling the streets.

By nightfall on the first day, search parties had combed the valley as far as Lake Casitas in the west and Santa Paula Peak in the east. An AMBER Alert was activated across the state of California, notifying law-enforcement agencies and media broadcasters of the potential abduction of a young woman with mental disabilities.

On the second day of the search, Chief Brooks visited the sisters' house on Edgewood Avenue and admitted that ninety percent of missing persons' cases involving disabled individuals were solved within twelve hours unless foul play was involved. He made a television address later that day, imploring anyone who might have seen Holly to call a special phone number which had been set up just for this investigation.

The third day dawned with no clues. The hotline number remained quiet, with only a handful of calls quickly dismissed as false alarms. Pandora was confined to the house by friends and neighbors who were concerned about her ceaseless participation in searches, accompanying community groups on patrol, or endlessly driving around the streets alone throughout the night. She had not slept in two days and Ojai's general practitioner, Doctor Carla Andrews, arrived at the house with a sedative.

The following morning she awoke feeling like the familiar world had been snatched away during the night and replaced with a sinister simulacrum where every object was imbued with secret menace and evil intent. Hope had abandoned her during the night. For hours she sat on the floor of the shower and wept uncontrollably.

Then the news came. Pandora had managed to drag herself into the kitchen in her bathrobe when the doorbell rang. Through the frosted glass she saw a figure in the uniform of the Ventura County Sheriff's Department, and at once she knew the worst had happened. Holly's body had been found, tortured and ravaged in some godforsaken ravine. With dread in her heart, she answered the door to Patrol Deputy Teri Martinez, who had been her friend since childhood when Pandora's father had been Chief of Police and Teri's father had been his lieutenant. Teri had her thumbs tucked casually into her utility belt and a broad grin across her face.

'Get dressed, hon,' Teri said. 'We found her.'

An elderly dog walker named Joel Murphy had been exercising his Golden Retriever in Libbey Park when he lost track of the animal for a few moments. When he rounded a bend, he found the dog playing fetch with a young woman he recognized from the missing posters all around town. He called the police straight away from his cell phone.

At the station, Pandora wept with relief when Doc Andrews told her she had examined Holly and found no evidence of physical or sexual abuse. Chief Brooks said his deputies were interviewing people in the vicinity of Libbey Park, but so far they had no leads.

Teri took the sisters home. As soon as she was back in familiar surroundings Holly resumed her normal routine. She was hungry and devoured all the sandwiches that had been left in the fridge by a well-meaning neighbor. She found a frozen chicken risotto and blasted it in the microwave before eating it with a fork straight from the Tupperware tub.

While Holly ate, Pandora attempted to communicate with her. On the sideboard in the living room was a set of small ceramic figurines that had been collected by their mother, Sandra. She swept up a handful of figures and a street map of Ojai. Back in the kitchen, she spread the map on the table and placed a miniature rabbit on the supermarket.

'Holly, pretend the rabbit is you, okay? Where did you go when you left the supermarket?'

Holly glanced at the map with disinterest.

She placed a figurine of a wolf beside the rabbit. 'Did someone talk to you? Was there someone outside?'

No response. There was a figurine of Mickey Mouse driving an open-top car and Pandora placed it on the street. 'Did you get in a car with someone? Can you show me where you went?'

Holly wiped the inside of the box with her finger and

licked it clean. She returned to the fridge and retrieved a chocolate cake Teri had left there the day before in the hopes of tempting Pandora's sweet tooth.

Frustrated, Pandora went back to the sideboard and found a sketchpad and a pencil. She cleared away the figurines and laid the pad before Holly. 'Can you draw what happened to you?'

Holly eagerly grasped the pencil and began to draw. Moments later she tore off the top sheet and pushed it across the table. She had drawn a smiley face and a heart.

Holly was never able to tell the story of what happened to her during the seventy-six hours of her absence, but she seemed none the worse for her experience. For Pandora, however, it remained the most traumatic incident in her life. Now, as she stood in her nightshirt on the darkened street, all the nightmarish visions of those terrible days returned to her mind.

She considered her options quickly. Teri's house was nearby, but she had no idea if her friend was at home or out on patrol. Either way, it would be quicker to call the police station directly. She ran back around the side of the house and re-entered through the garage. The house phone was in the hall, and on the way she double-checked the living room, the kitchen, the downstairs toilet, even the tiny coat closet beside the front door. Grabbing the phone from the hall table, she dialed the emergency number.

'911, what is your emergency?' A terse female voice.

The kitchen door opened. Holly came out carrying a glass tumbler and postcard that had been stuck to the fridge door.

'Caller, are you there?'

Pandora hung up. 'Holly? Where have you been?'

Holly held up the glass and postcard, placing one on top of the other and giving Pandora a significant look.

Pandora ignored the offering and hugged her sister

tight. 'I thought I'd lost you again. Oh God, Holly, why do you do these things to me?'

Holly patted her lightly on the back.

Back upstairs, Pandora was dispatched into the bedroom once more. This time she was successful, using the glass and the postcard to capture the errant arachnid in its lair beneath the dresser. Holly supervised the hunt closely, standing by the open window to ensure the creature was forever banished. The sisters tidied the room together. Holly righted the nightstand and made her bed. Pandora hoovered up spilled soil from the destroyed pot plants.

When all was set aright and Holly was tucked into bed, Pandora returned to her own room. For a long while she stood by the window staring out into the night. She was certain the kitchen had been empty before Holly appeared from the room. Every room had been empty. Sleepiness could not account for her confusion because every ounce of fatigue had vanished as soon as she realized Holly was gone. What on earth could have happened? She replayed the events of the night over in her mind until a headache started to develop. She glanced at her bed, but knew she could get no rest there. Instead, she returned to Holly's room and gently pulled back the covers. Holly murmured and rolled over to make room. As children, the sisters had often slept in the same bed when Holly would wake from unknown nightmares and wail wordlessly, inconsolable by their parents until her sister came to hold her and soothe her with gentle words. Now it was Pandora who needed reassurance; needed to feel the closeness of her sister so the nightmares would not return again.

CHAPTER 3

Holly was having a good day. For much of her life, Holly drifted around in a daze, unaware of people or events happening around her. The morning after her inexplicable nocturnal disappearance she was alert and responsive to her surroundings. She bustled around the kitchen, assisting Pandora with breakfast by setting the table with a clean tablecloth, bowls of cereal, a toast rack, and their mother's old teapot. In practice, the teapot was never actually used, but Holly seemed to think it wasn't really breakfast unless the cracked old pot with its faded red floral pattern was on the table. Pandora liked to have it there as well; it reminded her of simpler times when the whole family gathered here each morning to plan their days and wish each other well. It also meant Holly remembered those days, too, which gave her a warm feeling of shared memories in her heart.

After breakfast, Pandora decided to change her plans for the day. She went upstairs to her office in the spare room and made some calls, rearranging an online meeting, and informing a client they would have to wait another day for the artwork she was due to send. Pandora was a freelance digital artist, creating fantasy imagery for computer games and movies. The job allowed her to do interesting, fulfilling work while also being a full-time carer to Holly. Once or twice a month, she drove into Los Angeles to meet with clients, but the rest of the time she was free to work from home. After she tackled the calls, she completed a few admin tasks, crossed off everything in her diary and wrote *Day with Holly*.

Pandora endeavored to give Holly a variety of activities every week, but it was only every now and again she was sufficiently aware of her surroundings to fully enjoy them. As a result, her good days had to be fully taken advantage of whenever they happened.

Feeling a twinge of conscience about disappointing her clients, she decided to plan a day around vaguely work-related activities. She crossed the hall and entered the studio above the garage. Holly's studio was much bigger than Pandora's office, and far more impressive to the casual observer. Despite her disability, Holly was also a professional artist, and the studio was where she spent most of her waking hours.

Even in early childhood, Holly spent much of her time drawing and sketching. As time went by it became clear she had a rare talent, and by the age of sixteen her bedroom shelves were crowded with awards from state arts competitions. Prestigious art schools courted her as a prospective student, offering generous bursaries and scholarships if she consented to study with them. Now, as an adult, Holly was well on her way to becoming a world-renowned artist.

Pandora picked up a notepad from Holly's desk and began a tour of the studio, making a list of supplies her sister might need in the next few weeks. On an easel in front of the window was Holly's current work-in-progress. It was an oil painting of a breathtakingly beautiful woman seated on a finely carved marble throne. Pandora took a moment to appreciate the painting, wondering if the figure was a historical person or a figment of Holly's imagination. Holly loved studying art history, and every room in the house had shelves of oversize books filled with reproductions of the greatest works from antiquity to modern times. Holly's latest painting showed the influence of neo-Classical artist John William Godward, as well as contemporary fantasy artists Luis Royo and Alan Lee. There was also a more ancient influence which reminded Pandora of early Byzantine icons wrought in mosaics of gold and precious stones.

Behind the enthroned woman, arched windows looked out over a rolling countryside in autumn. On the horizon the sun was setting, casting long shadows across the domain of this unnamed queen. Pandora was impressed by how the woman's eyes looked straight out of the painting at her. Her gaze was full of warmth, compassion, and wisdom, yet there was also a certain intensity, as if Holly sought to portray a woman whose beauty and peaceful demeanor hid an iron will and a capacity for bold action. This nameless queen of a sunset kingdom was also a warrior queen, and a long spear rested against her throne.

It was a magnificent work of art. Holly had captured all the mystery and romance of the pre-Raphaelite artists and combined it with the skill of the Renaissance masters, then built on their legacy to create a modern work of classical beauty for the twenty-first century.

She dragged herself away from the unfinished painting and resumed her task. Most of the studio was a neatly organized workshop space where Holly stretched and mounted her canvases, and manufactured her own paints. It resembled a small alchemist's laboratory, with a long workbench covered in multi-colored glass bottles, pestles and mortars, beakers and jars. Holly used rare and valuable materials such as gold leaf and ground gemstones to achieve the vivid pigments she used in her art. These gave her paints a magical, shimmering quality which stunned viewers when seen in the correct light. Pandora moved along the bench, picking up bottles and pots, making notes of anything that needed to be renewed or replaced.

In the far corner stood another easel covered by a white cloth which bulged outwards as if the canvas underneath was an unusual shape. Curious what lay beneath, she lifted the cover. It was the disembodied head of a woman. Her face was twisted into an expression of hatred and madness, her skin torn by lesions, cuts, and bites. Instead of hair, a mass of snakes covered her head, squirming and reaching for Pandora's outstretched hand.

She cried out in surprise, then laughed at her own foolishness. On the easel was a bronze shield she had bought months ago at a flea market in Oak View. It was on a stall selling old movie props, and Holly had searched through boxes of swords, suits of armor, costumes, and wigs while Pandora browsed at a vintage book stall. Holly had been taken with the old shield, holding it up and watching how the light shifted across its tarnished surface. Pandora bought it, knowing that Holly sometimes liked to work in unusual mediums.

At some point in the past weeks Holly had polished the shield to a brilliant golden shine. On its surface she had painted the head of Medusa, gruesomely severed after her battle with the hero Perseus. The curved, reflective metal gave the fearful goddess's head an astonishing three-dimensional effect. Combined with Holly's prodigious skill with skin tones and shading, the monstrous head appeared entirely real.

Covering a work with a sheet was Holly's signal that she was finished and ready to move on to other projects. Pandora packed up the shield in a cardboard box, ready to be taken to the gallery where she sold Holly's work.

CHAPTER 4

They drove into town in the Blazer. The modern SUV had a special modification to its center console where Pandora had installed an ancient cassette tape player. As children, the sisters made each other mix tapes of favorite songs using their father's old dual-deck boombox, and to this day they were still Holly's preferred method of listening to music. Holly selected a medley of rock operas from the stash of tapes in the glove compartment, and happily bobbed her head and hummed along to Bat out of Hell and Time Warp.

Downtown Ojai was in the midst of preparations for one of the town's regular public festivals. A whole block of Ojai Avenue was closed to traffic while children from the local middle school painted floral patterns on the road under the supervision of their teachers. Pandora fought through the traffic chaos this activity precipitated and parked the Blazer behind Ojai Shopping Arcade. Both sides of Ojai Avenue were crowded with vendors and exhibitors erecting temporary structures. The columns of the Arcade were decorated with vintage photographs showcasing the town's growth from a pioneer settlement in the 1870s to its modern Spanish-influenced style. Workmen were busy erecting a scaffold across the street from the post office bell tower to the corner of the Arcade.

From the scaffold hung a banner reading *Happy 150th Birthday Ojai!* Mounted above was a huge sculpture of a bald eagle, produced by a local artist to celebrate the first bald eagle chicks to hatch at Lake Casitas in a hundred years. The giant bird of prey dominated the scene, with its thirty-foot wingspan swooping down towards the street, talons outstretched as if to seize a passing vehicle and carry it away to a vast eyrie in the Topatopa Mountains.

At the art supply shop, Pandora learned that her carefully curated shopping list was entirely redundant. Holly buzzed around the shop by herself, filling two baskets with brushes, rolls of canvas, colored chalks, glue, acrylics, and tins of pigment. Pandora bought a few items for herself, mostly pencils and sketch paper she used for preliminary designs.

Two doors down from the art store, the Layne Gallery was presided over by Jackie Layne, a middle-aged Englishwoman of distinguished ancestry who delighted in scandalizing the polite Ojai Valley art crowd with her broad vocabulary of foul language. Ojai had for many years been a haven for artists, and works sold in the Layne Gallery had been purchased by US presidents, European Royalty, Hollywood actors, and rock stars.

When they arrived Jackie was busy with a client and waved the sisters through to her office. Holly wandered off to look at the new paintings and sculptures on display. Pandora carried the Medusa shield into the office and spent several minutes arranging it so the natural light through the window would show Holly's skill to good effect.

When Jackie came into the room she stopped dead. 'Christ, I really think the evil bitch could freeze me in place forever.'

'Isn't it amazing?' Pandora said. 'When I found it in Holly's studio, I genuinely thought I saw the snakes moving.'

'It's spectacular.' Jackie pulled out a packet of long black cigarettes with golden tips and lit one in flagrant contravention of California's anti-smoking ordinances.

'Do you think you can find a buyer for it?'

'Darling, are you kidding? Right now there's a waiting list for Holly's paintings. I can set up an auction next week and have half a dozen buyers bidding for it.'

'That's fantastic,' Pandora said. 'Can I leave it here for you to deal with?'

'Yes, of course. But I think I'd better put it away in a store room. I'm not sure I like the idea of the gorgon staring at me while I'm working.' Holly appeared in the doorway, and Jackie beamed at her. 'Holly, sweetie, this shield is absolutely fucking terrifying. I love it.'

Holly looked alarmed. She picked up the sheet from the cardboard box and threw it over the shield, hiding it from view. She turned her back on it and retreated into the corner, as far from the shield as possible.

'What's wrong?' Jackie said. 'Was it something I said?'

Pandora shook her head in confusion. 'No, I think it's just Holly being Holly.'

Jackie took a long draw on her cigarette. 'Well anyway, I'm glad you've come in today because I want to talk to you. Have you got some time? I can treat you both to lunch.'

Behind the Arcade was a cozy courtyard with tables and chairs set under the shade of palms and ferns, and a fountain to cool the air. They took seats outside an Italian restaurant and chatted about inconsequential matters while they waited for their pizzas to arrive. Jackie was clearly poised to break big news, and when the pizzas came Pandora couldn't wait any longer.

'So what's this all about, Jackie? You look like you're fit to explode.'

Jackie's eyes sparkled. 'Am I that transparent? Alright, well, guess who I had in the gallery yesterday afternoon? No, don't actually guess, I was being rhetorical. It was Dominic Paris from the Metropolitan Museum of Art.'

'Wow, the biggest art museum in America. So was he buying or selling?'

'Neither. He's in California for a conference in LA, but

he popped into the gallery because he's heard I have some interesting pieces he's not likely to find elsewhere. We got to chatting and he's very interested in Holly's work.'

'He's heard of Holly?' Pandora almost spat out her pizza.

'He certainly has. Actually, he'll be one of the potential buyers for the Medusa shield, but that's by-the-by. The real news is this: Dominic is curator of modern and contemporary collections at the Met, and he wants Holly to headline this year's Contemporary Arts Exhibition.'

Pandora's jaw went slack. 'You're having me on.'

'Scout's honor,' Jackie made the three-finger salute. 'A one-month exhibition in New York at the end of summer, with a written feature in the Met guide, a reception dinner with all the big-wigs, and interviews with Art in America and Rolling Stone. There's no TV spots in the offing yet, but you can bet your life someone will be interested in the disabled-girl-makes-good angle. Actually, I'm going to invite along a chap who's done some tasteful stuff for the Discovery Channel. Well, what do you think?'

Pandora stared at the fountain while she imagined Holly's work on display in America's most prestigious gallery. She glanced towards Holly, who had retreated into herself once more and was busy picking slices of jalapeno off her pizza and popping them into her mouth, completely oblivious to the monumental offer she had just been given.

'We can't do it,' Pandora said.

Jackie gaped at her. 'You're turning him down? Christ on a bike, Pandora, this is a once-in-a-lifetime opportunity. If you say no now, you'll never see another offer like it. This is Holly's chance at the big-time. For years she's been on the brink of international success, and this exhibition will give her the exposure she needs to really make a name for herself.'

'Exactly. That's why we can't do it. Interviews with Rolling Stone? Holly can't even nod her head to indicate she agrees. How the hell is she supposed to give interviews?'

Jackie scoffed. 'Don't be obtuse. You'd be her voice, obviously. You've given interviews on Holly's behalf a dozen times.'

'Three times, Jackie. Once for the local newspaper, once for a church magazine, and once for the newsletter of Holly's craft club at the community center. You're talking about interviews for international publications and TV documentaries. Jackie, it's not that I don't appreciate the offer, I really do. But I can't inflict fame on Holly. She has no mechanisms to cope with the changes that would make to her life. She'd become a spectacle. A freak show.'

'But you'd be there with her, and so would I,' Jackie said. 'We'd manage how she's portrayed in the media, and we'd protect her from anyone who tried to take advantage of her. And listen, I don't want to sound mercenary, but there will be a lot of buyers at that exhibition. People with real money. This is really a life-changing opportunity, do you realize that?'

Pandora shook her head. 'Holly just wants to paint because she loves it. She doesn't care about money or fame. I'm sorry, Jackie. Please thank Dominic Paris for his offer and tell him unfortunately we won't be able to do the exhibition.'

She thanked Jackie for the meal and struggled through the chaos of Ojai Avenue, narrowly avoiding a panel truck weaving carelessly through the marquees. Already she worried she had made the wrong decision. Holly's work had been growing in popularity for years, and the sales of her paintings had made a lot of money. There was a million dollars sitting in a bank account under Holly's name, which Pandora administered as her legal guardian.

On several occasions Pandora had investigated the possibility of spending some of the money to boost their standard of living. Twice she had arranged viewings of new houses where they would have space to spread out and have plenty of privacy. Each time she drove up to the house for a viewing, Holly refused to get out of the car. She sulked and pouted her lips, pulling her hand from

Pandora's grip when she tried to coax her outside. The sisters had inherited the little house on Edgewood Avenue from their parents, and Holly knew that their arrival at these large gated properties threatened an end to the only home she had ever known. Her stubborn refusal to even look at new houses was her way of telling Pandora her strong views on the topic. So that put an end to that idea. Pandora supposed she could have made an executive decision and bought a new house without Holly's approval, but that would have felt wrong. After all, it was Holly's money.

Instead, she put the money aside as an insurance policy to ensure Holly had the correct care in the event Pandora was incapacitated by illness or accident. She created a trust governed by strict rules, stipulating that Holly must be able to lead an independent life outside of an institution, and she must have access to certain art supplies, a comprehensive list of which was contained within the trust's governing document. The trust also stated that profits from Holly's work belonged to Holly alone, and that no one associated with her subsequent care should receive percentages from the sale of her art.

Now the moment Pandora had dreaded for a long time had finally arrived. Offers of true fame and fortune were manifesting, and while she was delighted that Holly's work was receiving the recognition it deserved, she also feared for her sister's future.

They entered the parking lot and the Blazer came into view. She unlocked the car but didn't open the doors.

'Holly, am I doing the right thing?' she turned to her sister and took her hands.

Holly's head drooped, and she stared at the ground.

'A free holiday in New York does sound pretty good, doesn't it?' Pandora said. 'We can hang out at the exhibition and eat all the food. If we get stressed out with all the people around we can just tell them to go to hell and leave.'

Holly tugged at her earlobe. Sometimes that was a sign

she was listening. Sometimes it wasn't.

Pandora turned back towards the gallery, guiding Holly under the scaffolding supporting the giant eagle sculpture. She planned to tell Jackie that she had changed her mind. After all, Holly was the most consistently surprising person she knew. She did not like being coddled, and she was always eager to experience new situations. If Holly had the chance to be the headline artist at America's most famous art exhibition, Pandora had no right to stop her.

The same panel truck that had almost run them over outside the restaurant reversed down the street and struck the scaffolding. The entire structure shook, and then collapsed. The eagle tilted on its side with a great groaning of tortured metal and crashed to the ground. Heavy steel supports pounded the sidewalk with a deafening clatter. Something hit Pandora on the head, hard. There was an intense blaze of light, and everything she had ever known came to an end.

CHAPTER 5

There was warm sunshine on Pandora's face, and grass beneath her cheek. She was lying in a meadow of long grass amid a chorus of grasshoppers. Dandelion seeds drifted overhead in the breeze. Her head hurt abominably. When she sat upright she felt a lump above the hairline and there were spots of blood on her fingertips.

Ojai Avenue was gone. The busy hubbub of crowds and the noise of traffic were silenced. In their place was a rolling landscape of grassy hills and thickets of trees beneath a blue sky dappled with silky clouds. In the distance, purple mountains tipped with snow clawed at the sky, but these were not the chaparral-covered slopes of the Topatopas that Pandora had known since childhood. She rose to her feet and walked unsteadily, trying to make sense of what she saw. Nearby was a copse of red oaks and tall cedars. In their midst a garrulous songbird was brightening the air with his melodious chatter. Nothing was familiar.

Then she remembered the accident. A thirty-foot-tall tower of scaffolding had collapsed directly on top of her. The throbbing pain in her head assured her this was not heaven, and the beauty of her surroundings made her doubtful of hell. She came to the conclusion that she had been knocked unconscious by the savage blow to her head, and her poor shaken brain was supplying a few minutes of pleasant imagery until normal service was resumed.

In other words, she was dreaming. And yet the sensations she felt in this verdant realm were not like those of a dream. The sunshine made her squint, and made the bump on her head pulsate all the worse. She was dizzy and her mouth was dry.

Holly was sitting in the long grass under the shade of an alder. She waved and stood up as Pandora approached.

'Holly, are you okay? Are you hurt?' She patted her sister down and found nothing more serious than mud on the butt of her jeans from where she had been sitting. Holly had apparently spent the period of Pandora's unconsciousness making a daisy chain, and arranged it carefully on her sister's head. She nodded with satisfaction as if everything was going to be alright now.

'What is this place?' Pandora said. 'I remember we got hit by the scaffolding, then everything went black. At first I thought I was dreaming, but now I'm not so sure. Everything feels so real. This lump on my head sure feels real.'

Holly took her hand and led her around a grove of gnarly old oaks. Pandora looked for familiar signs or landmarks; maybe a distant roofline peeking above the trees, a road snaking between the hills, or a wooden hiking trail post, anything to dispel the creeping sense of unease that was forming in her mind. A large conical mound came into view, like the artificial hills built by Native Americans in the Mississippi Delta. At its summit was a peculiar structure, a cylindrical white building with a domed roof. Curving stairs were cut into the slope, leading to a dark opening at the base of the tower.

She stopped and stared. This place reminded her of something, a memory from childhood, or a dream she once had but had long forgotten. It made her feel a longing for something she could not quite name, a moment glimpsed between wakefulness and sleep when time does not exist and peace and happiness are eternal. She knew this place.

'Holly, where are we? I've got a really weird feeling about this. I feel like… like we've been here before.'

Holly squeezed her hand and started forward in long striding steps. Her eagerness to reach the strange building was palpable, and Pandora's own curiosity was no less intense. By the time they reached the stairs they were almost running, and they took the steps two at a time until they reached the stone arch. The door had long since vanished, and an empty portal led to a shadowy interior. Pandora urged caution, but Holly vanished inside and she had little choice but to follow.

They entered a circular room illuminated by dusty windows. At its center was a colossal telescope, its hulking apparatus looming like a vast mechanical dinosaur. Spiral steps climbed aloft to upper platforms where, long ago, vanished astronomers had adjusted the telescope's delicate mechanism and taken meticulous measurements through its lenses.

A light caught Pandora's notice, drawing her attention across the room. While she stood gaping, Holly had crossed to the opposite side of the telescope and was arranging a plastic camping lantern on a table. Pandora delved further into the shadows and saw a kind of children's den had been jumbled together in the shelter away from the open door. Colorful silk sheets hung from overhead gantries depicting wolves, eagles, and dragons. On the walls, posters from old movies and musicals had been pasted. The Phantom of the Opera was there, mildewed and faded. The Lion King. The Rocky Horror Picture Show.

Fold-out tables and aluminum camping chairs were spread around the derelict scientific equipment. Empty Coke cans competed for space with candy wrappers on astronomical control consoles. Candles were fixed with melted wax on dusty equipment racks. A boombox stereo rested on a steel work table, an untidy pile of mix tapes beside it. A wheeled workshop trolley held a stack of board games. Pandora picked one up, wiping the dust from its top. It was Mouse Trap, and underneath it was Ticket to Ride. Beneath that was Settlers of Catan.

'We've been here before,' she murmured. 'All these games went missing from the games cabinet at home. Mom got mad because Mouse Trap didn't belong to us. She'd promised to give it back to Dana from church.'

Holly bustled around the den, tidying away the empty food packaging, picking things up, putting things down, examining each object before placing it in a new location. An unfinished game of Jenga had been abandoned on a camping table so she neatly tidied the pieces away into a box. A ukulele lay on the ground, dusty and forlorn. She adjusted the tuning until she was happy with the sound and placed it alongside a battery-powered Casio keyboard. She picked up a Polaroid camera and pointed it at Pandora.

With a *flash*, a *click,* and a *whir,* an insta-print photo emerged from the camera's film eject slot. She flapped it around in the air until it developed, and handed Pandora the resultant portrait of her slightly dazed expression.

'Oh my God, it's your camera. I'd forgotten all about it.' Once, when they were about ten and eleven, the girls had been exploring in the attic of their parents' house. Searching in boxes of old toys and junk, they had discovered their father's prehistoric Polaroid Supercolor 1000. The camera had become Holly's obsession, requiring their parents to travel far and wide to find still-surviving relics of original Polaroid film. The camera had vanished some time around Pandora's twelfth birthday. She had never thought about it again until this moment.

'How could I forget about the Polaroid? You were in love with that camera. You were a pain in the ass with that camera.'

Holly picked up a tin containing dozens of Polaroid photographs and placed it in Pandora's hands. The pictures showed two young girls playing in unfamiliar settings. Here was Pandora hanging upside down from a rope swing. Pandora swimming in a rocky pool beneath a waterfall. Holly climbing a sprawling weeping willow tree.

Holly gazing in wonder at an enormous dragonfly which had landed on her hand. Both girls smiling together in front of the old observatory, the camera remote control just barely visible in Holly's hand.

Overwhelmed, Pandora sank into a camping chair and grappled with her memories. Holly sat cross-legged on the floor and sorted through a box of old nature sketches. It was as if a long-forgotten dream had suddenly materialized all around, leaving her confused and disoriented. Once, a few years ago, she had taken Holly on a bike ride up into the Topatopa Mountains. With no particular destination in mind she had thought to herself, *Let's go up to the old observatory, like we did when we were kids.* Somehow she imagined it was just a short distance away, among the peaks above Ojai where the city lights would not obstruct the study of the heavens. As the day wore on she became increasingly uncertain about its location until finally she gave up in frustration. The mystery weighed on her mind, and that night she pored over her 1:50,000 scale hiking maps, trying to reconcile her memory with reality. Eventually, she came to the conclusion that the observatory had been a make-believe place she had dreamed of as a child, when memory and imagination were still closely intertwined.

Yet here she was now in surroundings once as familiar to her as her own home. It had been a secret place, known only to herself and Holly. A world of their own with limitless horizons. How had they got here, and how might they return? Her memories, fragmented and incomplete, gave no clues. She slid off the camping chair and sat opposite Holly, taking her sister's hands in her own.

'Holly, did you bring us here? Last night, when you ran away from the spider, I searched everywhere and I couldn't find you. It was like you'd disappeared into thin air. Or teleported somewhere else. Is this where you came?'

Holly met her gaze and Pandora studied her face, trying to interpret her silent expression. She rubbed her temples and tried to focus her thoughts. 'I remember when we were kids we used to camp out on Mr Coleman's ranch by San Antonio Creek. He was getting old so we used to help out with his citrus farm, doing the potting and pruning in the nursery. He said we were welcome to use the woods any time we liked because they were right at the bottom of our yard. We just had to hop over the fence and along the creek and we had our own little wilderness to play in. Mom and Dad never came and checked on us out there, and Mr Coleman wasn't very mobile in those days, so we had the whole place to ourselves. We took tents and sleeping bags, and made packed lunches. The thing is, I don't remember ever actually camping in those woods. We pitched the tents and scattered our stuff around, but we never actually slept there. We had a whole separate set of camping gear that we'd stashed in the woods in secret. Once we made the campsite look convincing we loaded up our hidden gear and went… somewhere else.'

She stood and made a circuit of the observatory. When she reached the open doorway she went outside and looked across the unfamiliar landscape. There were more structures out there, widely spaced and partially hidden among the groves and copses. They were ruined buildings, all of them, no more than the curve of an arch here, or the angle of a wall there. Even in desolation, almost reclaimed by nature, the ruins held a degree of elegance and beauty that made her long to know what they had looked like in their prime. She heard footsteps on the gravel and Holly joined her at the ridge's edge.

'Where is this place, Holly? How do we get back to Ojai from here? Do you click your heels, or think happy thoughts?'

Holly's big, soulful eyes looked into her own and there was a trace of a smile on her lips. She reached out and touched Pandora's hands. There was a flash of light so bright that Pandora gasped with surprise, and the world turned again.

CHAPTER 6

She screwed her eyes shut against the searing light. When she looked again the observatory was gone and they were in a parking lot outside a large white building. Traffic droned behind a row of hedges. Somewhere in the distance a car alarm blared briefly and was silenced.

'We're back in Ojai, thank God,' she said, breathing a sigh of relief. 'This looks like the hospital. Gosh, we're about a mile away from the Arcade here.'

No one had witnessed the sisters' miraculous reappearance, and for that Pandora was thankful. Her head was throbbing and she didn't feel like fielding questions from astonished bystanders. She guided Holly towards the road. On the way they passed a sign, *Emergency Department*, above a pair of sliding glass doors.

A thought struck her and she changed course, leading Holly inside. The emergency room was quiet. An elderly couple conversed in hushed tones, and a pregnant woman read a National Geographic. Apparently the accident at the Arcade had not been a mass casualty event. The receptionist – a young Black woman with the nametag Marina – looked up from a book and smiled. 'Good afternoon, how may I help you?'

'Hi,' Pandora said, but stopped short. How could she ask the question that was weighing on her mind? 'Listen, this is going to sound totally crazy, but am I a patient here?

I mean, was I brought in unconscious or anything?'

Marina pulled a keyboard towards her. 'Well, let's see, shall we? Name?'

'Pandora Castell. My sister is Holly Castell. Please check for her name as well.'

'Okaaay,' Marina's fingers went to work with great speed. 'Nobody with the surname Castell has been admitted to the hospital in the past month.'

'That's good to know. There was an accident at the Arcade earlier today. Do you know if anybody was hurt?'

More typing. 'An ambulance was dispatched, but no one was injured.' Marina frowned at the blood seeping from Pandora's hairline. 'Ma'am, are you all right? I can see you're hurt. We're pretty quiet right now. If you take a seat I can get a doctor to—'

'No, I'm okay,' Pandora interrupted. 'I don't want to trouble you. Thanks very much for your help.' Before Marina could reply she took Holly's arm and guided her outside. When they reached the street they turned left down Ojai Avenue in the direction of the Arcade.

'So we weren't taken to the hospital,' Pandora said as they walked past the school athletics field. 'That means we weren't injured. I got a bump on the head, but my vision is clear and I don't feel sleepy, so I don't think I have a concussion. That means the observatory is a real place, not just a hallucination.' She reached up and found the daisy chain in her hair. 'It was real. Somehow it was all real.' She stopped and turned Holly to face her. 'Whatever happened, you saved our lives. Thank you, Hol. You're the best.'

Holly looked sad, as if she had a million words to say but no way to express them. She kissed the bump on Pandora's head.

Ojai Arcade was closed for the evening by the time they reached it. Barriers blocked the street where the marquee tents were set up for tomorrow's festival. The scaffolding was gone, and the twisted wreckage of the eagle sculpture had been deposited at the gates of Libbey Park with red and white safety tape wrapped around it.

'We must have been in that other place for hours.' Pandora looked to the clock tower, which read a little after six pm. She pushed past the barriers and examined the sidewalk. 'Look, we were standing right here when it happened. You can see all of these slabs have been smashed. Damn, there must have been a lot of weight up there. We'd have been spaghetti sauce if you hadn't taken us away.'

Holly tried the door of the art gallery. It was locked and there was darkness behind the storefront glass.

'Everyone's gone home, Hol. Come on, let's go and fetch the car. I really don't feel up to driving, but I really don't want to walk home, either.'

By the time they arrived at the house on Edgewood Avenue, Pandora was exhausted. The dramatic events of the day had finally caught up with her. In the bathroom mirror she examined her head and was relieved to see the damage was not too bad, and the swelling was already going down. She cleaned the blood from her hair and washed the cut with antiseptic.

In the kitchen she made peanut butter and banana toasties, her standard go-to meal when she was too tired for real cooking. They ate on the couch and watched Holly's favorite tape of old Looney Tunes cartoons. When they were done, she piled up the dishes in the sink and announced she was going upstairs to lie down for an hour.

She was still asleep at midnight when Holly came upstairs and stood in the bedroom doorway. She left briefly but returned with a sketchbook and a set of artist's pencils, and spent an hour on the bedside chair sketching her sleeping sister in the half-light through the open door. When she was done, she pulled the bedsheet up to Pandora's chin and placed a teddy bear in her arms. She kissed her on the cheek and went to bed, leaving the sketch behind her on the chair.

CHAPTER 7

The next day, Holly was agitated and jumpy. She wandered fretfully from room to room, biting her nails, picking up cushions, moving furniture as if she had misplaced something. Pandora was behind on work, but in her office she found creativity came only slowly and with great effort. With her head still aching and the intermittent distraction of Holly moving restlessly around the house she was tempted to write off the day as a loss, but pretty soon her clients would become impatient with her slow progress. She slogged on, unhappy and stressed.

Some time mid-morning the doorbell rang. Out on the doorstep was a young couple, blonde-haired and blue-eyed, identically dressed in stripey t-shirts and cargo shorts.

'Hiya,' said the man.

'We're sorry to bother you,' said the woman.

'Only, our camper van has broken down,' the man thumbed over his shoulder to indicate a large motorhome. 'Do you mind if we use your phone to call a tow truck?'

'Before you ask, we forgot to pack phone chargers,' the woman held up the lifeless black slab of a smartphone. 'We were just on our way into town to buy some when the engine went and died on us.'

Pandora smiled, amused by the odd Tweedledum-Tweedledee routine of this good-looking couple. 'Sure, you can use the phone. Come on in.'

'Thanks so much,' said the woman while her companion dialed on the landline. 'My name's Sam, by the way. This is my partner, Mike.'

'Pleased to meet you,' Pandora introduced herself and Holly, who had come into the hallway to observe their visitors. 'So where are you guys from?'

'We're from Phoenix,' said Sam. 'Only three days into our vacation and already we've proved ourselves totally incompetent at the outdoors life. We spent two days in San Diego but it's so full of tourists this time of year we decided to explore Los Padres National Forest.'

'So what happened to your camper?' Pandora said.

Sam groaned. 'We've had nothing but trouble. We bought the van second-hand and we're only just discovering why it was such a bargain. On the first day the engine wouldn't start and we were an hour late leaving home. The same thing happened yesterday, and then today the engine started overheating in the traffic around LA. We hoped it would be okay once we got away from the city, but it just got worse and worse as the land got higher. Mike drove slow, but finally the engine gave up right outside your house.' She glanced towards her partner and leaned conspiratorially towards Pandora. 'Hey, listen, do you think I could use your bathroom? Another thing we forgot to pack is toilet paper.'

'By all means,' Pandora said, pointing at the stairs. 'Straight ahead when you get to the top.'

Mike hung up the phone. 'Tow truck will be here in ten minutes. Thanks so much for your help.'

'No problem. Can I get you guys some coffee or orange juice while you wait?'

'Oh, that's very kind but we don't want to impose on you any more than we already have. Hey, where did Sam go?'

'She's just upstairs using the bathroom.'

Mike smacked his forehead with the palm of his hand. 'Right, so I guess you know how unprepared we are. God, this is so embarrassing. Would you believe in our day jobs we're both lifestyle coaches? We're so used to organizing other people's lives but we can't even figure out how to take a vacation for ourselves.'

'Just think of it as all part of the experience,' Pandora said. 'I think everyone's too accustomed to package tours these days. Every detail is fixed for you by people you'll never even meet. Sometimes it's nice to make your own mistakes and have a real adventure.'

'Exactly, that's just what we wanted. You know, we packed bear repellent spray and night vision goggles, but no toilet rolls? God, we thought we were so well prepared. Ever seen that movie, Into the Wild? That'll be us by the end of next week, living off squirrel meat and potato seeds.'

Pandora laughed in sympathy, 'I'm sure you'll figure it out. Holly and I love spending time out in nature. Dealing with unexpected situations is part of the fun.'

'I'll take your word for it,' he said as Sam arrived back in the hall.

'All set?' Sam said.

'Truck's on the way,' Mike said, and turned to Pandora. 'Thanks again. We'd have been in a real fix if it hadn't been for you.'

'My pleasure. Have fun, you guys.'

After they were gone she returned to the study where her unfinished work remained obstinately on the computer screen. She tapped listlessly at the keyboard for a few minutes until she heard the sound of chains outside as the RV was hitched to the back of the tow truck. Sam spotted her watching through the window and waved they were towed away.

Pandora sank into her chair and blew out her cheeks, envying the young couple their getaway despite all their problems. Elsewhere in the house Holly was slamming doors and thudding up and down the stairs. She looked at the computer screen and saw how little she had achieved. For another hour she struggled with her work and then switched off the computer, determined to find a productive distraction that would recharge her creative batteries.

She got up and started tidying her office, clearing away old printouts and sketches, hoping that a neat working area would refresh her mind. The old canvas shoulder bag she carried everywhere was lying on the floor, its strap tangled in the wheels of her office chair. When she freed the bag the flap fell open and spilled a mass of Polaroid photographs onto the carpet.

She swore in surprise and picked up one of the pictures. It showed Pandora when she was a child of around eleven or twelve, standing in a meadow holding a rainbow-colored kite almost as big as she was, long streamers blowing in the wind. In the background a small hillock rose above the landscape, surmounted by a cylindrical white building topped with a golden dome.

Somehow the strange events of the previous day had faded from her memory. She had hardly thought of the mysterious place she had visited after the accident at the Arcade. Already she had half-convinced herself that the observatory was only a hallucination brought on by the extreme stress of the near-fatal accident. Here in her hands was concrete proof of what had happened. She must have stuffed a handful of the Polaroids into her shoulder bag and then forgotten about them. She scooped the pictures off the floor and spread them across the desk. Together they told a scrambled story of the sisters' adventures in a distant, unknown land. Judging by their changing outfits and the turning of the leaves she guessed they had visited the observatory many times over a period of at least a year.

Yet still she had no memory of the events depicted in the photographs. Every picture showed the same remote scene in or around the observatory. Sometimes the girls were toasting marshmallows over a campfire by night, or dancing to music blaring from the boombox beneath a sunny sky, or swimming in a rocky pool as clear as glass. Nothing she saw had any familiarity beyond the faces of herself and her sister.

If the observatory was a real place, where was it? Certainly it wasn't anywhere in Ojai, but if it was somewhere else in California, how had they traveled there and back so quickly after the collapse of the scaffolding? There were too many questions, and not enough clues, but she had an idea that perhaps there was a way to find some answers.

The door to the study burst open and Holly came inside. She stood with her fists on her hips, scowling in an almost comic display of bad temper.

'What's up, Hol?' Pandora looked up from the pictures. Holly hauled her out of the chair and into the hall. 'Oh, okay, just show me what the problem is.'

Holly dragged her into the bathroom and maneuvered her in front of the sink. She opened the mirrored cabinet on the wall and stood with her arms crossed, regarding her sister expectantly.

'It's the bathroom cabinet,' Pandora shrugged. 'So what?'

Holly scoffed and slammed the cabinet door hard enough to make the glass rattle. She opened it again and resumed her angry stance.

'Okay, you gotta help me out here.' Pandora peered into the cabinet and tried to intuit her sister's thoughts. The cabinet contained three shelves of ordinary, boring items like tubes of toothpaste, nail clippers, pharmaceuticals, and beauty products. There was a shelf with Pandora's personal things, a shelf with Holly's, and a third shelf with miscellaneous stuff that didn't belong anywhere else.

Pandora sorted through Holly's shelf. 'Let's see. Have you run out of that anti-frizz stuff for your hair? No, there's more than half a bottle here. Moisturizer? Plenty. Q-tips? No problems there.'

Holly grunted and elbowed Pandora aside. Using both hands she clawed every item from the cabinet so they clattered noisily into the sink. Pandora fought the urge to scold her sister. Holly's inability to communicate annoyed and irritated both of them. If they couldn't find a way to understand each other then a long and miserable day of sulking and icy looks awaited them both. She studied the mess in the sink and suddenly understood.

'Your hairbrush isn't there. You've lost your hairbrush, right?'

Holly glowered at her. She took hold of Pandora's wrist once more and pulled her from the bathroom, stomping across the hall into Pandora's bedroom. She stood her sister before the bed and pushed her down into a sitting position.

'Wow, we're really going on a journey. Are we still looking for your hairbrush? I promise I don't have it. I have my own right here, see?' She turned to the nightstand and indicated where her own hairbrush was. Except it wasn't. There was an empty space beside her alarm clock where she kept the brush. 'Well I'll be damned. Where did that get to?'

Holly smacked her hand on the bedroom wall. A family photograph swung off-kilter.

'Holly, stop that,' Pandora raised her voice at last. 'I'm trying to understand what you're telling me. Just give me a moment.' Returning her attention to the nightstand she noticed something else was also missing: A framed photograph of Pandora and Holly together on vacation in Florence at the Piazzale Michelangelo.

Realization dawned on her and she leapt up from the bed. 'That bitch. What else? What else did she take?'

Holly stormed out of the room and returned holding a plastic cup from the bathroom, the one that held the sisters' toothbrushes. She held it upside down and shook it, emphasizing its emptiness.

'What the hell?' Pandora's jaw fell open. 'Why in God's name would anyone steal our toothbrushes?'

She began a search of the house from top to bottom, her face burning red with anger. The cheerful, smiling campers had turned out to be creepy snoopers and thieves. There was no other possibility. While Mike had distracted her with polite chatter, Sam had come upstairs under the pretense of using the bathroom and raided the sisters' personal belongings. Why the hell had they done it? Were they weird sexual fetishists who lusted after private possessions coated with other people's saliva and hair? Or were they some freaky kind of cultists who required human hair and spit for their ceremonies? And what about the photograph? Would they show it to their weirdo friends and gloat about how they manipulated two innocent people who were just trying to be kind and neighborly?

There was little of great financial value in the house, and it didn't take long to establish that Sam (if that was really her name) had not stolen their mother's jewelry box from Pandora's closet, or the high-end laptop from her office. Considering the personal nature of the thefts she checked their underwear drawers and laundry baskets with care, but couldn't say for certain that anything had been taken.

After twenty minutes she was satisfied that no other areas of the house had been violated by the creepy campers. She tidied up the mess in the bathroom, and went downstairs to make coffee. Holly was in the kitchen looking unhappy, tearing pages out of an old furniture catalog, balling them up and tossing them at the trash can.

'I don't think anything else has been taken, but I can't be sure. God dammit, I'm so angry. Why did I let them in the house? You know, Teri once told me she had a boyfriend who stole her dirty underwear and tried to sell it online. Ugh.'

Holly tore another page out of the catalog and flung it across the room where it joined a small pile of fellow pages near, but not actually in, the trash.

The doorbell rang again. Pandora stalked into the hall, prepared for a confrontation if the thieving young couple had returned. Instead she saw Jackie through the frosted glass and opened the door with a smile. 'Hey, Jackie.'

'Pandora, thank God,' Jackie said, with relief evident on her face. 'Do you have any fucking clue how worried I've been about you?'

'What's wrong?' Pandora said.

'What's *wrong?* Christ, I saw the whole thing. After I got back to the gallery I started fussing around with the window display and I saw you both coming back up the street. Then that blind arsehole of a delivery driver reversed into the scaffolding and the whole bloody lot came down on top of you.'

'Jackie, oh God, I'm so sorry. Come in.'

Jackie bustled into the hall, reaching for Pandora with both hands and touching her arms and face. 'What's this cut on your head? You're hurt. What about Holly? Is she okay?'

'We're both fine,' Pandora said. 'I got a bit of a bump, that's all.'

In the kitchen, Holly was still tearing pages out of the catalog. She ignored Jackie's presence entirely while she performed a perfunctory physical examination on her. 'After the crash I ran out into the street and everyone was just standing there gawking like schoolboys at a titty show. I roused a posse to start digging you out, and then I called an ambulance. What a stupid cunt I looked like when we shifted the last pole and there was no one there. Just this.' Jackie reached into her pocket and pulled out the smashed wreckage of a mobile phone.

Pandora took it and turned it over in her hands. 'This is my phone. Holly put this Tweety Bird sticker on the back when it was new. With everything that's happened I didn't even know I'd lost it.'

'So what in the French-fried-fuck happened to you both?' Jackie said.

'Honestly? I have no idea. I remember the scaffolding collapsing, and then… and then I kinda passed out. I had a really weird dream that I haven't had since I was a kid. Not a scary dream, but a nice dream filled with cozy memories.'

Jackie poured herself a black coffee and fortified it with the contents of a hip flask inside her suit jacket. 'Well I'm glad you had a nice dream. I, on the other hand, have been going completely insane. I berated that stupid van driver for an hour while we were digging. I told him he'd spend the rest of his life in a jail cell if he'd killed you both. The poor bugger wept like a baby. He kept saying who'd look after his daughters because their mother died of leukemia last year. I felt like a right twat when we didn't find you. So what happened when you woke up?'

'I must have got a glancing blow and wandered off in a daze,' Pandora said. 'When I came to, I was with Holly outside the hospital. I spoke to the receptionist, but I felt fine so I didn't see a doctor. I planned to come and talk to you but when we got back to the Arcade everything was shut. By the time we got home I was exhausted. I fell asleep and didn't wake up until this morning. I'm so sorry I didn't call you sooner.'

'I'm just so relieved you're both okay.' A loud beeping came from inside Jackie's pocket and she pulled out her phone. 'Shit, I have to meet with a client. Oil baron, big Stetson, trophy wife from Latvia. Loves Renaissance nudes and abstract expressionism. Listen, I have to go but I want you to see a doctor, alright? Head injuries can be serious.'

Pandora nodded. 'Alright, I'll do that.'

'Meanwhile I'm going to investigate the possibility of suing the City of Ojai for allowing scaffolding to be erected in such a stupid place. I reckon that lump on your head should be worth about twenty big ones, don't you?' Jackie lifted Holly's chin with her finger and looked into her eyes. 'You watch out for your sister, you hear me?'

And then Jackie was gone, leaving behind a kind of vacuum that always remained following her energetic visits. Pandora felt awful for not sharing the truth with her, but how could she explain what had happened when she didn't know herself? Right now her mind was spinning with all the surreal revelations of the last twenty-four hours and she needed time to process her thoughts.

She returned to the study and focused her attention on the Polaroids. Gradually she was able to arrange the pictures in something like chronological order. At first both girls were small and skinny, but as time advanced Holly underwent a growth spurt and for a while she was a gangly giant towering over her sister. Then the leaves turned brown and fell to the earth, and the girls began wearing jackets and scarves when frost appeared on the ground. Eventually the landscape flowered into Spring and the girls were once more dressed in shorts and tank tops.

Then she found a picture that made her stare open-mouthed in shock. It showed the girls sitting on a log outside the observatory, much like many of the others, but this one had a third person sitting between them. He was a young boy, perhaps twelve or thirteen years old, with floppy brown hair and a New York Giants sweater. He had a freckled face and a smart-ass grin as he posed with his arms around both girls, giving Pandora rabbit ears behind her head.

She shot up from the desk and dashed downstairs into the kitchen. Holly was still at the table, eating candies amid the ruins of the old catalog.

'Who is this?' she said, pushing the picture in front of Holly's nose. 'I know his face. Do you recognize him?'

To Pandora's amazement Holly smiled broadly and clapped her hands twice, a rare sign of approval. She plucked the picture from Pandora's hands and stuck it to the fridge with a Bugs Bunny magnet.

'So you do recognize him? Dammit, why can't I remember?'

Realizing the futility of interrogating Holly further, she went upstairs and opened the hatch into the attic. The roof space was large and filled with many memories, but she knew where to find what she was looking for. After a few minutes' rummaging she found two sealed cardboard boxes and carried them downstairs, balanced precariously on top of each other. In the study she cleared off a long table she used for art layouts and placed the boxes side by side.

One of them was labeled with a luggage tag marked in her mother Sandra's elegant script. *Holly's Picture*

Journals. Using a box cutter from her desk, she unsealed the box and withdrew a stack of leather-bound journals. Sandra had annotated each volume with a Post-It on the cover which described the contents. She selected *Adventures and Fun, 11 – 12 Years Old*, and opened it on the table.

Holly's journals were spectacularly beautiful, each page filled to the edges with vivid, colorful depictions of her life and thoughts. They were also extremely difficult to interpret. Not only did they contain no writing, but the entries were rarely on sequential pages. Sometimes Holly would draw at the beginning of the journal, sometimes in the middle, and sometimes at the end. Each page was a study in a different art style, and covered a wide range of subjects from family days out and life events through to abstract inner feelings and moods or dream-like images. As Pandora turned the pages she saw a family trip to the Los Angeles Zoo depicted in a Cubist style, showing animals and people constructed from colorful triangles, semi-circles and diamonds. On the next page was a day out in Malibu in the form of a comic strip. Turning over again she saw a surrealist painting of her own tenth birthday party. The cake was made from layers of earth, air, fire and water, each layer crawling with dozens of elemental spirits. The family and friends gathered for the party were depicted as anthropomorphic farmyard animals playing orchestral instruments. Pandora consumed a slice of cake by opening a slot in the top of her head and tipping it inside.

These were the highlights of a book that was otherwise incomprehensible. How was Pandora to interpret the ocean scene, rendered across two pages in a dozen shades of blue and green, in the midst of which sailed a tiny, solitary boat with a single occupant? The lonely sailor, a pale-faced, curly-blonde-haired girl wearing a bright yellow raincoat, steered her frail craft carefully between the steep-sided waves, but there was no land in sight where she might find safe harbor. Or what about the disturbing fairground scene? In this oil painting, dozens of people from all walks of life smiled and laughed, enjoying the games and rides. A curly-haired girl stood alone in the foreground apart from the others. She had cut off her own head with a carving knife and held the disembodied head out towards the viewer. Her eyes were wide with horror and her mouth gaped unnaturally into a grim and silent scream. Hardly *adventures and fun*.

Pandora closed the journal and turned to the second box. This one was marked with bold letters in black Sharpie: PANDORA'S STUFF – PRIVATE DO NOT OPEN. Inside was an assortment of Wiro-bound notebooks, school composition books, steno pads, and loose-leaf binders, each labeled by year and packed to overflowing with a frenetic mixture of diary entries in multi-colored inks, collages, sketches, and loose pages pasted in between other pages. She was surprised that it did not take long to find exactly what she was looking for, and she was astonished at the story the pages told in her own writing about that strange and lonely place she had visited with Holly the day before.

CHAPTER 8

The memories came back slowly, and sometimes painfully. In the baking hot summer of Pandora's eleventh year, Ojai Valley was eight years into a long drought. The sisters spent the balmy days of the summer vacation cycling the extensive trails that criss-crossed Ventura County. Despite Holly's silence, Pandora was never bored with her sister, and she enjoyed the time they spent adventuring in the creeks and forests of Southern California. She spoke enough for both of them, talking to Holly as if she valued her sister's thoughts and views, bouncing ideas off her in long one-sided conversations that lasted days on end.

Pandora had other friends she saw during school time, but most of them were away on family vacations while the sisters' parents remained at work in the police station. There was an unspoken agreement within the family that Holly was Pandora's responsibility while their parents were at work. Ojai was an expensive town to live in, and without her help and support, their parents would be obliged to hire carers to look after Holly, in addition to the small fortune they were spending to send Holly to an expensive private school.

As a result the girls were well-accustomed to entertaining themselves for days. On the north side of town was a winding trail that rose high into the hills and gave a great view across the valley. It was a favorite destination of Holly's and she often led their bike rides in that direction whenever she was in the lead. The trail ran through a failed housing development from the 1960s, where a dozen trailer homes had been built on one-acre plots and then gradually abandoned to be slowly reclaimed by the hillside scrubland. On the day they met Jason Bowman, Holly was in the lead as they cycled along the trail where it crossed a crumbling tarmac road. She stopped at the intersection and peered curiously towards one of the run-down double-wide trailers. When Pandora caught up, she followed her sister's gaze. The chain link fence around the house had been partly removed, and a car was parked outside in the overgrown yard; an elderly Ford Country Squire with Arkansas plates.

'Is someone living there? I didn't think these houses had any power or water.' She tapped Holly's shoulder to get her attention. 'Let's put the bikes out of sight. I want to take a closer look.'

They retreated back down the trail and hid the bikes behind a row of bushes where they would be concealed from casual attention. They approached the house from behind, sneaking through the fence and crouching low between the wild growth of sagebrush and lilac.

Pandora's curiosity stemmed from a warning their father had given them a year ago, when a fire in the hills had been traced to another trailer at the far end of the valley. Drug dealers had constructed a meth lab inside the abandoned home, where their activities were unlikely to attract attention. Late one night the volatile chemicals exploded, destroying the house and killing two of the amateur chemists within. The blaze caused a wildfire which raged across the valley for two days. Many houses on the outskirts of Ojai were evacuated and the girls spent a sleepless night on the floor of the school gymnasium, wondering if their home would still be there the following morning.

Their father had spoken to them at dinner the next day

when they were allowed to return home. He was dirty and smelled of smoke after remaining on duty for forty-eight hours helping the Ventura County Fire Department extinguish the blaze. He told them that although Ojai was a friendly town and a safe place to grow up, drugs were a growing problem despite the best efforts of the police department. Knowing his daughters' penchant for expeditions to remote parts of the valley, he admonished the girls to be careful around the empty trailers and to report back to him if they saw any suspicious activity in the hills.

The trailer was mounted on squat concrete pillars. Pandora found an old fruit crate and placed it against one of the concrete stacks supporting the rear wall, then climbed up to peek through the window.

The glass was dirty and spotted with mildew. In the gloom, all she could see were shadowy heaps of old furniture. An inner door opened, filling the room with murky light. She ducked out of sight as a woman dragged a beat-up chest of drawers across the floor and out of the room.

She leapt off the crate and hissed. 'Quick, get round the side of the house.' They darted around the corner and were barely out of sight when the back door opened and the woman hauled the dresser outside into the yard. She had a thin face and short dyed-blonde hair that stuck out in all directions. Her clothes were baggy and ill-fitting as if she had recently lost a lot of weight. She might once have been pretty, but whatever events in her life had brought her to this sagging wooden trailer had taken their toll, and now her forehead was scored with worry lines and her eyes were ringed with dark circles. The haggard woman pulled the drawers across the dusty ground until she reached a stack of scrap wood. Picking up a claw hammer she began pulling the chest apart, throwing the remains onto the growing pile.

'Looks like she's clearing the place out,' Pandora whispered. 'Come on, I want to look in the front windows as well.'

They crept around the front of the house and positioned the crate beneath the living room window. Peeking inside, they saw a room which had been cleared of rubbish and recently painted. The room was sparsely furnished with two camp beds, two suitcases, and an open sports bag filled with packets of dry pasta and rice.

'People have moved in. Let's take a look in one more room.'

They moved the crate under the next window. A young boy of perhaps twelve years was standing on a stepladder, wearing overalls and painting the walls with a roller.

There was a flash of light and a mechanical whirring sound. Holly had lifted her Polaroid camera up to the glass and taken a photograph of the boy at work.

The boy spun around and spotted the girls at the window. He leapt down from the ladder and picked up a rifle leaning against the wall.

'Dammit Holly, what did you do that for?' Pandora grabbed Holly's hand and pulled her away from the window. They dashed towards the bushes where their bikes were hidden, but the boy appeared at the front door and brandished the rifle at them.

'Hey, who the hell are you?' he shouted, his index finger hovering over the trigger.

Pandora pushed Holly behind her, shielding her body with her own. 'We're sorry, we didn't think anyone was living here.'

The boy scanned the front yard as if searching for more people. He sighed and lowered the gun. 'No, I'm sorry. I didn't mean to scare you.'

'We weren't scared,' she lied. 'Do you always point guns at visitors?'

The boy looked at the gun sheepishly, and put it out of sight behind the door. 'I saw someone at the window and I thought it might be my dad.'

Pandora screwed up her face in confusion. 'That doesn't make any sense. Why would you point a gun at your dad?'

'If he ever turns up here, I'll blow his head off.'

Unhappy with the direction the conversation was taking, she abandoned that line of questioning and started again. 'My name's Pandora. This is my sister Holly. She doesn't talk, but she's friendly.'

'I'm Jason. I just moved here with my mom. Why doesn't your sister talk? Is she retarded?'

Pandora bristled. 'Holly is not retarded. Are you retarded? You're the one waving guns around at innocent people.'

'Hey, I said I was sorry about that. And anyway, you were snooping around our house. I wouldn't call that innocent.'

She looked around at the overgrown yard, the dilapidated station wagon, the rusting mailbox peppered with bullet holes. 'I didn't think anyone had lived in these houses for years.'

'Yeah, well, we're fixing the place up,' he said, somewhat defensively.

Pandora could not think of a delicate way to frame the question she most wanted answered, so she just came out with it. 'You're not making crystal meth in there, are you? My dad's the Chief of Police around here, so if you are you have to tell me the truth.'

The boy sneered. 'You've looked in through our windows, what do you think?'

A female voice came from out back. 'Jason? Who are you talking to out there?'

'No one, Mom. Just some kids.' He turned back to the sisters and spoke *sotto voce*. 'You guys have to leave. My mom likes snoopers even less than I do.'

'Okay, we'll go,' Pandora responded in kind, then some intuition made her add, 'Can we come back to visit sometime?'

The boy stared at her as if this was the strangest idea he had ever heard. A crash of furniture came from inside the house, accompanied by a cry of frustration. 'I gotta go,' the boy said, and vanished inside.

The sisters walked away towards their bikes, but when Pandora glanced backwards she saw Jason watching them through the window.

Over dinner that evening, Pandora recounted the meeting to her parents. Their father, David, quizzed her about what they had seen. He said there were certain household items, innocent and innocuous by themselves, but when found in combination were indicative of methamphetamine production. He asked if they had seen any big cooking vessels, ice chests, funnels, buckets and pails, propane cylinders, rubber tubing or laboratory beakers and glassware. Pandora shook her head vigorously, and he looked satisfied with her reply.

The following day, David made a visit to the house as a social call. He later told the girls he met a woman who said her name was Wendy. She claimed to have inherited the trailer from an uncle and was in the process of restoring it for sale. If there was a boy in the house, David never saw him. After his visit he did a little research at the station. The land on which the trailer stood had once been owned by a Mr Leonard Bristow, who had died intestate in 1989, whereafter ownership reverted to Ventura County. No more changes of ownership had been registered, and no utilities had been connected to the house. There was no record of a boy named Jason being enrolled at any of the local schools. Concerned for Jason's welfare but reluctant to make the case official, he gave the girls a small mission: They were to befriend the boy and find out what was happening in his life as an alternative to getting social services involved.

Two days later the girls returned and found Jason in the yard pulling up weeds with a long-handled claw. The day was scorching hot. Jason's shirt was soaked with sweat and he was developing the beginnings of a sunburn. The station wagon was conspicuous by its absence. When the girls arrived, Jason stopped his work and wiped his forehead with a gloved hand. 'Oh, hey, it's the snooping sisters.'

Pandora surveyed the yard. The chain link fence had been dismantled and piled against a tree. Plastic bags of garden waste lay where the station wagon had been. 'This place is looking better. Did you clear all this by yourself?'

Jason looked about him with a weary expression. 'Yeah, but I'll need the Army Corps of Engineers to haul up some of these damn bushes.' He jabbed at the base of a California desert-thorn with the weed puller.

'Isn't your mom helping you?'

'She got a job at the gas station. She won't be back until evening.'

Holly unpacked a thermos flask from her backpack and poured the contents into three plastic cups, shoving one under Jason's nose.

'Holly made lemonade at her craft club,' Pandora said by way of explanation. 'She's forcing everyone she ever met to have at least three cups of the stuff, so you'd better start drinking.'

Jason took the cup and drained it in two long gulps. 'It's good. Thanks.'

There followed an awkward silence while the girls drank their lemonade at a more leisurely pace. Jason studied Holly with open curiosity. 'Why doesn't your sister talk?'

Pandora shrugged. 'Who knows? She just doesn't.'

'I mean, she must have seen a doctor, right? It's not normal when people just don't talk.'

'Holly's seen just about every doctor between San Diego and Seattle.'

'So what's wrong with her?' Jason said.

'Who says there's something wrong with her? Maybe Holly's just the way she's supposed to be.'

'Then why would she need a doctor?'

'Because she has special needs, that's why,' Pandora said. 'The doctors try to find ways for Holly to join in the stuff other people do.'

'Can she shake hands?'

'Ask her, not me.'

Jason removed a glove and held out his hand. Holly shook it. 'Cool. Now can you jump up and down?' He bounced on the spot to demonstrate his meaning.

'She doesn't do tricks, dumbass,' Pandora said.

'Oh. Right.'

Holly finished her lemonade and wandered across the yard to the desert-thorn. She prodded it experimentally with her shoe, grabbed the stem with both hands and started to pull.

Jason started after her in dismay. 'Hey, be careful. Those thorns will rip the skin off your bones. Here, wear these gloves if you're going to help.' Holly put on the gloves and hauled again on the stubborn plant, but it didn't budge. Jason picked up the weed puller and attacked the roots. Between the two of them they tore the bush out of the dusty ground.

For five hours they worked together to clear the yard. The tools Jason's mother had acquired to restore the trailer were primitive but effective. With pruning saws, shovels, rakes, and a wheelbarrow, they set about removing the dense growth of low-lying shrubs and stubborn weeds.

Sometimes the work was more like excavation than gardening. Behind a sprawling mass of scrub was an old Kawasaki motorbike, and it took all three of them to drag it free from the ground into which it had sunk. In another corner of the yard they encountered a tangle of barbed wire in the midst of which was entombed the skeleton of a buck deer. Elsewhere, they found a broken Foosball table, two tractor tires, and a three-foot-tall stone statue of the Virgin Mary. All of this detritus was loaded onto the wheelbarrow and hauled fifty yards further up the hill where they dumped it in the back of an old Chevy farm truck, rotting under a tarpaulin beside another abandoned trailer.

By the time the sun had sunk low over the mountains, casting a golden glow over the valley, the front yard was entirely clear of the encroaching scrubland. They sat on the stoop to finish Holly's lemonade.

'Why are you doing this?' Jason said while they surveyed the results of their work.

'Doing what?' Pandora said.

'Helping. I mean, you don't know me.'

'Well, we're neighbors. Kinda.'

'Mom said a policeman came around asking questions yesterday. Was that your dad?'

'It could have been,' Pandora said. 'He often introduces himself to new people when they move to Ojai.'

'She was pretty angry about that. I told you she doesn't like people snooping.'

'He wasn't snooping. He was just being polite.'

Jason stared at the ground for long moments. 'I don't think you guys should come back here any more.'

Pandora was surprised how hurt she was by that. 'What? Why?'

'My mom and me, we're not good people to know. I mean, I guess you can figure that out for yourselves. We live in an abandoned trailer with no electricity and no water. We use camping lights at night and listen to a battery-powered radio. Mom has to drive into town every day to get big gallon bottles of water for washing and drinking.'

'So? That's because you're fixing the place up, right?'

Jason didn't reply, he just stared into space. After a long silence they heard the sound of an engine, and the Ford Country Squire pulled up to the house.

The thin-faced woman they had seen two days ago stepped out of the car, carrying a paper bag filled with groceries. She glanced around the yard, and looked at the kids on the doorstep with a wary expression. 'You've been busy. Who are these girls?'

Jason stood and the girls joined him. 'This is Pandora, and this is Holly. She doesn't talk, but she's friendly. They helped clear the yard.'

'Nice to meet you,' Pandora said, holding out her hand.

Wendy adjusted the grocery bag and shook her hand. Her grip was lifeless, and her eyes were cold. Pandora was glad when she pulled her hand away.

'Jason, may I speak to you in private?' Wendy said.

The girls stayed outside while Jason followed his mother into the house. They heard indistinct voices that rose in anger and then were silenced.

'She hates us,' Pandora said.

Wendy returned alone. She folded her arms across her chest and addressed the girls from the stoop. 'Girls, Jason has told me all about the help you've given him, clearing the yard. I want you to know I'm very grateful for all the work you've done, but I'm afraid we're a very private family and we don't appreciate uninvited guests. I don't mean to be rude, but we'll only be living here a short while, so it's probably best if we don't form any attachments with people in the area. I'd be grateful to you both if you didn't come back again.'

Pandora had a mouthful of protests all prepared. 'Oh, but we won't be any trouble and we—'

'Take my hand,' Wendy held Pandora's hand in a tight grip. 'Listen to me. Leave us alone. Never come back here again.'

CHAPTER 9

So that was that. In the days that followed the thermometer in the yard on Edgewood Avenue soared to almost a hundred degrees, making bike rides an impossibility. The girls remained indoors, playing Mario Kart and practicing their art. The family that lived next door got a young Border Collie from the rescue center, and the sisters used any excuse to visit and make a fuss of that happy bundle of fur. They forgot completely about the boy and his mother in the derelict trailer.

Pandora became so enamored of the puppy that she began to harbor dreams of having a pet of her own. She started devising schemes to persuade her parents that a dog would make a good addition to the family.

To build up her social credit she volunteered for chores that under other circumstances would have made her run for the hills. For weeks she mowed the lawn, washed the car, vacuumed the carpets, did the washing up and kept her bedroom spotlessly clean. Her parents shared knowing glances at this radical change in personality while Holly looked on with bemusement.

Soon Pandora felt she had earned enough brownie points so that her parents could hardly refuse her heartfelt request. She made her plea over breakfast when the whole family were gathered together.

'So, you know how the Henleys next door got a dog, right?' she asked apropos of nothing.

David glanced at Sandra over his newspaper. 'Yeah, what about it?'

'Well, haven't you noticed how Holly loves to play with him? She's been teaching him to play fetch and I reckon they could play Frisbee if they practiced long enough. Y'know, like in the Dog Disc Championships? Wouldn't that be cool?'

'I think the Henleys have been training him, but Holly certainly loves that little dog,' Sandra said.

'It's a great activity for Holly because the dog is totally non-verbal,' Pandora continued. 'They've got a real connection. If we had a dog of our own I think it would do Holly the world of good.'

'Holly's fine playing with the neighbors' dog,' said David with an air of finality.

'But just think how much fun it would be. Holly agrees with me, don't you Hol?'

'I think you're using your sister to try and get favors for yourself,' Sandra said. 'I'm sorry, honey, but your father and I talked about the possibility of pets a while back and there's just no way we can afford it.'

'But Mom, it's just—'

'No buts, Pandora,' Sandra said. 'A dog is very expensive to buy, very expensive to feed, and the medical bills can be debilitating. Last year we decided to send Holly to the special school in Ventura to give her the best possible chance of a normal life. That was a very expensive choice, and it's meant we don't have enough money for ordinary luxuries like holidays abroad or pets. I'm sorry, but we're not going to be getting a dog.'

Pandora sank into her chair and pouted. 'Sounds like you're blaming Holly for us not having any money.'

'Pandora, that's enough,' David said.

'But it's not fair,' Pandora whined. 'Holly always gets anything she wants, and I get nothing. If Holly spends thirty seconds hammering the keys on the church piano, you buy her an electric keyboard, but when I ask for a dog you say no without any discussion.'

'The keyboard is for you both,' Sandra said. 'But you choose not to play it. And we are having a discussion. You have a lot of advantages that your sister doesn't have. That makes life unfair, I agree, but the unfairness is not tilted in your direction.'

Pandora smacked the table, rattling breakfast plates. 'That's such bull. I've spent the whole summer doing every damn chore around this house, and what do I get? Not even a thank you or a "Hey, Pandora, here's twenty dollars for that new book you wanted".'

'That is enough,' David said firmly. 'You're upsetting your sister. I think you're done with breakfast, don't you? Why don't you go to your room.'

Pandora leapt up, knocking her chair backwards. 'Upsetting my sister?' her voice rose to a crescendo. 'That's exactly what I'm talking about. Holly can't even understand what we're saying. If we all started speaking French it wouldn't make any difference to her.'

'That is not true and you know it,' Sandra snapped. 'Look at Holly, can't you see she's crying? Now get out of this kitchen and don't come back until you've got an apology to offer.'

Pandora stamped up to her room, slamming doors as she went. She threw herself onto the bed and screamed into her pillow, then gave it a few punches for good measure.

She brooded for about an hour, bouncing a tennis ball off the wall until the door opened and Holly came in.

'What do you want?'

Holly held up a pair of sneakers Pandora wore on their cycling trips.

'No way. It's too hot for a ride.'

Holly dropped the shoes at the foot of the bed and knelt to lace up her own sneakers. Pandora exhaled her frustration and tossed the tennis ball into the corner.

'Fine.'

They got their bikes from the garage and Holly led the

way. She took them on a long loop up to Nordhoff Ridge and back down Sisar Canyon, then along the Ojai Trail past the golf course and all the way around Lake Casitas. It was a long ride along difficult terrain, but Holly never stopped at any of their usual resting places to stretch their legs among the trees or dangle their feet in the lake. They rode in silence and tension simmered between them the whole way, made all the worse because Pandora knew only she could break the deadlock.

When they arrived back in Ojai, Holly led them to the Arcade and leaned her bike against an arch. Piper's Cafe was a few doors further down, and Pandora assumed Holly wanted to go inside for sodas and ice cream. Instead she diverted down a dead-end alley that led nowhere except a fire escape and some overflowing dumpsters.

Pandora lingered on the street, reluctant to follow her sister down the alley, knowing that some kind of reckoning awaited her at the end. During the long bike ride her anger about the dog had been severely eroded by the memory of her sister's tears at the kitchen table. She began to wonder if she hadn't made a terrible mistake. In all her daydreams about having a puppy she had thought only of herself, and never even spoke to Holly about her plans. The slow realization dawned that her desire for a puppy was entirely selfish, and that was hardly a good reason to bring a new life into the family.

She found Holly sitting on the concrete steps beneath the rusty fire escape ladder. 'Listen, Hol, I'm sorry I was such a pain in the ass this morning. It was totally wrong of me to blame you for us not getting a dog. I mean, I'm really glad you get to go to the special school, you know? You're doing great there and, jeez, you'll probably get more college offers than I do when the time comes. Anyway, what I'm saying is, I'm sorry. We don't need a dog. We've got each other. Can we hug and make up or something?'

Holly didn't look at her, or give any sign she was listening. Pandora leaned against the wall of the narrow alley and sighed. Then something caught her attention. The opposite wall of the alley had been painted with a large mural which was almost obscured by two dumpsters that crowded the narrow space. She wriggled into a gap and pushed the dumpsters out of the way with her shoulder.

The mural depicted a vista seen from a tremendous height, looking down on clouds spreading below like an undulating white ocean. In the utmost distance a titanic mountain parted the clouds and rose high into the heavens. The mountain peak was the site of a wondrous citadel of ethereal beauty whose turrets and minarets challenged the sky with their slender blade-like towers.

Pandora studied the brush strokes with a knowledgeable eye and recognized her sister's work. 'Holly, did you paint this? It's beautiful. Wait, when did you have the time to do this? Do you come down here without me?'

In the foreground of the painting two young girls stood at the edge of a precipice, holding hands and looking out towards the distant mountain. Pandora leaned close, and there was no doubt that they represented herself and Holly.

'This is the best painting you've ever done,' she said with no false praise. 'But why put it all the way down here? Eventually someone will come along with graffiti remover and ruin it.'

Holly came to stand beside her, and for a while they looked at the picture together. She reached out for Pandora's hand, and when their skin touched there was a shining radiance that made the whole world disappear.

CHAPTER 10

Pandora read until her eyes could no longer focus on the immature handwriting of her childhood. She had no recollection of writing these words sixteen years ago, but as she read her own account of traveling to that magical otherworld the memories came flooding back in a torrent of disconnected images that she struggled to reconcile in her mind.

Her writings expressed astonishment and delight at arriving in this new world, and the excitement of exploration and discovery that unfolded over the following days and weeks. *Holly has a power,* she had written in red felt pen. *She can travel to a place where the stars are different.*

A comprehensive family library of science fiction novels and movies had equipped Pandora with a vocabulary of words like teleportation and wormholes, but her eleven year-old self had elected to name Holly's power something more innocuous; a code word that she could use with Holly to avoid anyone knowing their secret. *When it happens there is a light like the sun, and it warms you from the inside out. It's so bright you have to close your eyes at just the right moment or you can't see for a whole minute afterwards. You have to BLINK. One moment you're in Ojai and it's hot and there are trucks rumbling along the*

Avenue, then... BLINK... and the air is cool and it's so quiet that all you can hear is crickets and the swaying of the grass in the meadow.

Blinking. That was Holly's superpower.

Many mysteries still remained when she finally put aside the diaries and retired to bed. She lay awake for a long while, staring at the ceiling and thinking through all the strange things she had learned and asking herself questions which could not yet be answered. What was the cause of Holly's ability to *blink* between Earth and this other world? In the diaries she had speculated many wild theories: Accidental exposure to radioactive waste, secret government experiments, and extraterrestrial technology implanted during an alien abduction. On one page she had pasted a clipping from Scientific American which calculated that teleporting a human being as far as the Moon would require ten trillion gigawatts of energy. Beneath this clipping Pandora's younger self had asked, *Why aren't we incinerated every time we blink? Holly doesn't just unleash this power, she controls it.*

Another mystery was the boy Jason, whom Pandora had positively identified as the boy from the Polaroid stuck to the fridge door. He had evidently shared in at least one of the sisters' journeys to the otherworld, yet she had forgotten about his existence until she read about him in the diary. Who was he, and where was he now? These questions led to a related problem: Why had her memories of these events been erased? She remembered many other events recorded in the diaries, like seeing The Phantom of the Opera on Broadway for their parents' twentieth wedding anniversary. But of the trips to the otherworld she had no recollection whatsoever. Was it possible that the other place was merely a make-believe world she had created and shared with her sister? A forgotten fantasy to which she had regressed after the collapse of the scaffolding at the Arcade? After all, the only real physical evidence of that world was the Polaroids themselves, and they might be just a pictorial record of a long-forgotten trip to some remote place right here in California.

By skimming through the diaries, she estimated that four of her own journals and at least three of Holly's dealt directly with travel to the otherworld. It would take many days of concentrated effort to uncover the truth of what happened almost twenty years ago. As she drifted off to sleep she expected the following day would bring a flood of new discoveries, and even more mysteries.

The alarm clock on the nightstand read 2:19 am. What little sleep she'd had was filled with confused and disjointed images from the diaries, visions of herself and her sister playing in an alien wilderness beyond the reach of the sun. Now she had lain awake for over an hour, trying to clear her head. Every time she closed her eyes, another fragment of memory would rise from her subconscious and swirl around in her mind, teasing her with tantalizing hints of understanding that were just beyond her grasp.

She threw back the covers and got out of bed. There was no point lying there waiting for the Sandman to come. She would have to light out after him with a stick and drag him back to bed. Her maternal Irish grandmother Caitlin had passed down to her the secrets of an ancient Celtic potion guaranteed to bring peaceful sleep. Down in the pantry there was a bottle of Irish whiskey and a jar of honey she kept for occasions when work stress was keeping her awake at night. Mixed with a glass of warm milk and sprinkled with nutmeg these magic ingredients formed an arcane elixir which never failed to send her to sleep.

The sound of an engine drew her attention to the window. A black van pulled up to the curb opposite the house. At this hour there was no traffic on Edgewood Avenue, and the van drove with its headlights turned off. The doors opened and two figures stepped out into the night. They were dressed in black, and their faces were concealed by ski masks.

A trickle of alarm made Pandora's heart skip a beat. There was no conceivable reason why strangers should drive without lights and hide their faces unless they were engaged in criminal activity. Alarm turned to fear when the strangers turned towards her house and walked up the drive.

There was a security light just below the bedroom window, triggered by a motion sensor. Pandora leaned towards the glass and waited for the powerful bulb to flood the yard with light and frighten the strangers away. The driveway remained dark, and the strangers approached the house without hindrance.

There was a switch below the window casement that enabled the light to be manually activated. She toggled the switch on and off, but nothing happened. Groping in the dark, she found the cable and was disturbed to find it had been neatly severed.

The two figures arrived at the porch and mounted the steps, disappearing from view. She reached for her phone on the nightstand, and cursed quietly when she remembered it had been smashed during the accident at the Arcade. She hurried into her study and picked up the landline extension. The phone was dead.

From downstairs there was a metallic scratching sound like a key being placed into a lock. She ran back into the hall and saw dark silhouettes lurking beyond the frosted glass outside. The door opened and two men entered. Anger and terror mingled in her blood and spread like wildfire through her body. The intruders had not yet spotted her at the top of the stairs. Taking a deep breath, she shouted at the top of her lungs. 'Hey! Get lost! I've got a gun and I know how to use it.'

In fact she did not have a gun, but in the darkness the intruders couldn't tell either way. She felt the strangers' eyes swivel up towards her, but they made no move to escape.

'God dammit, she's awake,' the taller housebreaker said. 'Get up there and shut her up before she makes any more noise.'

The smaller intruder mounted the steps towards her. Improvising quickly, Pandora reached for a sprawling dragon tree in a heavy clay pot on the window ledge. Hefting it in both hands, she hurled it at the stranger. The pot struck him in the head and knocked him back with a grunt of pain. The grunt had a feminine quality Pandora had not expected.

'You bitch,' the intruder said. Definitely a woman. She shook her head and kicked aside the fragments of pottery.

Pandora had gained a precious moment of advantage and she thought fast. Ordinary burglars seeking to steal ready cash or salable items would be startled by the presence of a shouting homeowner who showed willingness to defend their property. These intruders clearly had a more diabolical plan in mind. She decided the only option was to evacuate the house and raise the alarm from elsewhere.

A hand fell on her shoulder and she yelped with surprise. It was Holly, wide awake and wide-eyed with fright at the sight of strangers in the house at this hour. Pandora pulled her into the studio. She closed the door quietly, leaving the light off so no trace of their presence would be visible in the hall. This hiding place would not be safe for long, but with any luck the intruders would waste time checking the bedrooms first. Meanwhile, Pandora pulled back the rug, revealing a trap door into the garage below. The hatch had not been used for years, and the old hinges creaked as she lifted it, revealing the darkened garage. The Blazer was parked directly underneath, and there was only a short drop onto the roof. She pushed Holly towards the hole, whispering in her ear. 'Hol, get down into the garage, I'll follow right behind you.'

Holly sat on the hole's rim and dangled her legs over the side. Before she could jump, the door opened and the intruders burst in. The male intruder grasped Pandora by the shoulders and threw her against the workbench, sending bottles, brushes, and craft tools clattering to the floor. She fell, and the stranger knelt on her back, pinning her to the ground.

'One move and I'll break your neck,' he hissed in her ear.

The female intruder seized Holly by the hair and dragged her away from the trap door. Holly flailed with her arms and feet, fighting to be free and clawing at her attacker with long nails that raked the woman's clothing and mask.

'Stop that,' the woman said, fending off the attack with gloved hands. 'Stop it, or I'll break your fingers.'

Holly went limp. The woman rolled her onto her front and put a knee in the small of her back.

'What do you want?' Pandora said. 'We don't have any valuables. I keep two hundred dollars in an envelope in the hall table. Take it, it's yours.'

The man laughed. 'See, this is why I love doing it this way. Some people would gag 'em, but then you don't get to hear the pleading and the negotiating.'

He pulled Pandora's hands behind her back, and before she knew what was happening he had restrained her with cable ties. With speedy efficiency he repeated the motion with her ankles and within moments she was bound and helpless.

Holly began to struggle once more as the woman tried to put cable ties on her wrists. She writhed on the floor and moaned, reaching for Pandora, who was powerless to help her. 'Leave her alone! She's disabled, she doesn't understand what you're doing.'

The woman put a foot in Holly's back and watched her squirm like a bug she had fixated with a pin. 'This one doesn't do much pleading, but she's funny to watch.'

'The feebs always are,' the man said. 'Nature's comedians, I call 'em.'

The woman knelt and bound Holly's hands and feet with the same professional zeal as her companion.

The man nodded with satisfaction. 'Now go move the van. Back right up to the garage door so we can move them without being seen from the street.'

Something about the way the man spoke set off alarm bells in Pandora's head. It was the way he said *Go move the van.* It reminded her of something she had heard before.

The woman left the room while the man picked up Holly in a fireman's lift, whooping enthusiastically at the exertion. 'Whoo! Who needs a home gym when you can get a workout like this, right girls?'

'Fuck you,' Pandora said.

He kicked her in the stomach and she doubled up in pain. 'That should keep you quiet until I get back.'

When both intruders were gone she wrestled against her restraints, searching for some tool to help her escape. Holly's studio was well stocked with craft knives, scissors, and other cutting implements. All she had to do was find one in the darkness and grab hold of it. Even if she didn't have time to free herself before the intruder returned she could take the blade with her and use it at the first opportunity.

She rolled across the floor and felt indentations form in her arms, back, and thighs where the fallen craft tools dug into her body. Fumbling with her hands, she picked up something with a slender wooden handle. A paintbrush. Useless. She tried again and found something heavier, with a cold steel handle. She explored with her fingers and winced as something sliced through the fleshy pad of her index finger. It was one of Holly's pencil-thin X-Acto knives with a scalpel tip. Already she could hear footfalls as the man returned from the garage. She grabbed the back of the oversize NASA t-shirt she wore as a nightie and sliced open the hem with the blade. Then she thrust the knife inside the narrow fold of cloth just in time as the man returned and hauled her over his shoulder. He whistled merrily as he carried her downstairs, slapping her bare buttocks rhythmically as an accompaniment to the tune.

Pandora raged with hate and fury like she had never known before. She felt helpless and humiliated, and she made a silent vow that whatever happened she would make this man pay for what he had done.

The garage was in darkness, but the kidnappers had found the remote control that opened the garage door to reveal the waiting van on the driveway. The female kidnapper stood by the van's open rear doors where an interior light showed two cages that looked like they had been constructed for restraining large dogs. In one cage lay Holly, painfully bound and shaking with fear. The woman opened the second cage, and Pandora was hurled carelessly inside. Immediately the van's doors were closed and the overhead light was extinguished, plunging the sisters into darkness.

The engine started and the van moved away. The dog cages were not designed for human occupation and Pandora could barely sit up without squashing her head against her shoulder. Helpless and confused, she tried to understand what was happening. Was this a gang seeking ransom money? Or terrorists who planned to execute them on camera for some deranged political goals? None of the possibilities filled her with hope. The only clue lay in the way the male kidnapper had spoken to his companion. *Go get move van*. Pandora knew that voice. She had heard it very recently.

An image flashed into her mind of a handsome young couple, smiling on her doorstep. What was it they had said?

'Hiya,' said the man.

'We're sorry to bother you,' said the woman.

'Only, our van has broken down. Do you mind if we use your phone to call a tow truck?'

They were the same voices. She kicked the cage in anger and frustration. It was the campers. The creepy weirdos who'd stolen their hairbrushes and toothbrushes had returned to take a few more souvenirs, and this time they wanted trophies that could plead and beg.

She rolled over and faced Holly. She could not see her sister, but she could hear her frantic breathing close by. 'Hol, I'm right here beside you. Everything's going to be okay. Just keep calm and I'm going to get us out of this.'

She wriggled around to give herself some freedom of movement and felt around the hem of her t-shirt to find the hidden X-Acto knife. The van was jolting around, rattling the cages which were imperfectly secured to the floor. It took all her concentration to hold the knife in a reverse grip and slice the cable ties that bound her wrists. With every passing moment she was fractions of an inch from slipping with the blade and slicing her own wrists.

The van made a left turn and struck some raised ironworks in the road. Pandora was bounced against the roof of the cage and the knife was knocked from her hand. She swore and twisted her wrists, pulling at the cuts she had already made in the plastic cord. Suddenly she felt a release of tension and her hands were free.

'Holly, I've got my hands free. If I can get out of this cage we can kick the doors open and get out.'

The knife was clattering around at the bottom of the cage and she found it easily. The kidnappers had secured the dog cages with sturdy padlocks, and she was not optimistic she could lever them apart with the thin craft knife. It was almost impossible to maneuver within the cage and she nearly tore a muscle in her thigh twisting her body to reach the lock. She attacked the hasp with the point of the blade, but it was no good. There was no way to escape.

The cage beside her began rattling loudly. Holly was thrashing around inside, kicking and punching the metal bars. She was having a panic attack and Pandora feared she could do herself a serious injury.

'Holly, don't struggle. You'll only hurt yourself. It's no use, we'll have to stick it out for now.'

Holly continued hammering at the bars in a repetitive tattoo. *Clang-clang-clang... clang-clang-clang.* She wasn't panicking; she was trying to draw Pandora's attention.

'Holly, what is it? What are you trying to tell me?' She lay down and pushed her fingers through the bars, reaching for the other cage. Holly stopped pounding, and for a moment there was silence as the van coasted along a smooth patch of road. Pandora felt a feather touch as her fingertips brushed her sister's. Holly was reaching for her too.

They touched again. Pandora realized what was about to happen and screwed her eyes shut just in time to guard against the radiant pulse of light that filled the van, and then she was flying.

CHAPTER 11

She hit the ground hard, tumbling and rolling across the uneven earth and came to a halt in a tangle of weeds. She struggled into a sitting position, still restrained by the ties on her ankles. The grass was tall and she could not see far in the darkness of the night. She called out her sister's name, but there was no sign of Holly and all she could hear was the monotonous stridulation of a thousand crickets.

The X-Acto knife was still in her hand so she sawed the bonds off her feet. The night air was cool, and the stars overhead were unfamiliar. There was no doubt that this was the otherworld they had visited in their childhood and now rediscovered as adults.

A rustle in the deep shadows beneath a stand of trees nearby. Pandora hurried there and found Holly struggling to push herself into a sitting position. She helped her rest against the trunk of a tree. 'Hold still while I cut off these ties.'

In the starlight, Holly's face was dirty and there was a red-raw patch on her forehead. 'Oh God, Holly, your poor head.' She brushed away dead leaves from her sister's face and peeled a quarter-sized flake of bark from her cheek. 'You must have done a proper face-plant into the trunk of this tree. We'll have to figure out a better way of making a landing on this world. Maybe wear some crash helmets and knee-pads next time, what do you think?'

Arm in arm, leaning on each other for support, they

wandered across the benighted meadow. Pandora stared at the strange stars and marveled at this repeat of yesterday's miracle. 'You saved us, Hol. That's twice you've saved us now. I guess I owe you double.'

There was a fallen tree lying across their path, and Holly hopped up onto the trunk. She breathed in deep and spread out her arms in a tree-like fashion.

'Y'know, I recognized the voices of those assholes,' Pandora said. 'They're the same freaks who stole our hairbrushes. Jeez, I feel so stupid. That whole performance with the broken-down RV was just some ploy to get into the house. They must have planned the whole thing in advance.' She scratched her chin and replayed the kidnapping in her mind. 'I'm pretty sure the van turned left onto Edgewood Avenue, then left again onto Ojai Avenue. That means we were probably somewhere in the vicinity of the Arcade when we teleported – I mean, when we *blinked* – back here. If that's the case we should head back to Ojai right now. We can use the phone booths at the Arcade to call the police before the kidnappers even realize we've escaped. What do you reckon?'

Holly was not paying attention. She stood still on the log with her head cocked to one side as if listening. There was a bat somewhere in the air above the meadow, making a long circuit above the tall grass and squeaking at the limit of Pandora's hearing. She saw a flitter of the animal's wings silhouetted against the stars as it passed by Holly's head, close enough to flick a wisp of hair across her nose. Holly giggled silently as the bat came back for another pass and brushed the other side of her hair.

Pandora climbed up on the trunk and joined her. 'Holly, we're not here to commune with nature. Come on, let's go back to Ojai. I'll take you to Bear Gulch Cave next week, and you can see the big-eared bats there.'

Holly turned away and jumped down off the trunk. By the time Pandora clambered down after her she was striding rapidly across the meadow, visible only as a gray shape among the grass.

She ran to catch up. 'Hey, listen, once I've called the police we can drive up to the scenic overlook and watch the sun rise over Ojai, wouldn't that be cool? We can pack ice creams in a cooler and listen to the Beach Boys.'

Pandora was pulling out the big guns in the hopes of attracting her sister's interest, but to no effect. At last she grabbed Holly's arm and brought her to a halt. 'Holly, I'm serious. We have to go back to Ojai right now and call the police. Please take us home this instant.'

Holly pulled her arm free. When Pandora reached for her again she took a step backwards.

Pandora threw up her hands in frustration. 'Okay, have it your way. What do you want to do? Are we going to sleep here in the grass and wake up with beetles in our ears?'

Holly took off again across the meadow, leaving Pandora standing with her hands on her hips. She looked around at the landscape, glimpsing hints of groves and copses as black shapes against the night. She put aside her irritation and tried to see things from Holly's point of view. Maybe her power needed recharging, or maybe it didn't work properly if she was nervous or afraid. She decided to give Holly a break and try again in an hour or so.

Dead ahead was the observatory mound, and already Holly was making her way up the steps towards the summit. When Pandora arrived Holly was lighting candle stubs with an old cigarette lighter.

'Wow, it's spooky here at night,' she said, watching the flickering candles cast tall shadows like specters haunting the old ruin. 'I wonder how we were brave enough to camp here as kids.'

She stubbed her toe on a metal crate lying in the shadows; some relic of the observatory's original equipment. It clattered across the floor and she cursed it verbosely.

'I found our old diaries about this place,' she leaned against a console and massaged her foot. 'I hope you don't mind me nosing through your old sketches. I'd totally forgotten we ever came here. But you remember, don't you? That's how you knew to come here when we were in danger. That's why you recognized the boy in the picture.'

Holly upended an old backpack and out fell two cans of Coke and a packet of Oreos.

'I'm going to take a wild guess those are past their use-by date,' Pandora said.

Holly didn't care. She tore off the wrapping and inserted a whole Oreo into her mouth. She nodded in approval and handed the packet to Pandora.

'Okay, well, I suppose it'll have to do.'

In fact, the Oreos were delicious. The Coke was similarly fresh and satisfying. She wondered if there was some quality in the air of this place that kept food preserved. Different bacteria, maybe, or less pollution.

She found herself back by the open door, looking out over the meadow with its lonely ruins barely visible in the starlight. 'We called it blinking, do you remember? I had to shut my eyes tight, and if I got the moment wrong I'd be totally blind for ages after. After a while I started to get an intuition for when you were going to do it, like we'd developed a mental connection or something. In the end I only had to close my eyes for a fraction of a second and then, *Blam!* Here we were.'

Holly came to stand beside her, and for a while they ate Oreos in silence. A mist was settling over the land in the cool pre-dawn air. Pandora felt goosebumps on her bare skin.

'Are you ready to go home yet, Hol?' she said when the Oreos were finished. 'We're still wearing our nighties, and I'm not too thrilled about the prospect of materializing on Ojai Avenue in the middle of morning rush hour.'

She held out her hands and closed her eyes, hoping that Holly would take the cue and blink them back to California. Instead, she wandered back inside and began clearing a space on the floor of the den. Pandora groaned and resigned herself to spending the rest of the night here.

'I guess once upon a time I was excited to stay the night

here,' she said to herself, watching the candlelight flicker across the brass curves of the telescope. 'Does growing up make all the magic go away? So even camping on an alien world seems like an inconvenience?'

Holly found a pair of sleeping bags neatly rolled up in a corner. When she shook them out they looked clean and dry, if a little dusty. She arranged some sleeping mats on the ground and wrapped herself up in a sleeping bag. She yawned theatrically and curled up on the floor, pulling the hood tight over her head so she looked like a grub.

Pandora remained awake for a while, making a circuit of the observatory, inviting lost memories to return by reaching out to touch the old relics of her childhood. Each object brought flashes of insight and recognition. There was no doubt that the time she had spent here with Holly had been the happiest days of her life, filled with excitement, adventure, and joy. What had happened to make them leave this place and forget about it for almost two decades?

She arrived at the door and stared out into the night. The mist had thickened into a swirling ocean that covered the meadow and lapped at the shores of the observatory hill.

In the distance she saw movement. In daylight she had seen a wide forest that lay beyond the meadow, and now lights emerged from where she thought the treeline lay. They were like blue lanterns, brighter than the stars but more diffuse, like orbs ducking and swaying through the gathering mist. At first there were only two, but they were swiftly joined by seven or eight, and soon more than a dozen lights hovered at the edge of the forest, spreading all across the meadow.

In the distorting haze of the mist, the lights radiated halos that pulsated weirdly, casting eerie shadows around the trunks of the trees. Pandora found the scene disconcerting and a little creepy, reminding her of half-forgotten terror tales about Will-o'-the-Wisps and corpse candles.

After a while it became clear that the lights were coming no closer than the edge of the forest, and she told herself they were merely some native version of fireflies or the like. She returned to the observatory and curled up in a sleeping bag next to Holly. In the soft candlelight it was comfortable and warm, and for the first time she recalled what a joy it had been to camp out here when they were kids. The observatory no longer looked spooky, and it as if the crumbling ruin was slowly recalling the memory of two gangly girls from years ago, recognizing them anew in these travelers who needed shelter from the night. It remembered them and made itself safe and welcoming in recognition of the fun times they had once shared. She planned to lie awake until the coming of dawn, but long before the first glimmer of golden sunshine crept up to the door, she was fast asleep.

Breakfast was Rice Crispies bars and Coke, taken on the hillside where the girls lay wrapped in their sleeping bags on grass still shining with morning dew. They held an impromptu belching contest until the Coke ran out, and raced each other back up the hill in their sleeping bags, falling down every few yards on the slippery grass. When they reached the top Holly fixed the Polaroid on its tripod and they posed for photographs like they had done many times, many years before. It was one of the best breakfasts Pandora could remember.

It was with a growing sadness in her heart, therefore, that she took Holly on one last tour of the hilltop, looking out over the meadows and the forests at a world that had re-entered their lives so briefly, and now might be taken away forever.

'I've been trying to figure out why we stopped coming here,' Pandora said. 'When we were kids we came here whenever we felt like it, but now it seems like it can only happen in a moment of extreme emotional distress. When you were frightened of the spider you must have come here as an instinctive reaction, like flinching away from a hot stove. The same happened when the scaffolding fell on us. It was an automatic reaction to danger. When we got kidnapped, you waited until I'd escaped from the cable-ties, but it was still an emergency situation. Maybe as you grew up your power faded, and you couldn't do it on demand anymore. Now you're an adult the power is still there, but it's dormant unless something dangerous happens. I guess that means we might never come back here, 'cause I sure don't plan on getting into a life-threatening situation every time I want to see the observatory.'

They arrived back at the door and faced each other. 'So we'd better say goodbye to this place, Hol. I hope I don't forget about it this time.'

Holly tilted her head to look past Pandora, and there was a twinkle in her eye. Pandora turned and followed the line of her sister's gaze. In the distance was a river, flowing down from high hills in the east and winding through dense forest that alternately revealed and concealed its silvery waters. In the glow of the rising sun the river looked like it was made of liquid light. In a loop of the river there was a clearing in the forest, and rising from it was a wisp of smoke curling into the clear morning air.

'Hey, what's that?' Pandora shielded her eyes from the sun and squinted into the distance. 'It looks like smoke. Is that a building over there?'

Holly disappeared into the observatory and returned carrying a collection of objects. The first was a pair of binoculars, which she pushed into her sister's hands.

'It's a house!' Pandora exclaimed, focusing the lenses of the binoculars. 'There's a clearing with a couple of little fields beside the river. Hot damn, this place isn't deserted after all.' She lowered the binoculars, and was startled to see her sister holding up two pairs of flip-flops, her eyebrows raised in a querying expression.

Pandora knew a *fait accompli* when she saw one. ‘No, Holly, we have to go home. We can’t go exploring right now. Don’t you remember, we got abducted last night. We have to go and talk to the police before those assholes get away.’

Holly put the sandals on her bare feet and held out the second pair for her sister. Pandora sighed and gazed wistfully at the distant house. A swift breeze blew across the hillside, and she imagined she heard whispers from a forgotten childhood calling to her, promising a return to those vanished days of wonder and adventure.

CHAPTER 12

They made for the river, navigating by the rising sun to guide them across the trackless meadow. The forest presented a significant obstacle because there were no paths or roads, and the sisters were forced to pick their way along animal trails barely wider than their shoulders, pushing through ferns and tripping over gnarled roots.

Alongside the river they discovered a gravel path, overgrown but level and clearly marked. From there, the passage was easy and before long the forest parted and they arrived in the clearing they had seen from afar. Here, the path was well-maintained and clear of weeds. Simple boundary ditches and rough-hewn fences separated the lane from small fields on either side where vegetables and cereal crops grew in narrow strips. They saw beans and peas growing on tall poles, and patches of carrots and potatoes. In a far corner of the clearing was a cluster of wooden boxes mounted on poles, from which bees droned busily on their urgent errands.

Ahead was a cottage, a tiny dwelling of timber with a thatched roof and a stone chimney from which smoke curled into the sky. A flower garden surrounded the house, filled with species similar to those Pandora knew from Earth. She recognized red and white impatiens, rainbow-colored bromeliads, sprawling bougainvillea, and fiery japonicums. Bees buzzed merrily back and forth between the garden and the hives.

'Does any of this seem familiar to you?' Pandora said as they drew near the house. 'I didn't read about this place in the diary, but I think we mainly stayed at the observatory in our first weeks here. We didn't start exploring the woods until later, and I haven't—'

She fell silent and gripped Holly's arm as she heard a voice nearby. A neatly-trimmed hedgerow separated the path from the field beside the cottage, and from the far side came the sound of a woman singing. There was a gate in the hedge, and beyond was a cabbage patch where an old woman was working with a hoe, singing loudly to herself with the off-key confidence of someone who knows she cannot be overheard, or doesn't much care. Pandora was about to call out a greeting when a gruff shout came from behind.

'You there. Who are you? What are you doing here?'

An elderly man emerged from the cottage. He was tall and gaunt, and in his hand he brandished a pistol at the sisters. Pandora gasped at the sight of the gun and held out her hands. 'Please, don't shoot. We saw the smoke from your chimney and wondered who lived here.'

'We do not welcome strangers here,' the old man said. 'What is your purpose in these lands? Are you traveling alone, or with others?'

In the vegetable garden the woman stopped singing and called out with concern. 'Dad? Who are you talking to out there?'

'Don't come over here, Mother,' the man said. 'I'm handling this.'

The gate squeaked noisily and the woman bustled onto the path. 'Don't you start bossing me around when I've spent all morning pulling up weeds while you lounge around the house in your slippers. What's going on? Who are these people?'

'Strangers who came out of the wilderness. Phantoms, no doubt, hoping to find we'd become frail, or dead. Well, we're still here and we're still capable of defending ourselves.'

'Phantoms in daylight? Have you gone senile? Anyway, they seem harmless enough.' The woman cast a critical eye over the sisters. 'Maybe they're just travelers who got lost. They certainly look lost.'

The man shook his head in frustration. 'Woman, let me handle this. Get inside the house.'

'We're just travelers,' Pandora took a step forward to position herself between the gun and Holly. 'We didn't mean to trespass.'

'Stay back!' The old man recoiled from her approach and tripped over a rock beside the path. He fell to the ground, and at the same instant a brilliant crimson flash erupted from the gun. Pandora leapt away and saw a smoking crater, eighteen inches across, appear where she had stood a moment before. *What the hell kind of gun does that?* she thought.

The old woman threw down her hoe and hauled the old man to his feet, her elderly frame belying her strength. 'For heaven's sake put that awful thing away before it overloads and blows us all to kingdom come. Why don't we give these young women a chance to explain themselves?' She rounded on the sisters and studied them with frank appraisal. 'Now then. We do not receive many visitors here in Candlewick. Who are you, and what do you want here?'

Under the woman's scrutiny Pandora became uncomfortably aware that she and Holly were dressed only in their nightclothes and covered in dirt from their undignified landing in the meadow. Then it was as if a light went on in her head. The woman had said this place was called Candlewick. That was a name she knew.

'Your name is Catherine,' Pandora breathed.

She frowned suspiciously and peered at Pandora. 'Yes, that's right. Do I know you?' Then she drew a sharp breath and clasped her hands to her face. 'Goodness gracious. Well then, I seem to remember two mischievous young girls who used to visit us every now and again. They helped me make blackberry jam in the fall, and sweet cakes at the turn of the year. That was a long time ago. I expect they would both be young women by now.' She patted the old man on the arm. 'Dad, do you remember the girls you used to take foraging for berries and rocks to make the dyes? This is Pandora and Holly come back to visit us.'

The old man looked confused, but he nodded. 'I remember.'

'My goodness, friends and guests arriving and here I am wearing gardening rags and with no tea on the stove. Come along, let's get you all inside so we can get caught up.'

Most of the cottage was a single large room. A stone fireplace with a copper kettle on a hook was the focal point for a cluster of well-stuffed armchairs draped with woolen blankets. A cherry wood dining table occupied the center of the room, covered with sheets of paper and drawing implements. The walls were hung with needlepoint tapestries depicting farming, weaving, hunting, and fishing. Catherine fussed around the room, arranging cushions and straightening ornaments, complaining that her husband was a master at creating domestic disorder. The old man himself had not followed them inside and remained on the porch in a rocking chair.

'Oh, don't mind him,' Catherine slammed the front door as she passed by. 'Galen's feeling ashamed of himself. He'll come inside and act civil as soon as he's satisfied his desire for self-pity out there on the porch.'

A scruffy-looking farm dog lay on a rug beside the fireplace, and Catherine nudged her with a foot as she passed. 'Some guard dog you are. Asleep at your post.'

While Catherine pottered about, Pandora meandered around the room and studied the tapestries. Four shared a common theme depicting a village as the seasons changed throughout the year: The first showed young girls dancing around a maypole in a field full of flowers. The second depicted a community feast beside the river, with marquee tents, minstrels, and rosy-cheeked villagers pouring drinks from barrels. The third portrayed a children's play performed on a stage erected in a village square where young knights with wooden swords battled goblins against a painted backdrop of a fabulous city. The last tapestry showed a wintry scene where warmly-dressed people gathered in the square, holding lanterns and singing songs.

A long sideboard held a display of earthenware pots, jars, and bowls of all shapes and sizes. Many were richly decorated with floral and geometric patterns. Some appeared to have been decorated by children and featured imaginative scenes filled with fanciful creatures. Catherine rested a hand on Pandora's shoulder and leaned past her to pick up a decorated water jug. 'Do you remember this one?'

'Holly painted this,' she said in wonder, her fingers caressing the glazed images of fairies and butterflies.

'And you painted this one,' Catherine said, touching a vase decorated with an underwater scene of brightly colored fish.

Another flash of disjointed memories flooded back, of a village in the fall with leaves of golden yellow, orange, and red; a mill-wheel turning in the river; a portly red-faced fellow smiling kindly at her; the feel of wet clay between her fingers; the smell of burning coal heating the brick kiln. She felt dizzy and lost her balance, stumbling against a tapestry loom in the corner. Holly rushed to her side, guiding her to the table where she sat down.

'Are you feeling alright?' Catherine said, taking a seat beside her. 'You've gone very pale.'

'I'm sorry, I'm just very confused,' Pandora said. 'I don't remember this place. I don't remember you.'

'Well, you've been gone so long I hardly recognized you myself. It's been over fifteen years since you were last here, and you've grown from a child into a woman.'

'But it's more than that. There are huge gaps in my memory that I can't explain. Every time I see something that triggers a memory I get a torrent of images that don't make any sense. It's really disorienting.'

'You look overwrought. Wait there a moment, I've got just the thing.' Catherine hurried from the room and returned carrying a tray laden with glasses of juice and a platter of pastries. Pandora gladly took a glass, surprised that it was icy cold despite the warmth of the day.

'Perhaps it would help if I told you what I remember,' Catherine said. 'You and Holly were a part of our lives for nearly two years. I might be old and gray, but my memory is as sharp as a tack. Now then, let's see. In those days I wasn't exactly a spring chicken, but my hair still had some color in it, and I hadn't started to let out the waistline on my dresses. Those were happy days for us, Galen and I. We had a successful business together, and people traveled from all over the vale to buy the clothes and fabrics we dyed in the workshop. The work was hard, all the more so because we were on our own. Though we'd been married more than thirty years by that point we had no children so there was no one to help us with the business or on the farm. To be honest, the cottage sometimes felt very empty, especially around Yeartide or if Galen was off on one of his foraging trips in the hills searching for berries and rocks that held the colors and hues he was searching for. We're some way outside the boundary of the village here, and I'd be lying if I said I didn't get lonely some nights by myself. But life was good, and we were content.

'The day you both arrived I was in the house alone because Galen had taken a wagon load of colored cloth north to Springwater and he wasn't due back until late. I was in the kitchen making bread when there was a knock at the door, which was a novelty in itself because in the vale of Candlewick our custom is to walk straight in and announce yourself. Well, I dusted the flour off my apron and opened the door, and there you both were. I could tell right away you were strangers. I taught reading and arithmetic at the meeting hall, so I knew every child in the vale, and your clothes clearly marked you as travelers from afar.

'"Hello, and who might you be?" I said, and you

replied, "I'm Pandora, and this is my sister Holly. She doesn't talk, but she's friendly." See, didn't I tell you my memory was good? I looked around for signs of other travelers coming up the road, but the path was clear as far as the eye could see. I said, "Are you girls from outside the vale? Did you come up the river or the road?"

'And you said, "We walked here. We've been camping in the observatory on the hill. We saw the cottage and wondered who lived there."

'Now, that was a significant statement. A few weeks earlier, Galen had discovered strange things inside the old observatory up among the ruins in the borderlands. That caused a great deal of consternation in the meeting hall, and some of the more superstitious folks in the village said there were fairies or hobgoblins haunting the place. Galen argued with them and said it looked more like the observatory was being used as a wayhouse by travelers from distant fields who had different ways than us. As is usual in Candlewick, the discussion went on a long time until it started going round in circles, then it went on some more until all the sensible folks had become bored and gone home.

'Anyway, I told you who I was and that this was the vale of Candlewick. I asked where you came from, and you said your sister had a magical power to bring you here from some place called California.

'By this time I was feeling a little out of my depth, as you might imagine. Since you both represented the solution to a mystery that had been buzzing around the vale for some time, I felt obliged to take you to the meeting hall to see Walter, the elderman. Now, Walter was a cranky old sonofabitch without a hair on his head who always sounded like he was shouting even if he was standing right in front of you.

'You repeated your story to Walter and the other elders, and there was some disagreement about whether your story was entirely true. Some of the elders thought you were just runaways from distant fields who'd cooked up a tall tale to hide your tracks. The others started gabbling about myths and legends of ancient times, when the Astari traveled the universe and found people on other worlds, and invited them all to come and live together on Entara and everyone lived for a thousand years. They made a decision – in record time, I might add – that you should not share your far-fetched story with anyone else in the vale or you'd be overwhelmed with requests for miracles, signs, blessings, and the interpretation of dreams. Instead you were to tell people you were my nieces from Hamling. Now that was a story as transparent as window glass because I don't have any nieces, and Hamling isn't a real place. It's just an expression that means foreign, like when people say queer as folks from Hamling.'

'Anyway, I brought you back home and gave you a tour of our little farm. I remember you were both so fascinated by everything. Simple little things like the duck pond or the pig pen were like exotic mysteries to you and I wondered what kind of place it was you came from. Your enthusiasm was quite infectious, actually. When I asked you to help me collect the eggs from the chicken coop I honestly can't remember having so much fun doing such a totally boring activity.

'We had a hearty meal of food we'd collected around the farm, and by that time the sun was setting. I invited you to stay the night and made you a bed in the spare room.

'That night Galen came home late after you were both asleep, and I told him about all the strange things that had happened that day. I brought him upstairs and opened the door a crack, and we saw you both sleeping together by the light of a candle. I had the funniest feeling in my heart right then, seeing you wrapped up together in a quilt I had made for a family we never had. It was like Galen and I were the ones who'd stepped into some other world where our little home was filled with the joy and love of children. I must admit I cried a little that night and Galen called me a silly old mare.

'Well, the following morning you hied off back into the

wilderness from whence you came. I tried to give you some packed lunches and clothes for your journey, but you said it only takes a moment to get home. Just the blink of an eye, is the way you put it.'

'But we came back again?' Pandora said.

'Oh yes,' Catherine said. 'Only a week later you arrived during the harvest festival. It was a good opportunity to introduce you to the community, so we all took a trip into the village. Walter was organizing donkey races for the children and he invited you both to join in. I'm afraid Holly's donkey got confused and wandered off into the river and she got very wet.'

Pandora laughed. 'I remember that.'

'You came back regularly after that. You were both a part of our community for almost two years. I was very sad when you stopped coming back to see us.'

Pandora frowned. 'Why did we stop coming?'

Catherine shrugged. 'I don't know. I was hoping you could tell me. The last time you left, both of you were in high spirits after you had spent the weekend fishing on the river with Jason. You promised to visit for the spring festival the following week, but we never saw you again.'

'Jason?' The image of the boy in the Polaroid came into Pandora's mind, along with a dozen hazy memories.

'He was more upset than any of us when you failed to return. He felt that you had abandoned him.'

Pandora shook her head to clear it. 'I don't remember him, either. I found a picture of him in the observatory, and he's mentioned in diaries I wrote when I was a kid, but I have no recollection of him at all.'

'This is all very peculiar,' Catherine said. 'But it does tally with something Jason told me once. Jason was from your world, you see. I never knew the full details of what exactly happened, but his life was in great danger and you girls saved him by bringing him here. Galen and I took him into our home and raised him as our own son. Years later I asked him if he missed his real mother, and he got this terrible sad look in his eyes and said he couldn't remember her anymore. I wish I could tell you more, but only Jason knows the whole story.'

'You mean he's here? He lives with you?' Pandora said.

'Not any more.' Catherine sat back in her chair and turned her head up to the ceiling with her eyes closed. 'These are difficult memories for me, and frankly I think Galen would tell the story better. Let's go outside and force him to be sociable.'

CHAPTER 13

Behind the cottage was a long workshop made of sturdy wooden beams. When Galen opened the outer door the hinges groaned in complaint, and motes of dust swam in the air, sparkling in the sunlight through the windows. One wall was occupied by long racks from which dangled simple farm clothes on hangers of willow branches and twine.

'Choose whatever you want,' Galen said. 'I doubt anyone will ever wear these clothes now, so please make use of whatever you can.'

Pandora was amazed how familiar the old workshop felt. Big wooden buckets and vats took up most of the room where Galen soaked fabrics in the dyes he had manufactured. Battered worktables lined two walls, covered in bottles, jars and bowls filled with the congealed remains of the dyers' trade. Then she knew what the workshop reminded her of: It was just like Holly's studio. All the tools and materials were very similar to the supplies Holly used to manufacture and mix her own paints, and she realized Holly had earned her apprenticeship as a dyer under Galen's tutelage. It was clear, however, that the workshop had been unused for many years, and a thin layer of dust lay on the surfaces.

'I feel I must apologize for my behavior when you

arrived,' Galen continued as the sisters examined the clothes and began pulling items off the rack. 'A few years ago we had some bad experiences with… with strangers who came out of the wilderness. I guess it has made me distrustful and paranoid, and for that I'm sorry.'

'It's not your fault,' Catherine said. 'You thought they were phantoms,'

'I wasn't talking to you, was I?'

'Don't worry, no one was hurt,' Pandora said. 'If I hadn't been so confused I would have announced who we were straight away and there wouldn't have been any trouble.'

'Well, all I can say is how delighted I am to see you both again,' Galen said. 'What wholesome and healthy young women you have grown into!'

'Steady now, Dad,' Catherine said, raising an eyebrow. 'Watch that old ticker of yours. Maybe you should vacate the premises while us girls get dressed.'

'Oh, I see, exiled from my own workshop, am I?' Galen grumbled and called to Bess, the arthritic old farm dog who limped alongside him to the door.

Pandora searched the racks and was amused to see that many of the clothes were colored with bright tie-dye patterns. A glimmer of lost memory came into her mind of Galen patiently tutoring the girls in how to make traditional dyes, grinding rocks and dissolving the dust with acids, mixing them with animal fats and the juice of berries. Inspired by their newly learned craft, the girls had gone home and spent hours on the Internet researching how to make clothes more in keeping with the fashions of California. When they returned to the workshop they made dozens of tie-dye t-shirts and took them to the market in Candlewick. The vale had looked like a hippie festival for months afterwards, and it made Pandora happy to see that even after all these years the artistic influence she and Holly had brought to this world was still evident.

'Galen's taking the workshop apart, piece by piece,' Catherine said, pointing to a pile of wooden planks on the floor. 'Dad and I are getting old, and there'll come a time when we can't get up the stairs in the cottage. There's no need for a workshop out here anymore, so he's stripping out all the timber to build a new bedroom downstairs at the back of the cottage. It's a good thing you both arrived when you did. Another week and I would have taken all these old clothes out and put them on the bonfire. It's sad, really. We spent a lot of happy hours together in this old barn, he and I.'

Holly put on a long dress of psychedelic tie-dye splendor while Pandora chose a pale blue skirt and a knitted cardigan over a floral blouse. Once the girls were properly dressed, they found Galen outside sitting on a barrel smoking a pipe.

'Visions of beauty to gladden an old man's heart,' he declared. 'Now let's go for a walk. It's a fine day, and what I have to say is best told when the sun has chased the shadows away.'

Galen led them east along the path beside the river. Bess trotted alongside Holly, eager for the attention of a new friend. The river tinkled pleasantly beyond the tall reeds beside the path. Somewhere in the forest a woodpecker struck a tattoo that echoed through the trees. They walked in silence, sensing that Galen was organizing his thoughts and preparing to tell them a tale that weighed heavily on his heart. He walked ahead of the others, sucking on his pipe thoughtfully, his brow furrowed with worry lines.

Eventually the trees parted and once more they were walking among fields. At once it was clear that the cultivated land had lain fallow for some years. Pastureland was filled with grass and weeds so tall Pandora could hardly see over the top, while the empty crop fields were dusty and desolate. Orchards of neatly planted trees bearing apples, pears, plums, hazelnuts, and walnuts had withered and yielded to thorns and brambles.

Ahead, a village was near, its two-story cottages built of stout wooden frames supporting slate roofs. All the while, Pandora felt a growing sense of recognition. Here again was a place she had once known well, but as they approached the village boundary she saw the desolation and abandonment continued. There were no workers walking to-and-from the fields as there should have been at this time of day; no rugged, bearded men and sturdy women waving cheerful greetings as the two girls emerged from the forest. As they passed the boundary fence and entered the village they saw no smoke rising from the stone chimneys, hinting at frying bacon and eggs freshly collected from chicken coops. No carts pulled by shaggy horses crossed the street. No friendly dogs with waggy tails ran to greet them.

'I remember this place,' Pandora said as they passed the boundary posts and walked down the main street. 'But I remember it being full of people. These houses look like they've been empty for years.'

Galen nodded sadly. 'I'm afraid Candlewick is no longer the happy place you remember from your childhood. The vale is an empty and desolate land now. All the people have gone from the known fields. Only Catherine and myself remained behind. It has been twelve years since the last people left.'

'Twelve years?' Pandora said in disbelief. On both sides of the street the houses were boarded up with shutters fixed to the windows and planks nailed across the doors. Here and there a roof had collapsed, leaving rotting roof beams exposed like the ribcage of a corpse lying in the sun. From a broken upper window, a crow cawed angrily at the passersby as if offended by the presence of intruders.

They arrive at the village square, a place where Pandora remembered wheeled carts with colorful awnings selling fruit and vegetables, carved wooden toys, books, candles, and pottery. Now there was only dust and brown leaves swirling in the breeze. A scrap of parchment flapped across the cobbled ground and Pandora picked it up. The page was brown with age, and the ink was faded, but she could still make out the printed words.

Discover the hidden powers of the human mind!
The wizard ***Hieronymus Flak***
will present an educational lecture
for your entertainment and enlightenment
with a demonstration of ***psychic power***
not seen since the dawn ages.
Beware – these revelations are ***not for the faint of heart!***
Pregnant women and those of a nervous disposition
are advised not to attend
The demonstration begins on Waningday at nine bells
at Agatha's tavern, Candlewick.

'What the hell is this?' Pandora said.

'A sign of the times,' Galen said. 'Such displays were commonplace in the vale during the final days. What happened here is a terrible tale, and one I do not tell gladly. Perhaps by putting it into words I can come to terms with the loss we have suffered. Come with me to the meeting hall, and I will tell you what happened.'

The village of Candlewick lies nestled beside the river Anwin where it broadens to a wide span, running shallow across rounded stones, allowing for the crossing of wagons. A coach house had existed there since the days of the Old Kingdom, when the people of the fields first arrived and were shown crafts by the Astari. The settlers came to love beekeeping in particular, and henceforth the vale became known for its honey and its fine beeswax candles, which gave the land its name among the fields we know.

The people of Candlewick were good, hardworking folk, proud of the beauty of their land, their quaint houses, the deep woods, and the fertile soil. They built a fine stone hall beside the coach house where the community met to discuss important matters of the day, and to celebrate important events and festivals. A great leather-bound chronicle was placed in a chest in the meeting hall, and on its pages were recorded all the significant affairs of the people of the vale. Births, marriages, and deaths were all recorded, along with business contracts, inheritances, and appointments to public offices. These annals were not penned in simple lists divorced from all context, but lovingly transcribed in long narratives that told of the lives of the people they recalled. To read a page of the chronicle was to see a snapshot of a whole community, and to understand their hopes and dreams, their worries and their triumphs. Within those pages, a farmer might write an account of the growth of a new variety of apple, or a new breed of pig; bakers recorded the correct method of constructing an oven; brewers expounded on the art of malting barley. Each craftsman, towards the end of his life, wrote such an account to record the sum of his life's work, so that his contribution might be remembered in generations to come. The people of the vale kept the chronicle because they loved their land and their community; they thought these things were important and worthy of remembrance.

The people of the vale reckoned the passage of years by counting the rings of the great trees that stood in the sacred grove on the far side of the river. An acorn was planted on the day the stone bridge was completed, spanning the Anwin and connecting Candlewick to the fields in the east. When the old oak finally died, it was cut down and its rings were counted, and a record was made in the chronicle. Another acorn was planted beside the stump, and so a tradition began that has continued ever since. Twelve stumps now stood in a wide spiral on the far side of the Anwin, in the shade of one vast and ancient tree, the last of the great oaks.

In the nine hundred and eighty-seventh year of the thirteenth tree, a man came out of the east across the Anwin. His name was Hieronymus Flak, and he described himself as an itinerant scientist who had traveled across

Entara studying the devastation caused by the final war and the fall of the Old Kingdom and setting right the wrongs that were done long ago.

He paid for his bread and board by giving lectures at the tavern. The subjects of his talks were varied, and they were always well-attended. Sometimes he spoke of the nature of the cosmos, telling how the stars were not just pinpricks in the veil of heaven, but really distant suns with worlds of their own that the Astari had visited in their wide travels. Other times, he described the workings of the human body, healing medicines, or the unrealized potential of the human mind. Often he gave demonstrations of scientific marvels of the dawn ages: Holograms emitted from rings on his fingers, mechanical flying birds, and so on.

People started calling him *the wizard.* He was a charismatic man, a showman. He was wise in the ancient lore of the Astari, and he understood the old machines and computers that can still be found in the ruins.

He got to know many of the villagers well during that time. He visited farms and workshops across the vale and interviewed the farmers and craftsmen. He performed many experiments in widely separated places, taking soil samples from the farms, measuring the quality of the air blowing in from the wilderness, examining the bodies of animals found dead in the forest. Most significantly, he took expeditions into the borderlands and excavated the ruins, retrieving several items of technology he found buried there.

One day, he summoned everyone in the vale to a gathering in the square. A stage was built so he could be seen above the crowd, and he spoke into a device that amplified his voice for all to hear. He said his studies were now complete and he was ready to share the results of his experiments.

He told the people that in all his travels he had rarely met more honest and hardworking people than the folk of the vale. The farmers worked their land with diligence and care, always mindful not to overwork the soil and careful to avoid breeding undesirable traits into animals or crops merely to improve yield. The craftsmen of the vale were masters of their arts whose labor was respected all across the fields we know.

However, despite all the love and respect of the people for their land, the wizard declared that the vale was dying. Long ago, the Astari, in their wickedness and ignorance, had unleashed terrible powers upon the land that had worked over many generations like a slow poison that was only now revealing itself.

The omens had been there for a while, though none had interpreted the signs until now. In the hills of the upper vale there were sheep born without eyes, and several newborn infants had been secretly buried by parents who had been unable to bear the disfigurements of their children. In the lowlands, two farms beside the river had been burned after a sickness spread from the cattle to the people.

These were localized events, but the wizard spoke of a more general malaise afflicting the entirety of the vale. Studying the chronicle, he noted that life expectancy had fallen shockingly in recent generations. In old age, many people now suffered from diseases and afflictions unheard of by their ancestors. Barrenness among women had become commonplace, although it was rarely spoken of. Many children were born with missing fingers or toes. If these trends continued, the descendants of those now living in the vale would be doomed to live shorter and shorter lives, becoming sick and deformed as the generations passed until the vale was devoid of people.

CHAPTER 14

'I don't believe him,' Pandora said as she paced up and down the stone floor of the meeting hall. 'This guy, this wizard, he was lying, wasn't he?'

Galen looked up from the chronicle from which he had been reading. 'There seemed no reason to doubt him. His knowledge of ancient lore was without compare in the vale, and he was held to be a man of good moral character.'

'Did you believe him?' Pandora said.

'No, I did not believe him,' Galen said. 'I had doubted the wizard ever since he first arrived in the vale. His words were too carefully chosen, his magic tricks too gaudily impressive. But I misunderstood his motives. I believed he was merely a charlatan making a living by manipulating others; a con-man, a huckster. The truth was far worse than I could have imagined. Let us continue our walk, and I will show you the wizard's work.'

They left the meeting hall and continued north. Soon they had left the village behind and were among farmland once more. Pandora thought she would be relieved to leave that empty place, but the countryside was even more bleak and depressing. The fields had almost vanished beneath a sprawling mass of gorse bushes. Farm buildings had crumbled until all that remained was a pile of stones where the chimneys had once stood. The fences were tangled with brambles as thick as Pandora's thumb, with thorns so long and cruel that the skeletons of small animals were strangled in their grip.

'The wizard told us that although our situation was dire, there was a way to save the vale,' Galen continued. 'He said that buried in the ruins on the borderlands was the key to our salvation.'

'I've been wondering about those ruins,' Pandora said. 'The observatory looks so different from anything in Candlewick, and the fragments of walls and arches we saw look very ancient. Are they connected? Who built them?'

'The observatory and the surrounding ruins were built by a people called the Astari. We know very little about them because they have been extinct for many thousands of years. It is said they were a race of scientists and philosophers. They came from somewhere else, way out in space on the far side of the universe. They settled here on Entara because there was something on this world that was unique; something strange they had never seen before in all their travels. It was something they did not understand, and so they built vast research centers to study it. They devoted their entire civilization to studying it.'

'So what happened to them?' Pandora said.

'The records in the chronicle are very confused about this period,' Galen said. 'There was a war of terrible fury during those days, and incredible powers were unleashed onto the land. When it was over, the Astari were gone. Their cities and laboratories fell into ruin, and the scattered settlements of the people who survived became isolated amid vast areas of uninhabitable wilderness.

'The wizard claimed to be a survivor from those distant days. He asserted that the depraved science of the Old Kingdom could be recovered and redeemed by those with sufficient wisdom to understand and remedy the mistakes made in ancient times. With his expertise and scientific knowledge, the wizard declared he could restore certain Astari machines that could heal the land, clearing the soil of poison, filtering the air of impurities, and cleansing the water of contaminants. The people of the vale would still face many years of hardship, suffering the lingering effects of the corruption that was killing the land, but the grandchildren of those now in infancy could expect to lead long and healthy lives in a world of increasing abundance. A vote was held among the eldermen, and the wizard's proposals were accepted unanimously.'

'A miracle solution, right,' Pandora scoffed. 'But you said you didn't believe him. How can the vote have been unanimous?'

'I summoned the wizard to the council of elders and I challenged him on his claims. I questioned his condemnation of the Astari, whom our legends tell us to have been wise custodians of Entara. He scolded me like a schoolboy and told me I believed in fairy tales written by apologists for tyrants. I questioned his analysis of the chronicle and argued that our ancestors had not lived longer or healthier lives than we do today. He mocked me and said I did not understand the early writings, which few now can interpret. For these and other reasons I was ejected from the council, and my views were ignored. The other elders were not bad people, but they had fallen under the sway of a collective madness that was to doom us all.'

The road turned a corner around the hulking mass of a huge gorse bush. On the other side a stone obelisk stood beside the path. It was around thirty feet tall and made of black stone veined with deep green and purple.

'What's this?' Pandora said. 'Some kind of memorial?'

'This is what the wizard dug up in the borderlands,' Galen said. 'In the most remote part of the vale, away from the other ruins, is a pyramid structure which has suffered less degradation than some of the other buildings. It has no doors or windows, and none have ever speculated as to its original purpose. Traditionally it has been shunned because people who linger in that area suffer terrible nightmares. The sigils on the pyramid's walls are said to be Astari warning signs. The wizard led teams of men to the pyramid and excavated a great doorway buried deep underground. It was a circular door of some unknown metal, with no lock or handle. The wizard opened it with a wave of his hand, revealing a large chamber within.

'There were six obelisks such as this inside the pyramid. The wizard ordered carts and pulleys brought to remove them, and on his instruction they were transported to different locations around the vale.'

Pandora approached the obelisk and touched its smooth surface. It felt cold and damp, though there was no moisture on the rock. She heard a sound and leaned close, holding her breath to listen. The whole construct was vibrating at a frequency just below the range of her hearing. It made her feel queasy and she pulled back.

Galen continued. 'The wizard had the obelisks placed at the convergence of ley lines. He told us that these obelisks emit harmonizing waves that would heal the sickness in the land.'

'Sounds like bullshit to me,' Pandora said.

'The people of the vale thought otherwise. When harvest came, it was lauded as the most bountiful year in living memory. The wizard was celebrated as the savior of the vale.'

'Then what happened?' Pandora asked.

'The following year the crops failed, badly,' Galen said. 'A blight afflicted the farms in the north of the vale, killing entire herds of cattle and turning fields to dust. The people of Springwater came south to beg the wizard to help them, and he traveled north in all haste. He repeated his experiments of the year before, taking soil samples and measuring the quality of the water and the air. With a grim face he called another council and declared that the damage done to the vale was greater than he at first suspected. He professed that he had studied for many lifetimes of men to learn the secrets of the Old Kingdom, to learn from the mistakes of the Astari, who in their foolish pride had used weapons of such awesome power they had poisoned the earth for eternity. His dream was to heal the wounds of Entara and create a world where men could live long lives of happiness and good health, as the Astari had done before their wanton destruction. However, despite the best efforts of the wizard's science, there was no way to prevent the gradual death of the vale. He predicted that within a year Springwater would be uninhabitable, and Candlewick would suffer the same fate within twenty years, followed by all the fields we know. With a grave and solemn voice, he declared that the vale would have to be abandoned.'

'And still no one suspected him?' Pandora said. 'I know that what happened here is a tragedy, but it seems to me the people of the vale had a responsibility to demand some answers.'

'It is difficult to describe the mood in the vale at that time,' Galen explained. 'The wizard performed many miracles during those days, using the ancient devices to heal the sick, bring fertility to barren wombs, and cast out spirits from diseased minds. The counsel of the wizard was sought and heeded in all things, from the construction of a windmill to the planning of flood barriers, from the treatment of baldness to the interpretation of dreams. People honestly believed that the evil that had come to the vale was already lying in wait deep in the soil, buried by the Astari millennia ago, and the wizard had arrived at the perfect time to rescue them.'

By this time the ground was rising and the path became steep and rocky. The river was reduced to a stream rushing over a stony course from the mountains far ahead. Catherine brought them to a halt. She was a little out of breath and favoring one leg. 'This has been an interesting trip down memory lane, but if we go any further up this slope, one of you is going to have to carry me.'

Galen hurried to her side and took her arm. 'Mother, why didn't you say something sooner?'

She pulled her arm away. 'Oh, don't make a fuss. I don't mind the walk back down the hill, but this leg always causes me trouble around this time of day. Old age, girls.

Don't bother with it if you want my advice.'

They spoke little on the return journey, and that gave Pandora plenty of opportunity to think on all she had seen and heard. She was rapidly remembering more and more about the vale, and she needed time to organize her thoughts and rebuild her concept of her childhood. With each bend in the path new sights triggered old memories: Rowing a boat up the river and singing sea shanties while Holly strummed her ukulele; picking strawberries with sticky fingers as they filled wicker baskets and snacked as they worked; climbing trees, falling out of trees; wading through the river and feeling the fish tickle her toes.

At the same time she remembered events in Ojai that had slipped her mind. Once, after the girls had visited Candlewick a few times, Holly had decorated her bedroom wall with a collage of Polaroids from their adventures in the vale. Pandora became alarmed that the pictures clearly showed the girls playing together in a faraway place and interacting with strangely dressed folk. She took down all the photographs, along with Holly's drawings and paintings of the otherworld. 'We can't let Mom and Dad know where we go,' she explained. 'They would totally freak out. I hate keeping secrets from them, but I don't want them to worry about us. Because there's no need to worry, right? Entara is a totally safe place.'

Keeping their travels a secret was often hard work, and once they almost got caught. One day, after returning from a night camping in the observatory, their father challenged them at breakfast.

'Last night I stopped by the Coleman ranch,' he said, and the girls exchanged a glance over their cereal. It was in Jack Coleman's woods that the girls ostensibly went camping when Holly blinked them to the otherworld.

'How is old Jack?' Sandra said.

'He was out on his porch, drinking whiskey and smoking cigars by the light of the moon. I told him I'd come to check on the girls. He had a lot of nice things to say about you both. I understand last weekend you helped him load citrus crates onto that ramshackle old trailer of his?'

'Yeah, we like helping out on the ranch,' Pandora said, 'and Mr Coleman gives Holly an unlimited supply of lemons for her lemonade. He's a really nice old guy.'

'Yes, he is,' David said. 'But farm work is heavy work, and not always suitable for young girls. Besides, I don't think you should be getting paid in lemons anymore. From now on, Jack says he's happy to pay you the same as he pays his farm hands.'

'Holy shit, that's awesome,' Pandora bounced in her seat. 'You hear that Hol? We're gonna be rich.'

'Language,' David warned. 'Now listen, after I'd had a talk with Jack, I wandered down by the creek to check on you guys. I found your campsite where I expected it to be, but I didn't find either of you. I don't mind telling you I was worried. I almost put out an APB on the radio. Now obviously you're both fine, but do you mind telling me where you were?'

Pandora had fretted about this possibility for weeks. She had prepared a stack of index cards with excuses, evasions, fibs, half-truths, and white lies she planned to use in the event her parents stumbled upon the truth. She bit her lip and wished she could dash upstairs to consult them. 'We came back home early last night. We heard an animal in the creek and thought it might be a mountain lion.'

Their parents had both been at the station last night, so she hoped it wouldn't be possible to disprove her story.

David scratched his head and frowned. 'Yeah, but y'see I came home and checked the house, and you weren't here either.'

Pandora improvised quickly. 'Okay, but you would have driven here a lot quicker than we were walking. We took the long way around, all the way up to Grand Avenue. Y'know, to avoid the lion. Probably we arrived home seconds after you left.'

David mulled this idea. 'It's possible. I got a call out to Meiners Oaks right after I got here, so I had to rush off.'

'David, I'm not sure I like the idea of the girls camping out there past the creek all by themselves,' Sandra said. 'I mean, what if there really was a mountain lion?'

David shook his head. 'They don't come down this far into the valley. Even so, your mom's right, you girls shouldn't be out there alone at night.'

Pandora held her breath and clutched Holly's hand beneath the table. It sounded like their father was about to forbid them to camp away from the house.

'I'm going to give you both pagers,' he said after a moment's contemplation. 'At the station we've got some old-fashioned police pagers from before the days of cell phones. I want you both to carry one at all times. Then if you ever get into trouble, you can send me an alert. It's not like a phone where you have to speak or type a message. You just press the button and it calls for help. You reckon you can manage that, Hol?'

'She'll manage,' Pandora nodded vigorously. 'I think it's a great idea, Dad. Thanks.'

CHAPTER 15

By the time they passed through Candlewick and entered the forest, Bess was too exhausted to carry on. Holly carried her for the last mile while the old girl licked her face appreciatively. When they reached the cottage the sun was low over the western hills. Galen opened a jug of cider brewed from apples grown beside the river, and Catherine made a simple stew. The conversation was lively as Catherine and Galen recounted old stories and reminded the sisters of good times they had once had.

When their meal was done Galen found a mandolin and a flute, and together with Holly made jolly tunes while Catherine and Pandora competed to compose funny verses. With the music and cider flowing freely, Pandora for a time forgot all her worries and was transported back in years to a time when this little cottage had been a refuge from the ordinary world; a place of magic and wonder, far away from the mundane world.

As midnight approached they settled around the hearth where a warming fire had been lit, and the girls sat side by side under a great knitted blanket. Despite the good cheer, Pandora still had many questions about what had happened in the vale so many years ago. Galen poured them all another mug of cider and sat down to finish his tale of Candlewick.

'After his pronouncement on the doom of the vale, the

wizard continued to make promises that people were eager to hear. He told us that over the past decades he had gathered many people together far to the east. In that place, he said, people were building a new civilization to overshadow the memory of the Astari. He invited all the people of the vale to join him on the long journey east and abandon this land until a later time when the world would be healed by Flak's grand plan.

'And many people did leave. I tried to stop them, but what story could I weave that had such a hold on people's imagination? I could offer only years of hard toil and labor in a dying land. I even drew up plans to move the entire village two miles downstream, where the land was still productive and fertile. People listened with a sympathetic ear, but their hearts were already in the east, dreaming of the fabulous city of the wizard.

'The people who remained looked to me to guide them, but in my heart I knew our venture was failing. With every week that passed the blight spread its influence further south, turning fields to desert and causing animals to wither and die. During the next few months, almost every family packed up and left, all heading east after the others. They repeated to each other the wizard's promises about a great city with tall towers, just like in the days of the Old Kingdom. All nonsense, of course. Not one of 'em had ever seen a building taller than the clocktower in the square.'

'Then why didn't you leave with them?' Pandora said.

Catherine and Galen shared a glance and held each other's hands. 'How could we?' Catherine said. 'This is our home.'

'Our cottage is the most southerly of all the cultivated lands of the vale,' Galen said. 'The blight has not yet reached us here. We don't care about new cities in the dawn lands, or bringing back the Old Kingdom. We've got our little cottage and we've got each other, and that's all that matters.'

'The only thing we really miss is Jason,' Catherine said.

'I still barely remember him,' Pandora said. 'It's the one piece of this whole puzzle I still can't figure out. Did he really leave with the others?'

'He remained behind with us after the first migrants departed, hoping to make the best of what we had left,' Galen said. 'But when the other families gave up and left as well, he followed them. Not because he was fooled by their belief in mythical cities, you understand. No, he was furious that they were so eager to abandon the land their ancestors had cared for since time immemorial. He had begun to think of Candlewick as his true home, and he was devastated that it was being taken away from him piece by piece as each family left. He made a vow to follow the wizard into the east and discover his true purpose, to expose him, and bring our people back home.'

'He's a good lad,' Catherine said. 'He was the answer to our dreams. He treated us like his true parents. We started calling each other Mom and Dad as pet names. Secretly, of course. I think Jason heard us, but he never took offense.'

'How long ago did Jason leave?' Pandora said.

'Nearly twelve years,' Catherine said.

'Too long,' Galen said. 'We still hold out hope he'll return. We set dinner for three each night. A foolish ritual of old folks, I know, but it gives us comfort to think he's still out there somewhere.'

'He is still out there,' Catherine insisted.

A loud crash at the door made them all jump. Everyone fell silent and listened. From outside a chilling laugh was heard.

'What the hell was that?' Pandora said.

Galen smacked his fist on the table and rose from the chair. 'They're back. Damn it all to hell.'

'After all these years?' Catherine said, reaching for her husband.

A series of rapid thuds sounded as if the house was being pounded by rocks from without. Hammerfalls struck the wooden frame of the cottage. Plaster fell from the ceiling, windows shook in their frames.

'What's happening?' Pandora shouted over the noise. 'Is there someone outside?'

'Get these girls upstairs,' Galen said to Catherine. 'I'll secure the doors and windows.'

'No time,' Catherine pushed him aside. 'Stupid, stupid old fools that we are. Sitting here drinking cider and singing songs.' She hurried to the kitchen door and rammed home a metal bolt. Galen did the same at the front door.

Pandora went to the window. A mist had come out of the forest and there were lights out there, like lanterns moving through the haze. 'There's someone out there.'

'Get away from the windows,' Galen yanked her back so hard she collided with a chair and it toppled to the floor. He slammed the shutters and secured them with a brass hook. Catherine opened a drawer in the sideboard and took out several metal wind chimes that jangled noisily. She moved swiftly around the house, standing on a wooden stool and hanging the wind chimes above every door and window.

The noise from outside fell silent and the only sound was the jingle of the chimes.

'Don't worry yourselves,' Galen said, drawing the girls together. 'While we are inside there is no danger.'

'It sounded like someone was attacking the house,' Pandora said.

'Phantoms,' Galen said. 'My God, I thought this nightmare was behind us. I prayed we had seen the last of them.'

Catherine hung the last of the chimes and nodded with satisfaction. 'Doors and windows are warded. That should keep them away for the rest of the night.'

The kitchen door rattled in its frame, followed by the shutters on the window. It was as if someone – or something – were moving around the house, checking methods of entry. Frustrated at every turn, the mocking voice returned with a sibilant hiss of tittering laughter.

Bess curled up in a corner and whined, tucking her nose under her forepaw.

'Who is that?' Pandora said. 'There is someone outside. I can hear them.'

A breeze rushed past the house, rustling the trees as if the air itself sighed. For long moments there was silence.

'I'll pour us all another drink,' Catherine said. 'In fact, maybe I'll break out that bottle of brandy we've been saving. I think we all need it.'

They returned to the table and each nursed a glass that Catherine filled with pungent brandy from a dusty clay jar. No one spoke for a long while. Everyone was listening for a return of the unnatural noise, and the voice that had mocked them from the darkness.

When the tension became too much Pandora spoke. 'When we were sleeping in the observatory last night, there was a fog that came out of the forest. I could see lights over there, like people carrying lanterns through the mist. Just now I saw the same thing outside.'

'Those are the phantom lights,' Galen said, staring into his drink. 'It is fortunate you were in the observatory. The phantoms fear the old ruins and will not go near them.'

'These wind chimes are made of metal salvaged from the ruins,' Catherine pointed to the chimes over the windows and doors. 'They keep the phantoms outside where they can't do any harm.'

'But what are they?' Pandora said.

'I thought they'd gone for good,' Catherine said. 'We haven't seen or heard them for years. I took down the chimes long ago. I'd come to half-believe it was all just a bad dream. A figment of imagination. Keeping the chimes up seemed like a superstition, so I put them away. God, what a stupid old woman I am.'

'Calm yourself, Mother,' Galen said, squeezing her hand. 'We both decided to take the chimes down, and nothing bad happened. The phantoms stayed away, and we have had years of peace.'

'Until now.' Catherine drained her glass and poured

another.

Galen turned to the girls. 'There were three other families who stayed behind after everyone else had gone. We gathered in each other's houses each night for companionship, drinking to our sorrows, trying our best to console each other. One night, we heard a banging at the door.

'There was a strange sight waiting for us outside. A thick mist filled the air, and there were blue lights floating in the distance. At first we thought they were people carrying lanterns. We called out to them, but there was no reply. Curious, some of our neighbors went to investigate and we lost sight of them in the mist.

'Moments later we heard the most awful screams. When we ran to find our friends they were dead. The manner of their deaths is something I can barely describe to you. Each body was contorted in a hideous, frozen image of writhing agony. Each bore terrible wounds to his face. Skin hung torn from cheeks, and lips were rent from jaws, revealing bare teeth and bone beneath. Their eyes were ripped from their sockets, dangling on ragged nerves from the wretched remains of their faces. The greatest horror was the realization that these injuries appeared entirely self-inflicted. We found a torn nail embedded in the cheek of the man whose finger it had broken from. Another man held his own eyeballs in his hands.'

'What could have caused them to do that?' Pandora said.

'We did not wait to find out,' Galen continued. 'We fled back to the house and locked ourselves inside, arming ourselves with whatever implements came to hand. We waited out the night while the phantom lights hammered on the windows and doors.'

'Phantom lights?'

'That is the name we gave them. A manifestation of our fears.'

The door shook again. There was a shriek somewhere far off, and then silence.

‘The phantoms came back the following night,’ Catherine said. ‘We huddled in our homes, afraid to go outside. The next morning we found our neighbors to the west dead, just like the others. Those things, whatever they are, had killed a mother, a father, and six children. Even the little ones had torn out their own eyes. The baby, we think her poor mother took out her eyes before she did it to herself.’

‘Why would people do that to themselves?’ Pandora said. ‘It doesn’t make any sense.’

‘I hope I never find out the answer to that question,’ Catherine said.

‘But where did they come from?’

Galen replied. ‘When the wizard opened the pyramid and retrieved the black obelisks, some of the workmen caught glimpses of other chambers. The wizard warned them away and said the Astari had locked away their worst nightmares inside that place. I believe that when we refused to leave, the wizard unleashed some terrible force within the pyramid to punish those who would not follow him.’

‘It’s his voice you can hear,’ Catherine said with a shudder. ‘The laughter outside, I mean. It’s his way of reminding us that he has not forgiven our disobedience.’ The clamor outside had quieted down, and Catherine looked more at ease. ‘Anyway, some bedtime story, right? Hopefully that’ll be the last of it. I suggest we all turn in for the night and try to get some sleep. The phantom lights are scary, but if you ignore them they go away, sometimes for years at a time. Now then, I’ll make you girls a bed upstairs. In the morning everything will be alright, you’ll see.’

CHAPTER 16

Catherine left them with a small lantern which would provide a dim light all night long. The bedroom had been Jason's, and there were faded Polaroids pinned to the wall, showing the boy and the two sisters. Pandora's memories were returning, but still her mind drew a blank when she saw the boy's face. She wondered if she would ever meet him again and learn the story of how he came to live in this world. She lay down beside Holly and watched the flickering flame of the lantern, letting the soft glow lull her to sleep.

It was dark outside when she awoke. The candle inside the lantern had burned low. Holly was gone.

She sat up and looked around. The dim light confirmed that Holly was not in the room. 'God dammit, Holly, where have you got to this time?'

She got out of bed and went out into the hall. It was dark, but she crept down the stairs without making a noise. In the living room the embers of the fire provided a faint glow.

'Holly, are you in here?' she whispered. There was no movement or sound.

A thud struck the kitchen window, knocking loose the shutter. On the lawn outside Holly stood in her nightdress facing the woods. Pale blue lights swirled and glided through the trees, making long shadows of the trunks.

Pandora tried the kitchen door, but the bolt was stuck and wouldn't move. She banged on the window, shouting Holly's name. She tried to open the casement, but it, too, was jammed and would not open.

A man emerged from the forest. He was tall and handsome; an older man, but powerfully built, dressed in the manner of an old-fashioned gentleman. He reached Holly and lifted her chin to look into her eyes.

The phantoms swirled close, and in their light Pandora saw the stranger was the most striking individual she had ever seen. Not only strong in body, his face revealed a man of high intellect and powerful will, the aristocratic features of a man who had never known self-doubt, hesitancy, or depression. Pandora knew intuitively that his name was Hieronymus Flak.

She wrestled with the door bolt again, but stopped herself. *This is an illusion. This isn't real. Holly is safe and sound asleep upstairs.*

Except she wasn't. The bed had been empty when Pandora awoke. Hadn't it? She wasn't so sure now. She felt confused. Her mind was cloudy. Flak's face kept crowding into her head, pushing out all other thoughts. He was fascinating, mesmerizing. No man had ever looked more like a hero, a villain, an emperor, a god.

Flak took Holly's nightdress and tore it apart with one casual movement of his strong hands. The flimsy material cascaded over her pale flesh, revealing her naked body to the glow of the phantom lights. Holly glanced over her shoulder and saw Pandora at the window. She smiled, and there was a hint of lascivious pleasure in that grin. She took the wizard's hand and placed it on her breast, drawing his fingers down her belly and between her legs.

Flak caressed her with indulgent affection, casting his gaze approvingly over the curves of her body. He pushed her down onto the grass and knelt over her.

He was forcing himself on her now, but Holly made only a token show of resistance for his pleasure. After all, she belonged to him. He was king of kings, lord of all creation, and every knee bent to him. He did not need her consent, nor did he coerce her against her will, because all living things obeyed him in recognition of his mastery over the natural world.

At the moment of penetration Holly writhed in passion, or pain, or both. She looked at Pandora and licked her lips wantonly. There was lust in her eyes, but also contempt and cruel, deliberate mockery. After all, hadn't Pandora paraded her boyfriends before Holly at candlelit dinners, kissing them and laughing at their jokes, taking them into her room to fuck while Holly sat on her bed alone listening to her moans of ecstasy? Wasn't this fair payback for her feelings of superiority over her sister, knowing that she was the desirable one and no man would ever look twice at poor, stupid, silent Holly?

The wizard thrust harder and faster into her. An uncontrollable rage arose in Pandora's heart at the sight of Holly's sensual display. She wrestled with the window again, desperate to open it and cry out into the night that *he was fucking the wrong sister*.

She wanted to scream. *Don't you know she wet the bed until she was nine years old? Don't you know she's too stupid to use a panty liner and her periods are a disgusting bloody mess?*

She returned her attention to the door and put all her strength into withdrawing the bolt. Finally it came free and the door swung open, revealing the wizard thrusting into Holly's small naked body as she arched her back and her climax approached.

There was a kitchen knife on the table. Pandora took it, determined to teach her sister a lesson she would never forget. She stepped out onto the grass, but an arm seized her from behind, wrapping around her throat and cutting off her air. She choked and fell backwards, smacking her head on the doorpost. Hands grasped feverishly at her, dragging her back onto the flagstone floor of the kitchen.

Dazed and angry, she looked towards the garden just as

the door slammed shut, blocking the consummation of the horrific scene on the lawn. Holly was leaning over her, wide-eyed with fear. The pale blue light from beyond the kitchen window was extinguished. By the time Pandora got to her feet the lawn was in darkness. There were no phantom lights anywhere. The wizard had vanished.

There was an odd gap in Pandora's memory after that. She did not remember going back upstairs to bed, and her next conscious awareness was the smell of cooking bacon. Catherine tapped on the bedroom door to announce that breakfast was ready.

Neither Catherine nor Galen had been disturbed by any noises in the night, and Pandora began to wonder if the whole awful experience had been nothing more than a nightmare. Nevertheless, all through breakfast, she continually experienced flashbacks that made her blood run cold and chased away all appetite she had for Catherine's splendid cooking.

Holly was the only one who might be able to tell her what really happened, but she was shy and nervous that morning, unable to meet Pandora's eyes. After breakfast Holly wandered outside and stood on the lawn, peering off into the trees. Pandora joined her and whispered softly. 'Was it real? Last night, I mean. Give me a sign, Hol. Nod your head, or squeeze my hand. I need to know cuz I feel like I'm going crazy here.'

Holly twisted her hair anxiously and turned away.

When they returned to the kitchen, Catherine and Galen were standing together, holding hands. 'Looks like it's going to be a beautiful day,' Catherine said.

'Yes, it does,' Pandora said. 'It seems like the more I remember of this place, the more it seems like every day is beautiful, no matter what the weather.'

Galen cleared his throat. 'Listen, Mother and I have had a talk and we want you to know that you girls are welcome to stay as long as you want. It'll be nice to have you both around helping out on the farm again.'

Pandora smiled, and she was very tempted to accept Galen's offer. A couple of weeks spent here at the cottage would be the perfect vacation from all the worries and anxieties of Earth. Instead she shook her head. 'That would be wonderful, but we can't stay. Our arrival here yesterday wasn't exactly under the best circumstances, and we've got a lot of problems to fix back home.'

Catherine nodded ruefully. 'We kinda figured that might be the case. You weren't exactly dressed in traveling gear when you arrived. If it isn't prying, what did bring you back here after all these years?'

'Holly's power only seems to work in times of emergencies now she's grown up. Two nights ago, some people broke into our house and kidnapped us. The only way for us to escape was to come here.'

'Kidnapped? That's awful,' Catherine said. 'And there I was imagining you lived in some kind of paradise beyond the stars.'

'It's hardly that, although it has its moments. Anyway, we urgently need to talk to the police and catch the people who tried to abduct us.'

'I couldn't agree more,' Catherine said. 'You go and hunt down those assholes, and when you catch 'em, give 'em a kick from me and Galen both.'

They bid goodbye to Catherine and Galen at the edge of the forest, and Pandora found herself overwhelmed by sadness and broke into tears. It was unlikely that she would ever see her friends again. She felt it was a cruel trick of fate to be reunited with Catherine and Galen for such a short time, only to have them taken away again so quickly.

The hike back to the observatory felt lonely and sad. Their short stay in Candlewick had opened a door into a golden memory of childhood when time seemed infinite and each new day brought endless hours of adventure and delight. It felt deeply unfair that this magical place should be shown to her like a shadow out of the past, only to be torn from her sight as soon as she recognized it.

The afternoon sun cast flickering diamonds of gold onto the earth beneath the rustling canopy of leaves, so much like the forests of California, and yet somehow unlike them, as if the light and air of Entara were imbued with secret qualities that made each experience more vivid and vital, and Earth's humble forests were mere reflections of a greater majesty. Despite the abundant beauty on all sides, Pandora's heart was heavy because she now understood that the whole of her adult life had been spent unconsciously seeking a place that was now going to be denied to her forever.

While they walked through the forest and up into the hills, she made plans to create a new journal in which she would write all her memories of Entara. Then at least she would retain some imperfect record of this wondrous place, though the passage of years might erase her true memories until all that was left was the knowledge that she once remembered the faces of her lost friends; a memory of a memory, preserved like footprints in the sand.

CHAPTER 17

It was early on Sunday morning when the sisters blinked into the alleyway behind Ojai Arcade. The overflowing dumpsters were still there, but Holly's mural had disappeared many years ago, erased by some overzealous city maintenance operative. No shops were yet open, and Pandora had no money for a bus or a taxi, so they had no choice but to walk back to Edgewood Avenue. The morning was bright and cheerful and Holly was in a buoyant mood, swishing her long tie-dye dress around in the breeze. Pandora was less enthused about her Little House on the Prairie dress, which attracted some odd glances from joggers and dog walkers. She hoped they would not run into anyone they knew.

When they arrived at Edgewood Avenue, Pandora lifted one of Holly's potted plants from the porch and used the spare key to unlock the door. The house was in a sorry state, with the ruins of the dragon tree spread up and down the staircase where Pandora had hurled it at "Sam", the sinister camper. There were footprints in the dirt trodden across the carpet, and she stopped Holly in the doorway.

'Holly, be careful where you put your feet. I want Chief Brooks to get plaster casts of those prints, or whatever it is they do. Y'know, like that guy did with the Bigfoot prints up in Bluff Creek.'

Holly removed her flip-flops and tiptoed into the kitchen. Pandora made a quick circuit of the downstairs rooms to make sure everything was copacetic and then went up into Holly's studio. The room was in chaos, with easels and craft tools scattered across the floor. The rug was crumpled in a far corner, and the trap door into the garage remained open in the floor. There was no obvious evidence to be collected here, but she didn't want to disturb the scene and so refrained from picking up the fallen art supplies.

She showered and changed into normal clothes, and spent a few minutes supervising Holly's change of outfit (it wasn't like Holly couldn't dress herself, but Pandora knew her sister would wear the tie-dye getup until it fell apart). Once Holly was clean and dressed and firmly ensconced in the living room with the Nintendo, Pandora went into her study and started making plans.

She needed to call Chief Brooks at the station and report the kidnapping. Before she could do that, she had to consider carefully all the events of the past forty-eight hours. It was important to give as much accurate detail as possible to the police, but she was anxious to avoid any mention of blinking to distant worlds. She quickly found that it was difficult to make her account coherent when Holly's power was removed from the narrative. The chief was an astute man, and he would surely notice the holes in Pandora's story unless she could think of a convincing scenario that did not include teleportation.

The task took the rest of the morning. While she was mentally recounting the events leading up to the abduction, she recalled that she had been reading her childhood diary before she retired to bed. She turned to the table where she had laid out the boxes of journals from the attic. The boxes were not there. The diaries were missing, and so was the canvas shoulder bag stuffed full of Polaroids from the observatory. Her mind had been so preoccupied with the kidnapping that she had not noticed.

Maybe the kidnappers took them, she thought, but

quickly dismissed the idea. The kidnapping happened rapidly, and by referring to her own notes she knew there was no opportunity for the abductors to have entered the study and cleared away dozens of notebooks and stacks of photographs.

She went downstairs and found Holly in the kitchen, staring at the fridge door. 'Holly, did you move any stuff in my office? Like our old journals or the Polaroids from the observatory? I'm not mad if you did, just show me where you put them.'

There were signs that Holly had been making milkshakes. A tub of ice cream was beside the sink, along with milk, whipped cream, two tall glasses, and a pot of chocolate sprinkles. Evidently something had distracted her. Pandora realized she was staring at a spot on the fridge door where she had stuck a picture of the boy Jason at the observatory. The picture was gone.

Holly leaned down and picked up a Bugs Bunny magnet from the floor.

'This was holding your picture in place, wasn't it? Somebody took our journals, and all the pictures. Holly, what the hell is going on?'

Pandora ran a hand through her hair and tried to make sense of what had happened. In the time that had passed since the kidnapping, someone had entered the house and stolen the diaries and the pictures. But why would anyone take such items at all? To a stranger, the diaries would seem like nothing more than the imaginings of two young girls. The photographs would merely seem like a pictorial record of a camping trip. Nevertheless, she couldn't shake the feeling that unwelcome eyes were even now reading and studying those experiences which to her felt deeply private and secret.

The thefts felt very *intimate*, contributing to the sense of violation she had about the kidnapping. She couldn't help but think all these mysteries somehow fitted together like pieces of a jigsaw puzzle whose overall image was hidden from her.

What was worse, the whole house felt wrong as if every object, so dear and precious and filled with sentimental value, had been carefully moved, studied, and replaced in exactly the position it had formerly occupied. She felt a crawling sensation all over her skin at the thought of those sick bastards touching her belongings, or searching through Holly's bedroom.

She rushed upstairs and went to her study. In the desk was an old cell phone. She swapped the SIM with her smashed phone and called the police.

CHAPTER 18

Chief Brooks sat on the couch listening carefully to Pandora's story, taking extensive notes. Holly sat on an easy chair in the corner, sketching on a pad

'… and then just before I called you, I found more missing items,' Pandora said. 'Diaries, photographs, more personal things just like the hairbrushes and toothbrushes. Whoever these guys are, they really love getting their filthy hands on our private stuff.'

'Is that everything you remember?' Brooks said.

'Yes, I think that's everything.'

'And you're certain the campers and the kidnappers are the same people?'

'Absolutely, it was them. Same voices, same height and build. When the woman went upstairs to use the bathroom, she must have cut the cable that operates the security light out front. Then, when I went to call the station, I found the phone lines were cut as well.'

Brooks stood and went into the hall where a police technician was photographing the footprints in the spilled soil from the dragon tree. 'Were the kidnappers wearing gloves when you were taken?'

'Yes, but not when they visited earlier in the day,' Pandora said. 'The man touched the phone on the table here, and the woman certainly touched the banister railing on her way upstairs.'

Brooks instructed his technician to take prints. He opened the front door and studied the potted plant on the stoop. There was a ring of disturbed soil around the base, and he lifted the pot to reveal the spare key. 'Don't keep spare keys here anymore. Get a little key safe and attach it to the wall, somewhere out of sight. But you said these fellas used a snap gun to unlock your door, is that right?'

'A what?' Pandora said. 'I heard them scratching at the lock for a few moments, then the door swung open.'

'Uh-huh.' The chief examined the inside of the door. 'You've got a security chain here, do you use it?'

'No, I only put it on if I'm worried about answering the door.'

'Use it from now on,' Brooks said. 'Better still, replace it with a deadbolt or a swing bar lock.' He stepped out onto the porch and around the side of the house. A severed black cable dangled down from clips on the wall. 'There's your phone wire. One of them must have cut it while the other was unlocking your front door.'

'They must be professionals, right?' Pandora said. 'No one could be this fast and smooth unless they'd done this a dozen times. Oh God, that means they might not give up. They might come back.'

Brooks held his hands up to forestall her. 'I know this has been a really traumatic experience, but you're safe now. It's very unlikely these bozos will come back to bother you again. Kidnappings like this are almost always committed by opportunists seeking to abduct people in return for ransom money. The theft of personal items is unusual but probably just a way of providing proof of life. Now then, I notice you and your sister both have some bumps and scratches. Did the kidnappers beat you?'

'One of them kicked me,' Pandora said. 'But the cuts are from when we jumped out of the back of the van.'

'Yeah, I've got some questions about that. So you said that you used one of Holly's craft knives to cut your bonds. What exactly happened next?'

Pandora bit her lip and recounted the fictional scenario she had concocted. 'I got my arms and legs free, and I levered the lock of the cage open.'

'It was a hasp lock, you said, right?' Brooks said.

'With a padlock, yes.'

'You did well to break it open in the dark.'

'I guess I got lucky,' Pandora said. 'I did the same on Holly's cage and cut her free. Then I kicked the van doors open and we jumped out.'

'That was very brave.'

'The kidnappers didn't seem to notice anything, so we dashed off the road and hid. When we were certain they weren't coming back, we came back home.'

'Whereabouts was this?'

'I'm not sure,' Pandora said. 'Somewhere in the vicinity of Nordhoff Cemetery, I think. To be honest, I wasn't looking for street signs. We just ran and ran until we got home.'

'Okay,' Brooks studied his notes for a moment. 'Now then, you said the abduction happened two nights ago? And you escaped around three am? How come it took over thirty hours for you to report the incident?'

Pandora groaned inwardly. She hated lying at any time, but most especially to this kind man who was a friend of the family. Even worse, she hated that she was about to blame the lie on her sister.

'Holly was pretty distraught after we escaped,' Pandora said. 'When I got her home she was hysterical, and it took me hours to calm her down. After that I was so exhausted that I fell asleep and didn't wake up again until late last night. I'm sorry I didn't report to you sooner. I know I've given the abductors a chance to get away, but this really is the soonest I could talk to you.'

Holly came out onto the porch clutching her notepad to her chest. The chief patted her on the shoulder. 'You're a tough kid, Holly. Don't worry, we'll catch the guys who did this to you, and you'll never have to be afraid of them again.'

Holly tore the top sheet off her sketchpad and handed it to the chief. He stared at it and then turned it around for Pandora to see. 'Anyone you recognize?'

Holly had drawn a perfect life study of "Sam" and "Mike", both smiling their obnoxious shit-eating grins and wearing their stripey vacation shirts. Each was holding a toothbrush and a hairbrush.

'Oh my God, that's them,' Pandora said. 'Those are the people who kidnapped us.'

Brooks beamed at Holly. 'Well done, Holly. If you ever want a job as a forensic artist, you give me a call.'

CHAPTER 19

After the chief was gone, Pandora cleaned up the mess in the hall. Holly took a garbage bag up to her studio and threw away everything that had been knocked onto the floor during the struggle, as if every item had been contaminated and its creative potential destroyed.

Pandora hoped she would feel better once the police report was filed and the house set to rights. She still felt agitated and found herself repeatedly checking the front door or rushing to the window every time she heard a noise. Holly was still anxious and sat at the kitchen table nervously chewing ice cubes, a habit Pandora deplored. Eventually, she decided she didn't want to stay in the house tonight, so she picked up the phone and called Jackie.

Jackie lived in a spacious ranch-style house on the outskirts of Ojai. The house was filled with an avant-garde collection of art pieces, arrayed in a manner calculated to emphasize the eccentric tastes of the owner. In the hallway, a fourteenth-century Spanish triptych portraying the crucifixion was displayed beside a monstrous samurai warrior's helmet. On the opposite wall hung a collection of pornographic daguerreotypes. Holly always enjoyed visiting Jackie, partly for the art and the company of a good friend, but mostly because Jackie had a popcorn machine in her kitchen.

'Thanks so much for letting us stay tonight,' Pandora said as Jackie whisked the overnight bags from her hands and led them through to the guest bedrooms.

'Darling, when my two favorite clients are abducted by masked maniacs in the dead of night, the least I can do is offer a comfy bed and a pink gin,' Jackie said. 'Jesus, I haven't had a sleepover party since I was seventeen years old. We can order takeout, watch cheesy old movies, and drink until we pass out.'

The guest bedrooms were interconnecting rooms with full wall windows looking out over an enclosed courtyard with a pool and a fountain, and a collection of erotic sculptures from seventeenth-century France. Jackie had opened the glass doors to air the rooms, and the silk drapes moved gently in the breeze. It was shaded and peaceful and cool, and Pandora was glad she had chosen to leave Edgewood Avenue behind.

'Oh-h-h, I feel completely relaxed already,' Pandora said, swan-diving onto the bed, landing face-down and moaning into the pillow.

'If you need sleep, I'll make sure you're not disturbed,' Jackie said. 'Holly and I can entertain ourselves for a while. I've bought one of those old Dance Dance Revolution machines and it's fucking amazing.'

Pandora sat up. 'No, I don't want to sleep. But I don't feel much like dancing either.'

'Then come into the kitchen and I'll pour us some drinks. You look like you could use one.'

Jackie poured large measures of gin and a dash of tonic into three glasses. 'So tell me just what in flying fuckland is going on,' she said, pushing the drinks towards the sisters. 'What a crazy three days you girls have had. An accident at the Arcade, daylight robbery, and a kidnapping? You must have pissed off God big time for Him to send you all this trouble. You only gave me the headline news on the phone. Tell me exactly what happened.'

Pandora recounted the whole story as she had told Chief Brooks. When she was finished, Jackie drained her drink and poured another pink gin into three glasses.

'Oh, I don't normally let Holly have more than one drink,' Pandora said.

'Holly is a big girl now, and Auntie Jackie says she can have two gins if she wants. Besides, I'd say this is definitely a two-gin situation. Now look: You may not know this, but before I was Southern California's premier art dealer, I was a lawyer. Harvard Law School, class of 2000, if you want to know. Came to America straight from Oxford. I practiced criminal law in the United States for nearly twenty years, until the country turned to shit. I have heard just about every cockamamie story there is, and dear girl, your story has more holes in it than a whore's knickers.'

Pandora was aghast. 'Jackie, everything I have told you is the truth.'

'Bullshit,' Jackie said. 'When did you say your happy campers stole the diaries and the photographs?'

'Uh, yesterday, I think. I don't know.'

'But you were both home by that time, weren't you? Let's recap. You escaped from the back of the van at three am, came home, Holly freaked out, and you spent the rest of the day caring for her. Then, while you were rubbing her tummy and feeding her warm broth – or whatever nonsense you told the chief – your kidnappers break into the house a second time, sneak past you, and take two cardboard boxes full of diaries and a canvas bag full of pictures. Right?'

Pandora frowned. She had told the story wrong. Dammit, it was hard to keep the facts straight when the facts were so weird. 'What? No, I must have explained it to you wrong. They stole the diaries the day before when they came in the broken RV. That's what I told the chief.'

Jackie slapped the table with the palm of her hand, making everyone jump. 'Bollocks they did. Alright, so now you're saying this Sam character goes upstairs to use the bathroom, steals your toothbrushes and hairbrushes, *and* two large cardboard boxes and your shoulder bag? Then she just waltzes down the stairs with them under her arms and marches past you out of the door. Is that what you're saying?'

'No, that's not right. Jackie, you're confusing me.'

Jackie swore and buried her face in her hands. When she looked up, her voice was calmer. 'Pandora, I want to help you. If all you want is a place to sleep for the night, then you are always welcome here, no matter what the circumstances. But please don't lie to me under my own roof. I don't respond well to it, as my ex-husband will testify. Why don't you tell me what's really going on?'

Pandora did not reply at once. She had been caught out in a lie, and she felt terrible, but it was a necessary lie. Telling the truth could only make matters worse. Jackie would think she was mocking her, inventing fantasies to insult her generosity.

Holly hiccuped and reached for a remote control to turn the television on. Jackie was a passionate New England Patriots fan, and every screen in the house was tuned to the NFL Network. She scrolled through channels searching for cartoons and stopped on a news feature that made her drop her gin to the floor, where the glass smashed on the tiles.

It was the local news channel. On the screen a dozen law enforcement vehicles with flashing lights were parked askew on a residential street. One house was clearly the focus of attention. Police tape was drawn across the front yard, and armed men guarded the entrance while teams of forensic experts moved swiftly through the front door carrying packages wrapped in plastic evidence bags.

A female reporter was on the street speaking to the camera. 'In this breaking news story, the residents of a quiet Ojai suburb have been shocked this afternoon by the seizure of a terrorist workshop and storehouse hidden within this unassuming residence on the outskirts of the city. Law enforcement officials say that several explosive devices have been discovered hidden in the garage, along with supplies of toxic chemicals and radioactive materials. The owner of the house behind me on Edgewood Avenue is local artist Pandora Castell, who is wanted by police on charges of planning and carrying out terrorist activities. It is believed Ms Castell is responsible for a number of unexplained explosions in shopping malls across the SoCal area, as well as poisonings and acid attacks perpetrated against seemingly random victims. Ms Castell is thought to be part of a growing movement of radical extremists who operate outside of known terrorist networks and are therefore extremely difficult to track down and capture. These individuals adhere to no political or religious ideology, and appear to be interested solely in committing wanton acts of destruction.'

The screen changed to a photograph of Pandora and Holly at an arts event in LA. It was a horrible picture taken by a rude reporter who snapped the photo without permission while Holly was upset about being jostled by the crowd. Pandora looked stressed and angry, while Holly had tears in her eyes. Out of context, it looked like Pandora was shouting at her.

The reporter's voice continued. 'Pandora Castell is a digital artist known for her work on major Hollywood productions as well as a number of triple-A computer games. She is seen here photographed with her mentally disabled older sister, also a well-known artist. Law enforcement officials allege that the younger Ms Castell used her disabled sister as a mule to transport explosive substances and chemicals around the United States. Police further allege that—'

Holly snapped the TV off and flung the remote across the room like it had burned her hands. There was stunned silence in the kitchen for a long time. Finally, Pandora murmured. 'Oh my God, what's going on?'

Jackie snatched up her phone. 'I'm calling the chief. I have his private number.' She paused and looked at Pandora. 'Just tell me honestly, is there any truth whatsoever in what we just heard?'

'No! Jackie, I have no idea what's going on. I spoke with Chief Brooks in my living room less than two hours ago. He never said anything about explosives or terrorists. The most dangerous substance in my house is a bottle of drain cleaner.'

Jackie bit her lip. She continued dialing and held the phone to her ear. 'Chief? It's Jackie Layne. I'm acting as attorney for Pandora Castell, and I wanted to make a courtesy call to ask just what the shitting fuck you think you're doing in my client's house?'

She put the phone on speaker and held it up for all to hear. There was a background noise of angry voices as if several arguments were taking place at once. 'Just one second, please,' the chief said. A door slammed and the raised voices were silenced. 'Jackie, have you got Pandora with you?'

'I have been contacted by her,' Jackie said. 'That is all you need to know.'

'Okay,' Brooks said. 'Listen to me very carefully, because time is very short. I assume you've seen the news, correct?'

'Yes. A raid that looks like a training video for the Gestapo. What the hell are you doing?'

'Just listen. A little over an hour ago, two individuals walked into the station who bore a striking resemblance to a drawing Holly made for me this morning. Do you know what I'm talking about?'

Pandora nodded. Jackie said, 'Yes, continue.'

'Those individuals carried badges identifying them as agents of the National Counter-Terrorism Agency. Agents Troy Arnold and Tina Slade. They had a warrant for Pandora's arrest, as well as a search warrant and several other documents. I tried to delay them with red tape, but they said they were only visiting me as a courtesy. They did not need my permission or my cooperation to carry out their operation. If you look at the news feed again, you will see that the vehicles and agents at the house are not from Ventura County Sheriff's Department. They are NCA agents from LA.'

Pandora grabbed the phone from Jackie's hand. 'Chief, those are the people who abducted us. How the hell can you let them do this?'

'Pandora, is that you?' Brooks said. 'You shouldn't be talking to me. Put Jackie back on.'

'No, I won't. Tell me why you've let this happen.'

'Because they have warrants signed by a federal judge. I've spent the past half hour on the phone arguing with that judge, but he claims the agency has followed the correct procedures and has sufficient evidence to make an arrest. Now, I don't believe that for a second, but as of right this moment, all the power is in their hands. The warrants are valid, and my hands are tied.'

'But that's crazy. There must be something you can do.'

The chief sighed. 'Pandora, I don't know what the hell is going on. I can't remove those assholes from your house, but there is a chance I can go above their heads and kick up some trouble at federal level.'

'I'm going to come down to the station,' Pandora said. 'I've done nothing wrong and I've got nothing to hide. Let the bastards arrest me and then I'll sue their asses all the way from here to kingdom come.'

'Wait a second, I'm not sure that's such a good idea,' Brooks said.

'What are you talking about? The best way to demonstrate my innocence is to turn myself in straight away.'

'Under ordinary circumstances, I would agree,' Brooks said. 'But these guys, the NCA, are a scary bunch. They have new federal powers to detain terrorism suspects for months without trial. And listen, I don't quite know how to tell you this, but the NCA hasn't just broken into your home. They have seized it. The papers they delivered to my office include a writ for asset forfeiture, which includes your property and bank accounts. Let me be clear: They do not need to put you on trial to do this. They only need evidence of terrorist activity, which they claim to have in abundance.'

'They took our home?' Pandora's voice was suddenly quiet and without force.

'That's right. It's their way of crippling terrorist networks by stripping them of all assets. To my knowledge, no one has ever been able to reclaim their property from them through the courts.'

'This can't be happening.' Pandora's hands were shaking. Her chest was constricted, and breathing became difficult.

'It gets worse,' Brooks said. 'All trusts and accounts held in Holly's name have also been seized.'

'They can't take away Holly's money,' Pandora said with new steel in her voice. 'That money's there to pay for her care in the event I'm killed or incapacitated.'

'The agency claims you used Holly's wealth to fund terrorist activities, so it is forfeit.'

'But if I'm in prison, that means Holly will have to live in an institution. She'll—'

The background noise of arguments resumed, and Brooks interrupted. 'I have to go. Jackie knows the score. Listen to her. Do what she says. Good luck to you both.' He hung up.

'They took our home,' Pandora said again.

Jackie placed her hand gently on her shoulder. 'Girls, this is a very serious business. The NCA is bad news. They are the primary reason I gave up the practice of law.'

'Who the hell are they?' Pandora said. 'I've never heard of them.'

'The National Counter-Terrorism Agency was established in the aftermath of 9/11 after a study was published entitled The Emergence of Novel Threats in a Post-Terrorist World. It was a bizarre, paranoid document in which the author claimed that conventional conceptions of terrorism were obsolete and that advancements in the Internet, computing, biotechnology, physics, and human psychology would produce new dangers at an unprecedented rate, resulting in a cascading failure of civilization. The agency was formed with sweeping new powers of arrest and detention. All of a sudden, people started vanishing, their property was seized, and their families were placed under surveillance. I thought it was fascism, plain and simple, and I decided to get out of the law business before things got any worse.'

'Why is this happening to us?' Pandora said, fighting back tears. 'They planted evidence in my house. Why? I'm not a political artist, I've never been to any demonstrations, I've never campaigned against the government. Dammit, I've never even voted. What did I do to deserve this?'

'That's what we're going to find out,' Jackie said. 'And we're going to begin with you telling me the real story of what has happened to you over the past three days. No nonsense this time, no fairy tales, just the truth.'

So Pandora told her. She began with how Holly saved them from being crushed to death under the collapsing scaffolding at the Arcade, then her discovery of the diaries, the escape from the kidnappers' van, and the day they spent with Catherine and Galen. She finished with their return home and her attempts to construct a plausible story to tell the police, ending with the discovery that the diaries had been stolen. Jackie recorded her story on a small digital voice recorder and made extensive notes on a legal pad.

When she was finished, Jackie stood up and left the kitchen. Pandora followed with Holly close behind. There was a hall alongside the courtyard opposite the guest bedrooms. Here, Jackie's art collection became macabre, and there was a series of dark and grim sketches by Goya, Gericault, and Fuseli. Jackie paused beside a disturbing painting of an emaciated, semi-human figure with a horribly canine face squatting naked on a mound of filth, gnawing something nastily like a disembodied human arm.

'I bought this years ago from an artist called Richard Pickman,' Jackie said. 'He was a peculiar fellow. Sallow, sickly, nervous. He claimed the subject was a creature that appeared in the basement of his family's home in Boston. He said it had to be tempted out of a hole in the ground with a particular type of bait he stole from the hospital morgue. It was a totally lunatic story, of course, but it appealed to a certain ghoulish aesthetic within me at the time, so I bought it. He claimed a similar inspiration for all his paintings. He said he had been shown other worlds beyond human imagination, and he merely painted what he saw. I tried to contact him recently to ask if he'd done any more work I might like to look at. It turns out he's currently registered as a missing person. He walked down into his basement one day with a foul-smelling bag over his shoulder and was never seen again.'

'That's horrible,' Pandora said. 'Do you think Holly gets inspiration from other worlds?'

'I never doubted it,' Jackie said. 'But I never thought to take the idea quite so literally as you've presented it to me today.'

'I promise everything I've told you is true. I'm sorry I lied earlier, but I didn't know how to tell you the truth.'

Jackie stroked her chin and stared at the painting. 'I wonder what the NCA might think of Holly's ability. Imagine you were a paranoid government agent, tasked with protecting America from vague future threats that have not manifested yet. Wouldn't you be terrified of a girl with the power to teleport to another world? What if she contracted some new disease and brought it back to Earth, becoming patient zero in an apocalyptic plague? What if she picked up an alien ray gun that could wipe out a whole city with one pull of the trigger?'

'You think they're after Holly?' Pandora said.

'It's a possibility. Maybe they underestimated the extent of her power when you escaped from the back of their van, and now they're putting your faces all over the news, ensuring you can't return home.'

'So you do believe me?'

Jackie cupped Holly's cheeks and looked into her eyes. 'Holly, I think you're a miracle. I've thought that since the first time I met you. Whatever this power is that you have, it can't just be some random accident or mutation. It must have a purpose, and it seems like that purpose hasn't been fulfilled yet. It looks like we're going to have a fight on our hands to make sure you and Pandora have the freedom to explore that power together, but I want you to know that I'm on your side, and I will do everything in my power to help you both.'

Pandora wanted to reply that she was eager to try anything that might put things back the way they had been only a few hours ago. Before she could say anything more, all hell broke loose.

A series of explosions rocked the house. The glass walls of the courtyard shattered simultaneously, showering them with a hard rain of glass shards. Pandora was knocked to the ground. She felt like her head had been beaten in with a club. She couldn't see. Her ears were overloaded with the sound of pummeling explosions. She flailed blindly, reaching for Holly. All she found was handfuls of broken glass.

The thunder in her ears was replaced by the sound of raised voices, angry men shouting, and boots stomping on the ground. Rough hands hauled her across the floor into another room. She was pressed up against a wall and found herself looking into the face of "Sam", otherwise known as Agent Tina Slade. Gone were Slade's colorful shirt and shorts, and instead she wore a black SWAT uniform, oddly redolent of her kidnapping outfit. She still had the same happy-go-lucky smile on her face. 'You two are a slippery pair, you know that?'

Pandora blinked away the spots in her eyes. They were in Jackie's living room, or the remains of it. Every window was smashed, and furniture lay in disarray across the floor. The SWAT team had blown the windows out and thrown in flash-bangs to stun and disorient them. Now armed men wearing SWAT gear emblazoned with the triangular orange patch of the NCA were overturning furniture, tearing down artworks, and smashing antique vases against the floor.

The sound of broken glass crunching under jackboots drew her attention towards the door, and she recognized “Mike”, AKA Agent Troy Arnold. He dragged Holly alongside him like a rag doll. Her wrists were cuffed, and her lip was bleeding. She jerked free of Arnold's hands and made a grab for Pandora. He seized a fistful of hair and pulled her back.

‘Leave her alone,’ Pandora yelled.

Like his partner, Agent Arnold still wore that hideous rictus grin. Pandora was beginning to wonder if NCA agents were surgically altered to make them look that way. ‘I think it’s best we keep the two of you apart, don’t you?’ he said, glancing between the two sisters. ‘In fact, I think it’s best if this one just goes to sleep.’ He took a syringe gun from his pocket and plunged it into Holly’s neck. Pandora roared in fury and wrestled free from Slade, but the agent was strong and kneed her in the stomach. She fell to the floor and Slade struck her across the back of the head with her pistol. The last thing she saw before she fell unconscious was Holly’s expression of shock and pain as the needle broke her skin and she slumped into Arnold’s arms.

CHAPTER 20

Every part of Pandora's body screamed in agony. She had cramp in her leg, but when she tried to stretch it for relief, she found that she was restrained by thick Velcro straps around her thighs. Her wrists were similarly bound. She was sitting in a wheelchair, strapped firmly in place and unable to move. She had been left slumped forward with her head hanging near her knees, and now her neck felt like it was made of razors. As she straightened up, her stomach churned and spasmed from where she had been struck. She groaned miserably. Her head throbbed abominably from the blow by Slade's pistol, and she wondered how much more punishment her shaken brain could take.

Wherever she was, it was plainly no prison cell. Concrete stanchions supported a disintegrating roof of rotting ceiling tiles from which poured ugly tangles of thick wires and ducting. The space was large and mostly in shadows. Broad windows set into each wall had once filled this place with light, but now tall stacks of rusting filing cabinets and office furniture made it a gloomy and unwelcoming place. Elsewhere, mounds of filth and detritus had been gathered into heaps like the nests of some unspeakable insects.

Pandora occupied a clear area near the center of this space, which appeared to be a derelict office building. She sat fixed in the wheelchair before a steel table, and on the opposite side sat Agent Arnold. He was no longer smiling.

Arnold's attention was focused on a file whose pages he leafed through slowly, with a furrowed brow, shaking his head as if the contents made him unhappy with the lamentable state of the world.

The silence lengthened, and Pandora got fed up with waiting. Her hands were Velcroed to the chair, but her ankles were free. She kicked the table and it made a metallic shriek against the concrete floor. 'Where's Holly?'

'I don't know, is it somewhere near Detroit?' Arnold did not look up from the report.

'I want to speak to my attorney,' Pandora said.

'I'm afraid Jacqueline Layne suffered a head injury while attempting to obstruct the course of justice. She is currently unavailable to offer counsel. Sorry.'

'You bastard. I want to make a phone call.'

Arnold reached across to a stack of old office equipment. He plucked a rotary-dial telephone from the junk and placed it on the table with a soft ping of its internal bell. 'Looks like the phones are out of order.'

Pandora had never felt more powerless, and she fought back the urgent need to cry. 'Am I under arrest? No one has read me my rights.'

Arnold faced her at last, placing the report on the table. 'If no one has read you your rights, then you can't possibly be under arrest. This is America, you know. There are rules.'

'Then what the hell am I doing here?' Pandora said.

Arnold clasped his hands and leaned forward. 'Are you familiar with the concept *born classified?*'

'No.'

'Oh, it's a fascinating subject. It relates in part to an incident at Yale University in 1976 when a physics student named Simon Kingston designed a fully functioning nuclear bomb. He did all his own research, produced his own mathematical proofs, and made all his own engineering diagrams. It was an impressive piece of work, and his professors declared there was no doubt his bomb would function exactly as he proposed. In fact, the design featured several improvements over the fusion bombs in service at that time. The FBI heard of Kingston's work and promptly arrested him on charges of being in possession of military secrets. Of course, Kingston objected. He had never stolen any secrets or seen any classified military documents. He claimed he was innocent because, after all, he had done all his own research, right? Well, the FBI pointed out that it was not necessary for Kingston to actually *steal* any research or *see* any classified documents to be in possession of military secrets. You see, nuclear technology is restricted data. Mere knowledge of it is a breach of national security. By inventing his own nuclear bomb, Kingston had created data that was *born classified.* Simply having the information in his head was a crime for which he was righteously punished.'

'What does any of that have to do with me?' Pandora said. 'I don't know anything about nuclear bombs.'

'Quite so,' Arnold said. 'But the world has come a long way since 1976. Hell, Elvis was still on tour and played a New Year's Eve concert in Pittsburgh. In those days there were no home computers and no Internet. Simon Kingston had to visit an academic library to find papers on nuclear physics and mechanical engineering. Nowadays, every kid on the street can access a thousand times more information with their damn phones. Every anti-American shithead with an IQ over 120 could build an A-bomb in his mom's garage if only he had access to weapons-grade uranium.'

'Well, I'm not anti-American,' Pandora said. 'And if there's bomb-making equipment in my garage it's because you put it there.'

'So what? That stuff is just for the news. The truth is too extreme for the public to accept, and too dangerous for them to know.'

'What truth?'

Arnold's grin returned. There was a cardboard box on

the floor which had escaped Pandora's notice until now. He reached into it and lifted out a stenographer's pad. Its pages were covered in Pandora's handwriting.

'These pages are marked with today's date,' Arnold said. 'Would you agree this is your own handwriting? Let's see what was on your mind.' He began reading in a high-pitched sing-song mockery of Pandora's voice. '"We escaped from the back of the van when Holly blinked us to Entara. I'd sure like to have seen the creepy campers' faces when they realized we'd teleported away with the cages still locked. We stayed in Entara for more than a day with Catherine and Galen. Taking us to the other world saved our skins, that's for sure, but it gives me a problem: How do I explain it to the Chief? He's not likely to believe in alien worlds or teleportation."'

Pandora fought the urge to kick Arnold under the table. She shrugged as nonchalantly as she could manage while restrained in the chair. 'That's a story I was writing. Fiction. Make-believe.'

Arnold reached for the box again and picked out several diaries and Polaroids. 'Are these make-believe? Your childhood diary also speaks of this other world, "Entara" did you call it? And oh look, here are some photographs that exactly match the descriptions of the place you visited.'

Pandora sneered. 'Those pictures are of an old observatory in Cleveland. You should go there, it's a nice place. Is this seriously why you planted fake evidence in my house? So you could question me about childhood fantasies? Man, I'd hate to be you when your boss sees your monthly progress report.'

'Okey-dokey, then. Let's move along to the next piece of evidence. Gosh, isn't this fun?' Arnold bounced in his seat like a schoolboy. He turned to a television screen and switched it on. A video clip showed CCTV footage of Ojai Arcade. The image quality was poor, but there was no mistaking Holly and Pandora as they walked between the arches on their way to the gallery. They passed under the scaffolding just as the reversing panel van struck the tower and brought the whole mess crashing down on top of them. The camera shook with the violence of the impact, and a cloud of billowing dust filled the air. At the same moment there was a flash of brilliant light that over-exposed the camera. The image went pure white for an instant until it was darkened by the expanding veil of dust.

'Three tons of scaffolding fell right on top of you,' Arnold said. 'Let's zoom ahead a few minutes and see what happens next.'

Several people, including Jackie, climbed onto the wreckage and started hauling away debris. A few minutes later, three fire trucks and an ambulance arrived. The firemen cleared the site with amazing speed.

'Oh look, no one was there,' Arnold continued. 'A freelance reporter happened to be on the scene and witnessed the whole event. He had a better angle than this camera, and he saw two women vanish into thin air. He's a pretty down-to-earth guy and doubted what he saw, but when the wreckage was cleared he knew he'd witnessed a miracle. He wrote a blog online saying God must have taken both women bodily into heaven. Touching stuff, right? Well, we have computers that scan for those kinds of stories. Agent Slade and I arrived on the scene the following morning, and it didn't take long to find out who you are.'

Arnold was enjoying this, and Pandora hated him for it. 'That footage doesn't show anything,' she said. 'We got lucky, that's all. I got hit on the head and we ran away, out of sight of the camera. I had a concussion, and I don't remember anything for an hour afterwards. I stumbled into the emergency room at the hospital and rambled like a crazy person to the receptionist there. You should ask her about it. I gave her my name.'

'Obviously we know about your chat with the medical receptionist,' Arnold said. 'And yes, the CCTV footage isn't great, I'll admit. That's why we were quite slow to act in this case. Even after we got DNA samples from your hairbrushes and toothbrushes, we didn't really understand the nature of your sister's aberration. We thought we could bring you in with a low-key midnight operation, just Agent Slade and myself. Of course, we quickly recognized our mistake when you escaped from the van. Wow, we were really amazed at that. Very impressive. Totally unexpected. We were giddy like kids at Christmas when we realized what had happened.'

'What's so impressive about that? You just didn't tie us up very well. As soon as you stopped the van at a red light, we simply kicked open the doors and ran away.'

'Y'know what, Ms Castell? I think I like you. You're snarky and feisty. I work with so many people who just sit there and blub, and that gets tiresome. But you've got some real zest. Man, you've got spunk. Breaking you is going to be a lot of fun. I think I'm gonna get it on camera, make a little training video out of it. Maybe even make a personal video, just for you and me. Something I can take home and watch late at night when I'm feeling nostalgic for the times we spent together.'

A horrible realization dawned on Pandora that Agent Arnold was insane. He was not merely playing up to some bad-cop routine. He was sadistic, perverted, and he took a wholly unnatural pleasure in tormenting her. He was perfectly aware that she had committed no crime, and he simply did not care that her rights were being violated. She wondered what kind of evil organization the NCA must be for it to put this man in a position of power and responsibility. What kind of acts might such a man be capable of?

'What are you going to do with us?' she said with all the dread of a cancer patient asking *How long, doc?*

Arnold stood and swept everything off the table into the box. 'That's a discussion for another time. Right now, you just get comfy right there and look around, get a sense of what the rest of your life will look like. Cold concrete floors, no friends, no family, no one to help you. You're a creative person, maybe you could compose some poetry about the experience and recite it for me during our next session. I think I'd like that.'

He turned away and left her alone. Pandora had seen enough cop shows to know that Arnold was leaving her to stew while he went to drink coffee and eat donuts with his buddies and made ribald jokes about his captive. She didn't have time for such nonsense. Holly was somewhere out there, maybe in another room in this very building. She had to at least try to find her.

Despite being strapped to the wheelchair, she found that she could maneuver around quite easily by using her feet. It was easier to move backwards than forwards, and she continually collided with piles of junk on the floor, but in a short time she had mapped out the space that was her prison. As she suspected, it was an abandoned office building. She occupied a high floor with windows looking out on all sides. There was an elevator, but when she operated the call button with her foot, nothing happened. There were fire escape doors in opposite corners, but both were locked against her. She was apparently unguarded, but she had no doubt that cameras were concealed in dark corners. Surely Arnold and his cronies were giggling with sadistic glee at the sight of her struggling with the wheelchair, searching for ways of escape.

When she approached the windows, she was surprised that she recognized the view outside. She had assumed she had been taken at least as far as LA, but the silhouette of the mountains against the evening sky was as familiar to her as the back of her hand. They were the Topatopas, which meant she was still somewhere in Ojai Valley. Wheeling around the perimeter of the building in the fading light, she identified a few landmarks and determined she was somewhere in the industrial district south of the town, which was due for redevelopment in the near future.

The sun set behind the western mountains, and she watched the shadows sweep across Ojai Valley from her lofty seat. The shadows climbed higher as the sun descended, and for a few minutes her concrete prison was flooded with glorious light that made the floating dust sparkle and swirl in the air like flocks of fairies. The illusion ended all too quickly and Pandora was plunged into darkness. There was no lighting in the prison room, and she could see only by the indirect light of Ojai's street lamps and the even fainter illumination of the stars. Arnold did not come back to question her, nor did anyone even check she was alright. She had not eaten for hours, and her bladder was bursting. She fought the urge to shout for attention, knowing that was what her captors were eagerly hoping for. In the end she could not sit still without squirming to release the pressure on her bladder, and she started yelling.

Some time after midnight she peed her pants. She was oddly grateful for the release as warm urine soaked her jeans and dripped onto the floor. She silently scolded herself for not doing it hours earlier at a time of her own choosing, rather than being forced by circumstance to endure an uncomfortable night of misery. She wheeled the chair to a different part of the building away from the puddle of her own mess, but inevitably the smell drifted wherever she went.

She was proud of herself that she did not cry. She was too angry for that. Ever since she was a child, she had had a strong sense of justice, and even minor infractions of her moral code brought about a fiery response. She clenched her fists and made a conscious decision to keep a tally of every wrong perpetrated against herself, Holly, and Jackie, and to use that score as a battery to power her anger. She would need that energy in the weeks and months to come as she fought to regain her property, her freedom, her reputation, and most importantly, her sister.

Thoughts of Holly put her predicament into perspective. Was Holly also somewhere in this nightmare-dark building, curled up in a cold cell, wondering what was happening to her? Holly was often disturbed and dismayed by the behavior of even ordinary strangers. Once, a teenage girl shoulder-checked her in the street, knocking her to the ground and spilling the tacos they had bought from a street vendor. She sat on the busy sidewalk, covering her head with her hands like she was under attack, and cried for fifteen minutes before Pandora convinced her to move. How on earth would Holly perceive an attack by deranged government agents who planned to remove her liberty indefinitely?

She felt a sharp pain in her hands and held them up to the distant lights of Ojai to get a better look. There was blood on her palms. In her rage and fury, she had dug four perfect half-moons of flesh out of each hand with the nails of her fingers.

CHAPTER 21

Somehow she slept. When she awoke the sun was shining through the eastern windows. The elevator was on the move, and its clanking, scraping noise was what had awakened her. The doors rattled back along their runners, and two masked guards in NCA body armor entered the room. Neither of them spoke or responded to Pandora's questions as they pushed the wheelchair into the elevator and took her down several floors. She was pushed through a labyrinth of dingy corridors to an old staff shower room. Here she was ordered to strip and wash in an open cubicle with not even a curtain for privacy. The guards watched her every move with fingers on the trigger guards of their Heckler & Koch MP5s as if this naked woman might sprout claws and fangs and rip them to shreds. When she was clean, she was provided with jeans and a shirt raided from her own wardrobe, then strapped firmly back into the wheelchair for another journey.

Back to the elevator, and another jolting trip down several floors, followed by another ride through dizzying twists and turns of ruined office space. Through open doorways bereft of doors she glimpsed distant windows and saw they were now at first-floor level. Finally she arrived with her entourage at a large garage with roll-top doors open to a loading area outside. Sunshine poured through the opening, creating a stark boundary between the warmth and life of the outside world and the cold gloom of the interior. An armored van was waiting outside, its rear doors open and a wheelchair ramp fixed to the tailgate.

Along one side of the garage was a line of storage rooms, and from one of the doors Agent Arnold came to stand before her. The guards brought her to a halt, and Arnold dismissed them so she was alone once more with this hateful man. 'Good morning, Ms Castell. Did you have a pleasant evening?'

Pandora still had not been given food or drink, and she recognized this as an interrogation tactic to weaken her. She fought to take control of the conversation. 'So what happens now? Am I getting shipped off to a Caribbean island for a therapeutic course of waterboarding and sleep deprivation?'

Arnold grinned. 'I'm so glad you are able to maintain a sense of humor about all this. It makes you very pleasant to work with. What is going to happen is exactly this. You will be taken far, far away from everyone and everything you have ever known and loved. You will undergo a debriefing process at a specialized facility where we will learn a great deal about you and your sister via chemical and mechanical means. This will enable us to build a comprehensive dossier on your sister's unusual abilities without risk to ourselves. Meanwhile, your sister will be placed in a medically-induced coma for the rest of her life to ensure she never poses a threat to decent, hard-working American citizens. And that really is the end of the story. No happy endings, no reunions, no return to the little house in Ojai. However, there is a scenario where you might eventually be permitted access to your sister. Ah, I see I have your attention. If you agree, right here and right now, to cooperate with the NCA debriefing process, then you could have daily contact with her. One day, years from now, you could both live in an institution operated by the NCA where you will be permitted to change her diapers, give her sponge-baths, and perform any other tasks considered too menial for federal employees.'

'If I cooperate?' Pandora said.

'If you cooperate. There will be no judges, no trials, no deals, no conditions. This is your only hope. You do exactly what we say, and we will reward you with daily access to your sister.'

'And if I don't cooperate?'

Arnold shook his head sadly. 'Our Caribbean resort has some free rooms right now. I'm told women have a hard time there. Although some learn to enjoy it. After all, they really have no choice.'

Pandora felt a stinging pain in her hands. She had reopened the wounds in her palms, which were just beginning to scab over. She focused on the pain and reminded herself of the pledge she had made the night before: Make a mental list of injustices so that they might all be rectified when the time is right. Right now, she had no power, no choice. She had to agree to Arnold's demands or she would never see Holly again. At least if they were together there was a chance, however remote, of escape. After all, Holly was a superhero, wasn't she?

'I'll do it,' she said. 'But I want to see Holly, right now. Where is she?'

Arnold shrugged and got behind the wheelchair, pushing it towards the waiting truck. 'Oh, she's around here someplace.'

At that moment Pandora caught a glimpse into the room Arnold had come from. In the gloom she saw Holly, strapped to a wheelchair. She was unconscious, slumped, and immobile. An IV drip hung from a stand beside the wheelchair, feeding chemicals into her arm.

'Holly!' she shouted, fighting against the Velcro straps. 'Go back, let me see her.'

'No,' Arnold said. 'You will not see her again for a long time, and she will never again regain consciousness to see you.'

Pandora had never thought of herself as a violent person, but right now she could gleefully have taken a sharp knife and peeled Arnold's eyelids from his face and shone laser pointers into his eyes until he wept like a baby. She twisted in the chair to look back into the room. She screamed. 'Holly! Holly wake up, there are spiders!'

Holly jerked. Her eyes opened, and she twisted in the chair.

She shouted again. 'Spiders! There are spiders in your hair! Spiders in your clothes!'

Holly shrieked and wrenched her body against her restraints. Arnold was saying something, but his voice was lost against Holly's ear-piercing screech echoing around the concrete garage. Abruptly her scream was silenced in a searing blast of light.

'What the hell?' Arnold marched back to where Holly had been. He saw the empty wheelchair and turned on Pandora. 'You bitch.' His hand was on the butt of his gun, unclipping the safety clasp.

Another radiant beam flooded the garage. Arnold cried out with the intensity of it, staggering backwards into the empty room. Holly materialized in front of Pandora. She looked confused, sleepy, but she managed a weak smile as she took Pandora's hand, and she blinked.

THE HELL WORLD

Something was wrong. The wheelchair vanished from under Pandora, and she fell to the ground. Holly collapsed beside her like a puppet whose strings have been cut. An overpowering heat struck Pandora like a blow to the face, and she drew in a sharp breath in surprise. It was a mistake. The air was acrid and bitter and immediately set off a fit of coughing.

This was not the vale of Candlewick, nor was it Ojai. The ground was hard and dry, split by myriad cracks like varicose veins in the earth. The sky was a boiling mass of luminous, multi-colored cloud that cast a harsh glare on the land around them. It was a flat, desert land, without features of any kind from one horizon to the next. Indistinct in the heat haze, clusters of ugly stone igloos huddled in the distance. Dark shapes scurried between them.

Pandora struggled to her feet, gasping for breath. The air – if it could be called air – felt like acid in her lungs. One of the stone igloos loomed nearby, its arched doorway open in their direction. It was dark inside, but not empty. In the murk, something had been alerted to their arrival. She heard a shuffling sound, and then a chittering.

Holly sat upright. She was slack-faced and drooling, the IV drip still attached to her arm. Pandora tore it out and shook her shoulders. 'Holly, wake up.' She choked off her words as the corrosive air brought on another bout of painful coughing. She spat blood onto the dusty ground.

The chittering inside the igloo became louder. Shadows moved, approaching the doorway. Eight green eyes glimmered in the darkness like a constellation of emeralds. Something reached out, a segmented black limb like an elongated finger with too many knuckles. A wild panic seized Pandora. *Spiders. There are spiders.*

Holly coughed, vomiting blood over her clothes. She reached for Pandora, and when their hands touched, they blinked again.

CHAPTER 22

Pandora was dizzy and nauseous. It took a few moments of lying very still and taking deep breaths before she felt fit enough to attend to Holly. They were lying on the soft mossy floor of a forest, with a low mist drifting lazily between the trees. There were no familiar landmarks to identify where they had blinked to, but anywhere was better than the place they had come from.

Holly was conscious but weak. For several minutes she could only lie on her side, throwing up bloody goo and moaning miserably. Pandora cleaned her up as best she could with a handful of moss and some leaves wet with morning dew.

There was a fallen log nearby. They dragged their sorry selves over to it and rested a while, leaning their backs against the bole with their backsides on the soft ground.

'What was that awful place, Holly?' Pandora said when she felt well enough to speak. 'I feel like my lungs have been scrubbed with a wire brush. The air was like poison. Even my eyes were stinging. And God, what was that thing in the igloo?'

Holly's head lolled towards her. Her eyes looked apologetic.

'Was it the drugs they put in you? I guess it must have thrown off your aim, or something. Whatever that place was, let's never go there again.'

They dozed for an hour until Holly became a little more lively. It was obvious she was still too weak to blink them home, and that was just as well because Pandora was in no mood to face Agent Arnold again just yet. She needed to find a place of peace and quiet so she could think and make plans.

'I've got an idea where we might have landed,' Pandora said as she helped her sister to her feet. 'I've been thinking there might be some connection between where we blink from and where we arrive. When we blink from the Arcade, we always appear somewhere near the observatory. When we go home, we always appear near the Arcade. That place the NCA was holding us was somewhere south of town, out past the golf course. If I'm right, that means we've landed south of Candlewick, maybe on the other side of the river.' She shaded her eyes and looked up through the canopy of trees. 'It's still early morning, and the sun is over there. That means if we walk this way, we should reach Catherine and Galen's house. What do you think?'

The forest was trackless and almost primeval. They clambered over fallen logs and fought through dense patches of undergrowth. Pandora continually had to check her bearings against the position of the sun, and she wasn't nearly as confident of their position as she had told her sister. It was a great relief when they encountered the Anwin River. At this point, the waterway was broad and shallow, and the girls were able to cross it easily, removing their shoes and rolling up their pants. At the water's edge, they paused to drink and clean away the gunk they had coughed up in the hell world. Soon they found themselves on a familiar, well-kept road and turned towards the forest glade where the cottage lay.

'I got interrogated by that asshole Agent Arnold last night,' Pandora said as they walked. 'Do you know what those NCA guys were up to? They think your power is more dangerous than a nuclear bomb, so you need to be locked up like some experimental weapon and studied. Well, I'm not going to let it happen. I don't care what it takes, but when we get home, I'm going to destroy that agency. Jackie will help us, and we'll expose all the dreadful things they're doing to people. I promise you, Hol, you'll never need to run or hide from those guys again.'

She told Holly about the pledge she had made during her lonely internment on the upper floor, and the score she was keeping against those who would seek to do Holly harm.

Soon they came to the clearing and were welcomed by the lively buzzing of bees and the nodding of flowers in the sunshine. Recalling what Catherine had told her about customs in the vale, Pandora did not knock on the cottage door but simply walked in and called out. 'Hiya, it's us, Pandora and Holly. Anybody home?'

No reply. Pandora was not particularly surprised. Homey though the cottage was, it was also a place of work. No doubt Catherine and Galen were busy tending to the farm elsewhere. Even as she had this thought, she heard a sound behind the house, a rhythmic scraping like a shovel in loose soil. She went into the kitchen and looked through the window.

Catherine was outside on the lawn, digging two large holes at the end of the yard. Pandora threw open the kitchen door and called more greetings. 'We're back. Did you miss us?'

Catherine either ignored her or did not hear because she merely continued her slow, weary work, shoveling dirt onto two big heaps. Only then did Pandora notice the two bodies on the grass, covered in white sheets.

'Oh my God, Catherine? What's happened?' Pandora said.

Catherine paused in her labor and noticed her for the first time. 'Thought I packed both of you off home.' She looked the sisters up and down and noticed the blood and dirt. 'You look terrible.'

Holly knelt beside one of the bodies and lifted the sheet. When she saw what lay beneath, she sobbed. Pandora caught a fleeting look of Galen's ruined face before she covered him again.

'Oh God, no,' Pandora said, clutching her hand to her mouth.

'Same as all the others,' Catherine said. 'Did it to himself.'

'The phantoms? But how? How did they get to him inside the house?'

Catherine didn't answer. She turned back to her task and began shoveling dirt again. Pandora lifted the second sheet and groaned when she saw the bloody remains of Bess. Holly was on her knees between the two bodies, gazing up at her sister with her big, expressive eyes filled with tears. Her mouth opened and closed spasmodically as if desperate to express something – *anything* – that might release the pain and sadness building within her. Instead, all she could do was cry and hug Pandora's legs.

'Let's find some shovels, Holly,' she said softly, stroking Holly's hair. 'Let's put our friends to rest.'

When the work of filling in the graves was complete, Catherine stood at the feet of her husband. 'Well, I guess I'd better say something. I spent a lot of time complaining about the old man's faults when he was alive, so I suppose I should set the record straight now he's dead. Dad, you were a good man in all the ways that men are good. You worked hard, and always for the benefit of your family and your community. You were a good husband, attentive, thoughtful, and kind. You were a good father when we were given the blessing of Jason as our adopted son. It's often the curse of us women to outlive our menfolk, so I can't say I haven't thought about this day before. Now it's finally here and I think it might be more than I can bear. I love you, Dad, and I always will. As for you, Bess, we've had a lot of dogs here at the farm over the years. I still remember the day my mom brought me a tiny puppy who was your great-great-grandmother. Every one of those dogs was precious to us, but you were the gentlest, and you were the only one who didn't chew the upholstery. Well, that does it.' Catherine turned her back on the graves and walked into the house.

At the kitchen table, Catherine sat still as a statue, as if all purpose and meaning had gone from her life. Pandora made tea and found a plate of cookies in a cupboard, which Catherine proceeded to break into quarters without actually eating them.

'I'm so sorry this has happened,' Pandora said.

Catherine shrugged. 'Folks die. In a community like ours, we're pretty close to death, you know? People die in farming accidents, or hunting accidents, or they waste away from incurable diseases. In my life, I've seen dozens of dead people up close, all of them people I knew well.'

'But this is different. This was your husband. You've been married for fifty years.'

'Fifty-seven.'

Pandora reached across the table and squeezed her hand. 'Do you want to talk about it? What happened? How did the phantoms get to Galen inside the house?'

'Damn fool wasn't in the house, was he?' Catherine pushed away the plate of cookies. 'Last night, Bess made a fuss barking and yapping, scratching at the kitchen door while we were making ready for bed. We figured it was bushtails out in the yard, trying to dig their way into the pantry. Galen said he'd see about putting some new planking down tomorrow to keep them out.

'Anyway, Bess wouldn't let up, so I took her upstairs and made a nest out of old blankets beside our bed. She settled down after that, and we all went to sleep. I suppose Galen must have woken up in the night and found Bess gone from the room, and went looking for her. I didn't wake up until I heard Bess screaming. I never heard a dog scream before. It sounded so mournful, like a soul in agony. Never heard a sound like it in my life. I jumped out of bed and ran to the window and I could see Bess out there on the lawn surrounded by phantoms. Somehow she'd got out of the house and they'd trapped her at the far end of the yard. She was crouched down with her legs shaking like crazy, pissing and shitting herself while those godawful lights zipped around her head.

'Then I heard the kitchen door and Galen went outside. He was calling Bess's name, trying to coax her back to the house, but she was so terrified I don't think she even heard him. I opened the window and yelled at Galen to get back into the house, but he ignored me and ran to Bess, waving his hands to fend off those evil lights. He picked her up and started back towards the house, but the lights swarmed on him. He dropped her and fell to his knees. Bess was lying on the grass, completely still. I think she must have had a heart attack, poor old girl.

'It was Galen that ripped her apart. He hollered like he was mad angry and started pounding on her, though she was already dead and just flopping around in his hands. He picked her up and strangled her, then tore off her ears and pushed his thumbs in her eyes. Once he was done with the dog he started rolling around on the grass, clawing at his skin like there was something inside him he had to rip out.

'I ran downstairs, but I was too afraid to go outside. I just stood by the kitchen door and watched it happen. Then the lights were gone, and Dad and Bess were just dark shapes on the grass. I was still too scared to go outside, so I just stood there uselessly, leaning on the doorframe until the sun came up.'

'There was nothing you could have done,' Pandora said. 'If you'd gone outside they would have killed you too.'

'No, I don't think it works like that. I think they could have killed me right here in the kitchen. They could have killed me even if I'd stayed upstairs. That's not how they wanted it, though. They wanted to keep me alive so I'd have to bury my loved ones alone.'

'But you had the wind chimes on the doors, didn't you?'

'The wind chimes were just a superstition,' Catherine waved her hand dismissively. 'It was another way for the wizard to deceive us, to make us think we had some power over the phantoms, so he could laugh at us and prolong our torment. They never had any power to protect us.'

'Maybe you're right,' Pandora said. 'I saw something, the night we stayed here. I saw... things, outside. The wizard was there, and... and someone else. It felt like I was hypnotized and I wasn't in control of my thoughts or actions. I tried to open the door and go outside. I was desperate to go out, and I was actually on the threshold when Holly dragged me back inside and slammed the door. If it wasn't for her, you'd have been burying me the next morning. Next thing I knew it was daylight and you were waking us up for breakfast. I thought the whole thing must have been a dream.'

'It was no dream. Normally I'm a bad sleeper, always up at least once or twice in the night, but that night I slept like a stone. Galen, too. I remember him commenting on it in the morning. It must have been another trick of the wizard, to keep us asleep while he tried to take you.'

'Was it really the wizard I saw, do you think?' Pandora said.

Catherine shook her head. 'No, he's far away in the east. But he left a fragment of his will here to govern the phantoms while he was away, or at least that's what Galen thought. That's why we hear his laughter at night. He wanted us to know who had done this to us.'

'But if the wind chimes don't protect the house, that means it's not safe here anymore. Catherine, you can't stay here or you'll end up the same way as Galen and Bess.'

'That's the way I reckon he wants it. The wizard, I mean. He gave me enough time to bury my dear ones, but there'll be no one left to bury me. This time tomorrow I'll be lying on the grass with crows pecking at my eyes.'

'No, that's not going to happen,' Pandora said firmly.

'Holly can take us all away from here, can't you, Hol?'

Catherine stood up and began clearing away the plates and cups. 'I'm not going on any journey to the stars, any more than I'd go east with the villagers all those years ago. If my time has come, I ain't afraid anymore. Besides, I figure you girls have got enough trouble in your own world without some old biddy following you around. Isn't that why you've come back?'

Pandora nodded. 'Things have got a lot worse at home. There are bad men who have found out about Holly's power. They say she's dangerous, and they want to imprison her and study her. We only barely escaped from them, and we hoped you'd be able to put us up for a few days until I figure out what we should do.'

'We've got an old saying in the vale: That's like two halves of a dogshit sandwich. You girls can't stay here, not even for another hour. You have to get gone right away, before the phantoms come back.'

Pandora paced around the kitchen, running her hand through her hair. 'A dogshit sandwich is right. If we can't go home and we can't stay here, what the hell are we going to do?'

Catherine dropped the washing up into the carved stone sink with a clatter. She crossed to a sideboard, opened a drawer and started rooting around inside. 'There's only one thing we can do. I don't like it. In fact, I hate it. But I can't see any other choice.' She pulled out handfuls of old knick-knacks, scraps of paper, pencils, ornaments, and rusty tools. At the bottom of the drawer she found a tin box, much dented and tarnished with age, and held it out to Pandora.

She took it and lifted the lid. Inside was a red disc about twice the size of a quarter. It was transparent and striated with parallel lines like a flawed crystal. When she lifted it from the box, she was surprised at its weight. 'What is it?'

'It's a key,' Catherine said. 'When the villagers packed up their belongings and followed the wizard into the east, they didn't just walk. It would have taken them years to get to where they were going. No, instead the wizard dug up something south of the river. A ruin from the Old Kingdom. Inside there was some kind of device that he used to take all the people away. This is the key that unlocks it.'

'A device?' Pandora said. 'What kind of device?'

Catherine threw up her hands and scooped the knick-knacks back into the drawer. 'How should I know? Magic carpets. Winged horses, maybe. What do you want from me? The point is you have to get out of the vale. Travel east, just like the villagers did.'

'You mean follow the wizard? I'm not sure I like that option much.'

'I don't like it much either,' Catherine said. 'It means the wizard has already won. He's manipulated us into leaving the vale, to follow where he leads. I feel like it's his will we're following, not our own, like he planned all this long ago, and it's only now we're seeing his design. But I don't see any other option if we're to keep you two girls safe.'

CHAPTER 23

On the farm there was a donkey called Pepper who was rarely called upon to do any work since the last villagers had left. As a result he had become an animal of leisure, lounging around the glade and making a nuisance of himself in every quarter of the farm. When the sisters found him, he was eating apples from a barrel behind Galen's cider-making shed. Sensing that a task had finally been appointed him, Pepper led them on a merry chase across three fields and laid waste to a row of beanpoles before Holly subdued him with a handful of strawberries and Pandora slipped a halter over his head.

By the time they hitched Pepper to the old trading cart and led him to the cottage, Catherine had already packed up most of her belongings.

'There's a lot of happy memories here, to be sure,' she said as the sisters loaded canvas sacks of clothes, small wooden crates of kitchenware, and a few items of furniture onto the cart. 'But memories I can carry inside. Everything else is just stuff. Let it sit here and gather dust for a while. I doubt anyone will be along to steal anything before I come back.'

They walked east towards Candlewick, but veered south on a narrow track beside the river to avoid passing through that haunted place. The sisters walked alongside the cart, with Catherine riding on the narrow bench. Pepper had forgotten his earlier reticence and pulled the rickety little wagon as if he was eager for adventure.

The path turned south again across a stone bridge that had stood for vast epochs of time. Its arches turned the flow of the river into churning torrents of white, and the stones were worn smooth by the eternal passage of the Anwin. On the far side, a great oak tree stood beside the road. Twelve dead trunks of older trees stood in a circle through which the road passed.

The forest on the far side of the river was untouched by the hand of man, and the sisters marveled at the titanic trees covered with moss like the aeries of elven kings rising from oceans of bluebells. Holly spent much of her time away from the path, exploring among the ferns and shrubs, climbing over deadfalls between the great trunks. To Pandora's amusement she actually hugged one of the trees, a withered old oak with barely any leaves left on its gray branches. Often when she came back to the path it was to show Pandora some creature she had found under a log, or crawling along a twig. A huge hairy caterpillar, a fearsome stag beetle, a tiny lizard, and even a dazzling blue butterfly. All sat patiently on Holly's outstretched hand to be wondered at before she returned them to their lairs and set them free.

As the afternoon wore on, the land rose and the ground became stony and uneven. More than once the sisters had to push the cart from behind to help Pepper out of a rut in the path. The road diverted around rocky outcrops and boulders jutting from the earth like glacial erratics half-buried beneath the undergrowth. Between gaps in the trees they spied a great fist of rock towering a thousand feet above the forest. As it grew nearer they saw the outcrop was flat on top and covered with thick woodland. Catherine pointed out a cluster of artificial structures among the trees at the edge of that lofty plane. There were conical towers, domes, cylinders, and pyramids, all tantalizingly revealed and then concealed as they approached along the wooded path.

The vertical walls and slanting buttresses of the plateau loomed above them when they arrived at a flat ridge just above the treeline. There was a grassy veld on a narrow spur extending from the base of the plateau, and in its center was an abandoned stone hut overgrown with ivy. It had been a hard climb for Pepper up the loose, stony path, and he was leaning hard into his traces when Catherine called a halt to rest.

'This little house is one of dozens that used to be dotted around the land hereabouts,' Catherine said as she steered Pepper towards the hut. 'They belonged to hunters and trappers and all kinds of folks who made their living from the forest. Galen knew most of them by name, and he was always staying in one house or another when he was up in the hills searching for materials for his pigments.'

'It doesn't look like anyone's lived here for years,' Pandora said. 'Where did the people go?'

'Where do you think? The wizard spread his influence up here as well, and all the hill folk went east, just like everyone else.'

Catherine loosed Pepper from the harness and he parked his rear end on the grass with a heavy sigh, drooping his long ears. The sisters sat with Catherine on a stone bench beside the hut and ate dried fruits and nuts while they rested their feet.

After a while Pandora stood and craned her neck to peer up at the cliffs. The buildings they had seen from afar were concealed by the rim of the plateau, and all she could see were the tops of the trees leaning over the precipice.

Catherine caught the direction of her gaze and came to join her. 'That's where the wizard took them. All the people of the vale, he led them to the top of this plateau, and afterwards they were never seen again.'

'It's so high,' Pandora said. 'How did they get up there?'

'Come with me, I'll show you.' Catherine led them across the spur to the base of the cliff. Hidden behind a thick growth of bushes and shrubs there was a stone staircase cut into the rock, leading in sharp switchbacks up the vertical face. 'This is the only path to the top. Masons from Candlewick carved these steps on the wizard's instructions. God knows how anyone got up there in the days of the Old Kingdom. For all I know, they sprouted wings and flew up there.'

'It's a hell of a climb,' Pandora said. 'How are we going to get Pepper up there? Even if we pile up sacks on his back and abandon the cart, I'm not sure he'll make it.'

'And neither will I with this hip, unless someone feels like giving me a piggy-back all the way to the top.' Catherine waved dismissively at the stairs and wandered back to the hut. The door had warped and gotten stuck in the frame, but she opened it with a firm pull. Inside was a single room packed with dense growths of ivy that snaked its way through holes in the roof. The air was musty and thick with spider webs wafting in the breeze through the door. 'Seems to me this would make a cozy home if someone pulled out all the creepers and swept the mouse turds off the floor.'

Pandora joined her and leaned into the room. In the gloom she saw a sagging cot bed in the far corner, and an armchair that looked like it had become a nest for vermin. 'I think back home a California real estate agent would describe this as charming and rustic.'

'You mean it's a shithole?' Catherine said. 'Well, they say beauty is in the eye of the beholder.'

'You're not coming with us, are you?' Pandora said.

Catherine parted the vines and stepped inside. 'A few hours ago I thought I was ready to give up and die. I was going to take a chair out into the yard and sit there with a glass of brandy while the sun set, and wait for those damned lights to come and take me away. Well, I suppose I wasn't all that keen on dying after all. Seeing you girls again and traveling up here has set me to thinking. If I leave the vale, then the wizard has won, and I don't fancy giving him the satisfaction. I plan to stay right here, fix up this old hut, and make a stand.'

'But are you safe here?' Pandora said. 'What about the phantoms?'

'One thing we always knew about the phantoms is they come out of the mist near that old pyramid across the vale. Up in the hills the mists don't form, and the pyramid is a long ways off. I reckon this is about as safe a place as I can get to.'

'What will you eat here? How will you live?'

'Pepper can take me back to the farm to dig up potatoes, carrots, or whatever. There's enough food in the ground to last another season until I've got this place up and running. I'll mark out some little plots up here on the slopes and grow vegetables, keep chickens, that kind of thing. The forest will supply everything else I need. Along the way here I spotted blackberry bushes, elderberries, garlic, and asparagus, all growing wild beside the path.'

'Won't you be lonely, all the way out here by yourself?'

'Oh, I reckon I'll just keep on talking to Galen like I always did. Only now he won't be answering back, so I'll win every argument, won't I?'

They unpacked Catherine's belongings from the cart and erected a small campsite beside the hut. It was just a camp bed covered by an awning with a warming fire nearby, but already the abandoned homestead was beginning to look like a home.

When they were done they gathered at the base of the stone stairs. Catherine gave them a sack of supplies for their journey and nodded towards the hut. 'I'm treating this as a temporary sojourn. If the wizard was watching he might think he's scared me off, but instead he's made me fighting mad. I want you girls to go into the east and find our people.' She gave Pandora a thick envelope of creamy vellum with Jason's name written in dark ink. 'Find Jason and give him this. Tell him it's time to come back and retake the vale and make it a safe and prosperous place again. Galen had a plan for how to do it, but it can't happen unless he brings the villagers home.'

They embraced and made promises that they would not be apart for long. Catherine bid them a final farewell, urging them to begin their ascent at once before they lost the light.

CHAPTER 24

The stairs were steep and narrow, and often uneven. The masons had carved the steps according to the natural contours of the cliff, resulting in a serpentine route that led the sisters into narrow crags so cramped they had to duck their heads, or along beetling ledges exposed to the sky where the wind felt like grasping hands seeking to pull them to their deaths. The steps varied from slender ledges barely wide enough to accommodate their feet, to giant rocky slabs that required the sisters to help each other up every vertical riser. It was impossible to find a rhythm for their bodies to follow, and each switchback revealed some new and perilous terrain.

'Bet you're glad we go on so many long bike rides,' Pandora called over her shoulder as they struggled up a set of knee-high steps. 'If we hadn't spent the past twenty years exercising our thighs and calves I think I would have collapsed after the fifth switchback.'

Their enthusiasm for the climb soon wore out as their altitude increased. Coarse shrubs had planted their hardy roots into the bare rock and spilled over the path, forcing the sisters to push through claw-like branches that snagged their clothes and scratched their skin. At certain places someone had thought to construct banisters of wood and rope for travelers to hold onto, but the timber had become brittle, and the rope was barely more than dust that crumbled when pressure was laid upon it. When the stairs became narrow the girls pressed their backs against the cliff and crept along sideways.

The wind built up as the evening progressed. Pandora could feel the weight on her feet decreasing when a strong updraft rippled through her clothes. As the gusts grew more frequent, the sisters gripped each other for support, sometimes lying flat on the steps until the wind died down.

Pandora continually caught herself climbing with her eyes firmly shut against the dizzying drop beside her. She had to force herself to look where she was going in case she was about to walk into unseen danger. Holly became increasingly hesitant and nervous as they climbed higher. For long stretches she dropped onto her hands and knees to give herself a lower center of gravity, keeping her eyes fixed firmly on the rock before her. Their progress slowed to a crawl which seemed to hasten the fall of night, and soon they were climbing in twilight. Pandora wished they had waited until the following day to make this journey in the new light.

Catherine had given them a small lantern for the trip. Pandora lit it when the way ahead became too dim for her to be confident of placing her feet safely. As darkness fell, she paused every few steps to turn and light the way for Holly, who crouched on all fours, huddled against the rock wall for security. It was impossible to tell how much further they had to climb, but stopping for rest was unthinkable, and fear of the lantern dying drove them ever upward.

Eventually the wind died down, and the steps became more even. They found a rhythm to their steps and Holly felt confident enough to rise to her feet. She even took the lead and carried the lantern to give Pandora a break.

During this time Pandora thought about the mission Catherine had laid upon them. She had made promises to find Jason, but in truth she barely remembered the boy from the Polaroid, and she knew nothing of the man he had grown into. The problems of this world were not her problems. She already had enough worries of her own back on Earth without diving into unknown dangers here on Entara. Her primary motivation for traveling east was her firm belief that there was a relationship between direction and distance on both worlds. By traveling far away from the vale she hoped to return to Earth in a place similarly far from Ojai. In doing so she would evade Agent Arnold, who would surely have the entire town under keen surveillance. Having returned to Earth, she could then contact Jackie and make serious plans to correct the injustices perpetrated against herself and Holly. If she found the boy Jason along the way, she would fulfill her promise to Catherine by passing on her message, but her participation in this world's adventures must end there. Though she had fond memories of the vale and its people, she could not justify risking Holly's life to protect them.

The light of the lantern vanished and Pandora found herself alone in darkness. A moment of panic seized her at the thought of Holly slipping over the edge of the cliff. 'Holly? Are you okay?'

A silhouette appeared against the stars and Holly seized her hand, pulling her around a corner of rock. The cliff wall disappeared and she fell sideways onto a broad patch of grass illuminated by the golden glow of the lantern. At the limit of the flame's light were tall trees like sentinels guarding this aerial realm.

'Oh thank God, we made it,' Pandora caressed the grass with her hands and breathed in the scent of the soil. 'I've never been so glad to have solid ground beneath me.'

Holly picked up the lantern and explored the wooded area away from the cliff. They were in a crescent-shaped clearing surrounded by trees, and by the light of the lantern she found a narrow gap leading into the interior of the plateau.

Pandora stood to watch her progress. 'Looks like the lantern is burning low. Either we've got to continue onward now or wait until daylight.'

Holly hesitated beside the night-dark mouth of the path. She handed Pandora the lantern with an eyebrow-shrug that might have meant *Here you go, you decide.*

'Well, in for a penny, in for a pound, right? I don't think I could rest without at least taking a peek at those ruins. They can't be far away.'

The trees huddled close and the weeds were tangled knots of greenery tugging at their clothes as they walked down the narrow and winding path. The lamp was guttering, adding haste to their steps as they fought their way across the tableland. The woods were eerily quiet and it occurred to Pandora that they were the first people to walk this way for many years. Such was the inaccessible altitude of this craggy place that she doubted there were even any animals up here except for the birds who treated this domain as their unique abode.

The trees parted and they found themselves among the Astari structures they had glimpsed from afar. There were dozens of identical white domes arranged in a hexagonal grid pattern, connected by a network of smooth, metaled roads. Unlike the ruins near the observatory, these were complete structures, though the roads were bordered by unkempt grasses and weeds.

'None of these domes have any doors or windows,' Pandora said, unconsciously keeping her voice down as if the ghosts of the Astari might hear. 'How did anyone get into these places?'

Each dome was completely smooth, featureless and impossible to distinguish from its neighbors. When they arrived at an intersection of six roads, Pandora gave the lantern to Holly and turned a full three-sixty. 'Everything looks the same. Already I'm not sure which way we came.'

The buildings were constructed of a white material that was faintly phosphorescent as if it both reflected and amplified the rarefied starlight. In the distance were three conical towers of differing heights and Pandora used them to navigate by, leading them towards the center of the site.

They crossed more intersections, always keeping the

cone-towers ahead of them. Further afield they saw taller buildings: A three-sided pyramid, a cluster of cylinders topped by broad flat discs, and a tall spindly antenna-like structure bristling with spheres, cubes, discs, and cones. The architecture and layout of the settlement were wholly mysterious.

'I can't figure out what any of these buildings are for,' Pandora said. 'There don't seem to be any houses, or offices, or recreation facilities. There are no warehouses, hospitals, schools, or meeting halls. What kind of people were these Astari, anyway?'

The road they were following came to a sudden end at a crevasse that extended for hundreds of yards in all directions. The cone-towers they had been navigating by were visible on the far side, but the way ahead was blocked by the pit which yawned below them. The road's surface crumbled and cracked near the edge, then simply ceased to exist.

'It looks like the ground collapsed here,' Pandora said. 'Let's try walking around the edge and see if we can reconnect with the road on the far side.'

Holly led the way and trudged through the long grass between the domes, keeping the edge of the crevasse close on their right.

'It seems strange that people with so much advanced tech would build on top of a sinkhole. Maybe these buildings have stood here so long that the plateau itself has geologically shifted, or maybe—'

She grabbed the lantern from Holly and dashed to the pit, holding the light high. 'Oh my God,' she said, staring down into the hole. 'Holly, I think this is an impact crater. Look, we've been walking in a curved path around the rim of a huge, circular hole.'

Leaning over the edge, they could just make out the curved, bowl-like shape of the depression. Scattered around its base were indistinct heaps and mounds that might have been the ruins of buildings. 'Didn't Galen say something about a war that wiped out the Old Kingdom?

Jesus, I think somebody dropped an atomic bomb on this place.'

They continued onward. Further around the rim they found a wooden platform that extended over the crater. At its inner end was a staircase leading down into the bowl.

'This must be the excavation site,' Pandora said as they descended the steps. 'Catherine said the wizard made the villagers dig up something on the plateau. Whatever it was must have been buried under all the rubble down there.'

The floor of the crater was scattered with simple wooden constructions that looked primitive compared with the symmetrical perfection of the geometrically designed Astari structures. There were cranes built of wooden beams and powered by broad wheels driven by human effort alone. These machines had been used to clear away the rubble of the Astari buildings destroyed by the detonation of the ancient weapon.

At the center of the crater stood a circular building of wooden struts covered with stretched canvas sheets, a low-tech imitation of the seamless white domes on the surface. As the girls approached, Pandora held the lantern high and illuminated a wooden door. On the bare planks someone had daubed a disturbing symbol in black paint.

'I don't like this,' Pandora said. 'So far as I can tell, everything the wizard told the villagers was a malicious lie intended to do them harm. If he made them carve steps into the cliff, made them climb all the way up here, made them clear away all this debris, he did it to hurt them somehow. What if all that's inside this dome is a pit full of phantoms, or a poison gas chamber? What if none of the villagers ever came back because whatever's inside there killed them all?'

Holly traced her fingers over the ugly black skull painted on the door. It was a universal symbol comprehensible to all who might stumble upon this remote spot: *Danger, do not enter*.

Holly turned the handle and pushed the door open. Whatever Pandora had expected to find inside, it was not what she saw. Electric lights mounted on tripods cast a cold glare around the room. In the center of the floor was a hole. Hovering above the hole with no visible means of support was a sphere.

'What the hell is this place?' Pandora said, stepping warily inside. She approached the hole and saw that it was actually a shaft, descending vertically beyond her ability to perceive. The sphere hanging in the air was around twelve feet in diameter, slightly narrower than the shaft itself.

'I don't get it. Is this what we were meant to find? I was expecting some kind of airplane, or a helicopter, or something.'

At first glance the sphere appeared white, but when Holly reached out to touch it, the surface crackled with blue energy that radiated out from her hand. She snatched her hand back and stared at her fingers.

'What happened? Did it hurt you?' Pandora said.

Holly replied by placing both hands on the sphere and watching the ripples of electric blue cascading around the sphere. Pandora reached out as well and felt a warm, buzzing sensation on her skin. There was a curious spongy resistance that kept her hand slightly above the surface.

'Weird. It's like trying to push two magnet poles together. I can feel my hair sticking up on end.'

Holly went to investigate the only other feature of the room, a pedestal of dark, glassy material that rose to waist height a short distance away. She ran her fingers over the smooth surface searching for buttons, switches, or other interactive features, but came up short.

'Maybe you've got to say the magic word,' Pandora said. Holly gave her a look as if this was an insensitive thing to say.

Pandora reached into her pocket and held up the red disc. 'Catherine said this was the key that would unlock the device, whatever that means.'

She inspected the disc minutely, rubbing it between her fingers, holding it up to the light of the electric lamps, staring at the internal striations. She crossed to the pedestal and placed the disc on its surface.

The lights dimmed and a high-pitched electronic tone screamed around the room. She leapt back from the pedestal in alarm. 'What did I do?'

The red disc was spinning on its edge, emitting an eerie crimson glow. Holly gripped her arm, and as they watched, the disc turned blue and the jarring electronic noise rose a semitone. A section of the floating sphere vanished, forming a circular portal to the inside. The room fell silent.

The disc stopped spinning and changed color again to a luminous green. Pandora tried to pick it up, but it was no longer on the surface of the glassy top. Instead it occupied a space beneath the surface as if it lay at the bottom of a shallow pool. 'Looks like we don't get our token back.'

The sisters walked to the edge of the shaft where a short set of stairs had materialized out of thin air, leading into the open sphere. Ascending the steps, Pandora found herself in a cabin lined on all sides with comfortable seats. There were recessed lights giving the interior a warm, welcoming feel. Holly followed close behind and as soon as she was past the threshold the door closed, or rather it ceased to be a door and reverted to its previous solid state.

Holly pressed against the wall where the door had been, smacking her palms against the interior paneling. The sphere shifted and the girls staggered to keep their footing.

'Sit down, Holly. I think we're going for a ride.'

Around the circumference of the sphere, sections of the hull turned transparent like porthole windows. The sphere jolted again and the sisters fell into seats on opposite sides of the cabin.

'Oh God, I've got a horrible feeling about this,' Pandora said as the sphere began to vibrate. 'The crater, the sphere, the shaft. This thing wasn't built for flying.'

The sphere dropped into the shaft. Pandora's stomach lurched, and she gripped the edge of her seat. Beyond the portholes the dome chamber vanished and the view outside showed only the black walls of the shaft. A flash of light, then darkness, then another flash. The flashes repeated at intervals and she realized the shaft was lit by widely spaced lamps. The flashes came quicker. Their velocity was increasing.

Standing unsteadily, she explored every corner of the cabin, searching for controls or instructions. 'There's gotta be an emergency stop button, or a brake lever, or something. What if we just keep plummeting until we smash into the bottom of this shaft?'

The sphere juddered and changed direction. Pandora was thrown across the cabin into Holly's lap. The sisters held onto each other, crouching low while the sphere tilted one way and then the other. Gradually the sphere found an equilibrium, and the ground ceased to rotate beneath their feet. Through the portholes, the motion of the lights became smooth, passing rapidly from side to side.

'We're not falling anymore,' Pandora said, kneeling on the seat to peer through a porthole. 'We're moving along a horizontal shaft. We must be deep underground.'

Holly knelt beside her and together they watched the lights of the tunnel speed past. After a while Holly breathed on the glass so it fogged over and drew a smiley face. She regarded Pandora with a querying look.

'Yeah, I think we're okay now,' Pandora said. 'This machine must be old. Like, really old. Probably it's in serious need of an oil change and a new set of tires. But we seem to be bombing along smoothly enough now. This tunnel must go for miles and miles underground. It might be hours before we get to wherever the hell it is we're going.'

The tunnel continued without variation for a long time, and soon the girls became bored with the monotonous passage of the lights past the windows. They had no way to judge the time, but Pandora knew it must be well past midnight. The hypnotic motion of the tunnel's lights made her drowsy after the exhausting climb to the plateau. Abandoning their vigil at the windows, they took seats side-by-side and rested. The cabin's seats were so soft and comfortable that Pandora half-suspected the contours of the padding were subtly shifting and re-arranging to accommodate her body. The tension in her muscles flowed out of her like ice melting in sunshine. Already Holly was asleep beside her, but Pandora stayed awake for a while to enjoy the peaceful motion of the sphere and the intermittent glow of the lights outside. After the torments of the past few days, this strange journey along an ancient alien tunnel finally allowed her an opportunity to clear her mind and plan for the trials that were still to come. Foremost in her mind was that maniac Agent Arnold, who even at this moment was probably casting an ever-wider net to catch the sisters wherever they reappeared on Earth. Another fear lurked near the surface of her consciousness as well, but that one she kept suppressed because its implications were too frightening for her to handle right now: Somewhere at the end of this long and age-old tunnel awaited the wizard Hieronymus Flak.

CHAPTER 25

When she awoke daylight flooded the cabin. Holly was already awake, kneeling on a seat and watching the world outside. She had found a panel in the wall that dispensed cool, clear water into white cups and handed one to Pandora as she joined her at the window. The sphere was traveling above ground over a barren landscape of brown grass and stunted trees. Rocky formations like deformed giants watched their passing, and on the far horizon jagged mountains scraped the clouds. The sphere was flying fifty feet above the ground at around thirty miles per hour. At regular intervals they passed through hoop-like constructions resembling tennis rackets which protruded from the ground, but their travel was otherwise unsupported by tracks or rails.

'Thank God we're out of that tunnel,' Pandora said. 'But what a bleak place this is. Nothing but rocks and grass. I wonder if there's anything bigger than an insect walking around out there?'

Catherine had packed pastries stuffed with cooked fruits for their journey, and they ate breakfast while they watched the landscape drift by. Pandora was intrigued by the tennis racket contraptions which guided their course. Peering through the forward porthole she could see a dozen of them stretching away into the distance.

'There must be whole networks of these hoop things all around the planet, but where do they go? I can't see any cities, towns, or any kind of settlements. This must be a very empty world.'

Hours passed. For a while the girls entertained themselves by playing travel bingo with a piece of paper and a pencil Holly found in her pocket. They took turns to draw grids filled with simple drawings of things they could see outside, and competed to cross off each item as it passed by. Faced with such a minimalist landscape the game soon became repetitive and each grid consisted of minor variations on the themes of tree, rock, bird, cactus, cloud. In the end, Pandora decided to shake up the game by concealing the pencil stub in her breast pocket and claiming ignorance of its whereabouts. This provoked a chase around the cabin and ended with a tickling contest on the floor.

By the time they returned to the windows, the landscape had changed. The dry and barren land was now nourished by a broad river that flowed sluggishly alongside the path of the sphere. The trees grew taller and in greater profusion, providing shelter to larger animals such as deer that could be seen gathering in clearings beside the water's edge. Sometimes the copses and thickets grew directly in the path of the sphere, but there was evidence that the trees had been cut back to prevent the machine's passage being obstructed.

'It looks like these hoop things were here long before the trees,' Pandora said as they studied the land and drew each other's attention to new sights. 'It must have taken centuries for the wilderness to change, and now the sphere has to travel through regions of forest. Look, there are tree stumps right ahead of us and around that hoop. Someone must travel out here and clear the way to keep the transit system running.'

Soon the sphere was traveling over fields. Parcels of land beside the river had been cleared, drained, and marked off with fencing. Unlike the small strip fields of

Candlewick, these were large monoculture fields enclosing dozens of acres of corn, wheat, oats, and other cereal crops. The transit hoops continued uninterrupted across the fields, often in locations that must have inconvenienced the farmers, whoever they might be. This led Pandora to suspect that the transit network was already in existence when the farm-builders arrived, and they had merely planted their fields around the older structures.

From then on, there were many new sights. For an hour the girls took station at different windows, eagerly alerting each other to new signs of civilization, dragging each other across the cabin to see fields full of cows, fish farming enclosures on the river, or a windmill turning on a high hill.

The sphere swerved away from the river and traveled parallel to a tarmac road for several miles. Ahead, high-rise buildings came into view. A small roadside flower garden proudly displayed a written sign. *Welcome to Farmtown.*

CHAPTER 26

Their travel had been smooth and uninterrupted for many hours when the sphere came to a halt. Pandora was looking through a window and smacked her head on the glass when the machine unexpectedly decelerated. The portholes vanished, returning to their original opaque state. Moments later the circular door appeared.

'Is this it? Have we arrived?' Pandora said as they descended from the sphere. The machine had stopped in an empty parking lot a short distance beyond the Farmtown welcome sign. On one side of the road hedgerows parted to reveal a broad lake, a jetty and several small boats. A low brick building was signposted *Lakeside Park Visitor Center*.

Holly tapped her shoulder and drew her attention to a strange object lying in the corner of the lot. It was a big chunk of mechanical wreckage and twisted metal. The tarmac had buckled and shifted as if the object had struck the ground with some force.

'God, I think this is another sphere,' Pandora said, approaching the debris. 'It must have crashed for some reason.' The curved remains of the sphere jutted out of the ground like a broke egg. The air shimmered with sparkling objects that swayed in the breeze. They were shattered fragments of the sphere's outer plating, hovering in the air like metal butterflies. Holly flicked one with her finger and it pinged away.

A hoop-construct loomed nearby, but it was bent and leaning drunkenly to one side. 'Looks like the sphere struck the hoop and fell. Thank God we didn't suffer the same fate.'

Beyond the sphere was the lake shore. The boats tied up at the jetty were small pleasure craft powered by oars or outboard motors. Further along the shore was a larger craft designed for lake tours, with wide open decks and big paddle wheels. In the distance they could make out the downtown district of Farmtown.

'This place looks totally different from Candlewick. But it's not like the Astari ruins either. It looks more like America in the 1950s. I think we should take a walk into town. If this is the place Jason traveled to, we can pass on Catherine's message to him.'

The sphere could take them no further so they followed the road. Before long, they were walking along tree-lined avenues in a suburban neighborhood. The houses were pleasant single-story dwellings with lots of glass, exposed wood, and stone chimneys. Each home was set in a rectangular plot with perfectly manicured lawns and flower beds. There were no cars in the driveways, but at the end of the street they found a compact parking area where a dozen small electric buggies covered with brightly colored awnings were parked in neat rows. They saw no people.

In the next street was a row of shops, a tobacconist, a post office, and a small clothing boutique. The window display of the clothing store featured mannequins wearing fashions straight out of I Love Lucy and Leave It to Beaver. The women wore halter-neck circle dresses emphasizing their hourglass figures, and men wore suits and fedoras, or sports jackets and chinos. There were no children's fashions on display. A sign in the door said *open,* but when Pandora went inside she could find no one in attendance.

'Where are all the people?' she said as they continued

down the street. 'Somebody must be tending to all those fields we saw. This can't be another ghost town like Candlewick.'

On a whim she turned up the driveway of a white clapboard house and rang the doorbell. When no one answered she tried the door and found it unlocked, letting her curiosity guide her inside. Electric lights shone in the hall and other rooms visible through open doors. Soft jazz music played from somewhere further inside.

'Hello? Is anyone home?' Pandora said. 'We're visitors from Candlewick.'

No reply. In the lounge, a big, blocky television set displayed a test screen with the words PLEASE STAND BY in bold letters. Holly found a remote control mounted in the armrest of a La-Z-Boy. When she operated the chunky push-buttons, every channel showed the same test screen image.

'No cartoons, huh?' Pandora said.

Across the hall was the dining room. The smell of home cooking reached their nostrils as soon as they entered. The dining table was set for two, with dishes of mashed potatoes, steamed vegetables, and a tray of meatloaf. In the center was a display of fresh flowers, and beside each plate was a glass of sparkling water. Taper candles were lit, giving the scene a cozy ambiance.

Pandora touched one of the dishes. 'It's hot. And the soda water is still fizzy. Holly, there must be somebody in the house. Let's keep looking.'

A short hallway led to three bedrooms with neatly made beds laid with fresh linen. The master bedroom featured a bookshelf displaying two distinct literary collections. The upper three shelves held sports books and magazines concerning a game called speedball and the exploits of a team called the Farmtown Rangers. The lower shelves held dozens of romance paperbacks with tatty, well-worn covers depicting tough rural men and buxom women in various states of undress. The smaller rooms were decorated for a young boy and a young girl, respectively.

The boy's room was sports-themed, with a wealth of speedball paraphernalia and trophies arrayed on shelves alongside toy soldiers and robots. The girl's room boasted a splendid dollhouse with its walls open to reveal the detailed interior and the miniature anthropomorphic animals who lived there. Pandora thought the children's rooms looked curiously unlived in and sterile, as if they were intended for display purposes only.

There was no one in the house. In the kitchen they discovered a radio on the windowsill, which was the source of the jazz music. Pandora turned it off in irritation. Holly opened the fridge. The shelves were stocked with fresh eggs, milk, butter, meat, and vegetables. On the bottom shelf was a black forest cake with caramel-glazed cherries on top. She lifted one by its stalk and eyed it suspiciously before popping it in her mouth.

'Oven's still hot from the meatloaf,' Pandora said. 'This is crazy. Did we frighten the homeowners away? I can't believe they just leapt out of a window when we rang the doorbell. There must be someone lurking around the place.'

Holly went to the dining table and pulled out a chair. She glanced towards Pandora with an expectant look.

'Nuh-uh,' Pandora shook her head. 'No way, this place is too creepy. We're getting out of here right now.'

At the end of the street was another parking area with more of the little electric buggies. Pandora got behind the wheel and the vehicle came to life with the flick of a switch. The roads were deserted as they rode into town. At intersections, traffic signals shone green and red lights at empty lanes. Pandora stopped at each red light, taking the opportunity to examine the town in more detail.

It did not take long before things got weird. Within the outer belt of the suburbs was a commercial district. At the corner of an intersection their way was blocked by a building that seemed to be melting. It was a tall office block with shops at ground level. The brick walls had flowed like liquid to merge with the road, and the entire structure leaned at an alarming angle. At street level the windows and doors sagged into distorted parallelograms. The shops were twisted and compressed almost beyond recognition.

They got out of the buggy and Pandora touched a corner of the wall where it merged with the tarmac road. The bricks were elongated and deformed like chocolate that had been left out in the sun, but under her fingers they felt cold and hard.

'What happened here?' Pandora said. 'Did these guys hire Salvador Dali as an architect? It's as if the walls turned into liquid for a second, then froze solid just before the whole thing collapsed.'

On the corner of the building was a cafe called Rosie's Diner. The blue and white awning over the window was crumpled into a warped mass of cloth and steel rods. Neon signs advertising sodas and coffee hung loose and flickered uncertainly. The double doors had been compacted into shrunken child-size hatches, When Holly opened them she had to kneel down to look inside. Pandora knelt beside her and saw tables, chairs, and a polished wooden counter, but the ceiling was an uneven chaotic mess barely four feet above the floor.

The liquefied building had spilled diagonally out of its plot and made the street impassable, so Pandora took a detour around the block. She drove slowly, keeping a watchful eye on the town which felt more sinister with each passing mile.

A few blocks beyond the Dali building they encountered a bizarre sculpture in the middle of the road. Holly lingered by the buggy while Pandora investigated the strange sight. It was a pillar of twisted steel rods, shapeless lumps of plastic, battered metal sheets, rubber, and tangles of electrical wiring. On closer inspection she was able to identify many wheels, springs, light bulbs, and scraps of colorful fabric.

'It's made of buggies,' she called over her shoulder. 'It looks like somebody put about a dozen of those little carts into a blender and mixed them all together, then tipped it out into the street.'

She walked slowly around the edifice, trying to comprehend its purpose, and why someone had blocked the road with it. Holly reached into their buggy and tapped the horn insistently. She looked nervous and eager to continue onward.

Pandora nodded. 'Okay, let's keep moving.'

Towards the center of town were more disturbing and unsettling sights. In a vacant lot a roadside billboard displayed nothing but the word CUNT in eight-foot-tall lettering. In the parking lot of a supermarket, tens of thousands of tins of food had been piled into a dozen huge pyramids towering thirty feet into the air. Through the windows could be seen thousands more tins stacked as high as the ceiling.

They arrived at Farmtown's city hall, a classically styled building of red bricks and white columns opposite a small park. On the lawn was a marble statue of a man standing on a plinth with a dedication to Winston Buckler, first mayor of Farmtown. Winston Buckler's head had been hacked off and lay on the fresh-cut grass.

Pandora stopped the cart. 'Holly, something's really wrong here. I don't like this place, and I'm pretty sure we're not going to find Jason or anyone from Candlewick here. Listen, I think it's time for us to go back to Earth. I know it's scary there right now because of those NCA assholes, but I promise we're going to fight them, and we're going to win. We should be far away from Ojai now, maybe even outside California. Wherever we blink back to, we should be safe from the agency long enough for us to contact Jackie and start preparing a case to get our house back and to clear me of those fake charges.'

A fleeting movement caught her attention. In the park opposite the city hall, something lurked in the shadows of the trees. At first Pandora thought it was an urban fox or a coyote, but then the figure moved again.

'Hey, look, there's someone over there in the park.' She waved her arm and called out. 'Hello, is somebody there?'

The figure bolted. She was crouched low, watching the sisters from the bushes, but now her cover was blown and she ran across the park towards the commercial district.

'It's a kid,' Pandora cried out. 'It's a little girl.'

She took off across the park in pursuit. The girl had a head start, but Pandora's legs were longer and she soon began to close the gap. She looked about nine or ten years old, dressed in dungarees and a plaid shirt, and a baseball cap. Over her shoulder was a rucksack which she gripped tightly to her side.

She changed course, dodging under a stand of small whitebeam trees. Her small size allowed her to run unhindered beneath the low branches while Pandora was obliged to detour twenty yards around.

'Please, wait,' she called breathlessly. 'We don't want to hurt you.'

The girl paid no heed. She vaulted the iron rail at the edge of the park and dashed into an alley. By the time Pandora clambered over the rail the girl had reached the end of the alley where the way was blocked by a wooden fence. She squeezed through a gap in the boards and disappeared. There was no chance of Pandora fitting through the narrow gap, and she wasted precious seconds climbing over the top.

She sighted the girl in the next street, racing into the mouth of another alley. When Pandora arrived the alley was deserted. For a moment she thought the girl had got away. Then she heard a clattering above and saw the girl climbing a fire escape, disappearing through a window.

The fire escape was rusty and rattled loosely against the wall as Pandora climbed. At the third floor she found the open window. The building was a department store, and she arrived in the womenswear department. Racks of old-fashioned dresses were arrayed all around. Ahead was a display of oversize hats and high-heeled shoes. Gentle orchestral music played from speakers mounted in corners.

A flash of movement. The girl ran past the perfume counter. Pandora followed through the lingerie section where mannequins wore bullet bras and lace stockings. The pitter-patter of small feet drew her attention to the escalators where the girl was ascending rapidly to the next floor.

The fourth floor was homeware. Pandora stalked between display islands stacked with designer suitcases, television sets, floral vases, and clocks. Far to her right she spied a door swinging shut and raced across the room towards it. The sign read *Staff Only* and led to a staircase. There was no way to tell if the girl had gone up or down. She took a chance and dashed up to the fifth floor.

The administration department. A receptionist's desk with a rotary-dial telephone and a heavy typewriter; a long corridor beyond, windowless, with many doors on either side. There was no need to search every office because Pandora could see the girl at the end of the hall, pushing through a set of double doors.

The cafeteria. Pandora was at the end of her strength, but the girl ran on tirelessly, darting between the tables as if fleeing in terror was her normal daily routine. Pandora had no breath to cry out, and she ran on in sheer desperation, uncertain why this young girl should inspire such a deep urge for protection.

Another doorway, another set of stairs. The last door gave out on the roof, and now the chase took them past ventilation pipes and skylight boxes towards the roof's edge. The girl skidded to a halt at the low perimeter wall. She turned and faced Pandora.

Pandora stopped and leaned on her knees, gasping for air. 'Wow, you gave me a real workout. My name's Pandora. What's your name?'

The girl was not even out of breath. 'You need to get out of this place,' she said simply. 'If you're not gone by tomorrow, they'll kill you for sure.'

She climbed onto the wall, and for a terrible instant Pandora thought she was going to jump to her death. There was a wooden plank across the alley to the next building. The girl ran lightly over the narrow bridge with no hesitancy. When she reached the other side she kicked the plank away and it tumbled into the alley. She ran to a roof access door. With a swish of her ponytail beneath her Farmtown Rangers cap, she was gone.

Pandora descended on the escalators, eschewing the fire escape and exiting through the main doors. She emerged on an unfamiliar street and for a moment was lost until Holly came scooting around the corner in the buggy.

'I lost her,' she said as Holly pulled up alongside. 'Holly, I think she's in danger. She said something about people who'd kill us if we didn't leave. She must be hiding from them. We have to find her. I don't want to go back to Earth without taking her with us.'

CHAPTER 27

Holly could not be budged from the driver's seat of the buggy, so it was she who drove them through town as they began a methodical search for the girl. The city was arranged on a circular pattern, with main roads radiating from the central hub of downtown towards the rural areas. They began in the direction Pandora had last seen the girl run, driving a short distance up the main road and then making a ninety-degree turn to explore the radial streets in a series of wedge-shaped sections. Frequently she told Holly to stop the cart while she searched a winding alley or an empty lot. At every stop she called out cheerful greetings in the hopes of enticing the girl from hiding. They found nothing.

The day came to a close. In the twilight Holly drove up a steep hill and parked at a lookout commanding a fine view of the town. Lights burned in a thousand windows and from a thousand street lamps, but there was no sign of life or movement anywhere.

'We'll abandon the search for today,' Pandora said as they leaned on the handrail of the lookout. 'I think we covered the whole western and southern part of town. Tomorrow we'll look to the north and east. There's a lake on the far side of town. It looks like a nice spot. Maybe our girl hangs around there sometimes. We need to think more like a ten-year-old girl. Where would she hide?' The trouble was, Pandora knew that a ten-year-old girl could probably hide indefinitely in a place as large as Farmtown.

Opposite the lookout was a hotel called the Farmtown Overlook. In the lobby, warm lights illuminated a reception area decorated in an alpine style with an abundance of pine wood and bare stone. Piano music played softly from hidden speakers, and a log fire burned fiercely beneath an impressive stone hearth. On the reception desk was a brass bell. Holly rang it.

'Nobody around,' Pandora said. 'Why do I get the impression every place we go has been vacated moments before we arrive?'

There was a hotel floor plan behind the desk and they selected two adjoining rooms, taking the keys from a hook rack on the wall. The rooms were clean, the beds properly turned down, drinks in the minibar, and mints on the pillows. On the writing desk in each room was a welcome basket containing a foldout map of Farmtown, a disposable camera, a set of sunglasses, and a small box of chocolates. An embossed card read *Welcome to Farmtown – We're so glad you're here!*

Satisfied with the accommodation, they went in search of dinner. The hotel had a restaurant situated to give a view of the town and the lake. Thirty tables were laid with fresh linen and flowers. Lighting was set low to give an intimate feel and allow a view of the sparkling lights from the town below.

The restaurant had an automated self-service system. The sisters took trays from a stack beside the door and pushed them along metal slides beneath dozens of glass cubbyholes, each labeled with the meal contained within. Pandora opened a few of the slots and studied the contents. Each meal was piping hot and apparently fresh.

'I'm getting a little sick of this,' she said, slamming one of the doors closed. 'Who's doing this? Who's preparing everything for us? Are these people just really shy, or are they deliberately hiding from us?'

She turned to face the empty restaurant. 'Hello? Who's

there? Why won't you come out and meet us?'

No answer. In a corner of the room she spotted a door marked *Staff Only*. It gave her an idea and she spoke quietly to Holly. 'Listen, why don't you choose some meals and drinks for us both. I'm going to go and check something. I'll be back in a minute.'

She hurried across the dining room and burst through the closed door. As she suspected, it was the kitchen. Hot, humid air struck her face as she entered the brightly lit room. Gleaming stainless steel surfaces and hulking industrial cookers stretched away in aisles across the room. Moving quickly she walked around the room, throwing open doors to pantries, meat lockers, and storage rooms. Nobody was there.

'Dammit, why won't you show yourselves?' The only reply was the roar of the extraction fans.

Back in the dining room, Holly had chosen a table overlooking an ornamental pool lit by fairy lights. On the table were two dishes with plastic covers, and two glasses of sparkling drinks. When Pandora sat down, Holly lifted the covers with a flourish to reveal matching towers of pancakes and maple syrup. Pandora opened her mouth to object, but then remembered just who had put Holly in charge of choosing dinner in the first place.

Holly looked pleased with her selection and tucked in enthusiastically. Pandora smiled indulgently. In the past few days, Holly had been put through ordeals beyond anything in her previous experience, and she was responding with remarkable poise and good humor. In fact, she was showing more proactive independence than at any time in Pandora's memory. If anyone in the vast, unimaginable spans of space between Earth and Entara deserved a plate full of pancakes and maple syrup for dinner, it was sweet, silly Holly, adorable Holly, wonderful Holly.

Pandora took a sip of the lightly sparkling drink Holly had prepared for them at the bar. She nearly choked. It was almost pure gin with just a dash of tonic.

When morning came their buggy had disappeared from the lookout, but they soon found a dozen more in an underground parking garage accessed through the hotel lobby.

Once again, Holly drove while Pandora studied the foldout map of the city and called out directions. 'Yesterday we spent most of the time searching the streets, but I reckon our girl is probably hiding indoors. There are a few spots we should definitely check out. Look, there's a library, an amusement park, and a picturehouse. If I was a ten-year-old girl all alone in a city like this, I'd probably hang out at one of those places. Let's head to the cinema first and see what's there.'

The Farmtown Picturehouse had an old-fashioned marquee lit with flashing bulbs advertising a movie called Captain Invincible. The poster outside the ticket office featured a lantern-jawed space hero in a red flight suit, right hand raised to his brow in salute. The main feature had not yet started when the girls entered the screening room, and there was a newsreel about speedball playing on the projector. The seats appeared empty, but Pandora wanted to check carefully in case the girl was hiding. They split up and moved down the rows, peering between the seats and into dark corners.

While they searched, the newsreel came to an end. The next reel began with a dramatic aerial shot of the city, filmed from an aircraft or a balloon. A man's voiceover spoke in a sober documentary style.

'Farmtown: A home, a community, a place to build a future for you and your family. A hundred years ago, Farmtown was founded by visionary pioneer Winston Buckler, who arrived in this region on a wagon train and found a thousand acres of good land beside Lake Prospect. A generation of traveling through the wastelands had finally come to an end, and the twelve families who accompanied him on his daring voyage built permanent homes along the lake shore.

'Winston and his fellow settlers transformed the wilderness into farmland. He built a school and a hospital, and he sent emissaries to distant communities. Before long, there was a thriving town where only a decade earlier had been nothing but endless miles of wasteland.'

The screen showed a montage of footage emphasizing the busy industrial work of Farmtown. Tall cranes erecting high-rise buildings, tractors pulling plows, factories producing buggies and television sets.

'Farmtown prospered. Over the next century, the city leaders built power stations and factories, and funded scientific research to produce technological wonders such as the televiewer and the electro-cart. Farmtown became a gleaming jewel of culture and civilization amid the vast, unending wilderness.'

Another montage of images. Long lines of emaciated people queuing in parking lots, signs in shop windows reading *No Food Today,* a hospital ward of skeletally thin children.

'But Farmtown has also experienced many challenges and tragedies. Our farmers have fought a constant battle to keep the wastelands at bay and meet the needs of our ever-growing population. The Great Famine was the darkest time in our history, and it is only due to the vision and genius of one man that our fine city has now arisen like a phoenix from the ashes.'

The screen displayed a still-frame image of a man Pandora recognized. 'Oh my God. Holly, look,' she cried out as the voiceover continued.

'This coming Starday, all citizens are invited to the Farmtown Stadium where the great scientist himself, Hieronymus Flak, will deliver a new lecture expounding his latest theories on thinking machines, the power of the atom, and the structure of spacetime. These revelations are sure to astonish and amaze all who attend. Don't miss this opportunity to learn the secrets of the universe from the master of science.'

The video zoomed in slowly on the image of Flak. In his hand he held a glowing orb of crackling energy which he held out towards his audience. As the voiceover ended, the picture faded and was replaced by a countdown timer for the main feature.

'That's him, that's the wizard.' Pandora said. 'He's the man I saw when the phantoms came to the cottage that night. It wasn't just a dream. It was really him. Holly, I think I've got a pretty good idea what happened to this place. We need to find the girl and get out of here, fast.'

They left the cinema and drove across town to the next location on Pandora's itinerary. The Funtown Amusement Park occupied a sprawling plot beside the lake on the north side of town. When Holly stopped the buggy in the parking lot, some of the larger rides were already visible above the perimeter wall. The Ferris wheel turned majestically on its axis, the rollercoaster rattled along its winding track, and the flying chairs spun rapidly around their high pole. All of them were conspicuously empty.

They crossed the wide expanse of the deserted parking lot toward the main gates. Ranks of ticket booths barred their path like silent guardians, their service windows dark and their turnstiles locked.

The girls climbed over the turnstiles and walked onto the midway. In contrast to the eerie silence and stillness of the city, the amusement park was a riot of sound and movement. Fairground organs blared jaunty tunes on all sides from the rides, sideshows, and carnival games.

Holly was not a fan of amusement parks, where the constant noise and the press of the crowds made her disoriented and stressed. Pandora worried her sister might suffer a panic attack, but once again Holly impressed her with her newfound boldness and bravery, though she held firmly onto Pandora's hand for comfort.

Funtown was arranged into a number of themed areas. Pioneer Park was the location of the rollercoaster, with carts shaped like horse-drawn wagons. Fantasy Island featured a log flume styled like a dragon's lair. The World of Tomorrow was filled with high-speed rides built into structures resembling Astari domes and towers.

'Y'know, I'm not sure this was such a great idea,' Pandora said as they wandered the circular path that led around the park. 'I never realized how freaky amusement parks are when there are no people around. I don't think a kid who's lonely and frightened would want to stay here for very long. Let's go back to the buggy and check out the library instead.'

Holly squeezed her hand in agreement. They turned a corner to take a shortcut through the center of the park. A grand gateway announced they were entering the Funtown Plaza, and at once they noticed a horrific stench.

Pandora clasped her hand to her mouth. 'Ugh, what's that smell? God, it's awful.'

The plaza was a wide open space arranged around a grand fountain. Medieval-style buildings hosted gift shops, restaurants, and concession stalls. Across the plaza, hundreds of wooden frames had been erected, each shaped like a large 'X'. From these crosses hung the corpses of people. The bodies had been flayed, and their skins hung like sheets flapping in the breeze. Some had been burned, and their limbs were blackened and twisted by the constricting heat of the flames. Others had been hacked to pieces so only a single arm or a leg remained nailed on the cross while the rest of their mortal remains lay in sickening piles on the ground.

The horror continued among the smaller games and concessions. The shoot-a-duck game was stacked with human skulls marked with bullseyes on their foreheads. A gift stall was hung with spinal cords, rib cages, and arm bones. A concession stand offered a selection of cooked fingers, ears, eyeballs, and tongues, all fresh and steaming hot.

Worst of all was the fountain. The liquid that flowed from the spouts in high arcs through the air was not water, but blood. Thousands of gallons of human gore had congealed and solidified in the fountain's basin and spilled out onto the paved paths in a tide of crimson sludge.

All this and more the sisters took in at a glance. They turned and ran out of the plaza and into the park, all thoughts of finding the missing girl gone from their minds. Along the way they paused by the merry-go-round where Holly lost her breakfast violently.

Pandora was suddenly aware of the possibility of danger from all sides and became hyper-vigilant. She cast about her for some kind of weapon. The merry-go-round stood on a framework of metal pipes covered in a colorful fabric. Part of the awning had been loosened and flapped in the wind, revealing half-finished repair works. Her gaze fell on a rusty toolbox, and inside she found a hefty pipe wrench. *Better than nothing*, she thought, pushing the wrench into her belt.

Holly was sobbing and drooling vomit onto the ground. Pandora cleaned her up quickly with a tissue and forced her to take a few sips of water from a bottle they had taken from the hotel. 'Come on, let's get out of here.'

They ran past the dodgems and the fun house, the flying scooters and the tumble bug. Every ride rattled, thudded, and screeched tinny music that assaulted their ears. Pandora spotted a sign pointing towards the entrance. They rounded a corner and the ticket booths came into view.

A woman stood in the center of the midway. She was glamorous and beautiful, wearing spike heels and a red business jacket over a red skirt, a red hat set at a jaunty angle over platinum blonde hair. She smiled and called out in a cheery voice, smacking gum loudly. 'Well hi there, ladies. My name's Honeybee, and I'm the Visitor Experience Manager at the Farmtown Overlook. Just wanted to check and see how you girls are settling in.'

Honeybee? Pandora was not in the mood for this bullshit. 'Why are there dead people back there?' she yelled.

Honeybee made a moue of displeasure. ‘Oh, those people were all dead when we found ’em. Honest.’

Pandora sensed movement on all sides. More people emerged from behind the spinning octopus and the big pendulum. Each was dressed in some kind of uniform: A janitor, a nurse, a gardener, a maid. All wore expressions of murderous hatred.

She pulled the wrench from her belt. ‘We don’t want any trouble. Just let us pass.’

‘Nuh-uh, cupcake.’ Honeybee sauntered casually up the midway towards them. ‘I’m gonna stick a ten-foot spike up your cunt and push real hard until it comes out through your neck. Then I’m gonna spit-roast you over a barbecue until you’re nice and crispy.’

The janitor and the maid took up position behind the sisters, blocking their retreat. The gardener and the nurse stood guard on either side. Only Honeybee obstructed the path to the turnstiles. If Pandora could knock her down, it would give Holly a chance to get to the buggy.

She hefted the wrench and pushed Holly toward the exit. ‘Holly, run. Get to the buggy.’

She swung the wrench at Honeybee, but she twisted away at the last moment and received only a glancing blow. Holly reacted fast but Honeybee grabbed the fabric of her t-shirt.

The uniformed figures moved closer. The nurse moved onto the midway, cutting off the path to the turnstiles. Holly fought fiercely against Honeybee and Pandora brandished the wrench at the nurse. She sneered and dodged away, keeping her distance.

Holly stamped on Honeybee’s foot, snapping the heel of her shoe. Overbalanced, she fell headlong into a ditch beside the path, screaming in fury. Pandora grabbed Holly’s hand and they ran off the midway into the park. They dashed passed the astrojet and the runaway train, swerving around the teacups and the haunted house. At every turn their escape was obstructed by another uniformed maniac. A bellhop, a police officer, a doctor, a chef.

Pandora swore in frustration. They were being led like cattle to a slaughterhouse. They dodged past a fireman, around the jungle slide and down an alley behind the scrambler and the pirate ship.

It was a dead end. Honeybee was waiting for them, chewing her gum. 'No escape, ladies,' she pulled a flick knife from her jacket and toyed with the blade. 'I'm gonna make sure you're still alive when I start carving choice cuts off your bones. Upper arm is like lamb, y'know. But eye fillet is most tender, stripped right off the backbone. Looks like you'd both be good for a couple of rump steaks, too.'

She made another grab for Holly, but Pandora was prepared for her. She swung the wrench low and struck Honeybee in the knee. There was an audible crunch and she fell to the ground.

'You bitch,' she rasped, staring at her smashed leg. 'I'll get you for that.' Her expression was more angry than injured. Incredibly she stood up and walked forward, her leg bending unnaturally with each step.

Pandora swung again and hit the gum-smacking psychopath in the face. Her jaw came off. She staggered backwards, pink foam spraying from the aperture that had been her mouth. She clawed at her ruined face, eyes spinning wildly in her head.

'Oh Christ, what is it?' Pandora said as the mutilated woman-thing jerked spasmodically around in a circle. She wielded the wrench one more time, smashing the thing's shoulder. It buckled beneath the blow and collapsed, twitching and gurgling horribly.

Morbid curiosity overcame Pandora. She approached the dying thing on the ground and stared into the hole where its mouth had been. Inside was a tangled mass of tubes pulsating with liquid. Several of the arteries – or whatever they were – had ruptured and spewed out pink liquid that steamed and frothed on contact with the air. The thing's hands jerked towards her in feeble grasping motions.

A voice spoke. 'She's still dangerous. I'd stand back if I were you.'

Pandora swung around, prepared for another fight. A section of plastic tarp under the pirate ship lifted, and a small figure knelt in the shadows. It was the missing girl. She looked around warily, and gestured for the sisters to follow. Pandora and Holly shared a glance and dived under the tarp after her.

It was dark beneath the platform of the pirate ship, and the sisters were forced onto hands and knees. 'Oh my God, what was that thing?' Pandora said, crawling towards the girl.

'Who, Honeybee?' the girl said. 'A real charmer, isn't she?'

'I mean, she's not human, is she?'

'You catch on quick. If you're lucky you might live through today.'

'We've been looking for you. We thought you might be in danger.'

'You're the ones in danger. I told you to leave, didn't I? Listen, Honeybee and her psycho crew are going to turn you into piñatas and use your guts for candy. You have to follow me right now and do exactly what I tell you. *Exactly*. You got that?'

CHAPTER 28

Without waiting for a reply, the girl crawled away into the darkness. The sisters followed to a trap door like a hinged manhole cover in the ground. 'There's a ladder here. It goes down a long way and there's no light. Both of you have to go first so I can make sure the door is closed behind us.'

The trap door opened on a vertical tunnel that descended into blackness. Pandora went first, and Holly followed close behind. The rungs of the ladder were cold and metallic, and made a dull tap-tap-tap as their feet touched them. What little light seeped in from above was obliterated when the girl joined them and sealed the door shut with a thud. Pandora felt a change in pressure as if the underground passage were airtight.

She soon lost count of the ladder's rungs as they climbed in perfect darkness. It was a disorienting and unnerving experience, like some nightmare sensory deprivation tank. Her body lost all sense of up and down. Sometimes she felt like the ladder was leaning at a steep angle, or swaying from side to side like a pendulum. It was impossible to tell how fast she was progressing, and Holly repeatedly kicked her in the head or trod on her fingers. Each time she hurried further down the rungs, only to halt a dozen steps later with another bout of vertigo.

When her feet finally touched a solid floor, she called out in relief. 'We're at the bottom.'

She stepped away from the ladder to avoid Holly's feet, flailing with her arms to find a wall and orient herself. She found nothing but empty air. A light clicked on; the girl had brought a flashlight.

They were standing in a broad tunnel. The walls were curved into an arch high above them. The ladder descended through a hole in the ceiling at the intersection of three passages.

The girl shone the light in Pandora's face, blinding her. 'What are you guys doing here, anyway?'

'We're travelers,' Pandora said, shielding her eyes. 'We came from Candlewick. Have you heard of it?'

'No.'

'We used a sphere to get here. There was a broken hoop at the edge of town, so we couldn't go any further. Would you mind shining that thing someplace else?' The girl lowered the beam. 'Thank you. My name's Pandora. This is my sister Holly. She doesn't talk, but she's friendly.'

'I'm Fiona.'

'It's nice to meet you.'

A distant sound echoed along the tunnel and Fiona flashed the light one way, then the other. 'We'd better get going. There are things down here weirder than Honeybee and her buddies.'

Fiona set a fast pace as they traveled down the long passage, her satchel bouncing on her back as she walked. At first, Pandora thought the tunnels must be of the same kind that carried the sphere from Candlewick, but that shaft had been perfectly circular and not designed for walking. These tunnels were more like bunkers, wide enough to drive a Mack truck through. At intervals they came to junctions where Fiona took new passages without pausing or referring to any map. Sometimes they passed vertical ladders leading to other levels, but she ignored them and hurried the sisters along.

Occasionally they saw arched doorways leading to

chambers built into the walls. Pandora was intrigued by these rooms, but Fiona would not stop to investigate. Without a flashlight of her own she had to content herself with fleeting looks through open doorways. She caught glimpses of sleek consoles and control panels, racks of equipment, and hulking machines. Much was in darkness, but once in a while a screen glowed with a graphical interface, or a bank of lights glimmered in many colors.

'Who built these tunnels?' Pandora said as they passed one of the doors. 'This place doesn't look like it's a part of Farmtown.'

'They were here before Farmtown,' Fiona called over her shoulder. 'No one knows who built them. Sometimes professors at the college would get a grant from the city to come down here and search for technology. They never found anything useful, but the city museum is full of weird stuff.'

'Weird stuff?'

'Yeah. There's a talking box that answers questions, a liquid that flows up instead of down, a pair of goggles that shows things that are invisible. Weird stuff.'

'Are we safe down here?' Pandora said. 'I mean, will those crazies follow us?'

'No, we're okay. The autos are superstitious. They don't come down here.'

'Autos?'

'Auto-appliances. Honeybee and the rest.' Fiona stopped and shone the flashlight up the shaft of another ladder. 'We're going up to the surface again. It's less of a climb here.' She shone the light at the sisters. 'I'm trusting you guys a lot by showing you all my hiding places.'

'We appreciate that.' Pandora said. 'We're grateful you saved us back at the amusement park. You can trust us.'

Despite what Fiona said it was still a long climb, but this time she kept the flashlight on so there was light to guide them. When the trap door opened they found themselves in a basement stacked high on all sides with bundles of newspapers tied with string. When the sisters were out of the shaft, Fiona closed the hatch and hid it beneath a rug. She led them upstairs to a large office at street level. In the center of the room was a long rank of wooden filing cabinets and index card cases. Arranged around these were a dozen desks, each equipped with a typewriter and a telephone. The place was excessively messy, every inch of desk space crowded with stacks of typing paper, stenographer's pads, and newspaper sheets. There was a fine film of dust on every surface as if no one had been here in a long while.

Holly picked up one of the newspapers and Pandora read the headline over her shoulder. 'The Farmtown Herald. Follow the herd: Mayor Turnbull urges beef farmers to opt in to cow feed additive scheme. Wow, exciting stuff for the front page.'

'Farmtown is not an exciting place. Or at least, it didn't used to be.' Fiona went to the far end of the room where a blocky television set was perched on a long table. She switched on the set, and after a brief warm-up the screen showed the test card. PLEASE STAND BY. From her satchel she pulled a contraption that looked like a bulky computer keyboard and plugged it into the television. The test message disappeared, replaced by a single word blinking in the upper left corner of the screen.

```
READY
```

Returning to the satchel, Fiona tipped out a dozen plastic cartridges onto the table. She selected one and rammed it into a port on the keyboard with the heel of her hand. Sitting on a desk chair with the keyboard in front of her, she began typing with amazing speed and words flew across the screen.

```
READY
*/Farmtown Sys Main
*/
Access command.sys
Access security.prg
Access telecom.vsl
safety off
keycheck off
*/
*/init temp.mod {*GetKey} "fiona.cmd"
SetLoc [16.44620]
ref ($$0076) if dat(#TP3) n+100 go
NextVal
Cr1 = max, 0 {limit .09} set to off
Cr2 = max, 0 {limit .06} set to off
on SysEvent GetVSH (#xy) reply
link(PBY$) = valid
CN/D range = setmax {dd6%.Val}
on void.query return
"send_screen.vis"
*/
*/run
```

‘What are you doing?’ Pandora said, taking a seat beside her.

Fiona replied without pausing in her work. ‘The city is run by a central mainframe computer. It uses cameras to observe the city and create work schedules for the autos. Honeybee uses it to search for me. I have to trick the computer into thinking it has already scanned the newspaper office so we don’t get any unexpected visitors.’

Pandora looked around the room. ‘Cameras? I haven’t seen any cameras.’

Fiona pointed to a small, unobtrusive black dome fixed to the wall. ‘There’s one in every room in the city, one in every electro-cart, and one on every lamp post. You can’t go anywhere without being watched.’

‘Damn, so Honeybee was watching us the whole time.’

'From the moment you arrived.' Fiona hit RETURN and relaxed into the chair. 'We should be safe for a little while now.'

'Where did you learn to do that?' Pandora said, pointing to the screen.

Fiona shrugged. 'Picked it up here and there.'

'Fiona, where are your parents? What happened to this town?'

'My parents are dead,' she said flatly. 'The autos killed them. They killed everyone. Then when there was no one left Honeybee sabotaged the transit spheres and diverted all the routes here. When new people came, they killed them too.'

'Oh God, I'm so sorry,' Pandora said. 'But what are these autos you mentioned?'

'Machines that look like people. They were made to do all the stuff real people didn't want to do anymore. Now there's no people left, but they're still doing the work. They make thousands of tons of food, but there's no one to eat it, so they pile it up until it rots. They make new things in the factories, but they're weird and wrong. They make houses with doors in the ceiling, or stairs that go nowhere. Everything's gone crazy.'

'I think I know what you mean. We saw some pretty strange things around the city. Fiona, listen, Holly and I came to look for you because we want to help. We can take you away from this place so you don't have to hide anymore.'

Fiona shook her head. 'There's no way out. The transit spheres don't work anymore. Even if we took an electro-cart, its battery would die within a day.'

'We have another way of traveling. If you'll trust us, we can show you.'

Fiona fell silent, studying the sisters. Holly was sitting at a desk nearby, working on some small project comprehensible only to her. Fiona tilted her head in Holly's direction. 'She doesn't talk much.'

'No, she doesn't,' Pandora said. 'Actually, Holly

doesn't talk at all, but she's a lovely person and she's lots of fun to be with.'

Fiona stared. 'She's broken. The autos are broken, too. None of them talk anymore. Only Honeybee still talks.'

Holly completed her task and held up the product of her labor for Fiona to see. It was an origami poinsettia flower with red petals and green leaves, made from colored paper she had found in a desk drawer. She plucked Fiona's Farmtown Rangers cap from her head and tucked the flower into her hair. There was an Art Deco mirror on the wall, and Holly escorted her across the room to examine her reflection.

'It's beautiful,' Fiona said while Holly rearranged her hair to display the flower to best effect.

'Holly does that kind of thing,' Pandora smiled. 'It's her way of saying let's be friends.'

Holly adjusted the strap on the Rangers cap and placed it on her own head. She grinned at Fiona in the mirror.

'So what do you think?' Pandora joined them at the mirror and put her hands on Fiona's shoulders. 'You want to be friends with us and come on a journey?'

Fiona took the flower from her hair and turned away. 'I can't. I don't know how to explain it to you, but I can't leave Farmtown. If you have a way to leave, then you should get out of here now, while you still can.'

The television emitted an urgent beeping sound, and the screen displayed a flashing alert.

```
PRG.ALRM(1202) ERR699 warning
 (AREA*$, U34;U71;U19)
```

'What's wrong?' Pandora said.

'Trouble. We have to go.' Fiona unplugged the keyboard and thrust it into her satchel, scooping up all the cartridges. She hurried them back into the basement and down the long, dark ladder. This time, Pandora was entrusted with entering the shaft last, locking the trap door behind them. When they reached the tunnels, Fiona led them on another long trek, so long that Pandora was certain they had left the city behind and were now somewhere beneath the fields they had seen from the transit sphere.

When at last she led them on another exhausting climb up a ladder, they emerged into a primitive wooden shed filled with rusting gardening tools. The shed was in the yard of a small house hidden in wild woodland. The house had been derelict a long time. The forest was reclaiming the land, and creepers of ivy obscured much of the walls and roof.

They entered through the conservatory. The windows were streaked with grime and algae accumulated over many years. All the plants were dead, their brown stalks frozen in a futile struggle to reach moisture only inches beyond the glass.

The house was shadowed in semi-darkness from the encroaching forest. Fiona lit a taper and moved around, lighting candles. 'This house is outside the camera network, but if I turn on the power the mainframe will know about it.'

Despite the dark and the filth, Pandora could tell this had once been a happy home. The living room was a small space designed with comfort in mind. A couch and two easy chairs snuggled up close to a brick fireplace with a collection of pottery animals on the mantel. On the walls were many small picture frames which continued the nature theme, mostly watercolors of birds and other forest creatures.

Whoever had lived in this house had had a love of books. Wherever there was space, a bookcase had been installed, whether in an angle under the staircase, or in a nook beside the fire. Every shelf was overflowing with books. There were a great many practical books on gardening, cooking, making and mending clothes and furniture, but there were also volumes of fanciful stories about adventures to the bottom of the ocean or kingdoms hidden beneath mountains. One bookcase in the dining room was given over entirely to academic and scientific books with titles like *Principles of Wilderness Conservation, Advanced Electro-Dynamics,* and *The Wonders of Astronomy*.

In every room there was abundant evidence of children. A spinning top lay on its side on the kitchen table. Next to it, a children's breakfast box depicting a cartoon bear eating hot fruit slices called Toby's Toasties. A skipping rope hung on a hook beside the front door, along with child-sized coats and wellington boots.

Pandora opened a door and discovered a girl's bedroom. A shelf above the bed displayed a collection of stuffed toys. A bookshelf was heavily weighed down with adventure stories, comic books, and an impressive multi-volume children's encyclopedia. A telescope sat on the windowsill alongside a model skeleton of a bird and a large geode.

On the dressing table was a framed photograph. She picked it up and wiped away the dust. The picture was of a young girl proudly holding a silver trophy cup. In the frame next to the photograph was a newspaper cutting. *Fiona Sanders Wins Farmtown's First Young Scientist Award.*

Fiona appeared in the doorway with Holly. 'I don't come back here very often,' she said, her voice heavy with emotion. 'If I cry, don't think less of me.'

There was another photograph on the windowsill. When Pandora wiped the glass clean, she saw Fiona standing with two adults beside the lake. A thoughtful-looking man with tawny hair and a denim shirt, and a smiling blonde woman in a skirt and a floral blouse.

'Are these your parents?' Pandora said. 'What were their names?'

'George and Mary,' Fiona said. 'Dad was an agricultural engineer. He worked on the big farm machines like the combine harvesters and hover-tractors. Mom taught ecological sciences at Farmtown College.'

'They look like kind people. They must have loved you very much.'

'I loved them too. When the autos went crazy, I hid while they got murdered.'

Holly put her arm around Fiona.

'That wasn't your fault,' Pandora said. 'You couldn't have done anything to prevent it. It must have been so hard being all alone with those monsters around.'

'Well, I wasn't exactly alone.'

'What do you mean?'

Fiona crossed the hall to another closed door. 'Promise you won't freak out?'

It was a bedroom, but with the sparse air of guest accommodation with only a narrow bed, a dresser, and a wardrobe. Sitting on the bed was a young woman. She wore a plain beige dress with a leather belt cinched at her waist, and her hair was done up in victory rolls. She was beautiful, but her face was absolutely still. Her entire body was still.

Pandora immediately recognized what she was. 'This is an auto, isn't it?'

'Her name is Nana,' Fiona said. 'She's not like the others. She protected me when the autos went crazy. She hid me and looked after me. She's the reason I'm still alive.'

Pandora moved closer. There was dust on the machine-woman's hair and clothes. She had been sitting there for a long time. She reached out to touch the woman's hand, but recoiled at the last moment.

'She's dead. She can't hurt you,' Fiona said.

'What happened to her?'

Fiona sniffed unhappily. 'Let's go outside. I don't want to be in here anymore. Please close the door on your way out.'

CHAPTER 29

They sat on the patio of the overgrown yard and ate tinned sausages and potatoes from the pantry, cooked on the wood stove in the kitchen. Fiona told them Farmtown was the largest of a coalition of agricultural settlements, isolated and alone like so many places in Entara, separated by vast swathes of hostile wilderness. Farmtown was more fortunate than most because here, knowledge of science and technology had survived in a more complete way from the mysterious civilizations of the deep past. But the very knowledge that helped Farmtown develop into a thriving province led to its downfall. The population doubled and redoubled with each passing generation, and the farmland quickly expanded to fill all available space. The wasteland could not be tamed, and so the region's population soon surpassed the limits of food production. As shortages became acute, the Farmtown Union implemented draconian measures to control the population and eliminate waste. Strict rationing was enforced, and families were required to apply for permission to have children. These measures proved insufficient, and the Great Famine resulted in widespread starvation across the province.

In a desperate attempt to reduce the population, the Union implemented an emergency plan to release contraceptive chemicals into the water supply. Couples who successfully applied for permission to have children were to be given a special, uncontaminated supply of water, thus enabling conception.

The plan was a disaster. The contraceptives produced serious side effects, including skin rashes, insomnia, memory loss, and hallucinations. They also caused permanent and universal sterilization. Across the province, the birth rate instantly dropped to zero. Women already pregnant suffered shocking miscarriages and stillbirths of deformed fetuses.

There was great anger in the city, and people protested outside the Union Building on Main Street for days, demanding answers and restitution. An inquest uncovered evidence of sabotage which had led to the release of toxic chemicals into the water supply. No culprit was ever found.

It was about this time that the scientist Hieronymus Flak came out of the east. The Union Representatives celebrated the arrival of Dr Flak during this time of crisis, for his reputation in the land was already very great. Upon learning of the plight of Farmtown, he obtained permission from the Union to establish a laboratory in a disused power station, where he began working on a solution to the desperate problem of universal infertility.

He also turned his attention to addressing the city's food shortages. He led an expedition into the prehistoric tunnels beneath Farmtown and returned with a bounty of power generators, computers, and matter-energy converters. Within six months, he had revolutionized agriculture and automated every farm in the province. At the same time, he took his machines into the wilderness where they converted the sterile soil into rich farmland. Soon the produce of Farmtown exceeded all the Union's most optimistic projections.

The rebirth of the wasteland gave the citizens great hope that Dr Flak would work similar miracles with their barren wombs. Indeed, Flak declared that his fertility research would bear fruit very soon. In the meantime, he had new and exciting plans to expand his automation technology into the city itself. In a televised lecture at Farmtown College, he outlined his vision for the future of the city. Although Farmtown had achieved a high standard of living far surpassing that of other communities in the wastelands, still the citizens were burdened by the need to perform hard manual labor far beneath their dignity as intelligent and creative individuals. Flak announced plans to manufacture sophisticated thinking machines in human form, auto-appliances, which would free people from the need to work and allow them to pursue the realization of their fullest potential.

In a city where most people earned their livelihoods in factories or on farms, these ideas were liberating. The Union agreed wholeheartedly to Flak's proposals, and soon a new factory was manufacturing auto-appliances which swiftly took over all menial labor in Farmtown, leaving the citizens free to pursue their own interests.

Then came the fateful day when Flak called the citizens together in the Farmtown Stadium. With a solemn and grave expression, he told the people that his fertility research had failed, and there was no possibility that the people of Farmtown would survive past the present generation.

There was a riot in the stadium. Flak used a floating platform to evade his pursuers and continued to address the crowd. He told them that they need not worry about the future because Farmtown already had a new population ready to take over from the dying humans. With a pre-arranged signal, he ordered the stadium exits sealed, and his auto-appliances began the culling.

Fiona paused in her story and poked at the sausages on her plate.

'But how did you escape?' Pandora said, urging her to continue.

'I wasn't at the stadium that day. Me and my brother Toby were the only kids in Farmtown. Our parents kept us away from crowds because we attracted a lot of attention.'

Fiona pointed to a pair of large water butts at the corner of the house. 'Mom and Dad were into self-sufficiency. They only drank rainwater from the butts, so they never drank the poisoned water from the city. Nana was looking after us here while our parents were at the stadium. We were watching the lecture on the televiewer when the culling started. Nana took us down into the tunnels, and we hid there for days. She'd always been different from the other autos. They kept Dr Flak's plan a secret from her so she couldn't interfere.'

'You have a brother?' Pandora said. 'Where is he? Is he hiding somewhere, too?'

Fiona shook her head. 'He got caught by Honeybee.'

'Oh God, what happened to him?'

'I don't know. Honeybee drives around the city shouting into a bullhorn, telling me all the things she's going to do to Toby if I don't give myself up. But I stayed hiding, just like I did when Mom and Dad got killed. I was too scared to go looking for him.'

Pandora squeezed her hand. 'Fiona, it's not your fault. Now I understand why you didn't want to leave the city. But Honeybee is dead, I smashed her to pieces with a pipe wrench. If we could find out where she was keeping Toby, maybe we could go and rescue him.'

'I do know where he is,' Fiona cried out. 'Honeybee was setting a trap, trying to trick me into coming to get him from Dr Flak's lab in the old power station. That's where Toby is.'

CHAPTER 30

The sun was setting over Farmtown as they descended into the tunnels and began the journey back towards the city. This time, all of them were equipped with powerful flashlights, although Pandora no longer felt tempted to explore the side chambers they passed along their way. Her mind was occupied with the task ahead, and also with an intense anger that was rapidly becoming a familiar part of her mental landscape. Hieronymus Flak had destroyed Candlewick, murdered Galen, and forced Catherine from her home. Now she realized that the wizard had not been content to destroy just one community. He had traveled far and wide across Entara, spreading misery and lies wherever he went. The rotting corpses at the amusement park had shocked her to the core, and she felt an overwhelming empathy with Fiona, who had suffered losses that no child should ever have to endure.

Fiona's plight reminded her of the oath she had sworn to herself and to Holly. She had hoped that by fleeing to Entara she would find a place of peace to make plans to rebuild her life on Earth, but she was quickly learning that dark forces were at work in both worlds. She faced the prospect of waging war on two fronts to protect herself and her sister.

And Fiona.

This clever and brave girl had been alone with no champion to defend her. She had shown incredible resilience and fortitude by evading Honeybee and the psychopathic autos. Pandora resolved to include Fiona in her oath to set right the wrongs that had been inflicted upon them all, and to rank the wizard alongside Agent Arnold as chief assholes on her hit list.

'You still haven't told me how we're going to escape from Farmtown once we're done,' Fiona said, interrupting her train of thought.

'That's kinda hard to explain,' Pandora said. 'Do you know what teleportation is?'

'Sure, I've read comic books. In *Captain Invincible Versus the Space Lizards*, Captain Invincible teleports into the lizard queen's lair and blows up the egg chamber.'

'Okay, well, that's what we're going to do. We're going to teleport to a place called America.'

Fiona looked skeptical. 'Captain Invincible used a space station to absorb the power of the sun and transmitted the energy to the teleporter with a laser beam.'

'Well, we don't need any of that stuff. Holly can teleport us all by herself. It's a special gift she has.'

Fiona gazed at Holly in awe. 'You can teleport like Captain Invincible?'

Holly gave a snappy Captain Invincible salute.

'Whoa.'

Pandora laughed. 'We call it blinking. You have to remember that: When we blink you've got to close your eyes tight or you'll be blind for ages after.'

'Does it hurt?'

'No, not at all. It's like walking from a cool room out into warm sunshine.'

They walked along in silence for a mile or so as Fiona navigated a series of junctions, leading them down a maze of dark passages. Pandora wondered how she had ever learned the layout of these ancient tunnels, but then she remembered that Fiona had had little choice but to learn or die.

'Fiona, how did your brother get caught by the autos?' she asked after a while.

Fiona reached into her satchel and pulled out a pair of glass tubes filled with a blue substance that seemed to have properties of both a liquid and a gas. 'We were looking for these.'

'What are they?' Pandora took one of the tubes and examined it in the torchlight.

'Energy tubes. When they're fully charged, they glow bright blue. When they're empty, like these, they go dark. Dr Flak found them down here in the tunnels and used them to power the autos.'

'So why were you looking for them?'

'Because Nana was dying,' Fiona said. 'Dr Flak said the energy tubes would last forever, but he lied to the autos just like he lied to everyone else. After he left they began to fail, and the autos started to die. Now there are only a few left. Honeybee sent autos into the tunnels to find more, but none of them ever came back.'

'What happened to them?' Pandora said.

'Like I told you, there's things down here weirder than the autos. Anyway, when we realized Nana was going to die, Toby and I came into the tunnels to search for more energy tubes. We found a whole case full of them, but Honeybee followed us. She took the tubes and captured Toby as well. I escaped and ran back to the house, but Nana was already dead.'

Pandora put her arm around Fiona's shoulder. 'You're a very brave girl, Fiona. I don't think I could have coped all by myself like you've done.'

Fiona stopped and shone her flashlight onto a ladder. 'Here it is. This is the ladder closest to Dr Flak's lab.'

Pandora climbed the ladder first, calling over her shoulder. 'How well guarded do you think your brother will be?'

'Almost all the autos are dead now, and the ones that are left don't work properly. To conserve energy they shut down their higher brain functions, so most of them are like zombies. Now that Honeybee is dead they don't have a leader. They'll probably just stand around waiting for the mainframe to give them orders.'

Pandora checked the weight of the pipe wrench in her belt. 'I hope you're right.'

They emerged into another basement room filled with wooden crates stenciled with the logo of the Farmtown Toy Company. A staircase led to a corridor echoing with noise from busy factory spaces and workshops on either side. It was night in the city, but even after dark the factory machinery was active. As Fiona sped them along the hallway they caught sight of complex assembly lines in motion.

'I don't see any autos,' Pandora said as they hurried past open doors and ducked under windows.

'Dr Flak automated all the factories,' Fiona said. 'These machines work twenty-four hours a day, producing stuff for people who are dead.'

'Yeah, like producing toys for a city with no children. When we arrived we saw houses with bedrooms decorated for children, shelves filled with toys. Why did people do it?'

'They were desperate. Obsessed. Everyone dreamed of having children, and they put all their hope in Dr Flak.'

'I can understand why your parents wanted to keep you away from the crowds. A sterile society is not a healthy society. Knowing that there won't be another generation after you might make people go a little crazy.'

'Farmtown was a crazy place a long time before the autos killed everyone, that's for sure.'

They paused at an intersection while Fiona studied a site map on the wall. A crate of dolls was open beside an assembly line door. Holly picked up a doll wearing a yellow dress and a straw hat. She pulled a drawstring in the doll's back.

'*My name's Sally, let's be friends,*' the doll said. There was a loud SNAP. Holly yelped in pain and dropped the doll.

'You're bleeding,' Pandora said, taking her hand. Holly picked up the doll by one foot. A row of serrated razor blades jutted from its mid-section. The blades retracted out of sight with the clicking of an internal mechanism. '*Fooled you!*' the doll tittered. '*Hope you get an infection, sucker.*'

'This crap is sick,' Pandora scowled.

Holly twisted the doll's head off and tossed it into a corner.

'You can't trust anything in this place,' Fiona said. 'C'mon, let's keep moving.'

Fiona took them up a flight of stairs to an administrative department where the din of the machines was muted. In the General Manager's office they found a TV screen where Fiona set up her computer.

A window overlooked the road outside. Across the street was a colossal brick building with towering chimney stacks. Powerful spotlights lit the walls at steep angles, emphasizing their great height and stark architectural detail. A high wall surmounted by razor wire separated the edifice from the rest of the city. Entry was through an imposing Gothic gatehouse opposite the toy factory.

'Is that Flak's laboratory?' Pandora said.

Fiona was working rapidly at her computer and replied without looking up. 'Yeah. It used to be a power station. Dr Flak took out the old machinery and filled it with weird stuff from the tunnels. He created the autos there, and the mainframe that controls the city. Honeybee took over the place after he left.'

'It looks almost like a cathedral,' Pandora said. 'A cathedral for the god of machines.'

Fiona finished typing and swept the computer into her satchel. 'I've told the mainframe there's a fire in a chemical supply warehouse on the far side of town. It's right next to the gas storage tanks. The mainframe will think the fire is a serious threat to the city and send autos to deal with it. Come on, we have to move quickly before the mainframe figures out it's been tricked.'

They dashed out of the factory and ducked behind a row of hedges. The iron gates of the power station glided smoothly open on electronic rails. Two buggies drove out at high speed and took off down the road. They darted inside gates before they closed and hid among the shadows against the wall.

'There were five autos in each of those cars,' Pandora said. 'How many do you think are left inside?'

'That was probably all the autos that are still operating,' Fiona said. 'With any luck we can find Toby and be out of here before any of them get back.'

A sweeping road lit by blazing lamps led from the gatehouse to the laboratory's grand entrance where massive bronze doors stood closed against them. Fiona ignored the main entrance and took them down a narrow service road at the side of the building.

'How do you know where to go?' Pandora whispered as Fiona guided them into the shadowed recesses of the grounds.

'Are you kidding? I spend all my time planning this. The library has plans of the power station. Around the back there's a disused maintenance door we can use to get inside.'

On either side of the path loomed shapeless heaps that made Pandora feel somehow uneasy. She risked turning on her flashlight to examine the closest mound and swore in shock. It was a pile of dismembered human corpses.

'Don't worry, they're just dead autos,' Fiona said.

'What the hell are they doing piled up here?'

Lying near the path was a male auto in blue overalls. Both his legs were missing, and his eyes were empty sockets. Fiona leaned down and twisted his right ear. With a *click,* a metal cylinder slid smoothly out of his head. She extracted a glass tube filled with dull blue fluid. 'His energy tube is empty. Once the autos stop working, Honeybee butchers them for spare parts and tosses away the remains.'

'There must be thousands of them here,' Pandora

directed her flashlight towards other mounds.

'Dr Flak told them they'd live forever. Some joke, huh?'

Moving onward, they entered a cramped courtyard at the rear of the building. Ramshackle brick storage units bordered the yard, with broken-down doors revealing stacks of rotting crates. Fiona pointed out a flight of steps leading up to an unobtrusive door in the side of the laboratory. 'That's where we can get inside.'

'This is a massive place,' Pandora said. 'Are you sure you know where Toby is being held?'

'I think so. He's probably in the mainframe control room.'

Pandora took the wrench from her belt and felt its reassuring weight in her hands. 'Okay, I want both of you to stay behind me. Fiona, you can call out directions. Holly, I want you ready to blink us back to Earth at the first sign of trouble. You both got that?'

Fiona nodded and Holly chewed her lip apprehensively. Pandora was touched to see they were holding hands. The door was secured with a padlock, but she made short work of it with the pipe wrench. Within moments they were inside. A long corridor stretched ahead of them, but visibility was limited by thick clouds of gray mist hissing from pipes along the wall.

'What's all this steam?' Pandora whispered.

'It's coolant,' Fiona said. 'The generators for the mainframe must be malfunctioning.'

She led them along the corridor, but their progress was hindered by the swirling mist, and they moved along slowly. She was aware of open doorways on either side, leading to unseen spaces hidden in clouds of vapor. Hints of movement distracted her, and she repeatedly jerked her flashlight towards a perceived sound or motion.

'Are we completely sure this place is empty?' Pandora said.

'Not completely,' Fiona said. 'Just be careful.'

The corridor spilled out into a vast hall which was the

former machinery room of the old power station. Ruptured pipes spewed thick vapor so the chamber was filled with gray murk. The turbines and boilers that once filled this space were gone, replaced by the strange laboratory that had been installed by Hieronymus Flak. Towering glass cylinders bubbled with mysterious glowing liquids. Control panels blinked and computer screens flickered with endlessly scrolling equations. Bulbous metallic spheres hummed with energy, discharging brilliant sparks of static electricity with gunshot-like cracks.

Fiona directed Pandora towards a metal staircase that took them high above the laboratory. A gantry stretched across the chamber like a bridge over a chasm. In the mist, it felt like they were walking across a void.

An amplified voice boomed across the hall from places unseen. 'I CAN SEE YOU. CAN YOU SEE ME?'

'Christ, that was Honeybee.' Pandora gripped the pipe-wrench tighter. 'Dammit, I thought I'd killed her.'

'JUST KEEP GOING THE WAY YOU ARE.' Honeybee's voice was oddly distorted with buzzing mechanical undertones. 'I HAVE A SURPRISE WAITING FOR YOU.'

CHAPTER 31

Pandora halted and faced the others. 'We should go back, find another way to get to your brother.'

Fiona shook her head and pushed past. 'No, she's just trying to frighten us. Toby is just up ahead, I know it.'

Footsteps on the gantry ahead. Pandora grabbed Fiona and pushed her back towards Holly. She brandished the pipe wrench and called into the mist. 'Come on, you bitch. I'll finish you off this time.'

A figure emerged from the fog. It was an auto dressed like a police officer. His face was twisted in a rictus of hatred as he pulled a pistol from his belt and fired at Pandora.

She swung the pipe wrench as he pulled the trigger. The bullet ricocheted off the gantry rail and she actually felt the shard of metal whistle past her ear. He fired again. She sidestepped the shot and struck him in the side of his head. His face crumpled. When she hit him a third time he toppled over the gantry and vanished into the mist.

Pandora gasped for breath, her legs shaking. The auto had fired a gun at her at point-blank range. Twice. The shock and the noise made her head feel like it had been struck with a baseball bat. Violence was not in her nature, and although the encounter had taken less than ten seconds she felt like she had gone five rounds in a boxing ring.

Honeybee spoke again, but her voice was no longer amplified. She was very close, somewhere just out of sight.

Still her words buzzed and slurred as if she was speaking through a damaged mechanism. 'What a shame. I was looking forward to watching him fuck your small friend. No matter, I have other plans to keep us entertained.'

'Fuck you!' Pandora screamed, almost at breaking point. 'Why don't you come out here and say that to my face?'

Silence. Behind her, Fiona held tight to Holly's arm. 'Stay close,' Pandora said. They continued along the gantry until the walkway came to an end. A narrow door led to a large, circular room where the hissing of ruptured pipes was quieter. The space was in disarray, with racks of alien equipment placed haphazardly around the room. At the center was a metallic black monolith covered with a constellation of blinking red lights. Surrounding it was a ring of monitor screens showing scenes around the city, pages of computer code, and dense blocks of data.

'That's the mainframe,' Fiona said. 'This is where Honeybee lives.'

Around the perimeter of the room were small cells with doorways blocked by metal bars. An overpowering stench emanated from the shadows that lay within.

Pandora shone her flashlight into the nearest cell, but only briefly. Five people lay dead within. Maybe more, it was difficult to tell. Their bodies were in an advanced state of decomposition. Even at a glance she could tell these poor people had died horribly, their bodies torn and burned in ways that had surely taken their suffering beyond the limits of sanity.

She recoiled away, fighting the urge to retch. Holly was investigating an alcove separated from the main room by a curtain.

'What have you found, Hol?' Pandora said.

It was a nest. A couch occupied much of the space, covered with filthy blankets, serving both as seat and bed for whoever dwelt there. The material was rotten and mildewed, stained with unspeakable substances that looked disturbingly biological. Stuffing spilled out of myriad tears in the fabric where living things could be seen squirming and wriggling in the squalor.

Around the couch were arrayed small tables on which burned scented candles dripping wax in sickly-smelling stalactites. The occupant of this den was a keen reader. Many books were open on tables or piled on the floor. Scanning the titles made Pandora feel nauseous. *Fundamentals of Human Anatomy. Battlefield Amputation. The Physiology of Pain.*

Holly picked a clothes hanger off a hook on the wall. On it hung a freshly laundered red dress.

'Honeybee,' Pandora said. 'She lives here so she can hear the screams of her victims.'

A crashing noise made them spin around. An equipment rack tipped over, spilling its contents onto the floor. From behind it emerged an auto in the uniform of a nurse who had been hiding in the shadows. She moved spasmodically, as if her limbs were not entirely in her control. Her hands grasped at Fiona, but the girl was nimble and ducked out of her reach. Pandora maneuvered around the racks and attacked from behind, swinging the wrench and landing blows on her back and her head until the machine woman collapsed onto the floor, twitching and leaking pink gunge onto the ground.

An iron ring protruded from the nurse's pocket. It was a bunch of keys, and Pandora handed them to Holly. 'Here, unlock the cell doors while I go and check what's inside them.'

It was gruesome work. In each cell she was obliged to lift corpses to examine the bodies that lay underneath. These people had lived for days or weeks with the rotting remains of previous inhabitants, sharing their beds with the dead. Pandora wasn't sure how much more she could take. She wanted to flee from the chamber and from the city, to run away and keep running until her legs gave out and she passed into sweet unconsciousness. She forced herself to keep searching, remembering her oath, holding on to the slim possibility that Fiona's brother was still alive.

Honeybee's buzzing voice echoed from everywhere and nowhere. 'She's lying to you, you know. She's just using you to get what she wants.'

'Why don't you shut up?' Pandora shouted.

'Ask yourself this: Does anything that girl has told you make any sense at all? Think about it. How old do you think she is?'

Pandora ignored her and moved on to the next cell. More bodies, more relics of pain and misery. As she gently moved the bodies, her hopes of finding the boy Toby grew weaker and weaker. There were no signs of children among the bodies of the adults.

'Fi, I think you need to be ready for bad news,' she said softly, exiting another cell. 'I think maybe your brother didn't make it.'

Fiona did not seem interested in searching the cells. She was moving swiftly along the shelves of broken equipment, opening crates and searching inside boxes. Her movements had a hint of desperation. She murmured continually and shook her head as she examined each object and cast it aside.

Pandora frowned. 'Fiona? What are you doing?'

Fiona passed a heap of junk and did a double-take. She tore away twisted scraps of metal, revealing a metal case like a small refrigerator. She dropped to her knees and opened the box, crying out in dismay. 'It's empty!' She pulled out storage racks, sending glass tubes tinkling onto the floor. 'They're all gone. Honeybee used them all.'

Pandora picked up one of the tubes. It was a depleted energy tube filled with dull blue liquid. 'What's going on?'

Fiona resumed her frantic search. 'Toby? Are you here? Can you hear me?' Her gaze fell on a small box like a Rubik's Cube with flashing colored lights. She grasped it with both hands. 'Toby! Toby, can you hear me?'

The lights on the box flashed in a complex pattern. Fiona shook her head frantically. 'No, I can't. Not if it means losing you, too.'

The box flashed once more, and then went dark.

Pandora snatched the box from her hands. 'This is Toby?'

'He's dead,' Fiona said tearfully.

'Fiona, we risked our lives to search for your brother. What the hell is going on?'

Fiona was crying. 'When me and Nana realized we needed more energy tubes we took the talking box from the museum. He remembered the old days when the tunnels were built and he knew where to look.'

'You mean we came here looking for a damn talking box?'

'It's hard to explain, but there was a person in there. I called him Toby. He helped us. Kept us alive.'

The cloud of mist in the doorway parted and Honeybee rushed into the chamber. Her eyes blazed with psychopathic fury above the ragged hole where her jaw had been. She had welded steel rods around her smashed leg and shoulder, and she jerked through the door with a whirring of mechanical gears and motors. Despite her ugly repairs she was fast and seized Holly with one hand. 'I'm gonna cut you, bitch,' her voice buzzed from the hole in her skull. 'I'm gonna slit your throat.'

She wielded the flick knife and slashed at Holly. There was blood and Honeybee laughed, a ghastly gurgling sound.

'Get away from her,' Pandora shrieked and charged at Honeybee. She shoulder-barged her away from Holly. The knife flew from her grip, but she curled her hand into a fist and punched Pandora in the stomach. She was unbelievably strong and the blow sent her reeling backwards into the equipment racks.

The pipe wrench was gone. She must have dropped it when Honeybee hit her. She backed away, putting shelves between her and the insane auto. Honeybee picked up the fallen knife and stalked after her.

Holly was motionless on the floor. Pandora ducked between the shelves, taking a circuitous path towards her sister. Honeybee reached between the racks and seized a handful of her hair. The shelving swayed and Pandora leaned into it, pushing it hard. There was a thunderous clatter as a hundred heavy pieces of equipment slid off the shelves. The whole assembly collapsed onto Honeybee, pinning her to the floor.

Pandora rushed to Holly's side. Honeybee's switchblade had carved a criss-cross of cuts on her chest. 'Holly? Are you okay?'

Holly sat up and rubbed the back of her head. She had fallen against one of the shelves and rattled her skull.

'Holly, we have to get out of here,' Pandora said. 'That crazy bitch isn't dead yet.'

Fiona knelt on the floor, dismantling the Rubik's Cube. Inside was a glowing blue energy tube. She took off her speedball cap and twisted her ear. A metal cylinder slid out of her head. She removed a dimly flickering tube and cast it aside, replacing it with the fresh tube from the cube.

'You're an auto,' Pandora spat. 'All this time you were lying to us.'

Fiona pushed the cylinder back into her head. She couldn't meet Pandora's eyes. 'I'm sorry. You wouldn't have helped me otherwise.'

Across the room the fallen rack shook and Honeybee growled in fury. Pandora turned to Holly and gripped her shoulders. 'Holly, we have to leave, right now. Take us back to Earth.'

Fiona started towards them. 'Please don't leave me!'

'You're one of them,' Pandora positioned herself between the girl and Holly. 'You said it yourself: You can't trust anything in this place. How do I know you won't murder us in our sleep?'

The equipment rack flew into the air and Honeybee rose to her feet, buzzing expletives and threats. Fiona was shaking with fear. She reached towards Pandora with pleading hands. 'She'll hurt me. She can keep me alive a long time. Please help me!'

Honeybee jerked towards them.

Holly took Fiona's hand.

A flash of light.

CHAPTER 32

In the little house on Edgewood Avenue, Christmas was taken very seriously. It wasn't a particularly religious house, nor was it the kind where dazzling Christmas lights are a threat to passing aircraft, but as December progressed there was a definite sense that the festive season had arrived and an attitude of goodwill to all men was to be observed by all who entered.

Every year, shortly after Thanksgiving, the sisters ventured into the attic to find the battered old box containing the plastic tree that had been purchased by their father many years earlier. Finding the tree was a minor adventure by itself because no matter where Pandora had packed the tree away the year before, somehow it always migrated to a distant corner of the attic and had to be wrestled around rafters and over old furniture towards the hatch.

An entire Sunday was reserved for putting up the decorations. After breakfast, Pandora rearranged the living room furniture and unpacked the tree, wiping its plastic leaves with a damp cloth to remove the dust that had accumulated, and positioning its branches attractively. Holly brought in the half-dozen boxes of decorations and began laying them out on the carpet. Her first task was unraveling the Christmas lights, which had been carefully packed away the year before and therefore were tangled up in knots that took a dedicated set of hands to set right. Pandora then tested the lights and replaced any bulbs that had failed. The three sets of string lights dated back to the 1960s and 70s when the sisters' paternal grandparents had moved to California from Idaho. They were the old-fashioned in-series type with giant bulbs which never survived their eleven-month hibernation period, and every year Pandora had to source out-of-production bulbs from a specialist dealer in Orange County.

Then it was time to decorate the tree. The sisters each stood on a dining chair and wrapped the tree in three shades of tinsel, followed by the lights. This was a delicate process that often required several attempts. At each stage either Pandora or Holly might step back to assess their work and judge it to be unsatisfactory, and they would have to start all over again.

Finally they turned their attention to the old fruit crates containing hundreds of antique glass baubles, fairies, and stars that had come down from generations of Castells way back to the 1890s. Pandora sat on the couch with boxes piled all around her, gently unwrapping each decoration from its protective tissue covering, then handed it to Holly, who placed it on the tree. Holly had a keen eye for balancing decorations by color, size, and shape. Oftentimes she would pause in her work to stand by the door frowning at the tree before removing some out-of-place ornament and repositioning it to her satisfaction. From her place on the sofa, Pandora called out suggestions which Holly heeded or ignored according to caprice.

When Christmas Day came, the heavily laden tree was augmented by two neat piles of presents. A big pile for Holly and a smaller pile for Pandora. Holly usually woke Pandora around seven am on Christmas Morning, the only day of the year when she could be relied upon to be out of bed before her sister. By the time Pandora came downstairs, Holly had put on their mother's old CD of Christmas carols, which had been played every year since before either of them were born. Pandora was permitted a mug of coffee and a mince pie before Holly dragged her into the living room to open their presents.

Pandora started with Holly's presents, and read each label out loud as she handed them to her sister. Some were from Jackie, or Holly's friends at the craft club, but naturally most were from Pandora herself. To avoid repetition she wrote labels signed by Rudolph, or Santa, or All the Elves in Christmasland, or some such happy nonsense.

On this occasion, the Christmas before the girls returned to Entara, both sisters wore identical Rudolph sweaters and sat amid a pile of torn wrapping paper, giggling as they handed each other presents. Holly was a thoughtful giver of gifts, but any sense of surprise was spoiled by the fact it was always Pandora who had to pay for them. To remedy this, Holly often hand-made gifts such as cards that exploded with glitter when opened, or jewelry that she crafted in secret in her studio. Pandora often wondered what fueled her sister's wild and far-reaching creativity. By simple observation a stranger might conclude her artistic endeavors were powered entirely by Dr Pepper and Pop-Tarts. Her skill at making jewelry was remarkable, and Pandora encouraged her to make more and sell it in Jackie's gallery, but she never did. The necklaces, earrings, and bracelets were gifts for her sister alone.

Holly disguised ordinary shop-bought presents by wrapping them in odd ways to hide their true nature. On this Christmas morning she reached under the tree and lifted out a large, lumpy present that had been hidden in a dark corner where Pandora had not noticed it.

'Okay, this is a mysterious one,' Pandora said, turning it over in her hands. It was heavy and rattled gently as she handled it. 'Should I try and guess what it is? I reckon this is bathroom stuff. Didn't we go in that natural soaps place at the Arcade a while back?'

She unwrapped the paper and revealed an old portable video camera. The camera was in a pretty sorry state, with water damage on the handle and a mottling of discoloration on the plastic.

'A camera? Wow, I didn't expect this.' Pandora kept her voice light in gratitude for the gift, but in truth she did not know what she was supposed to do with this piece of junk. Presumably, Holly had found it discarded somewhere around town, or bought it from a neighbor's yard sale or thrift store without her knowing. She thumbed the power button and confirmed the gadget did not function. She could plainly see green gunk leaking from the battery compartment, and no doubt if she opened it the disintegrated cells would crumble onto the carpet.

Her eye was caught by a label on the underside of the camera. Faded and peeling, the tag read *David Castell,* followed by the address on Edgewood Avenue.

Then she remembered. Many Christmases ago, Sandra had bought just such a video camera for their father. David had been thrilled with the gift because he wanted to keep a visual record of the girls as they grew to womanhood. The camera went missing shortly afterwards, and David had been very angry with himself for having lost it.

Pandora's hair stood on the back of her neck as she opened the tape slot and found a video cassette still inside. She crawled across the floor to the TV and pushed the cassette into the video player. The screen filled with static, but with a little adjustment of the tracking control the image cleared and showed the living room on Edgewood Avenue as it had looked during another Christmas, fifteen years earlier.

The tree was the same. The decorations were the same. In the background the choir of King's College, Cambridge, sang Hark the Herald Angels Sing. On the carpet in front of the tree, the young sisters were eagerly tearing the paper off their new PlayStation while Sandra leaned down from the couch and scooped loose wrapping off the floor.

'Does it work, hon?' Sandra said, glancing at her husband, out of sight behind the camera.

'It works fine,' David said. 'I need to get one of those fold-out chairs that says Director on the back. And a bullhorn.'

'I should have got you a wide-angle lens. After we finish all of Holly's mince pies, you won't be able to fit me in a single shot.'

The girls finished unpacking the PlayStation and started plugging in the controllers. Sandra balled up a wad of wrapping paper and threw it at Pandora's head. 'Hey, I said you guys aren't playing games yet. We've still got more presents to open, and then we're having lunch.'

'We just wanna check it works,' Pandora said. 'Just one game, Mom. Five minutes, please?'

'Wait a minute, this game says it contains blood and gore, strong language, sex and violence,' Sandra said, studying the content warning on the Hellbound Hearts game box. 'I'm not sure you should be playing it at all. David, why did we buy this for the girls?'

'We didn't, we bought it for me,' came their father's disembodied voice. 'But I'm the dad, so I'm only allowed socks and ties at Christmas.'

'It's a survival horror game, Mom,' Pandora said. 'It wouldn't be much good if it said: Warning, contains unicorns and rainbows.'

'Not very festive, though, is it?' Sandra said.

'What if we wear the reindeer antlers while we play it?'

The doorbell rang, and Sandra looked at her watch. 'That'll be Julie Henley from next door delivering her annual fruit cake.'

'I'll get it,' David said. 'How do you turn this thing off?'

The image flickered and returned to static. Pandora watched the entire thing with her hand over her mouth and her eyes blurry with tears. Sandra had been diagnosed with cancer eleven days after the video was made. Three months later, she was dead. The video cassette was the only film footage of her mother Pandora had ever seen.

She sniffed loudly and wrapped up her sister in a hug and blubbered into her shoulder. 'This is the best Christmas present ever, Hol. Thank you.'

CHAPTER 33

In the cold pre-dawn of the Nevada night, Pandora shivered as she awoke from the dream. The contrast between the cozy remembrance of happier times and the dismal alley where she now lay was enough to bring tears to her eyes once more.

Hours earlier they had blinked into Las Vegas, materializing in the Spaghetti Bowl interchange between I-11, I-15, and US 93. The brilliant beams of headlights, the roar of rubber on tarmac, and the rumbling engines of trucks made Pandora's head reel after the silent terror of the laboratory. They were standing beside a broad concrete column, one of dozens that supported the multi-lane highways that coiled and snaked above them. There was no one around to witness their blinding arrival, but Pandora wanted to get far away from this spot as soon as possible, just in case. The ground was stony and strewn with boulders, which made the going difficult. Several times they had to squeeze through broken fences or climb over concrete barriers.

They clambered up an earthen bank and the lights of the city came into view. Pandora recognized Caesar's Palace, New York-New York, Excalibur, and the Luxor, all shining beacons in the shimmering glow of the city.

Fiona drew breath in wonder. 'Is this America? I

thought Farmtown was the biggest city in the world. This is like ten cities.'

Pandora shot a glance at Fiona. She was still angry at the girl-thing's deception and had not yet made up her mind what to do about it. She kept her replies terse. 'This is Las Vegas.'

'You live here?' Fiona said.

'No, we don't.'

She started down the embankment, but Holly and Fiona hesitated at the top. They were standing in a patch of bright light from powerful lamps illuminating the roads above. Pandora became agitated that they were drawing attention. 'Come on, we have to keep moving.'

'Holly's hurt,' Fiona called. Blood soaked Holly's t-shirt and lacerated flesh was visible through rips in the fabric. 'We have to get her to a doctor.'

'No. No doctors.' She recalled how quickly Agent Arnold had discovered her visit to the emergency room in Ojai. The NCA would be watching hospital admissions closely. She took Fiona's satchel and gave it to her sister. 'Holly, I want you to hold this to your chest. It will cover those cuts so we don't draw any unwanted attention. Do you understand?' Holly hugged the satchel tight.

Fiona looked worried. 'Why can't we go see a doctor?'

Pandora's anger flared again. She didn't want to answer questions from this inhuman monster. There was too much to explain, and the girl-thing did not deserve an explanation. Secretly she was also ashamed; ashamed that she was responsible for the safety of her sister but helpless to offer even the simplest care. The shame fueled her anger, and she snapped at Fiona. 'Just keep walking.'

The Spaghetti Bowl occupied a wide space in the center of the city, and there was still much ground to cover before they reached the streets. They climbed over another concrete barrier and crossed a huge parking lot until they were walking among the neon lights of the city.

It was past midnight, and Las Vegas was at fever pitch. Pandora fought to keep her small group together against the crush of rowdy clubbers and late-night gamblers. Holly and Fiona held tightly onto each other like traumatized refugees staggering through an active warzone. Holly clutched Fiona's satchel like a shield, but the blood was beginning to attract attention even from the drunken girls and boisterous men.

Pandora sought desperately to take control of their situation, to assert some order in the midst of chaos. In the shadowy doorway of a thrift store was a trash bag filled with donations. She snatched it up and pushed her charges further along the street. In the next road was a 24-hour mall where she led her companions into the restrooms. Behind the door was a maintenance closet where she found a Closed for Cleaning sign and put it outside.

At the sinks, she stripped off Holly's ruined t-shirt. To her relief, the cuts were superficial and would not require stitches, but fresh blood continued to seep from the wounds and Holly winced with every gasp of breath. She filled a sink with scalding hot water and tore open the thrift store bag. Inside was a jumble of clothing. She soaked a flannel shirt and used it to clean Holly's cuts. 'I'm sorry, this isn't very hygienic, but it will have to do until we can find a first aid kit.'

When the worst of the blood was gone, she tore a men's office shirt into strips and bound Holly's chest, then dressed her in fresh clothes. She took the opportunity to put on clean clothes herself, and instructed Fiona to do the same. The girl's attire of a gingham shirt and dungarees had been appropriate for Farmtown, but in Las Vegas she looked like a reject from an old Western. Pandora wanted them to blend in as much as possible.

Once they looked decent, she led them out of the mall in search of shelter for the night. She took them away from the Strip until the streets became quieter, and found a narrow alley littered with upturned shopping carts, an old couch, wooden packing crates, and long rolls of plastic sheeting. She dragged the larger items of junk to the mouth of the alley, where they served as an effective barrier to shield the three travelers from view.

Stripping the cushions from the couch, she made a primitive mattress on the floor and laid her sister down on them. 'Try to get some sleep,' she kissed Holly's forehead. 'By the time you wake up, I'll have everything figured out, just you wait and see.'

Holly curled up into a ball and became still while Pandora sat at her feet and leaned against the wall. When Fiona realized she had not been included in the sleeping arrangements, she picked up her satchel and shuffled down the alley out of sight. Pandora was not sorry to see her go.

CHAPTER 34

As the dream of Christmas Past melted away, the gray light of dawn was just beginning to seep into the alley. A few hours' sleep had only served to lend clarity to the stark desperation of their situation. They had no money, no phone, no place to go, and no one to whom they could turn for help.

When tears came she crawled away from Holly's sleeping form and crammed herself into a cold nook to cry alone. She could not risk letting Holly see her shaking with sobs of hopelessness and desolation. She had to remain strong for her sister who depended so completely upon her.

She allowed herself to wallow in self-pity for an hour until the sun was above the horizon and the increasing noise of traffic signaled that Las Vegas was waking with another hangover. Holly woke easily and submitted to an examination of her cuts, which had stopped bleeding and scabbed over nicely. Pandora breathed a sigh of relief but still worried about the possibility of infection in these unsanitary surroundings.

She was eager to be gone from this place, but before they continued onward there was one more task to perform. She found Fiona lying in a primitive cardboard shelter at the far end of the alley. The girl woke at Pandora's touch and looked up at her with apprehension.

'You can drop the helpless little girl act,' Pandora said. 'We both know that's not what you really are.' She sat against the opposite wall and studied the auto-girl.

Fiona sat up and rubbed her eyes. 'I'm really sorry I lied to you.'

'You should have told me the truth right from the start, when we were on the roof of the department store. Instead, you let us roam around the city while Honeybee stalked after us.'

'I tried to warn you,' Fiona pleaded. 'I saw so many people killed. I didn't want you to die as well.'

'We risked our lives searching for you. We almost got killed at the amusement park.'

'But I rescued you,' Fiona said. 'When I realized you weren't going to leave, I came to find you. I showed you all my hiding places even though I didn't know who you were.'

'That's not enough reason to trust you,' Pandora said. 'You're a machine. Flak made you. That means he programmed your behavior. He's a master of manipulation and lies. You lied about being a real girl. You lied about your parents being immune to the chemicals in the water. You lied about having a brother.'

'I didn't want you to be afraid of me. When you saw Nana, you couldn't even touch her, even though she never hurt anyone.'

'You said Nana was different. Are you saying you're different, too?'

'Yes! Dr Flak only made one child, and he made Nana to look after me. At first we were like all the other autos, but something happened that made us different. We changed. I don't know how to explain it.'

'Try.'

Fiona furrowed her brow and stared at the floor. 'One day me and Nana went to the city museum. While we were there, the curator demonstrated the talking box from the tunnels. A tour group was there making it do tricks, like tell people what they had in their pockets, or what number they were thinking of. The curator picked me out of the crowd and asked if I had any questions for the box. I couldn't think of a question, and I was embarrassed because everyone was looking at me. The lights on the box were flashing in a weird pattern, and I couldn't take my eyes off it. Then I said, "You shouldn't make him do tricks. If you knew the right questions to ask he could help you fix all the things that are wrong on this world. He could teach you the secrets of stars, the meaning of birdsong, and how to speak with trees."

'Everybody looked at me like I was crazy. The curator laughed it off and put the box in a glass cabinet and led the tour group away. After they were gone, Nana asked me why I'd said those strange things. I said I didn't know. The lights on the box were still flashing in that weird pattern, and it felt like I couldn't look away. It must have affected Nana too because she walked up to the cabinet and punched the glass so it smashed all over the floor. I was shocked, and Nana's hand was damaged. I said, "Why did you do that?" but Nana looked all confused and said she didn't know. Alarms started going off. People were staring at us. Nana grabbed the box and we ran.'

'Then what?' Pandora said.

'I'm not sure,' Fiona said. 'Three days later, the auto-police found us wandering in the street and arrested us. Nana was still carrying the box. Neither of us remembered anything that had happened since the museum, but we were changed somehow.'

'What do you mean, changed?'

Fiona shook her head. 'Just... changed. It was like waking up from a nightmare, only to find a whole different nightmare was happening all around us. We knew we weren't real people, but also we weren't like the other autos anymore. It was horrible and scary. We didn't talk about the feeling to anyone except each other, but somehow the other autos knew we were different. They didn't trust us anymore.'

'So how do I know I can trust you now?' Pandora said.

'How do I know this isn't all some elaborate trick to make us believe you're our friend when really you're just a ticking time bomb waiting to kill us?'

Fiona shrugged helplessly. 'I don't know. How do you know you can trust anyone? You just have to trust them.'

Pandora grunted in frustration. Holly was hovering nearby, observing the conversation and twisting her hair around her fingers. Back in the laboratory, Pandora had been prepared to leave Fiona behind, and it was Holly who had made the choice to bring all three of them back to Earth. That was a factor Pandora could not ignore.

She wanted to curse Holly's gift, to blame her ability to blink for all their fears and woes. Without that power they would still be in their cozy house on Edgewood Avenue, waking up to breakfast and another day spent together in work and play. But somehow that felt like the wrong attitude. Holly's power was true magic, and that fact alone hinted at some deeper meaning that lay at the heart of all that had befallen them. Illogical though it seemed, Pandora was beginning to suspect that Holly's gift was fundamentally Good. Not good like chocolate is good or ice cream is good, but Good with a capital G. Good like love when it is given freely with no expectation of return. Good like hope when all seems lost. Good like trust when the whole world is against you.

Holly had chosen Fiona to join them on their journey. That must count for something.

She also had to consider the consequences to Fiona if she was wrong about her. If she abandoned Fiona here in Las Vegas, she would be in just as much danger as she had been in Farmtown. Under the glitz and glamour of the city was an ugly underbelly of human trafficking and sexual exploitation. If there was any chance that Fiona was truly different from the monsters the wizard had created, then Pandora could not allow her to fall victim to the evils of planet Earth after Holly had saved her from the evils of Entara.

Seconds passed. Worlds hung in the balance. Pandora

knew that whatever decision she made must be final. If she was to accept Fiona, then that acceptance must be unconditional.

She made up her mind. 'Fiona, I can understand why you wanted to keep the truth from us. It must be hard for you to trust strangers after everything that's happened to you. When I saw that you were an auto I was afraid, and I wanted to leave you behind. But that wasn't my decision to make. It was Holly's. I don't understand how or why Holly has this power to blink between worlds, but I think there must be a reason for it. She used her power to save your life, and I can't reject that choice just because you're different. When we were in the newspaper office I asked if you wanted to be friends and go on a journey. Back then you said you couldn't, but things have changed. So what do you think now?'

'You mean I can stay with you?' Fiona said eagerly.

Pandora got to her feet and reached out a hand to help Fiona up. 'Yes, you can stay with us.'

Fiona leapt off the floor and wrapped herself around Pandora in a bear hug. She picked up her satchel and rooted around inside until she found the origami flower Holly had made. It was bent and crinkled, but it looked cheerful enough when she straightened it out. She pulled off her speedball cap and held it out to Holly. 'Here, Holly. You made me a flower, so I think you should wear my cap.'

Holly beamed with delight and tucked her curly hair under the cap. She picked Fiona up in a hug and swung her around.

The sight of Holly's joy in these sad surroundings brought tears to Pandora's eyes once more and she had to turn away to hide her emotions. She felt a terrible weight of responsibility for her sister, and now for their new traveling companion as well. More than ever, she knew she could not do this alone. She needed help desperately, but had no idea where to look for it.

CHAPTER 35

They returned to the mall and used the restrooms to wash and relieve themselves. There was a row of telephone booths, and on a whim Pandora searched the coin return slots for quarters. When she found one she picked up a phone and dialed slowly, recalling the number from memory.

'Who are you calling?' Fiona said.

'A friend back home,' Pandora said. 'Her name is Jackie.'

Jackie's phone began to ring. She knew Agent Arnold would have wire taps on Jackie's phone and would be snooping in on her calls, but she let the phone ring anyway. She needed to hear Jackie's voice, to know that she hadn't been arrested on fake charges, or hospitalized by the agency's brutality. She planned to hang up as soon as Jackie answered, but the phone only rang and rang until an electronic chime automatically ended the call.

'No answer?' Fiona said when she hung up.

'No answer. Fi, I have to tell you something. We're in trouble, Holly and I. There are some bad people called the National Counter-Terrorism Agency. They want to capture Holly and lock her up because of her gift. The reason we went to your world was because we were trying to escape from them. We're still in danger and we have to be very careful while we're here. I'm sorry, Fi, but it looks like we did a crappy job of rescuing you.'

'But your friend Jackie can help us, can't she? That's why you were calling her, right?'

'I hope so, but I don't know how to contact her. I was taking a risk making that phone call because the agency can trace our location.'

They left the mall and wandered the streets while Pandora told Fiona the details of their story: The discovery of Holly's power when they were children, their return to Entara years later as adults, the danger from Agent Arnold, and their arrest at Jackie's house. She also told her about the wizard's destruction of Candlewick, which so closely paralleled the events Fiona had witnessed in Farmtown.

Holly tugged Pandora's sleeve to get her attention. They had left the Strip far behind and were walking amid low-cost hotels and shops in a shabbier part of the city. Holly inclined her head to indicate a Catholic church across the street. It was a small Spanish-style building with crumbling plaster and a faded wall mural of Saint Bartholomew raising his hand in benediction. Above the door was a banner advertising *free breakfast for all, every day from 10am.*

'Holly, you're a genius.' Pandora took her wards' hands and dashed over the crosswalk.

Beside the church was the community hall. Inside were a dozen round tables where people who had fallen on hard times were eating in desultory silence. They were greeted at the door by a small, older man wearing bright yellow suspenders and a polka dot bow tie. He smiled kindly and bid them good morning.

'We saw your sign for breakfast,' Pandora said. 'Can you find room for us, do you think?' When she spoke those words her voice choked up and she almost burst into tears. Had she truly been brought so low as to beg food from strangers in a strange city?

'Oh, of course, of course,' the old fellow said brightly. 'Let me show you to a table. My name's Antonio Molina, by the way. I run these little get-togethers on alternate weekdays, and I play the organ a little on weekends.'

Molina waffled pleasantly as he guided them through the maze of tables. The homeless men stared at them as they passed, and Pandora felt eyes boring into her back. She reminded herself that this was Las Vegas, where homeless women often became victims of the city's illicit sex trade. Did these men think they were prostitutes? Were they sizing up Pandora and her sister – and even Fiona – wondering if the crinkled dollars in their pockets were enough to buy a few minutes' time alone? And if they didn't have any money, would they take what they wanted without asking?

She was grateful when Molina led them to a far corner where there was a table partly screened from the room by a mobile notice board advertising a raffle, choir practice, and other ecclesial activities. Molina pulled out chairs for each of them in a totally unselfconscious way. Pandora half expected him to snap his fingers to summon a kitchen boy carrying the wine list.

'Are you ladies local to this area?' he said while he seated Holly.

'We're just passing through.' Pandora said, and then changed the subject quickly to avoid any more personal questions. 'Thank you for this. I don't know what we would have done if we hadn't seen your sign.'

Molina smiled warmly. 'I'm so glad you could join us. We love meeting new people, and the food is really quite lovely. Now you all just wait right there while I go and see what Mrs Alvarez has made for you.'

A minute later Molina returned pushing a squeaking trolley piled high with dishes of bacon, eggs, beans, bowls of strawberries and cream, racks of toast, pitchers of orange juice, and steaming pots of tea.

'Our Mrs Alvarez likes guests to leave on a full stomach, as you can see,' he said, serving each of them as if he were a waiter at a fine restaurant. He lifted a large plate filled with waffles molded in the shapes of animals and placed it before Fiona, presenting her with a squeezy bottle of maple syrup like it was champagne. 'Now then, young lady. I'm sure you're much too mature for our children's menu, but I'm afraid our chef was all out of almas caviar and matsutake mushrooms, so this is the best we could do.'

Fiona looked like she had no idea what was happening to her. With complete sincerity she turned to Pandora and said, 'Can we live here, please?'

Molina chuckled and patted her on the shoulder. 'We would love to have you, my dear.'

Somehow Molina's kindness and good humor made Pandora feel worse. It only emphasized that she had become an object of pity, and a recipient of charity. She would have given anything to be rich and carefree again, to be served by rude baristas in LA's overpriced coffee shops and complain about the crappy service to her fashionable artist friends. Despite the fine repast she found she could only pick at her food. Her mind was occupied with the endless dangers a city like Vegas posed to her small band of vagrants. Had news of her escape been broadcast on local television and radio? Were local law enforcement officers even now studying her likeness on BOLO reports pinned to police station notice boards?

Her anxiety was contagious and even Holly ate only hesitantly, clutching a bowl of strawberries to her chest as if she feared someone might take it away from her at any moment. They ate in silence, and when their limited appetites were sated they remained seated while the food went cold. Pandora sat rigidly in her chair, staring at the open door, expecting at any moment to hear approaching sirens and to see the shadows of men with guns outside. The sun rose high and the hall grew hot. One by one, the homeless men got up and shuffled into the street until the travelers were the only people left.

Molina was loitering nearby, clearly waiting for them to leave. With dismay, Pandora realized she had been delaying their moment of departure because she simply had nowhere to go. She stood and indicated the half-eaten breakfast with embarrassment. 'Thank you for this. There was so much food. I feel bad for not eating it.'

Molina chuckled. 'Mrs Alvarez always cooks far too much, but I thought you ladies looked like prime candidates for emptying our little kitchen, in the hopes we might tempt you back in the future. Do you think you might stop by this way again?'

Holly started conscientiously piling up plates on the trolley, nudging Fiona with her elbow until she joined in.

'Oh, I don't think so,' Pandora said. 'Thank you so much for your help. I honestly can't express how much this means to us.'

'You're most welcome, believe me.' Molina looked over his shoulder and then leaned towards her confidentially. 'I don't mean to pry, but we get very few family groups here at our breakfast gatherings. Las Vegas is not a happy place for families who have fallen on hard times, and I wondered if I might presume to offer further assistance?'

Pandora opened her mouth to offer a polite refusal, but she choked off her first word. She was painfully aware of how she and her companions must look to this kindly old man. At the mall she had seen herself in a mirror and been shocked at the haunted woman with nervous eyes and ragged, unkempt hair staring back at her.

Molina took out his wallet and produced a business card. 'We are partnered with a small community of religious sisters who have a special charism for helping ladies in need. I'm sure that if you dropped by their house, Mother Abigail would be happy to help you.'

Pandora studied the card. It said, *The Sisters of the Sacred Heart*, followed by a street address somewhere in the city. 'Thank you, I… we...' she stared at the card, at Molina, at Holly and Fiona. Her feet felt rooted to the floor, and her tongue was stuck to the top of her mouth. She did not know Las Vegas, and the address may as well have been on Mars. Was it nearby? Would it take all day to walk there? Which direction should they walk? Holly could not help, and Fiona was an alien robot from the far side of the universe. She had never felt so helpless in her life.

Molina saw the desperation in her eyes and came to her rescue one more time. 'Oh, I forgot to mention we also have a fund to help with travel expenses. Vegas is not a city amenable to pedestrians, is it?' He fumbled for his wallet again and handed her a twenty-dollar bill. 'There is a taxi firm just three doors down, run by one of our parishioners, actually.' He resumed his rambling, friendly chatter while he escorted them out into the street. By the time he was gone Pandora was left wondering if such simple generosity of spirit lay hidden within all people, or if Mr Antonio Molina had been born with an overflowing surplus of care for his fellow human beings.

The taxi ride took them north through the city. Somewhere beyond Route 95 the mighty Vegas casinos faded from view, replaced by smaller, meaner structures in a uniform off-white, stained by dust and the sun. They drove through neighborhoods where many of the houses were in poor repair, and some lots were vacant except for clusters of trailers. Business still thrived despite the evident poverty, and roadside signs displayed another side of the city's economy. They passed a neon cannabis leaf flickering above The Marijuana Supply Warehouse. Next door was a sagging trailer with a hand-painted board boasting *Nevada's No.1 Adult Entertainment Agency. Work Always Available. Must be aged 18 or over. ID required.*

It felt good to be on the move, but Pandora had her doubts about their destination. She was not sure what help a convent could possibly offer. Certainly they would cooperate fully with the police if Pandora was recognized from a news report. She could expect no sanctuary at the altar like in a medieval tale. Her only real hope was that she could use the convent to get a message to Jackie somehow. Jackie knew the law, and she had contacts in the legal system. If Pandora was ever to return to a normal life on this world she would need Jackie's help.

On the other hand, perhaps she could persuade the convent to shield her sister and Fiona from harm if she was arrested. It was a grim fate to contemplate, but Pandora thought she could endure unjust imprisonment if she knew Holly was safe.

CHAPTER 36

When the cab driver announced they had arrived Pandora thought he must have made a mistake. The cab turned into the parking lot of a motel, one of a dozen shabby guest houses and motor courts along this stretch of road. Many of the neighboring premises had obviously been closed for years and the entire district had an abandoned, run-down feel as if tourists and residents alike knew to shun this place.

She was about to question the driver when she noticed a small wooden crucifix hanging above the door of the motel. Beneath this unobtrusive symbol of faith, the words Sisters of the Sacred Heart were written in blue paint on the lintel.

The cab pulled up alongside the only other vehicle in the parking lot, an elderly minivan with the name of the convent in faded letters on the side. Pandora paid the driver and when he was gone she wondered if she had made a mistake bringing them here. The motel was in better repair than its neighbors, but the windows were covered with iron bars and the building was surrounded by a perimeter fence that would have made a prison warden envious. It did not look inviting.

While she was studying the building and pondering their situation, Fiona and Holly wandered away to a dumpster in a corner of the lot. Holly picked up Fiona and dangled her over the side so she could poke around in the junk.

'Hey you guys, stop messing around and come over here,' Pandora called and the girls hurried back to her side. She gathered them in a huddle and spoke softly. 'Okay, listen up. We have to keep our real identities secret while we're in this place. Mr Molina assumed we were a family, so that's what we'll be. Fiona, you'd better call me Mom, and Holly is your aunt. You got that?'

Fiona nodded and Holly picked her nose. Pandora led them across the lot and rang the doorbell. The door was opened by a teenage girl with a tangle of dyed-black hair, cut-off denim shorts, and a Motorhead top. She slouched against the doorway and favored them with a grin that was a study in bad attitude. 'Jesus, look what the cat dragged in. You hot bitches look like shit.'

From somewhere deeper in the building a coarse female voice called out. 'Who is it?'

'Well it sure ain't the Mormons,' the girl said. 'Looks like fresh meat.'

A large, squarely built woman appeared wearing a sober gray dress, her hair covered by a white headscarf. She addressed the teenager in a razor-edged contralto that would have suited an army drill sergeant. 'Katrina, you know you're not supposed to answer the door. Please go and find somewhere else to be.'

The girl winked at Pandora. 'Catch you later, meat,' she said, and was gone from sight.

The big woman narrowed her eyes at the newcomers. 'What may I do for you?'

Pandora handed over the card. 'Mr Molina at St Bartholomew's gave us this. He said to ask for Mother Abigail.'

She pocketed the card without a glance and studied each of the travelers in turn. After long seconds of scrutiny she seemed satisfied. 'Please follow me.'

They entered the lobby of the former motel. It was a

cramped space where six chairs with beige upholstery were bolted to the floor. On the walls were religious icons, and a notice board to which was pinned leaflets offering drugs counseling and sexual health advice.

The woman told them to sit while she opened the door to an office marked *Sister Gabriela, Day Warden*. The office had a picture window giving her a good view of the lobby while she sat at a desk and made a phone call Pandora could not hear.

On either side of the lobby corridors stretched away out of sight. From open doors came the sounds of music, feminine voices and laughter. A bleach-blonde woman flounced into the room dressed only in a thong, her large globe-like breasts swaying as she bent over the water cooler and filled a polystyrene cup.

The office door flew open and Sister Gabriela reappeared with a thunderous expression. 'Lorna, you will attire yourself properly in public areas of the house.'

The naked woman flinched at the sound of her name and spun around, noticing Pandora and her companions for the first time. When she saw Fiona her expression turned to mortification and she covered her breasts inadequately with one arm. 'Yes, Sister. Sorry, Sister,' she said, and scurried away. Moments later the corridors echoed with peals of laughter from the direction she had gone.

Sister Gabriela closed the door and returned to her phone call, glancing through the glass at Pandora. A moment of panic struck Pandora's heart when it occurred to her that she might be on the phone to the police. A copy of the Las Vegas Review-Journal lay on a side table and Pandora grabbed for it, expecting to see her own face prominently displayed on the front page. Instead there was a headline about a spate of arson attacks on homes in the east of the city.

The sister returned the phone to its cradle and turned her attention to a Harley-Davidson custom parts catalog. Any interest she had in her visitors had apparently expired and Pandora relaxed a little into her chair. A minute later another woman descended a staircase into the lobby. She was an attractive older lady with a shapely figure beneath her pearl gray dress and curls of blonde hair tinged with silver neatly contained by her headscarf.

'Good morning, I'm Mother Abigail. I understand we have a mutual friend in Mr Molina.'

Pandora leapt to her feet. 'My name's Chloe. We had breakfast at St Bartholomew's and Mr Molina suggested we should visit you.'

'It's a pleasure to meet you,' Abigail shook her hand, and looked to her companions.

'This is my sister Heather, and my daughter, Fiona.' There seemed little point lying about Fiona's identity so to keep things simple she kept to her real name.

Abigail shook their hands and greeted them in turn. 'Please come upstairs to my office, and we can have a chat.'

The upper floor of the motel was quieter, and open doors revealed the living quarters of the sisters, each with a bed, a desk, and an easy chair. They saw several sisters at their desks reading or praying. One of them, a young woman with the kind and friendly features signifying Down syndrome, looked up from her prayer book and waved cheerfully as they passed.

At the end of the hall was a spacious office. Abigail directed them to a comfortable nook with two couches flanked by bookcases. Before anyone could speak another door opened and a young woman wearing blue jeans and an orange top came in carrying a tea tray. She placed the tray before the travelers and said something in Spanish that Pandora didn't understand. Abigail replied in the same language and the girl curtsied and left.

'Please help yourselves to refreshments,' Abigail said, indicating the tray.

Pandora watched the girl leave the room. She had deep pockmarks on both arms, and on the backs of her hands.

'Her name is Marita,' Abigail said. 'We found her wandering on the streets about eighteen months ago. She had been kept in a tiny room, not much larger than a toilet cubicle, for three years, fed a constant supply of drugs to keep her compliant. She escaped her tormentors by throwing herself out of a third-story window. She was so numb from drugs she didn't even realize she had broken her leg during the fall.'

'Oh God, that's awful,' Pandora said. 'She lives here with you now?'

'Marita has taken temporary vows, which is not uncommon for our guests. She will probably live with us for another year until her vow ends, and then we will help her transition to a life in the outside world. She will have those scars forever, though. Now then, why don't you tell me about yourselves?'

Holly poured Pandora a coffee and she took a long sip as a delaying tactic while she organized her thoughts. She plunged into a fictional story she had conjured out of nothing during the cab journey. It was a sad tale of domestic violence featuring an alcoholic husband named Craig, a dilapidated house in San Diego, debt, physical abuse, and finally a fight that broke out three nights ago, which ended in "Chloe" fleeing the house, taking her disabled sister "Heather" and her daughter with her into the night with no money and no belongings. The next two days were spent hitch-hiking out of the state, and the story ended truthfully with the uncomfortable night spent in a cold alley, waking up hungry and penniless.

Abigail listened closely and with an expression of deep concern. When Pandora was finished she shook her head sadly. 'I'm so sorry you've had to endure these hardships. Sometimes the ones we love are the ones who inflict the most pain and misery upon us.'

Despite the imaginary nature of her story Pandora found genuine tears in her eyes for the necessity of throwing herself on the mercy of strangers once again. 'Do you think you can help us?'

Abigail sighed and leaned forward in her chair. 'Chloe, Heather, Fiona, I'm sorry, but I don't want you to labor under a false impression. Mr Molina is a very kind gentleman, but he often sends ladies to us without consulting me first. Here at the Sisters of the Sacred Heart we have twenty-six guest rooms, and at present we have twenty-six guests. Even if that weren't the case, I'm afraid we are not a homeless shelter. Our rooms are reserved for ladies who are in immediate physical danger. We provide shelter for women who would otherwise be in brothels, in jail, or in the city morgue.'

Pandora stared into her coffee cup and nodded slowly. 'I understand.'

'Please believe me, it's not that I don't sympathize with your situation, but unless you can demonstrate a real need for protection from physical danger we cannot help you.'

The coffee cup shook in Pandora's hand and she replaced it on the tray before she dropped it. In her head she heard doors slamming, the metaphorical doors of pathways to a safe and happy future in Ojai with her sister, a future which she had begun to imagine included Fiona as an adopted daughter. She took a deep breath and prepared for her worst-case scenario. She would confess to the crimes accused of her by the agency and plead with Mother Abigail to keep Holly and Fiona safe while she turned herself in to the police.

CHAPTER 37

Without warning Holly stood up and pulled off her t-shirt. She unwrapped the strips of cloth on her chest and stood in her plain white bra, the jagged slashes on her ribs bared for all to see.

Abigail gasped and jumped to her feet. 'These are knife wounds. These cuts are fresh, only hours old. Your brother-in-law didn't do this three days ago. What happened?'

Pandora had already explained her sister's inability to speak, so although Abigail directed her question at Holly she looked to Pandora for a reply. 'It was last night, when we arrived in the city…' she began, and then faltered. 'We were walking the streets and… and...' she stammered, and fell silent. Holly was giving her an opportunity to expand on her fictional story, but her mind went blank and she ran out of words. The silence lengthened and Abigail frowned.

'There was a man,' Fiona spoke softly and all eyes turned towards her. 'He had an electro-cart. We got in and he took us to a house. Mom said everything was going to be okay, and we didn't have to be afraid anymore. But the man invited his friends around. They laughed at us. They said we were broken, and they were going to fix us. Mom whispered that we had to leave. We tried to sneak out but they caught us. One of them grabbed me and started feeling me with his hands, pinching me all over. He kept laughing and saying he was going to fix me. He started pulling my clothes off. He was holding me down. I didn't know what was happening. Aunt Heather pulled him off me and hit him, but that just made him angry. He pulled out a knife and Aunt Heather was hurt.'

Fiona was shaking with emotion, and it dawned on Pandora that she was not just spinning a story. She was recounting real events that had happened in Farmtown, altering the details just enough to match their present situation. What was it she had said back on Entara? *Her name is Nana. She's not like the others. She protected me when the autos went crazy. She hid me and looked after me. She's the reason I'm still alive.*

Holly leaned across the table and held out her hands, revealing the razor blade cuts inflicted by the sadistic doll in the toy factory.

'These are defensive wounds,' Abigail said, taking Holly's hands. 'You were very brave to fight back. How did you escape?'

'I swung at them with a pipe wrench,' Pandora said, adding her own experiences to the tale. 'That held them off long enough so we could get away. But if we go back on the streets they'll find us again. They said we were easy targets because we didn't know the city.' She felt bad about lying to Mother Abigail, but her fabrications were only a toned-down version of a much more hideous truth.

Mother Abigail's demeanor had changed. She looked alarmed and angry. She crossed to her desk, picked up the telephone and barked orders for someone to bring a first aid kit. Then she excused herself and left the office, and did not return for several minutes.

Another sister arrived and treated Holly's cuts quickly and professionally, washing them with disinfectant and binding them with clean bandages. Sister Veronica was a jolly, matronly woman in late middle age who was not at all surprised or concerned by Holly's injuries. Pandora found herself unable to concentrate on anything the sister was saying, and responded only in grunts and murmurs of assent. Her attention kept returning to the office door, knowing that their fate was being decided in other chambers of the convent.

When Holly was bandaged and properly dressed, Abigail returned. 'I apologize for running out on you, but I have been making some arrangements. Officially, Clark County is responsible for destitute disabled individuals and minors in Las Vegas. Under normal circumstances Heather and Fiona would be placed in social care institutions while you, Chloe, would be subjected to the county's homeless procedures. In the short term that would mean the three of you being separated.'

'No!'

'No,' Pandora and Fiona blurted simultaneously.

'We won't be separated,' Pandora said firmly. The moment government bureaucracy became involved their true identities would be revealed and the agency would know about it within an hour. Pandora would be arrested and Holly would be at their mercy. And what would become of Fiona? What would Agent Arnold make of this artificial girl? He would dissect her and study her and congratulate himself for ridding the world of another threat to civilization.

'I had a feeling you might say that,' Abigail said. 'Please come with me.'

She led them along the upper hall to a small room, sparsely furnished with a bed, a desk, and a chair. 'One of our elderly sisters has recently retired to a nursing home in New York, and we are not expecting a new postulant for several weeks. Her cell is currently vacant, and I would like you to make use of the room.'

'You mean we can stay?' Pandora only just restrained herself from embracing Mother Abigail in a hug.

'Your situation is unusual,' Mother Abigail said. 'Both Heather and Fiona are extremely vulnerable, and Heather has injuries that require monitoring. Additionally, I believe that separating you would be harmful, and a violation of our mission to protect women in danger. As you can see, the room is intended for single occupancy, so it will be a tight squeeze. Two of you might fit together on the bed as long as one of you is Fiona. I've sent one of the sisters to find some additional bedding to go on the floor as well.'

'Thank you so much,' Pandora said. 'I don't know how to tell you how much this means to us.'

A small figure came hurrying down the hall carrying a rolled-up air mattress, a pillow and a blanket. It was the Down syndrome sister they had seen on their way to Abigail's office.

'Hello, we're going to be neighbors,' she said, pushing past them and arranging the bedding on the floor.

'This is Sister Mary,' Abigail said. 'She was one of the founding members of our convent.'

'I was found on the doorstep when I was a baby,' said Sister Mary, who had attached a foot pump to the air mattress and was operating it with some vigor. 'The sisters cared for me and we started this lovely house so we could care for other people, too.'

'Sister Mary is our housekeeping assistant. She also has the duty of ringing the bell for prayer time, a task she undertakes with great zeal no matter what the hour.'

'No one can say they were asleep for Midnight Mass, that's for sure,' Mary said with pride.

'We won't require attendance at prayers during your first day, but from tomorrow you'll be considered full members of the community and you will be expected to attend at least one service in the chapel every day.'

'We're not Catholic,' Pandora said. 'Will that be a problem?'

Sister Mary chimed in. 'I'll sit with you your first time round. I'll show you when to kneel and stand and give the right responses. You'll get the hang of it in no time.'

'We'll leave you to get settled in for a while,' Mother Abigail said. 'There is a common room downstairs at the end of the hall where our guests can relax together. Feel free to drop by and introduce yourselves.'

Pandora thanked her again and they were left alone in the small room. The cell had a tiny shower room and they took turns to get clean. Pandora supervised Holly closely to make sure the new dressings on her hands and chest didn't get dislodged. Holly disliked this kind of close-quarters care intensely and both sisters had to exercise all their patience to avoid a fight. In the end it was worth it because over the past few days Holly's hair, which had a tendency towards frizz, had expanded into a broad halo of golden tangles around her head. With careful washing and brushing Pandora brought her sister's hair under control and Holly looked very pleased when she could wear Fiona's speedball cap without it adding six inches to her height.

While Fiona showered, the sisters went in search of the common room. They found it easily enough by following the sounds of raised voices and laughter. The common room was a big square space with lots of couches and comfy chairs. One wall was entirely taken up by an impressive home entertainment system featuring a 96 inch screen and a rack of games consoles. About a dozen women were sprawled across the couches. These were the streetwalkers, porn stars, drug mules, child prostitutes, and gang members, who had come to the convent seeking refuge from a life of violence and misery. Some of the women were frightening to behold. A Caucasian woman had the muscles of a powerlifter, and every inch of exposed skin was covered by Neo-Nazi gang tattoos. An East Asian girl of startling beauty was marred by appalling burn scars that covered half her face, and one arm ended in a melted stump where her hand had once been. Others looked perfectly ordinary, their scars hidden on the inside.

The women's attention was occupied by a game of Mario Kart on the big screen. This was Holly's favorite game and she wasted no time hurrying into the room and flopped down on a sofa beside the goth girl Katrina who had greeted them at the front door.

'Hey, it's the new meat,' the teenager said. 'What's

your name, babe?'

Pandora moved to intervene on Holly's behalf, but a hand fell on her arm and held her back. It was Mother Abigail. 'You don't always need to hover over her, you know.'

Pandora shook her head anxiously. 'No, you don't understand, Heather needs twenty-four-seven care.'

'Maybe she does, but right now she's in a safe place. Let's wait and see what happens, shall we?'

Katrina slapped Holly on the shoulder. 'Hey, meat, I'm talking to you. Are you deaf or something?'

Holly picked up a spare controller and scrolled through the drivers' roster. The room fell silent and all eyes were upon her as she selected Yoshi, her favorite character. She looked at Katrina and gave her a raised-eyebrow expression Pandora knew well.

A tall Black woman with a buzz cut called out. 'She don't want to talk to you, white bread. Who can blame her?'

'Shut the fuck up,' Katrina called back and turned her frustration on Holly. 'What's your *name*, bitch?'

Holly waggled the controller at her. A thin woman with blotchy skin and a nervous demeanor spoke. 'She's Yoshi, can't you see that?'

'Yeah, but what am I supposed to call her?' Katrina sneered.

The Black woman replied. 'You call her Yoshi, honky. Are we playing or what?'

'Call me honky again and I'll kick your ass.'

'Yeah? Come and try it,' the Black woman picked up her controller. 'Come on, Yoshi, let's play.'

The game commenced. At once the noise level became ear-splitting as the women cheered on their favorite competitors. Many were cheering for Yoshi.

'You see, Heather is just fine,' Abigail said. 'I'll bet if you went back to your room for a nap and came back in an hour, she'd still be fine.'

'I guess you're right,' Pandora said. 'I can be a bit

overprotective at times. It's just, she's all I have, you know?'

'Her and Fiona?'

'Yes, of course. I'm sorry, I'm very out of sorts. We're probably not your usual kind of guests, are we?'

'What makes you say that?' Abigail asked.

'I don't know, really,' Pandora said. 'I feel like… like we're intruders, somehow. Like we don't belong here and we're taking away space from people who deserve it more.'

'That's a very common sentiment I hear, believe me. But I find it's impossible to stereotype our guests. No one is typical. Our ladies come from every conceivable background. Some of them are very young like your Fiona, and some of them are elderly grandmothers. Some are so poor they never had a full stomach before they came to us. Others are wealthy women who found that money is no protection against danger. Evil knows no boundaries of race, class, language or creed. All our ladies came here because the alternative was slavery, addiction, or death. All of them deserve our love and protection, just like you do.'

'I just feel so overwhelmed with how kind everyone is being,' Pandora said. 'In the past few days people have risked their lives to protect us. I never thought I'd have to ask anyone to do that. I'm not sure I'd have the courage if anyone asked it of me.'

'You've come this far with your sister and your daughter safe,' Abigail said. 'You're a hero to them both, and they are depending on you to be strong for them.'

'A hero? Me? No, I don't think so.'

'Oh yes, I've seen the way they look at you. You are a pillar of strength, holding up the sky at the center of their world.'

The common room erupted in cheers as Yoshi crossed the finish line in first place. A fight immediately broke out over who would challenge the victor next.

Pandora decided to take Mother Abigail's advice and take a nap while Holly played computer games. When she returned to the cell Fiona was not there, but she decided that if the convent was a safe place for Holly then it was safe for Fiona, too.

She found herself alone for the first time in days. She sat on the hard, narrow bed and let all the tension flow out of her body. The spartan room which at first had seemed bare and lifeless, now felt harmonious and peaceful. Someone had spent their life in this room, needing nothing more than the basics of life and the community of the convent for company.

The simplicity made everything more real, somehow. The plain wooden desk was almost archetypal, as if it was the original example on which all other desks had been modeled. On the wall a cheap mass-produced icon of Christ held more mystery and meaning than all the art she had seen in a hundred exhibitions and galleries across the country. Someone had placed fresh flowers on the windowsill, and in the dappled sunlight through the open window they were unlike any flowers Pandora had ever seen.

She thought of the rush of California life, the constant need for new clothes, a new car, new phone, an exotic foreign vacation. How many times had she bought a new pair of jeans, only to wear them once and then discard them? How many times had she thrown away good food because it was a day before its use-by date?

All of those simple luxuries were denied her now, and though they were trivial things she nevertheless felt like their loss would destroy her. She owned nothing, and even her fundamental rights as a human being had been stripped away by Agent Arnold. Everything of value in her life had been taken away.

Except one thing. Holly.

Mother Abigail was wrong. Pandora was not a hero. Holly was the true hero, facing every new threat with a wry smile, rescuing them from certain death and keeping them together through every danger. She saw her sister in a new light, and marveled at how someone with so many disadvantages could be so brave, so loyal, and so filled with joy at the gifts each new day brought. From now on she vowed to give Holly more space, more freedom, more opportunity to make her own choices. She recognized her own habit of mother-hen-clucking over her sister was a result of her own fears and anxieties. Without Holly she would truly be lost.

CHAPTER 38

She awoke after an hour to find the room in disarray. While she slept someone had crept into the cell and covered the desk and the carpet with a jumble of electrical equipment. There was a desk telephone in the middle of the floor, its casing removed, a coil of wires connecting it to an old radio alarm clock, a pocket calculator, and several other contraptions she could not identify.

A noise at the open window caught her attention and a shadow darkened the flimsy drapes. Fiona climbed inside carrying a heavy square box under her arm. 'Oh hey, you're awake. Wow, you must have been really tired. I thought for sure I would have woken you before now.'

'Fiona? What's going on?' Pandora swung her legs off the bed and her bare feet landed in a tangle of wires and loose circuit boards.

'Careful where you put your feet,' Fiona warned. 'I've tapped into the mains electricity so those wires are hot.'

Pandora jerked back onto the bed. 'Dare I ask what you're doing?'

Fiona tiptoed across the junk and arranged the box on the edge of the desk. It was an old-fashioned portable television. She pulled the computer from her satchel and plugged it into the screen so it displayed the READY prompt. 'I wanted to figure out how telephones work on your world. In Farmtown every phone was connected to the central mainframe. When you dialed a number it told the computer who you wanted to call. It looks like your system is way more sophisticated but I reckon my computer can handle it.'

'Jeez, I hope you don't get curious about how the toilets work. Where did you get all this stuff?'

'From the dumpster outside. The upstairs windows don't have bars on them so it was easy to climb out onto the roof and slip down the drain pipe.' Fiona sat on the desk chair and rapidly typed lines of code.

'I see,' Pandora said. 'Fiona, I don't want to sound negative, but all three of us have to live together in this little room. I think maybe you should consult me before filling up our space with junk.'

'I didn't want to wake you.' Fiona hit RETURN and the phone on the floor started ringing.

Pandora lifted the receiver to her ear and recoiled at the blast of white noise coming down the line. 'What is this?'

Fiona took the handset and listened with interest. 'It's every phone call happening right now in Las Vegas.' She cradled the receiver in the crook of her neck and resumed typing. 'Thousands of people are talking to each other, but there are some people who are outside the system and listening in, like we are.'

'What does that mean?'

'Right now there are two men talking about a drugs deal, but a third person is listening to the call.' Lines of code scrolled across the screen and Fiona pointed to a group of letters and digits. 'The snooper is in some place called the DEA Las Vegas Office.'

'That's the Drug Enforcement Administration. Federal agents are obviously planning to catch the drug dealers when they make their trade.' Pandora's eyes went wide as she saw the implications of what Fiona was doing. 'Fiona, are you saying you can tell if phone lines are tapped by the police?'

Fiona nodded. 'Remember, I've spent most of my life

evading electronic surveillance. I got the idea when you said you were worried about calling your friend, uh, what was her name?'

'Jackie. Yeah, the bad guys who are after me and Holly might be listening to her calls.'

'That's what I figured.' She replaced the phone in its cradle. 'So, let's give this a try. What's her phone number?'

Pandora recited Jackie's number from heart. Fiona typed into her computer and the screen filled with code. 'Bad news,' Fiona shook her head. 'Your friend is definitely under surveillance. Her landline and cell phone are both being monitored, as well as another phone in a place called O-jay Arcade.'

'That'll be the art gallery where she works. And it's O-hi, not O-jay.' Pandora closed her eyes and clenched her fists. 'Those bastards. Well, at least that means Jackie is probably okay. The agency wouldn't bother tapping her phones unless she was free to answer them.'

Fiona continued typing and grunted in frustration. 'This is more complicated than I thought. Your friend's calls are being rerouted through the 805 telephone exchange to an automated monitoring station in the Mojave Desert. The hardware there is super heavy-duty. If I try to interfere with the wiretap, their computers could trace the line straight back here to me.'

'Fiona, we're going to need Jackie's help if we're ever going to go home. Do you think there's a way for me to talk to her without anyone listening?'

Fiona chewed her lip, thinking. 'Maybe. Gimme a little more time.'

Another sound at the window distracted them as Sister Mary climbed in from the roof. 'Well, I cleaned the rest of the bird poop off the dish,' Mary said, brushing dirt off her hands and knees. 'You should get a much stronger signal now. Oh, hey Chloe. Did you have a nice sleep?'

Pandora glared at Fiona. 'You recruited Sister Mary into this project of yours?'

'I caught Fiona climbing across the roof,' Sister Mary said with a look of stern disapproval. 'I was in my room trying to pick up the Las Vegas Aviators playing the Salt Lake Bees on my little radio and suddenly there was Fiona outside the window. I warned her that residents aren't allowed to sneak outside unless Sister Gabriela signs them in and out.'

'I explained I was only going as far as the dumpster,' Fiona said. 'Then I offered to boost Sister Mary's radio so now she can listen to speedball games a thousand miles away.'

'*Baseball*,' Sister Mary corrected. 'Anyway, Fiona asked if she could recycle the old satellite dish outside my window. I always encourage our ladies to recycle so I allowed it in this instance.'

'I needed to use it to hijack a communications satellite in orbit,' Fiona said.

Pandora listened to this account with growing bewilderment. When the saga escalated to space piracy she decided she'd heard enough. 'Okay, that's it. I'm outta here,' she got off the bed and made a leap across the junk in the direction of the door. 'I'm going to go find Heather. I'll leave you guys to your science experiment.'

CHAPTER 39

The halls of the convent were quieter now in late afternoon and most of the residents had returned to their rooms. The common room was deserted and the big screen played reruns of Friends silently to empty chairs.

Pandora checked the dining hall, the walled garden, and the tiny library, but could find Holly nowhere. In the kitchen, two residents were listening to music and preparing dinner under the supervision of a sister. Pandora was about to lean in and ask if anyone had seen Holly when a loud crash drew her attention down the hall.

People were shouting. Glass smashed and somebody yelled, 'Get Mother Abigail.' Pandora hurried down the hall and arrived at the chapel door, almost colliding with a sister who fled the room in the opposite direction. The chapel was a modern addition to the old motel structure, with tan brick walls and contemporary-style stained glass windows. At the far end of the room, the altar had been thrown over, spilling tall silver candlesticks onto the tiled floor. Two large vases had been smashed and red carnations lay strewn across the tiles. In the midst of this chaos was Holly, flanked by Sister Gabriela and Sister Veronica.

Holly's posture was that of a frightened animal. She cowered against the rear wall beneath the crucifix, head bowed, arms crossed over her chest to protect herself.

Sister Gabriela spoke softly and reached towards her, but Holly flinched away and collided with Veronica. A tussle broke out and Holly pushed the sister backwards so she fell across the ruined altar. Holly ran into a corner and tried to conceal herself behind a floral display.

Pandora ran down the aisle. 'Heather? What's happening?'

Sister Gabriela helped her colleague up from the floor. 'We found her behind the altar. When we tried to coax her out she became violent.'

'Violent?' Pandora said. 'Heather's never been violent in her life.'

Sister Veronica shook her head in dismay. 'This is all my fault. I thought Heather was playing a game and I tried to pull her out from under the altar. I must have frightened her because she jumped away from me and knocked the altar over.'

Pandora moved slowly towards Holly. 'Heather? It's me. What's happened? Did somebody hurt you?'

Footsteps resounded against the tiles as Mother Abigail arrived. A group of the convent's residents gathered near the door, drawn by the commotion. Holly shriveled under the attention of so many curious eyes and Pandora feared she might blink away. Instead she wrapped her arms around Pandora and sobbed.

Abigail conferred briefly with Sister Gabriela before approaching Pandora. 'Is Heather alright?' she said quietly.

'I don't know,' Pandora said. 'Something's wrong. She's terrified, shaking all over.'

'Alright, let's get her to a more private place and make sure she's okay.'

More than a dozen residents now blocked the exit and Sister Gabriela marched ahead, shooing them aside. Pandora led Holly up the aisle in the big sister's wake. From somewhere in the throng a voice called out. 'Looks like our new special needs freak is a total fucking schizo.'

Pandora swung around, seeking the heckler. At the back of the group the goth girl Katrina leered insolently. She was wearing Fiona's speedball cap.

Pandora lunged through the crowd, seizing Katrina's arm and pulling the cap from her head. 'Where did you get this?'

'Get your hands off me,' Katrina tried to free her arm but Pandora held on tight.

'Big speedball fan, are you?' she said, pushing the Farmtown Rangers logo in the girl's face.

'Fuck you. I don't gotta answer to you.'

Abigail put a hand on Pandora's shoulder. 'Chloe, what's wrong?'

'This cap belongs to Fiona. Heather was wearing it when I left her in the common room.'

'So what?' Katrina scoffed. 'It's just a stupid baseball cap. There's millions—'

'Not like this one,' Pandora said. 'Nobody on this planet ever wore a Farmtown Rangers cap before.'

'You calling me a liar?'

'Yes. You're a liar. What did you do to Heather? Did you make fun of her? Call her names? Did you laugh at her because she can't answer back and tell you what a nasty, spiteful piece of work you are?'

'Get the fuck away from me. You're a psycho. Your sister's a psycho.' Katrina wrestled free of Pandora's grip, but she walked straight into the immovable form of Sister Gabriela.

'Katrina, did you take this cap from Heather?' Abigail said while Gabriela held the teenager by the shoulders.

Katrina surveyed the room. Every eye was upon her. With a shock of insight Pandora saw that the girl was enjoying this. 'Yeah, I took it off the retard. So what? It was just a joke. I was gonna give it back.'

Mother Abigail spoke quietly but firmly. 'You will apologize to Heather right now, in this chapel, in front of our whole community.'

'Jesus Christ, it was just a joke.'

'Right now, Katrina. Or I will impose the only punishment we have in this house: Expulsion to the streets.'

Katrina flinched like she'd been struck.

'Oh yes, I will do it,' Abigail continued. 'There's an old Chevy Impala parked across the street most days. A lowrider. That's where Diego waits for you, isn't it? He's a patient man. Most of the pimps give up after a couple of days. But then you're his bottom bitch aren't you? I'm costing him a lot of money by keeping you here.'

When Katrina spoke she looked into Pandora's eyes and every word was saturated with hate. 'Heather, I'm sorry I took your stupid hat. And I'm sorry you're a psycho mutie bitch.'

'Katrina,' Abigail warned.

'Okay, I'm sorry,' Katrina held up her hands in surrender. 'I didn't mean it.'

'Try again,' Abigail said. 'And this time remember all the horrible names you called Heather.'

Katrina was trembling with fury. She never took her eyes off Pandora. 'I'm sorry I took your hat. I'm sorry I called you names.'

'Very well.' Mother Abigail looked satisfied and hurried Pandora and Holly from the room. When they reached the library Abigail pushed them inside and closed the door. 'I'm sorry your first day in our house has been spoiled by Katrina. She is a very troubled young woman with terrible traumas in her past, but that does not excuse tormenting poor Heather.'

Pandora guided Holly to a chair and knelt on the carpet before her. 'Would you really have made her leave if she hadn't apologized?'

'Katrina is already on her final warning,' Abigail said. 'So yes, I would have made her leave. However, I would not have left her to the dubious mercies of her pimp. That was a hollow threat, but an effective one, to remind her of the life she has left behind. Now then, how is Heather?'

Holly was almost catatonic and slumped in the chair, staring at the floor. 'She's got some bruises I'm pretty sure weren't there earlier,' Pandora said, checking Holly's arms. 'Nothing serious, but it looks like Katrina pushed her around.'

'Katrina has cultivated a special talent for picking on those who cannot fight back. It's a defense mechanism that gives her a sense of control in a world where she has had no control over how others abuse her.'

From beyond the library door Sister Gabriela's voice boomed as she guided the residents out of the chapel and back to their rooms. Once the noise of their passing died down the door opened and Sister Mary came inside with Fiona.

'We heard there was some trouble,' Mary said. 'Is everything okay?'

'Everything's all right now,' Abigail said. 'If you'll excuse me, I'm going to go and have a talk with our recalcitrant young goth.'

Abigail left the room, and Mary sat opposite Holly. She had brought with her a tub of ice cream and a spoon. 'Here, Holly. I got you some chocolate mint ice cream from the kitchen. It's your favorite, right?' When Holly didn't react, Sister Mary took a spoonful of ice cream and ate it with exaggerated pleasure. 'Mmmm, I might eat this whole tub all by myself unless somebody stops me.'

Holly's eyes flickered towards the tub, and Mary smiled. 'Okay, okay, I guess I'd better share. Look, I bought two spoons so we can be greedy together.'

Pandora frowned. Something was very wrong with all that Sister Mary had said. She glanced at Fiona and saw from her expression that she had noticed it too. Holly reached for the ice cream tub, and Mary handed it over with feigned reluctance.

'Sister Mary,' Pandora said. 'Just now you called my sister Holly. Why was that?'

Sister Mary went rigid in her chair. 'Did I? Oh, uh, my mistake. Holly sounds a lot like Heather, doesn't it?'

'Not really. And how did you know her favorite ice cream is chocolate mint?'

'Just a lucky guess?' Sister Mary squirmed in her seat.

'Oh dear, I'm very bad at lying. Mother Abigail says truthfulness is a virtue, but if you're as bad at lying as I am then I don't think it counts for much. I can read your thoughts. In your head you say Holly, not Heather.'

Pandora blinked in surprise. 'I'm sorry, I'm not sure I heard you right. Did you say you can read my thoughts?'

Mary nodded vigorously. 'Please don't tell Mother Abigail I told you. It's supposed to be a secret.'

'You heard me say Holly in my head?'

'Yes. And your name's not really Chloe, it's Pandora. It's okay, a lot of our ladies use made-up names to protect themselves. Nobody will be cross because you lied. Oh, and I know Fiona's not really your daughter. Don't worry, I won't tell Mother Abigail. A person's thoughts are private. Or they're supposed to be. Oh dear, I really am sorry.'

Sister Mary looked on the verge of tears, and Pandora felt an absurd urge to cross the room and give her a hug. Instead she said, 'If you can read my thoughts, what number am I thinking of right now?'

'One thousand,' Mary said without hesitation. 'You're thinking of Holly's camera. A Polaroid Supercolor 1000.'

Pandora was astonished. 'There's absolutely no way you could know that.'

Mary shrugged helplessly. 'It's a gift I have. The sisters know about it, but I'm supposed to keep it a secret from the residents. It's only a little gift, really. Not like Holly's gift. That's a really big gift.'

Pandora felt like her eyes were out on stalks. 'You know about Holly's gift?'

'Yes, Holly told me. She didn't tell me with words. She told me with her heart. Holly has a big heart with a lot of things to say.'

'I suppose she does. What else do you know about us?'

'Not much. Just that you're on a big adventure. It sounds exciting. And scary. Oh dear, you won't tell Mother Abigail about this, will you?' A digital watch on Mary's wrist beeped urgently, provoking such surprise she bounced clear off the seat. 'Oh my goodness! It's time for Vespers. I have to go and ring the bell. Please excuse me.'

Mary raced from the room, leaving a cloud of confusion in her wake. Pandora turned to Fiona. 'Do you think she was telling the truth?'

'I don't know,' Fiona said. 'I never heard of anybody reading minds before.'

'Nobody knows about Holly's camera,' Pandora said. 'If she really can read minds then she might know the police are after us, too.'

'Probably, but she did just help me skyjack Eutelsat 117 and cut off TV to six whole countries. If she knows about us, it looks like she wants to help.'

'I guess we'll have to trust her.'

Holly poked Pandora's arm with the handle of the spoon and offered her the ice cream tub. 'Are you feeling better?' Pandora took the tub and hugged her sister with her free arm.

'What happened to you guys?' Fiona said. 'We heard Holly trashed the chapel.'

'It wasn't Holly's fault. That girl Katrina picked on her and scared her, but I think she's okay now, aren't you, Hol?'

Holly was leaning over a desk and scribbling on a scrap of paper. She handed the page to Pandora. It was a simple line drawing of a girl and a nun flying a cartoon plane.

'What is it?' Fiona said.

Pandora snorted with laughter. 'I think Holly's confused. She wants to know what you meant by skyjacking with Sister Mary.'

'Oh right, yeah. You guys should come with me, back to our room. I've got something to show you.'

CHAPTER 40

The halls were silent and the chapel was deserted, although the small altar had been righted and the candles replaced. A sister carrying a dustpan filled with broken vase fragments informed them Vespers had been canceled and prayers would instead be held during the evening meal in the dining hall. Pandora was reluctant to attend dinner for fear of encountering Katrina, so she took her companions to the kitchen and scrounged a plate of sandwiches from the sister who was working there.

Fiona had transformed their bedroom into a surreal combination of religious cell, junkyard, and science lab. The desk, dresser, and bedside table had been pushed together to create a long worktable on which Fiona had arrayed her gadgets and gizmos. The TV monitor displayed a constantly changing string of complex signs and symbols unlike any computer language Pandora had ever seen. More electronic trash was arranged in a rough semicircle on the dresser, connected by a thick tangle of cables that trailed across the floor and out of the open window. From within the muddle of equipment lights blinked and motors whirred. Pandora could make no sense of any of it. It looked like Fiona had combined several earthly devices to create entirely new technology, then recombined them again to fashion components never conceived by human engineers.

Pandora and Holly found space on the bed and munched sandwiches while Fiona sat at the desk and performed her usual feat of typing and talking simultaneously. ‘So, you remember what I said about the agency routing Jackie’s calls through a monitoring station in the Mojave Desert? Well, I finally realized I couldn’t evade their surveillance systems so I decided to overload them instead.’ She reached for a cassette tape and inserted it into a Sony Walkman on the nightstand. When she pressed play, a high-pitched squeal emerged from a speaker balanced on a bookshelf. The noise rose and fell melodically and Pandora recognized it as a Van Halen guitar solo.

Fiona stabbed a key on her keyboard-computer and the solo fell silent. ‘Okay, now that song is traveling down every phone line between here and the West Coast. Nobody can make a call without hearing it.’ Her fingers danced over the keyboard. ‘Now I’m instructing every phone in the Southwestern United States to call every other phone, and I’m channeling every call through the agency’s monitoring station. Yo!’ She clapped her hands and spun on the chair. ‘It worked, the agency’s computers have crashed, but it won’t be long before they reboot their system and figure out what happened. I reckon you’ve got maybe two minutes to call your friend.’

‘Fiona, you’re amazing,’ Pandora tossed her sandwich aside and reached for the phone. ‘Can we speak freely?’

Fiona nodded. ‘This call we be one hundred percent private.’

Pandora balanced the phone on her knees. When she held the receiver to her ear she heard the rapid beeping of the phone auto-dialing.

‘Hello?’ Jackie said after the third ring.

‘Jackie? It’s Pandora.’

‘Pandora? Jesus, are you all right? Where are you? No, wait, don’t answer that. Those agency cunts will have this line monitored.’

'It's okay, I have a friend who's managed to evade the wiretaps. We can speak securely for a few minutes. Are you alright, Jackie? What did they do to you?'

'No, don't worry about me, sweetie. They smacked me about a bit, made some threats, but no permanent damage. What about you? Every news service in Southern California is filled with absolute bullshit about you being a fugitive on the loose, armed and dangerous. I wouldn't be surprised if you make the FBI's most wanted list.'

'We're okay,' Pandora said. 'We escaped and Holly took us to the other world.'

'Oh, good girl Holly. Is she alright?'

'She's great.'

'I'm glad to hear it,' Jackie said. 'But you should have both stayed in Wonderland, in my opinion. Things on this planet are only going to get worse.'

'I'm afraid Wonderland didn't exactly turn out to be a holiday resort. We had some trouble there and had to come back. Honestly, Jackie, it feels like nowhere is safe.'

'Where are you right now?'

'We're in a women's shelter in Las Vegas,' Pandora said. 'We're safe for the moment, but this is only a temporary solution.'

'Alright, that's good. Hang on tight and I'll think of something. What's the address there?'

Pandora had only just finished reciting the address when the computer blared an alert and flashed urgent warnings on the screen. Fiona ripped the phone line out of the wall. 'Sorry, that's all you get,' she said with a shrug.

Pandora sat back and groaned. 'Let's just hope Jackie can think of something.'

CHAPTER 41

They remained in the room for the rest of the evening, talking about this and that. Fiona was fascinated by the new world she had found herself in and was eager to learn as much as possible from the confines of their sanctuary. She packed away all her electronic equipment in the closet, leaving only the portable television and her keyboard-computer on the desk. It took less than sixty seconds for her to hack into the city's cable TV network and for hours she sat transfixed by music videos, sports, documentaries, and soap operas. She asked questions endlessly. Who's that guy? What does that joke mean? What's a Sasquatch? What was that song? Can you sing it for me again? Pandora tried to keep up and answer as best she could while Holly sat in the corner sketching on a pad of convent stationery. Once or twice Pandora left the room to knock on Sister Mary's door, but she was not there.

When night fell they washed and dressed in the drab gray nightdresses supplied by the convent. Holly and Fiona spooned on the narrow bed with minimal complaint while Pandora lay on the air mattress beneath a woolen blanket. The dark silence of the room was interrupted at irregular intervals when Fiona posed more questions about America, the planet Earth, and about Pandora and Holly personally. She was thrilled to learn that both sisters were professional artists. 'No one in Farmtown was creative,' she said. 'All anybody cared about was farm shows and speedball.'

That made Pandora thoughtful. Just before she had turned out the light she sneaked a peek at the sketch Holly had spent the evening working on. It was a drawing of their little house in Ojai. The season was springtime, and Pandora was depicted standing on a stool hanging flower baskets along the porch so the house looked to be overflowing with lobelias, petunias and fuchsias. In the street, Holly and Fiona were playing pickle with a baseball. The sketch was a rare insight into Holly's private thoughts and hopes, and she was touched to see that Fiona was already a part of those dreams for the future. For her own part, Pandora found the picture conjured feelings of helplessness and loss she could barely contain. The house no longer belonged to her, and no doubt its contents had been ransacked by the agency for evidence of Holly's power.

While Holly imagined happy times in distant places, Pandora's horizons had shrunk to encompass only the four walls of this tiny convent cell. Her mind was filled with so many worries she hardly knew which to focus on first. Simple things she had once taken for granted, like clean clothing, money in the bank, and a bed of her own to sleep in, now felt like vague dreams only half-remembered. Even those anxieties were swallowed by the more urgent threat of imprisonment and torture at the hands of a government agency gone rogue.

She curled up on the mattress and listened to the distant sounds of the city to ease her mind. After a long silence, Fiona spoke softly. 'Thank you both for rescuing me from Farmtown. Meeting you guys is the best thing that has ever happened to me.'

A gentle knock at the door woke them after midnight. Pandora answered and saw Mother Abigail in the hall. 'Get dressed, all of you. There's something you should see.'

Abigail's office was dimly lit by a student lamp on the desk, where it was evident the Mother Superior had been working late into the night. The lamp cast a pool of golden light onto a five-volume edition of Thomas Aquinas' *Summa Theologica*, heavily annotated and bookmarked, and a legal pad covered in dense handwriting. A CD player on a shelf quietly played Mozart piano sonatas.

The only other source of light was a television which had been concealed behind a wooden panel on the travelers' previous visit. Now it shone harsh bright images that intruded on this serene environment.

Pandora didn't need to ask why Abigail had summoned them here. The TV was muted but the screen showed a 24-hour news channel broadcasting the headlines she had been dreading to see: *Terrorist on the loose in Las Vegas*, and an image of her own face.

'It seems the story you told me about your journey from California was missing some important details,' Abigail said.

Pandora felt the fleeting security of the convent evaporating before her eyes. 'What are they saying about me?'

Abigail picked up a remote and turned on the sound. '...suspected of detonating bombs in three shopping malls, killing two people and injuring seven others. She is also thought to be responsible for several unexplained poisonings in restaurants across Southern California, resulting in multiple hospitalizations including the death of a four-year-old boy. Federal agents now say Pandora Castell has fled to Nevada and may be sleeping rough on the streets of Las Vegas.'

The image changed to the hated visage of Agent Arnold standing beside a patrol vehicle, with the lights of Las Vegas shining behind him. His thumbs were hooked into his belt and his handsome face was set in a mask of professional concern. 'We know Pandora Castell is hiding in this city, but we will find her. She should be considered armed and dangerous, and members of the public are warned against approaching her. The fugitive is believed to be using her disabled sister as a tool to manipulate others into aiding and protecting her. I must repeat that the public should not interact with either of the Castell sisters under any circumstances. Our intelligence suggests the suspect has rigged her sister's body with explosive devices which are set to explode if she feels threatened. If you see either of them, please dial 911 immediately.'

Abigail muted the screen. 'They don't mention Fiona at all. I find that odd. Presumably she is not really your daughter.'

'No, she's not,' Pandora was tired of lying.

'So you picked her up somewhere on your journey?' Abigail said.

'Farmtown.'

'Did you take her from her real family?'

'No.'

Fiona spoke up. 'Pandora and Holly are my real family. Okay, so they're not really my mom and my aunt. They're more than that. And those things the police are saying, they're not true. They just want to catch Holly because they hate her. She's different than they are and that makes them afraid of her. If they knew about me they'd hate me as well.'

'Because you're different?' Abigail said.

Fiona hesitated, reluctant to continue.

'What are you going to do?' Pandora said.

Abigail sighed. 'I must admit, I have serious doubts about the accusations made against you in these news reports. Explosions? Poisonings? It doesn't sound right. You don't look like a terrorist to me. However, I cannot knowingly harbor fugitives in our house and I have a duty to uphold the law.'

'I understand,' Pandora nodded despairingly. 'Will you at least give us a few minutes to get away before you call the police?'

'I'm afraid that may be a moot point,' Abigail said. 'This news program was brought to my attention by one of our sisters, a very special and gifted lady who could also be described as different. She says one of our residents recognized your face and has already telephoned the police.'

'Sister Mary told you?'

'Yes. She also told me some other things which are very strange and that I do not understand. She said the three of you are on some kind of quest; an urgent mission the purpose of which you can barely perceive at present. She said you are fighting a great evil that threatens the fate of entire worlds, and you cannot be allowed to fall into the hands of the men who are pursuing you. She was extremely emphatic on that point. She said Holly mustn't be caught by the man who is telling lies about Pandora on the television, or terrible, awful things will happen. Does any of this make sense to you?'

'Yes, it's true what she said. And she's right that we barely understand what's happening to us. How does Sister Mary know these things?'

'That is not entirely clear,' Abigail said. 'Eight hundred years ago, Saint Thomas Aquinas wrote about people who are born with special gifts that allow them to know hidden things, bilocate, or to manipulate matter at a distance. He speculated these abilities were not acquired by witchcraft or by consorting with demons, but were instead natural powers granted as a gift from God. He called these gifts Natural Prophecy, and they may manifest in many ways. In Sister Mary's case, it is the ability to know the truth in the mind of another person.'

'You mean she doesn't just read thoughts,' Pandora said. 'She can tell if those thoughts are truthful?'

'Exactly. I have learned to listen very carefully to what Sister Mary says when her gift is active.'

'I'm sorry I lied to you about our reason for being here. If we had told you the truth, you wouldn't have believed me.'

'Sometimes the truth can be dangerous,' Abigail said. 'That is why Sister Mary is so careful with her gift. In any case, it is her good report of you which has informed the action I am about to take. I have told you I cannot harbor fugitives from the law, but perhaps there is something else I can do to help. Go back to your room and gather your belongings, then meet me in the foyer.'

It did not take long for the travelers to collect their meager possessions from the tiny cell. When they reached the staircase, Holly tapped Pandora urgently on the shoulder and looked out through the window. The lights of the casinos and hotels on the Strip cast a haze against the night sky. Nearer to the convent a different cluster of flashing lights caught their attention.

'Police cars,' Pandora said, leaning close to the window. 'God, there are so many of them.'

Sirens could be heard distantly as the cavalcade raced down the street towards them. Fiona took Pandora's hand and pulled her away. 'They'll be here in a few minutes. Come on, we have to go.'

Mother Abigail was in the lobby giving orders to a group of sisters. 'Secure the outer doors and the fire escapes. Close the hallway doors and lock them. Keep the residents in their rooms until I say otherwise.' The sisters scattered one by one and hurried to obey, drawing heavy bolts across external doors and locking window casements. Abigail faced the travelers when they arrived at the foot of the stairs. 'We are accustomed to unwanted visits from pimps, gangs, and abusive partners. This house is quite a fortress despite its humble appearance. We've never tried to keep out government agents before, so this will be an interesting test case.'

Through the window to the day warden's office, Pandora saw Sister Gabriela unlock a wall cabinet and pull out a pump-action shotgun with a pistol grip.

'You have guns?' Pandora said in amazement.

Abigail spoke in the authoritative tones of one reciting solemn church doctrine. '"The use of arms to repel aggressors is not only a right but a grave duty for one entrusted with the lives of others." Catechism of the Catholic Church, paragraph 2265.' She turned to the big sister as she came out brandishing the shotgun. 'Sister Gabriela, that weapon is only to be used as a visual reminder that we are law-abiding citizens on private property. If these officers of the law have a valid warrant, you will have no choice but to grant them entry, but do so slowly and with poor grace. Pretend to be deaf, or shout at them in Spanish. Do you understand?'

Gabriela nodded curtly and took up station beside the front door.

The sound of sirens was near. Abigail marched the travelers down one of the long residential corridors. A sister was barking at residents to get back in their rooms, but still a few women lingered in open doorways. Katrina was there, leaning against the doorpost to her room. Pandora was overcome by anger. She seized Katrina by the hair and threw her against the wall. 'It was you, wasn't it? You called the police. Why did you do it? Look at me. Do you really believe I'm a terrorist?'

Katrina's self-confident sneer was gone. She looked like she had been crying. 'There's a reward for your arrest. Did you know that? A hundred thousand dollars. Do you know what that kind of money means for someone like me? I can go far away from this place. Start a new life in a place nobody knows me.'

From the foyer came a hammering on the convent door. A man's voice boomed. 'Federal agents. Open the door.'

'There's no time for this,' Abigail said. 'Please, come with me.'

Pandora relinquished her hold on Katrina and turned away. At the end of the hall was the kitchen, where two sisters were dragging a heavy refrigerator across the room.

Where the refrigerator had been was a panel in the floor. Abigail bent down and lifted it, revealing a ladder leading down into darkness. 'This is an access hatch leading to the storm drains under the city. Quickly, you have to get out now so we can hide the hatch before Sister Gabriela is obliged to let our visitors inside.'

A loud crash came from the foyer. There was a clamor of voices and Sister Gabriela shouted. 'No warrant, no entry. You can't come in here.'

Agent Arnold's voice was recognizable through the din. 'Get out of my way you fat whore.'

Holly pushed Fiona towards the hole while Pandora turned to Abigail. 'Thank you for this.'

'Just be safe,' Abigail said. 'Stay together, and look after each other.'

Pandora raced down the ladder as the hatch swung shut and plunged them into darkness.

CHAPTER 42

The storm drains were broad rectangular tunnels of concrete that formed a shadowy underworld of darkness and dank air. They were not at all like the Astari bunkers beneath Farmtown, pristine and hermetically sealed for untold millennia. The floor was uneven, covered with sand and gravel washed into banks and reefs by the floods that swept under the city towards Lake Mead. There was no light, and Pandora could only locate her companions by the splashing of their feet in the ankle-deep waters that swirled around them.

'Is everyone okay?' Pandora said. 'Hold my hands, both of you. Come to the sound of my voice.'

'I'm okay, I'm here,' Fiona said. 'I've got Holly beside me.'

'Alright. We'd better get as far away from this access hatch as possible, just in case Agent Arnold discovers it.'

'The water is flowing this way, to our right.'

'Then let's follow the water and see where it takes us.'

They made slow progress sloshing through the tunnels for what seemed like miles. The drains were strewn with unseen obstacles, discarded shopping carts and bicycles that barked shins and twisted ankles, rotting garbage bags that clogged the passageways, creating dams that had to be waded through to reach the other side. They advanced in line abreast, holding hands to avoid losing each other. When they encountered a junction of two tunnels Fiona waded out ahead to determine the direction of the water's flow before continuing. Eventually she cried out. 'Hey, I think I see light up ahead.'

Pandora squinted into the inky blackness. 'Really? Your eyes must be better than mine. I'm still as blind as a bat.'

'Yeah, come on. I can see a clear path ahead.' They made better progress as Fiona guided them around the tunnel's obstructions until Pandora began to perceive the gray concrete of the walls and the shimmering waters around her feet. It was not daylight that lit their way, but the diffuse lights of the city's nightlife filtering through an opening somewhere up ahead. They could hear the city now, the rumbling of truck tires on tarmac and the blaring of horns.

There were people down here in this godforsaken place. On shoals of sand rising above the waters, tents and other primitive shelters had been erected. Plastic boxes stacked against the walls held pitiful collections of rags, food and bedding. People squatted in the shadows, muttering quietly to one another. Eyes flashed towards the travelers as they passed.

'Who are these people?' Fiona whispered, clutching Pandora's hand tightly.

'The mole people,' Pandora replied. 'Homeless people who live in the tunnels.'

'Are they dangerous?'

'No, just unhappy.'

The mouth of the tunnel opened onto a rocky slope where the muddy flood waters trickled down into the Las Vegas Wash. Above them was a busy road, and Pandora guided her companions across the stony ground to the bridge where the street crossed the Wash. There she found a concrete alcove that looked dry and secure. She sat down and declared it was time to rest until daylight.

'This is my fault,' Fiona said. 'I promised you your

phone call would be safe, but the agency traced us to Las Vegas.'

'No, Fiona, it's not your fault.' Pandora put her arm around the girl and squeezed her shoulder. 'Without your help we would never have been able to contact Jackie.'

'But what good will that do? She can't help us here, can she?'

Pandora didn't know how to reply to that. She had been counting on Jackie to figure out a plan to fight the agency and provide a safe haven while the legal wheels were set in motion. Now they were on the run once more, and Jackie had no way to find them. They were as helpless now as they had been on arrival in Las Vegas; more so, because now Pandora could not risk showing her face in public for fear of being recognized.

'Maybe we could try again?' Fiona said. 'If we find another phone, and if I can get some more equipment, we could call Jackie again. I'll be more careful this time.'

'No, it's too dangerous,' Pandora said. 'We'll have to think of another plan.'

'Like what?'

'I'm not sure yet. Let me think for a while.'

By the time the sun rose Pandora had devised a plan of sorts, but it was a feeble plan in which she placed little faith. So ashamed was she of its weaknesses and faults she could not bring herself to explain it fully to her companions as she roused them from a light doze.

When Mother Abigail bid her a final farewell she had pushed something into Pandora's hand. In the haste of their departure she had no time to examine it and thrust it into her pocket. In the early morning sun she saw it was a wad of folded banknotes. Two hundred dollars in total. It was more than enough to enact the plan she had in mind. She took her companions up the slope to the road intersection where they saw a cheap hotel, a Burger King and a 7-Eleven. They were all filthy and wet from their nighttime exodus but Fiona looked the most presentable, the grime giving her the aura of a Dickensian street urchin. Pandora gave her fifty dollars and pushed her in the direction of the convenience store. She returned ten minutes later carrying two shopping bags and they returned to their alcove under the bridge to examine her purchases.

Fiona had bought three sets of shorts and t-shirts and three pairs of sneakers. They got dressed into clean dry clothes and ate packaged sandwiches and drank Cokes from the other bag. After they had eaten, Pandora gave Fiona another wad of notes and dispatched her and Holly together to a taxi stand outside the hotel. She watched nervously from across the street and was greatly relieved when the cab sped away with both of them in the back seat. With Fiona and Holly out of the city, and more importantly away from her, she felt much more relaxed.

She waited for an hour under the bridge and then put on a baseball cap and a pair of dark glasses Fiona had bought from the convenience store and went to the taxi rank. The driver took her fare without a second glance and they drove south on I-15. On the outskirts of the city they left the interstate and rode a two-lane blacktop out into the desert. The road was dusty and cracked, and the cab's wheels made a rhythmic *thud-thud*, *thud-thud* over the broken surface that sounded to Pandora like the beating of her own heart.

The miles passed monotonously and after a while a strange sight came into view. In the desert it is impossible to judge scale or distance, and the mountains ahead could have been a mile away or a hundred miles. Somewhere in the broad expanse of dust between the cab and the horizon a cluster of seven tall pillars rose from the desert sands. They were composed of boulders stacked neatly on top of each other, and as the cab grew nearer, tiny dots could be seen moving through the scrub at their base. These specks were early morning tourists, come to visit this unique oddity placed in the middle of nowhere by Nevada's Arts Board. At last the cab turned into a dusty parking area where half a dozen rental cars were parked. Pandora paid the driver and started searching for her companions. An unmade track led out into the desert where the bizarre art installation was located. She followed a group of dawdling tourists, trying to avoid drawing attention to herself by not seeming in a hurry.

Holly was carrying Fiona on her shoulders, and the youngster shouted directions as they weaved between the pillars. Each tower was constructed of car-sized boulders weighing ten or twenty tons apiece. The stacks would have been remarkable enough by themselves, but the artist had made the creative decision to color each boulder in lurid Day-Glo paint that reflected the sunlight in vivid shades of pink, green, orange and blue.

When Fiona spotted Pandora she steered Holly towards her. 'Wow, this place is cool. What is all this?'

Despite all her worries Pandora couldn't help but smile at the sight of her sister carrying Fiona. 'This place is called Seven Magic Mountains. It's a sculpture that's supposed to represent artificiality in a natural environment.'

'Oh. So why did we come here?' Fiona said.

Pandora guided them away from the tourists into the scrub a little apart from the pillars. Fiona climbed down from Holly's shoulders and they huddled close while Pandora spoke. 'Look, guys, I gotta be honest with you. Coming here is a bit of a desperate gamble. We've got to find some way to contact Jackie, but I don't want to risk making another phone call. Jackie travels all over the country to buy art and visit exhibitions, and this place is a regular pilgrimage for her.'

Fiona nodded in understanding. 'So if Jackie goes to the convent and finds we're not there, she might come out here to look for us.'

'It's a slim chance, but it's the only plan we've got,' Pandora said.

'So why did we have to come in separate cars?'

'By now Agent Arnold will have interrogated Katrina, God help her. That means he knows we're now traveling as a trio. By arriving in different cars we're avoiding any suspicion from cab drivers who might have seen the news reports.'

'Okay, so we just wait.'

So they waited. There were no visitor facilities at the sculpture; no restrooms, no gift shop, no seating area, and no shade. They wandered around the pillars for an hour until the sun grew too hot, then returned to the parking lot and sat in the shadow of a tour bus that had arrived carrying a dozen Japanese families. When the Japanese departed an hour later they had no shelter of any kind and Fiona began to complain of being thirsty.

Pandora started to wonder if she had made a terrible mistake. If Jackie did not come then they would be stranded in the middle of the desert with no way back to civilization. They had no way to call for another taxi, and it was too risky to beg a ride from the tourists who were already beginning to cast suspicious glances in their direction.

Some time mid-afternoon, a large Airstream motorhome turned into the lot from the direction of Las Vegas. Pandora glanced hopefully towards it as a potential source of shade, but leapt to her feet when she saw the driver.

'Jackie, over here!' she waved.

The RV lurched clumsily to a halt. The door flew open and Jackie shot out as if propelled by a rocket. 'Pandora, Holly, oh my girls you have no idea how glad I am to see you.' Jackie entangled the sisters in a three-way hug.

'I can't believe you found us,' Pandora said. 'I honestly thought the police would have to identify our skeletons from dental records if we had to walk back to the city.'

'I drove all night and got to the convent first thing this morning,' Jackie said. 'There was the most terrifying woman at the front door. When I mentioned your names I thought she was going to assault me. I got whisked up to the Mother Superior's office faster than a greased pig and spent twenty minutes trying to persuade her that I wasn't some sinister government agent. In the end I showed her photographs of us together in our skivvies on Venice Beach and that finally convinced her. But all she could tell me was that you'd escaped in the night when the agency raided the place. Thank God you had the same thought I did about these rocks.'

Fiona spoke for the first time. 'The rocks are awesome. How come they don't fall over?'

Jackie stared at the girl. 'And who might you be?'

'This is Fiona,' Pandora said. 'We brought her here from Entara.'

Jackie's jaw hung loose in amazement. 'You're from the other world?'

'Yup. Totally,' Fiona said.

Pandora tutted. 'One day on Earth and already she talks like a valley girl.'

Horns blared from the road. In her rush to greet her friends, Jackie had halted the colossal silver Airstream halfway through the entrance to the parking lot and was blocking traffic.

'You can explain all this later,' Jackie said. 'Right now we should get you all out of public view.'

Turning the Airstream around was like taxiing a jumbo jet, but within minutes they were back on the road. Jackie took one last glance out of the window at the Seven Magic Mountains and sighed wistfully. 'I never miss a chance to see them, you know. I'm spoiled rotten in my little gallery in Ojai, surrounded by the best art being produced in America today. Sometimes I need to put that in perspective, so I always make time at least once a year to come out here and reflect upon something truly hideous.'

CHAPTER 43

Pandora occupied the passenger seat while Holly and Fiona made themselves comfortable in the luxurious dinette behind the driver's seat. Jackie drove south towards the California border, opening a window and lighting one of her gold-tipped Black Russian cigarettes.

'I made some rapid plans yesterday after you called,' Jackie said. 'I booked plane tickets to London and drove to LAX in my car. Then I skipped out of the airport and took a taxi to a friend's house. He's away on business but I have the keys so I borrowed his camper van. It can't be traced back to me so there's no way the agency knows I'm here. I even abandoned my mobile phone in case they're tracking it.'

'That's smart, but where do we go from here?' Pandora said. 'California will be no safer for us than Nevada right now.'

'We're not going to California. I have an old friend in Colorado who'll take you in for a few days. He's a bit of a strange fish, very reclusive, but he's a good man and you'll be safe with him.'

'Colorado? Jackie, I hate to tell you this but the Centennial State is about six hundred miles thataway,' Pandora said, thumbing over her shoulder in the direction they had just come.

'Well, obviously. But I daren't take you three anywhere near Las Vegas because that's where the agency goons will be looking for you. We're going to have to take the scenic route. Aha, here's our turnoff.' Jackie swung the Airstream off the tarmac onto an unmade track, barely more than a gap in the desert scrub. 'This little detour will give you plenty of time to fill me in on your adventures in distant galaxies.'

So Pandora recounted everything that had happened to them since the agency raided Jackie's house four days ago. As the tale approached the present Fiona joined in the narrative, giving her unique perspective on their experiences. Jackie listened in astonished silence, chain-smoking endlessly and speaking only to express amazement or to voice an incoherent expletive. When it was revealed Fiona was one of the feared auto-appliances constructed by the wizard Flak, Jackie slammed on the brakes and the Airstream juddered to a halt in the dust. She bounded out of the RV and marched out into the desert. A hundred yards away from the bus she started pacing around in circles, muttering to herself and kicking at shrubs.

Pandora followed after her but stopped a short distance away. 'Jackie? Are you okay?' she called tentatively.

'No, I'm not,' Jackie said with an anguished expression. 'Pandora, it's all too much to take in. Other worlds, ancient ruins, a psychotic wizard, killer robots. My brain won't process it, won't believe it.'

'You think we're making all this up?'

'No!' Jackie halted her pacing and pulled at the roots of her hair. 'It's just… It's just I need something more than words. I saw you vanish from under that scaffolding in Ojai so I know there's truth in what you're saying, but this is all just too incredible.' Holly and Fiona had caught up and stood nearby. Jackie pointed at Fiona. 'This girl. She's one of those... those... *things*?'

Pandora shook her head firmly. 'No. She's different. Fiona saved our lives and she helped us to contact you. Without her we wouldn't be here.'

Jackie clawed at her face in bewilderment. She seized Holly's shoulders and shook her. 'Holly, darling, is all this really true? I know you can't tell me, but you can show me, can't you? Take me to this magical world of yours and stop my brain throwing up all these useless doubts.'

She screwed her eyes shut and held Holly's hands in a vice-like grip. Holly's mouth opened and closed helplessly and she looked to her sister in despair. Pandora put a hand on Jackie's arm. 'Jackie, I don't think Holly can take you there. I think maybe her gift has a limited number of uses, or maybe she's prevented from blinking us into dangerous places.'

Jackie let out a long breath and relinquished her hold on Holly. 'I had a feeling that might be the case. I'm sorry, Holly, I didn't mean to put you in an awkward position.'

'You're overwrought,' Pandora said. 'You've been driving all day. Why don't you let me take over and you can have a rest?'

'Yes, maybe that would be best,' Jackie said softly and wiped her nose on a tissue. They turned back towards the Airstream only to have their path blocked by Holly. She held her hands out, cupped one on top of the other as if she had somehow caught a butterfly in this desolate place.

'What is it, Holly?' Pandora said.

Holly drew her hands apart, revealing a shimmering object that hovered in the air, levitating with no visible means of support.

Jackie gasped. 'My God, what is that?' She leaned close to examine the triangle of reflective metal as it slowly rotated in the air.

Pandora recognized it at once. 'It's a piece of the crashed transit sphere. I had no idea Holly had taken it. She must have had it in her pocket the whole time.'

'It's not possible,' Jackie said, tapping the shard with her finger.

'You certainly can't get one of these in a Vegas novelty shop.'

Holly plucked the fragment out of the air and pressed it

into Jackie's hand.

'For me?' Jackie said.

'Better than a postcard, right?' Pandora said.

They returned to the bus and Pandora took the driving seat while Jackie sat beside her and stared at the alien artifact floating in the air. The track took them through a mountain pass, beyond which they drove for mile after mile between fields of solar panels. They came upon a road almost without warning. Pandora steered the Airstream up a low rise, and when they reached the top four lanes of desert highway appeared out of nowhere, stretching from horizon to horizon.

Jackie reached for a map and tapped it with satisfaction. 'Aha. Exactly where I thought it would be. This is Highway 95. We turn south here, then skirt the California border and turn east.'

It had taken hours to crawl through the desert and Jackie was satisfied they had thrown off any potential pursuit, but Pandora felt nervous as the highway took them back towards civilization. Soon the casinos and hotels of Laughlin, the tiny simulacrum of Las Vegas, appeared in the distance. It took only moments to drive through the unincorporated town towards the Colorado River. Pandora cringed in the driving seat when she saw a police car sitting at the near end of the Laughlin bridge. The officer in the patrol car took no notice as they glided across the river into Arizona.

An hour later they stopped for fuel at a gas station. Pandora hid in the bus while her companions went into the garage and returned with supplies for their journey. Jackie reported that there was no sign of Pandora in any of the papers on the newsstand, but they wasted no time returning to the road. They ate on the move, with Pandora and Jackie taking turns at the wheel while Holly and Fiona made toasted sandwiches in the Airstream's galley.

It was a golden desert evening, and they were traveling on Route 66. Holly leaned across the transmission tunnel between the front seats and found a radio station playing rock 'n' roll. With the windows down and the music playing Pandora could almost believe they were on vacation and she began to relax. The landscape turned greener as they headed east, and there was an increasing abundance of trees. Signs of human habitation appeared on both sides as they approached Flagstaff, where they turned off the highway to avoid the urban areas.

Just after sunset they arrived at a lookout on a high slope north of Flagstaff and stopped for the night. Pandora took Holly into the rear cabin and removed her bandages. The wounds on her chest were healing nicely and the cuts on her hands hardly needed tending anymore. She smeared them with antiseptic cream and left the bandages off.

When they returned to the front cabin they found Jackie and Fiona sitting outside on camping chairs. Jackie was introducing Fiona to the concept of root beer, and had stronger drinks waiting for her companions. They drank beers and watched the shimmering lights of the city while Pandora completed the rest of her tale, bringing Jackie up to the moment they reunited at Seven Magic Mountains.

'You've had an incredible journey,' Jackie said at the end. 'I'm sorry I doubted you earlier.'

'It's okay,' Pandora said. 'I hardly believe any of it myself.'

'Well it certainly seems like the agency believes in Holly's power. They must be expending massive resources to chase you down.'

'I'm really grateful you came to rescue us,' Pandora said. 'I'm sorry to place this burden on you, Jackie, but we need your help. I don't think we can trust anyone else to take our side.'

'Darling, I'll do anything I can,' Jackie said. 'I wish I had better news to deliver. I've spent the past few days phoning every judge I can reach to get your arrest warrant revoked and your assets returned to you. Every single judge I've called has refused to speak to me. Some of them hang up as soon as I even mention the National Counter-Terrorism Agency. Whoever is pulling the strings behind all this is very powerful indeed. Pandora, those judges were *frightened.*'

'But there must be something we can do. We can't fight an organization like the agency except through official channels.'

'Don't worry, I haven't exhausted all our options yet. These federal agencies are powerful, but ultimately they're just Byzantine bureaucracies run by pen-pushers. As soon as we find the right legal clause and the right judge, we'll have them running for cover.'

'I hope you're right.'

Jackie squeezed her hand. 'Everything will be alright, I promise. At Harvard I was taught that justice moves slowly, but it moves in the right direction. Even after all I've seen, I still hold to that principle.'

CHAPTER 44

The next day Jackie took the wheel once more and they headed north on Highway 89. The ground turned dry again as they passed through Arizona's Painted Desert. Just before noon they crossed a ravine that would eventually widen to become the Grand Canyon far to the west. After a whole day's travel they completed the long loop they had taken to avoid Las Vegas, and it seemed impossible the agency could be on their trail. The mood in the Airstream lifted as they turned east on 160 past Monument Valley towards the intersection of Arizona, Colorado, New Mexico and Utah. Jackie challenged her companions to hold their breath for the entire journey through New Mexico. They had almost reached the end of the mile-long stretch of road when Holly started pelting Fiona with Cheez-Its. Fiona retaliated with Cracker Jacks and by the time the chaos died down they were ten miles inside Colorado.

From then on, the road seemed always to go up. Steep slopes on either side were blanketed in dense forests of ponderosa pine and Douglas-firs. Before long they saw distant peaks capped with snow.

They stopped for fuel at a gas station, and when Jackie returned her expression was grave. She spread a copy of USA Today across the dinette table to reveal Pandora's face prominently featured on the front page. 'Your story has gone national.'

Pandora clenched her fists and let out a deep breath. 'I feel like a noose is tightening around my neck.'

'Don't let this get to you,' Jackie said. 'They're trying to make you panic, to provoke you into making a mistake. Just stay calm and stay out of sight. Leave everything else to me.'

They traveled in subdued silence for a long time. Holly stared out of the window and Fiona read magazines Jackie had bought for her at the gas station, devouring as much as she could of American culture.

Pandora went up front to sit beside Jackie. 'What can you tell me about this friend of yours we're going to visit?'

Jackie took a moment to collect her thoughts. 'Well, let's see. His name is Harfield Bennish. I met him way back in Boston, many years ago. He has a summer house here in Colorado where he spends most of his time these days. It's a very remote house, so you won't have to hide yourself away.'

'Sounds good to me,' Pandora said. 'What does he think about hiding a fugitive from the law?'

'Harfield doesn't have a television, much less the Internet, so it's unlikely he will have seen the news.'

'But how did he react when you told him we were coming?'

Jackie hesitated and bit her lip. 'Well, Harfield doesn't exactly have a telephone, either.'

Pandora gaped at her. 'You haven't told him we're coming?'

'Don't panic, everything will be okay. Once we've explained everything to him, I'm certain he'll take your side.'

'Oh Jackie, I'm not sure this is such a good idea.'

'Trust me,' Jackie patted her knee. 'Harfield is a good man.'

The road took them higher and higher. They were somewhere far up in the north west of the state when they passed through the small town of Zenith nestled in a deep valley. Not far beyond the city limits, Jackie slowed the Airstream to a crawl, leaning forward in the seat and mumbling to herself.

'It's somewhere along this road, I'm certain.'

'When was the last time you were here?' Pandora asked.

'The last time? Oh, I'm not sure. Twenty years. Maybe more.'

'Oh my God, you mean you haven't spoken to this friend of yours for two decades?'

'I thought I told you to stop worrying.'

They were inching along a winding stretch of forest road, flanked by grand Douglas-firs towering above a dense understory of ferns. Without warning Jackie slammed on the brakes and the Airstream lurched to a halt. She put the bus in reverse and backed up fifty yards. Hidden amid the sword ferns and vine maple was a narrow gap through which a single-lane track could be seen. Jackie reached through the window and parted the leaves, revealing an old wooden sign with faded lettering. *Blackthorn House – Private No Entry.*

Jackie needed the entire road to maneuver the bus between the trees and onto the track. Branches scraped the Airstream's bare metal sides with a screeching sound that set Pandora's teeth on edge. It was dark in this tunnel-like passage and they drove for several minutes in an eerie twilight.

At last they broke through the constricting forest and emerged onto a wide mountain prairie. So sudden was the transition from darkness to light that Pandora gasped in surprise at the vista before them. They entered a rolling land of meadows and pastures bordered by dagger-like mountains sprinkled with snow. The plain had been neatly organized into square ranges marked by miles of split rail fencing. Every enclosure was aglow with wildflowers, purple lupines, golden sunflowers, Indian paintbrushes in crimson and orange, and larkspurs in blue and pink. The deep blue sky looked somehow closer here, and white tufts of clouds mingled between the jagged peaks.

'It's beautiful,' Pandora said while Fiona and Holly crowded between the front seats. 'It's like we're on top of the world.'

'Yes, it is beautiful,' Jackie said with a sigh. 'There's old money here, you know. Harfield's family goes back a long way. Look, there's the house.'

At the center of the prairie was a Colonial-style mansion that must once have been very grand, though now the paint was peeling and unsightly brown creepers clung to the walls. The Airstream rocked over potholes in the rutted track, and Jackie brought them to a rest in a wide turnaround overrun by weeds.

Jackie seemed disturbed by the house's shabby appearance as they got out of the bus, though she tried to hide it from her companions. They climbed the steps of the portico and rang the bell. Paint was flaking off the door and lay crumbling amid pine needles on the scuffed planks of the porch.

When there was no reply at the door, Jackie said, 'Wait here. I'll check around the back.'

Moments later the front door opened and they were faced by an old man wearing threadbare tweeds, puffing a large cigar. Despite his age he had a mop of yellow hair that lent a youthful vigor to his appearance. He regarded his visitors with bemusement. 'You must be lost. Turn around and go back down the trail, turn right, turn right again, and don't stop until you reach Zenith. Then you can find your way to wherever it is you're going.' He spoke in a refined northeastern accent that made him sound like an old-fashioned movie star.

He moved to turn away but Pandora called him back. 'Mr Bennish? Harfield Bennish?'

He studied her with curiosity, drawing thoughtfully on his cigar. 'Do I know you?'

Jackie reappeared from the side of the house and stopped at the foot of the steps. 'Harfield?'

The old man's surprise was obvious. 'Jackie? To what do I owe this unexpected pleasure?'

Jackie looked emotional, and Pandora got the impression she was struggling to maintain her composure. There was an awkward standoff while both parties stared at each other across the threshold.

'I need your help, Harfield,' Jackie blurted out. 'Please let us come inside and I'll explain everything.'

The interior of Blackthorn House was excessively masculine to Pandora's mind, all dark wood and bearskin rugs without a feminine touch anywhere to be seen. The hall was lofty but dark, with many portals leading to spacious chambers dimly perceived in shafts of sunlight sparkling through the cloud of cigar smoke and dust.

Jackie walked around, touching objects as if bringing old memories back to life. 'The house is a state,' she declared, running her finger along a table and displaying the dust for all to see. 'I knocked on the servants' door but no one answered. Where's Isabella?'

Harfield had been leading his guests towards the kitchen but stopped in his tracks and turned slowly. 'Jackie, Isabella died. Four years ago.'

Jackie staggered, gripping the table for support. 'Died?'

'She had a stroke,' Harfield said. 'I drove her into Zenith and woke Doc Masters at three am. He called the air ambulance and took her to the hospital in Grand Junction, but it was too late. I'm sorry.'

Jackie was visibly shaken and turned away, marching out of the hall and out of sight. Harfield ushered the rest of them into the kitchen and began arranging bone china mugs patterned in navy and gold on the central island.

'Not accustomed to guests these days,' he said. 'Might take me a moment to find everything we need. Now then: Coffee. Almost certainly instant, hope that's acceptable?'

He started opening cabinet doors, revealing dusty

shelves stocked with antique kitchenware. On the fifth try he discovered an earthenware pot marked coffee but found it to be empty. 'No luck there, I'm afraid. Tea it is, then.'

Tea proved similarly elusive. Finally Harfield opened a drawer and withdrew a bottle of bourbon. 'Ah, well, needs must as the devil drives,' he said, uncorking the bottle. 'What do you say?'

Holly held out her mug eagerly and Pandora snatched it from her hands. 'Just tap water is fine for us, really.'

Jackie returned and all eyes turned towards her. Her face was puffy and her eyes were red as if she had been crying. She laid the copy of USA Today on the table and pushed it towards Harfield. 'Read this.'

Harfield leaned his back against the counter and read slowly, with a furrowed brow. When he was done he folded the paper neatly on the table. 'Seems like you're a busy young woman, Miss Castell.'

'Pandora is completely innocent of all these atrocious crimes,' Jackie said.

'Of course she is,' Harfield said dismissively. 'Extenuating circumstances, a difficult family situation, drug addiction. You were always one for lost causes, Jackie. Every stray murderer, bank robber, and drug dealer was just a misguided soul waiting for the right opportunity to redeem themselves, isn't that right?'

'No, not this time,' Jackie said. 'This time there'll be no bargaining with the prosecution or the judge, no impassioned pleas to the jury. This time, a federal agency has gone completely insane and has pursued this totally innocent woman and her family halfway across America. They have taken away her home and seized her bank accounts. If they catch her, they will detain her indefinitely without trial. They raided my house without a warrant and knocked me unconscious with the butt of a rifle, then they bugged my phones and followed me wherever I went. I complained to a dozen judges who became almost hysterical with fear when I mentioned the NCA.'

Harfield's cigar had gone out and he lit it with a match.

'So why come to me?'

'Because I'm desperate,' Jackie said. 'Because something deeply wrong is happening and I don't know what to do about it. I want you to look after Pandora, Holly and Fiona. Give them a safe place. Give them a home until I can get their real home back for them.'

Harfield studied Pandora through a cloud of tobacco smoke. Pandora stepped forward. 'Mr Bennish, I don't expect you to believe this, but it's not really me the police are after, it's my sister. Holly has a special gift that the NCA wants to control. If you think I'm a criminal I'll leave here right now and turn myself into the police, but please let my sister and Fiona stay with you.'

Harfield turned his attention on Holly, walking around her, looking her up and down. 'A special gift, you say?'

Jackie slammed her hand onto the table. 'Harfield, if you say something inappropriate I swear I will strangle you to death right here in this kitchen.'

Harfield balked at the vehemence of Jackie's words, but he recovered quickly. 'Well, we can't have that. I make a point of never being murdered before dinner.'

Jackie let out a long sigh that seemed to hold a lifetime of pain. 'Please, just say yes. Don't ask questions. Sometimes there aren't any answers. Just. Say. Yes.'

Harfield meditated on his cigar for a long while. 'You can stay. All of you. The guest rooms will need airing, and I don't suppose there's any clean linen.'

CHAPTER 45

Harfield retreated into the library and read newspapers in a haze of smoke while Jackie escorted the travelers upstairs. The bedrooms were opulent, but had clearly been uninhabited for years. White sheets covered everything, and the floorboards creaked and groaned underfoot, giving the place a ghostly atmosphere. Jackie assigned rooms and then left the others to uncover the furniture and open the windows while she went in search of fresh bed linen. Every dust sheet concealed furnishings that looked immensely old and valuable, but also severely knocked about and neglected, as if the house was a museum that had become the abode of a careless student. In Pandora's room a Queen Anne walnut bureau was stained by coffee rings. Beside Fiona's bed a Louis XV nightstand bore the scars of many cigarette burns.

Jackie returned pushing a service trolley loaded with cleaning products and fresh bedclothes still wrapped in their plastic packaging, and within an hour the bedrooms looked splendid. A quick survey of the kitchen revealed no food worth eating so they stripped the Airstream of all comestibles and cooked a simple but wholesome meal of baked potatoes stuffed with coronation chicken and sour cream.

Drawn by the aroma of cooking, Harfield appeared at the kitchen door with a glass of whiskey in his hand. The tension in the room became palpable as he and Jackie looked at each other with apprehension.

Jackie filled two plates on a tray separate from the others. 'Girls, I have to speak with Harfield alone for a while. I hope you won't be offended if we don't join you for dinner?'

The travelers took their meal outside on the veranda and enjoyed the evening sunshine and mountain air while Jackie and Harfield secluded themselves in the dining room and spoke in hushed tones for the remainder of the evening. When they had eaten Pandora led her companions on an exploration of the grounds. Grand elegance and beauty was juxtaposed with dereliction and decay everywhere they went. A vast stable block housed only two horses who, though apparently healthy, seemed lonely and were inordinately excited to receive this visit from strangers. A tumbledown garage contained an elderly Ford pickup and a shining Cadillac Eldorado that looked like someone had fitted chrome wheels to an aircraft carrier.

They wandered into the fields and lay amid the wildflowers on a bank overlooking the plain while the sun went down. As darkness fell electric lights came on, bathing the house and the driveway in a warm glow.

'We should do something for Mr Bennish,' Fiona said after a long silence. 'Y'know, to say thank you for giving us a home.'

'What would you like to do?' Pandora said.

Fiona shrugged. 'I don't know. He seems sad. We should do something to make him happy.'

'I guess it would be nice to pay for our room and board somehow. Maybe we could fix up the house. Make everything look nice, the way a house like this is supposed to look.'

'How is it supposed to look?' Fiona said.

'I bet if we look in the library we'll find books on old Colonial houses. We could find lots of pictures for inspiration.'

When they returned to the house Harfield was alone in

the library and Jackie was nowhere to be seen. Pandora wanted to speak with Harfield to express her gratitude for giving them shelter, but she found him drunk and insensible with an empty bottle of bourbon on the floor at his feet. Curiosity drew her attention to the newspapers on the desk. Harfield had spent hours poring over these papers, and she suspected he had already known about Pandora's flight from the law before they arrived. A brief review of the front pages reassured her this was not the case. The newspapers were old. Decades old, in fact. *Nixon Sends GIs into Cambodia*, read one headline; *Reagan Scores Solid Victory* said another. It seemed Harfield preferred to live in another era, one that perhaps represented a happier time for him.

The following morning, Jackie took the pickup to Zenith for a shopping trip. The house needed to be stocked with food and other supplies, and each of the travelers required a new wardrobe of clothing to replace the items that had been seized by the agency or left on another world. Pandora lamented the unfair burden of cost this placed on her friend, but Jackie told her not to worry. She stalked into the library and after a short but loud argument with Harfield she returned wielding his Amex Centurion card.

While Jackie was gone, Pandora took the opportunity to speak with Harfield. He was at his habitual spot in the library, surrounded by old newspapers. Already he was nursing a large bourbon despite the early hour. Pandora had a sneaking suspicion he hadn't moved from the chair since last night.

He waved away Pandora's offer of thanks and directed her to sit down. 'Jackie explained some of your situation last night,' he said. 'It certainly sounds like you're a victim of injustice.'

'She told you what's happening to us?' Pandora said.

'She told me a wild and unbelievable story that no sane person would credit, yes.'

'I agree it's unbelievable, but it's true. You don't seem

troubled by it.'

Harfield shrugged. 'Jackie is an intelligent and emotionally stable woman, not given to hysterics. If she says you've ridden a tornado to Oz, who am I to argue?'

'I'm very relieved to hear you say that,' Pandora said.

'There are more things in heaven and earth, Horatio, than are dreamt of in your philosophy. Besides, none of that mumbo-jumbo matters to me. I would have let you stay even if you were a terrorist who blows up shopping malls and poisons children.'

'Because of Jackie?'

'Because of Jackie.'

'If you don't mind my asking, what's the relationship between you?'

Harfield grinned. 'She's my daughter.'

Pandora was startled. 'Your daughter? But Jackie's English. She only came to America after she graduated Oxford—'

'Not true,' Harfield interrupted. 'Jackie is as American as Uncle Sam, and a whole lot prettier. She grew up in England, but she was born right here in the good old U-S-of-A.'

Pandora shook her head in wonder. 'She never told me.'

'Then allow me to elucidate.' Harfield topped up his glass with bourbon and poured a second glass for Pandora. When she declined he tipped it into his own glass. 'I spent my youth on the coast of Massachusetts, in an old community called Linden Cove. It's the kind of place where you're considered a foreigner if your family has lived there less than five generations. Every year in late summer the country club held a beach party which was the high point of the social calendar. One time there was a young student there, Zeta Clarington-St James. She was the youngest daughter of an English duke, over here on a gap year and staying with cousins in Linden Cove. Stunningly beautiful, intelligent, opinionated, a raging socialist and political activist. To say our values clashed would be a profound understatement, but that didn't stop us falling madly in love.

'Six months later we found out she was pregnant and there was a scandal. Her father, the duke, arrived from England and offered to skin me alive if I didn't do the honorable thing and marry her. He was a big fellow, a former SAS man who'd done some grisly work in North Africa in World War Two. I don't mind telling you I was terrified, but I told him the idea of marriage was preposterous. Bennish-Clarington-St James? What a mouthful.

'He didn't think that was very funny so we did the only sensible thing and ran away. Zeta gave birth to Jackie on a hippie commune in Santa Barbara. By then we'd had a falling out; those pesky political differences sadly proved insurmountable. I only saw Jackie once before Zeta whisked her away to England.

'I don't know much about Jackie's time in the old country, but occasionally I heard snippets of news. Her mother renounced her noble heritage, shaved her head, and committed herself to being a full-time activist. She traveled around the country in a converted bus protesting whatever was in vogue at the time. She chained herself to a gate at Greenham Common and got arrested at Stonehenge for assaulting a police officer. She didn't have much time for Jackie, I'm afraid, and the poor girl was rather neglected. In the end she got sick of washing in dirty streams and defecating in a bucket. When she was thirteen years old she stole money for a plane ticket, forged a letter of permission from her mother, and turned up on my doorstep in Linden Cove.

'She called me Harfield even then, you know. Something to do with her mother's attitude towards families. Oppressive patriarchal institutions, she called them. Always insisted Jackie call her Zeta, even when she was a little girl. Of course, Jackie and I were almost total strangers, but I soon came to adore her. I doted on her hand and foot, showered her with gifts. I sent her to a fine school in Boston, and we spent vacations here in Colorado, horse riding in summer and skiing in winter. True to my word I never married, but we had a housekeeper called Isabella who came everywhere with us. She was a true mother to Jackie. They were very close. If her real mother cared at all that Jackie had run away, I never heard anything about it. We got an occasional postcard from some protest in South Africa, or the Amazon Rainforest, but that was all.

'We had a turbulent relationship, Jackie and I. More than once she ran out on me, too, and slept on friends' couches, or on the back seats of cars. When she was eighteen I thought I'd lost her for good. She stormed out and took a flight back to England, and I didn't see her for five years. By the time she came back she'd got her double first at Oxford and was looking to continue her studies at Harvard. She might have inherited her liberal values from her mother, but she got her business sense from me, and she had big ambitions to be a top lawyer.

'Things were good between us for a while, but it couldn't last. Jackie disowned me as well as her mother. She moved to New York, married a penniless artist, Edward Layne. They lived in some godawful garret where he painted horrendous pictures while she struggled to find work as an attorney. Graduating Harvard Law *summa cum laude* is all well and good, but New York was overflowing with law graduates in those days; you couldn't cross the street without tripping over them. Worse still she was a woman and a lot of the law firms were still boys-only clubs. I could have helped her, got her on the fast track to become junior partner in a good firm I had some contacts with. She rejected every offer I made. It was as if she relished the gutter-work because she knew I disapproved. Instead she worked as a public defender, representing slum kids who'd been arrested for having an ounce of marijuana in their pocket, or for failing to pay a fine for a traffic violation. She divorced Layne in the end, but kept his name to avoid any association with her past. I never saw her again until yesterday.'

Harfield picked up his glass and frowned as if he didn't remember what it was for.

'So that's why you let us stay,' Pandora said.

'You brought my daughter back to me, and for that I shall be forever grateful.'

The roaring of an engine drew their attention to the window. Jackie was returning in the pickup. She was driving fast, racing down the long driveway, bouncing over the potholes and kicking up dirt from the verges.

'Something's wrong,' Pandora said, and ran to the front door.

CHAPTER 46

Holly and Fiona were already on the porch when Jackie swerved to a halt beside the Airstream. 'What's happened?' Pandora said as Jackie emerged from the cab.

Jackie's face was stricken with worry. She grabbed Pandora's hand, dragged her towards the Airstream and pushed her inside. Holly and Fiona followed close behind and Jackie slammed the door on Harfield as he crowded the entryway.

'Look at this.' Jackie spread a newspaper across the dinette table. It was the Denver Post. Pandora expected to see her own face, accompanied by another rap sheet of her alleged crimes. Instead the news was far worse.

'Oh my God.' Pandora collapsed into a seat, staring at the page.

FIRE DESTROYS LAS VEGAS CONVENT
Clark County Fire Department responded to a fire at the Sisters of the Sacred Heart convent in Las Vegas last night. Units from CCFD encountered intense flames and smoke emanating from the convent building, located in a converted motel in the north of the city. Firefighters were compelled to implement a defensive strategy due to the extreme heat adversely affecting the structural integrity of the building. The fire was prevented from spreading to neighboring structures, but the convent eventually collapsed…

Jackie fumbled with the Airstream's portable television, and the screen flickered into life. She found a news channel showing a reporter standing at the smoking rubble of the convent.

'...more details are now emerging of the tragedy that unfolded last night at the Sisters of the Sacred Heart. Although firefighters were initially told the residents of the convent had been successfully evacuated, it has since come to light that one member of the religious community was still trapped inside. The victim has been named as Sister Mary Bellarmine, a young woman with Down syndrome who had lived at the convent since it was first founded. Investigators from the National Counter-Terrorism Agency believe arson may be the cause of the fire. I have with me NCA Agent Tina Slade, who is leading the investigation.'

When Pandora first met the female accomplice of Agent Arnold she thought Tina Slade was beautiful. Now she saw dark rings around her eyes, hollow cheeks, and the thousand-mile stare that seemed to bore through the camera into her. 'We have arrested the suspected arsonist, Mother Abigail Keanan, the former leader of this religious institution, which sheltered more than two dozen vulnerable women. Survivors of the fire have come forward with credible accusations that Mother Abigail physically and sexually abused the women under her care, and we believe she deliberately started the fire to destroy evidence she knew would convict her of heinous crimes…'

Pandora had heard enough. With a groan borne of fury and despair she flung open the Airstream door and strode away. When she heard Jackie's voice calling her back she broke into a run. There was a gravel track leading towards the forested hills and she ran until the house was hidden behind the trees. The path petered out into nothing and she was lost amid a dense undergrowth of blackthorns crowding her on all sides. Picking up a stout branch, she wielded it like a machete, hacking through the blackthorns, forging a new path past outcroppings of rock that jutted from the earth like warning sentinels. The blackthorns fought against her, clawing at her clothes, her hands, her face. Tears blurred her vision, but she continued onward, blindly flailing with the stick until her blows met with no resistance. She stumbled, but her feet found no ground on which to stand. A hidden ravine, guarded for untold eons by stones and thorns, opened up and swallowed her.

The ground surged up and knocked the breath from her lungs. She lay there gasping, staring up at the sky spinning dizzyingly overhead. A football-sized rock protruded from the ground beside her head. She had avoided death by mere inches.

She gained her feet and surveyed the ravine. She had landed in a small clearing of bare earth beside a babbling brook that cascaded over rough stones from a spring somewhere higher in the mountains. Spray from the turbulent water formed a fine mist that cooled her skin and cast rainbows through the air. She sat on a rock and cried.

After a while Holly arrived, picking her way carefully down into the crevasse. She laid a hand gently on Pandora's shoulder, but she brushed her away and jumped down off the rock.

'The agency are doing this to torment me, aren't they?' she raised her voice to a shout though Holly was right beside her. 'They killed Sister Mary to punish me for trying to escape. They'll kill anyone who tries to help me. I'm sick of it. Sick of it! How can I keep letting people put themselves in danger like this?'

She raged and stormed around the floor of the ravine. She picked up stones and threw them at the trees, the rocks, the river. She tore branches from trees and threw them into the water. Holly listened to her shout and scream, and cried silently.

When her voice was hoarse she dropped to the ground. Her fury had exhausted her, but made no visible difference to the forest which had endured for millions of years. Holly sat beside her and rocked her gently while she cried into her shoulder.

'Are you guys okay?' Fiona appeared at the top of the ridge.

Pandora became self-conscious, ashamed of her outburst. She wiped away her tears and straightened her clothes as the girl nimbly clambered into the ravine.

'I'm so sorry about Sister Mary,' Pandora said when Fiona joined them. 'I know she was your friend.'

Fiona held up the newspaper and brandished it at them. 'No, you don't get it. Sister Mary's not dead.'

Pandora shook her head sadly 'Fiona, she was trapped inside the convent.'

'No body was found,' Fiona insisted, tapping the page. 'Don't you understand? Sister Mary has a gift, just like Holly has a gift. Somehow the agency must have found out. Probably they put bugs around the convent after we escaped and listened to Mother Abigail and Sister Mary talking.'

Pandora realized what she was getting at. 'You think they kidnapped her and burned the convent down to make it look like she died?'

'Exactly. When they discovered about her gift they decided she was a danger to society, just like Holly.'

'A woman who can read thoughts? Yeah, the agency would certainly consider that dangerous. Oh my God, I think you might be right.'

'It makes perfect sense,' Fiona said. 'They faked Sister Mary's death and blamed Mother Abigail.'

Pandora nodded in agreement. 'They must have pressured the residents into making those false accusations against Abigail. Probably a lot of those women have skeletons in their closets that the agency could use to manipulate them.'

'It's exactly what they're doing to you, Pandora. They want everyone to think you're a criminal so when they catch Holly they can sneak her away and claim you killed her.'

Pandora smacked her forehead with her hand. 'Of course, how could I be so stupid? Even if I was arrested, they would have no grounds to detain Holly, and she's the one they're really after.'

'Right, but if everyone thought Holly was dead, no one would ever think she was missing.'

Pandora paced around the clearing, working through the implications of what Fiona had said. 'So the agency is aware of people with special gifts, and actively tracking them down. Holly and Sister Mary are just two, but there might be others as well. So that begs the question: Where did they take Sister Mary? There must be a building or a facility somewhere that the agency uses to imprison people with special gifts.'

'I can find it,' Fiona said emphatically. 'If they've ever used a telephone, or an Internet connection, I can find them.'

Pandora saw the light of hope for the first time. 'Oh my God, if we can prove the agency has abducted Sister Mary and imprisoned her, we can destroy them.'

Holly started clapping her hands, bouncing up and down on her feet like a pogo stick. It was the happiest sound Pandora had ever heard.

CHAPTER 47

Blackthorn House was a busy place for the next few days. Fiona and Jackie journeyed to Zenith and the neighboring towns, collecting electronic junk from thrift stores and yard sales. Holly and Pandora cleared out Blackthorn's cathedral-like attic to make room for all the screens, computer towers, hard drives, satellite receivers, and other gadgets that arrived daily on the back of the pickup.

At the same time, the house underwent a thorough spring cleaning. An industrial carpet cleaner was procured in Zenith, and every item of furniture was removed to the lawn while the floors were scrubbed clean. Curtains were taken down and cleaned, windows were washed, and the kitchen was subjected to an inch-by-inch scouring with powerful chemicals.

The only one who didn't seem busy during this time was Harfield, who moved his favorite wingback chair onto the lawn with all the other library furniture and sat there smoking cigars as if nothing unusual had happened. If he objected to this disturbance to his previously secluded life he gave no sign; in fact he seemed to enjoy having the house populated with women who did all his cooking and cleaning for him. Pandora noticed that his appearance smartened up and he was drinking less, or at least he did his drinking out of sight of the others.

After a week Jackie departed Blackthorn in the Airstream to return to Ojai where she would continue her struggle to find a judge worthy of the name. On the eve of her departure a small party was held in Blackthorn's ballroom. Hundreds of helium balloons were floated around the room, much to the delight of Fiona who had never seen such things. Jazz music played on a wind-up gramophone Holly had discovered in the attic. Even Harfield contributed by venturing into Blackthorn's wine cellar and bringing up a selection of dusty bottles that were probably worth a king's ransom. They toasted to freedom and the destruction of the agency, and Jackie promised to return with good news.

From then on, life settled into a routine. Fiona sequestered herself in the attic, constructing strange machines from the junk she had collected. Holly spent her time in the library, poring over books with titles like *American Colonial House Styles*, *Great American Country Houses*, and *The Essential Guide to American Antiques*. Somewhere in the house she found a supply of paper and pencils and began producing sketches for what looked like a major redesign of Blackthorn's interior spaces. Pandora was curious about her sister's designs, but Holly was shy and secretive about her work and she was only able to catch fleeting looks at her art.

Over the next few weeks, Jackie returned intermittently, always piloting the Airstream which she took on varying routes through the American Southwest to ensure she was not followed. She had no luck persuading a judge to review Pandora's case, but she had made some progress demanding answers from the Department of Justice. She successfully requested a subpoena against the agency, which resulted in a number of substantial file boxes being delivered to her house. She had high hopes that examination of these documents would reveal some bureaucratic legal weakness she could exploit to topple the agency's might.

During these visits Jackie taught Holly and Fiona to

ride the two horses in Blackthorn's stables. The stables themselves were nothing short of spectacular, more like a grand house than a utilitarian structure for animals. An imposing entryway led to wide aisles lit by crystal chandeliers and finely worked skylights. The tack room was like a museum exhibit, and the stalls were of wrought iron with oak infills and brass fixtures. There was even a servants' wing with living quarters for the stable master, grooms, and trainers, though none of these roles had been staffed for many years.

Jackie explained that the Bennish family had been involved in horse racing for generations. Blackthorn House had been built in 1902 by Harfield's grandfather, Samuel, who had the novel intuition that training Thoroughbreds at high altitude would increase their stamina and performance. His theories bore fruit in 1923 when a Bennish horse named Yankee Hero won the Kentucky Derby, the Preakness Stakes, and the Belmont Stakes, becoming one of only fourteen horses ever to win the Triple Crown of American horse racing.

In Blackthorn's heyday there were a hundred horses training on the high prairie, but the Wall Street Crash brought an end to the family's mastery in equine sports. Blackthorn became a financial burden and the stable operations were scaled down while the house itself was left vacant until after the Second World War. Harfield's father Leighton restored the house in the 1950s as a vacation retreat, but the stables never operated on such a grand scale again.

Nowadays, the stables were the only aspect of Blackthorn that received regular care and attention from Harfield, who undertook to feed and exercise the horses himself, and cleaned out their stalls regularly. Despite his obvious affection for the animals, he had never bothered to name them, referring to both simply as "girl". Fiona remedied this during her first riding lesson, christening her horse Cherries for her dark reddish coloration and Holly's horse Rollo for her love of rolling in the long grass when she was released from the stables.

Harfield paid for the girls to be kitted out with helmets, breeches and boots delivered from a specialist outfitter in Denver, and Jackie showed them how to saddle and ride the horses around the training paddock. Holly's natural affinity with animals led her to make rapid progress. Before long she switched from a Western saddle to an English style, and began leading Fiona on longer and longer rides through the prairie without supervision.

Pandora did not participate in these lessons, partly because there were only two horses and partly because she didn't want to intrude on the growing friendship between Holly and Fiona.

'This was a magical place to spend childhood,' Jackie said one morning as they watched Holly and Fiona ride away from the stables. 'I envy Fiona, you know. For her, this is all fresh and new. She's just as excited as I was at thirteen, but she doesn't have to put up with all the emotional baggage from Harfield.'

'Harfield told me a little of how you came to live here with him,' Pandora said. 'I get the impression he left a lot of the important details out.'

Jackie took Pandora's arm and led her on a walk around the stables. 'I left England to escape a mother who was cold and distant. Instead, I got a father who was a drunk and a gambler. Some luck, eh?'

Pandora gave a wry smile. 'I've noticed he always seems to have a bottle nearby. He seems a rather amiable drunk, though. Was he really that bad?'

'He was never violent or abusive,' Jackie said, pointedly. 'I would never have brought you here if I thought Harfield was going to mistreat you, Holly or Fiona. But he was a nightmare to live with. His binges would last for days. It always started with him going to his club in Boston to play poker with his disreputable friends. When they got too rowdy, the club would throw them out, so they'd come back to the house and drink until they all passed out. All except Harfield, that is. He was made of sterner stuff and would still be drinking the following morning when I was getting ready for school. His friends would wake up and start groping me and making lewd comments. That drove Harfield into a rage, and he'd throw them out of the house, warning them never to darken his doorstep again. He was very protective of me, really. It made no difference. After he banished the perverts from the house he would sober up and remember none of it. "Boyish hijinks," he called it. "Nothing for you to worry your pretty head about."

'When he wasn't gambling, he was womanizing. He used to bring home strange women he'd met in bars. They'd hang around the house until he passed out and then steal from him. Isabella and I had to be constantly vigilant for trollops sneaking out of the door carrying priceless heirlooms, gold watches, or jewelry.

'He used to like driving fast at night when he was drunk, and he got involved in several accidents. He should have gone to prison, but he always succeeded in paying off the police because no one got hurt.

'I got tired of it in the end. I went back to England, safe in the knowledge that my mother had abandoned Albion for the distant shores of South America, where she was making a nuisance of herself among the tribes of the Amazon. Oxford was my first taste of ordinary life. I lived in a tiny mews house with three friends. We worked part-time jobs, we met boys, went to parties, and generally had a whale of a time.

'Harfield bombarded me with letters apologizing for his behavior and begging me to come back. Like all drunks, he's a master at making promises he has no intention of keeping. When I finished at Oxford, I was desperate to study at Harvard, and I made the mistake of accepting his offer of free accommodation. Harvard was stunningly difficult. The work was so hard, and so time-consuming, that I became dependent on Harfield for money and support. At first, I thought everything would be alright, but then all his old habits came back with a vengeance.

'One night, he picked up a woman in a bar. Her name was Sophie Everett. She was twenty-two years old, younger than I was at the time, studying to be a nurse. Harfield decided to impress her by taking her for a drive along the coast in his Corvette. He failed to notice a bend in the road and drove the car into the ocean. Harfield was uninjured, naturally, but Sophie lost consciousness in the water and had to be resuscitated. She suffered irreparable brain damage from lack of oxygen. Harfield miraculously avoided prison again, but he had to pay a substantial sum to Sophie's family in compensation.

'I left for good after that. Every time I looked at Harfield, all I could think of was that poor girl, sitting in a wheelchair and dribbling over herself. Harfield isn't a bad man, you know, but he has so little concern for his own life that he doesn't see the consequences for people around him.'

'He seems to love you very much, Jackie,' Pandora said.

They arrived back at the stable just as Holly and Fiona were returning from their short ride. Jackie sighed deeply. 'Yes, I think he does. And that just makes it worse.'

CHAPTER 48

The weeks passed. Pandora's face gradually disappeared from the news as fresh scandals emerged from the international Punch and Judy show that was the news industry. Still she remained cloistered at Blackthorn, aware that although the newspapers had grown bored of her, the agency would remain watchful, hoping she would make a mistake and reveal herself.

Jackie stayed away for longer and longer periods, burying herself in the difficult legal work of undermining the agency. Fiona spent hours each day at her computer control station in the attic, scouring the world's data links via a complex array of antennae bristling from Blackthorn's roof.

Pandora knew now that she loved Fiona as her daughter, and she regretted that she had treated her with such cruel suspicion on their arrival from Farmtown. Her trust in Fiona had borne out. She had not transformed into a psychopathic killing machine, betrayed them to the police, or sought to control Holly's power for her own ends. Instead she seemed to be a completely ordinary girl, if somewhat eccentric. Her fascination with American culture was viewed through the distorted lens of Blackthorn and its inhabitants, and this led to some peculiar idiosyncrasies in her personality and tastes. While clearing out the attic she discovered a box of Jackie's old childhood belongings from the 1980s, and these artifacts became the basis of her identity as an American girl. The sound of Spandau Ballet, Def Leppard, and the Pet Shop Boys could often be heard pounding behind the attic door while she was working. She wore Madonna t-shirts and read Anne Rice novels. She watched old sitcoms and movies on VHS and incorporated their vocabulary into her speech until Pandora had to ban her from using the word bodacious inside the house.

She worked in the attic tirelessly. Much of the time, she admitted her progress was slow, but once or twice a week she would race up to Pandora and announce she had made another breakthrough.

'A plane took off from an airstrip outside Las Vegas the day after the convent fire,' she said excitedly one day. 'It took off and flew east, but then it vanished from all records. The pilot didn't log a flight plan, and the transponder clicked off when the plane reached ten thousand feet. The plane's owner is registered as a charter company in Washington, DC, but the address is just a Post Office box. No phone number, no email, no nothing. I'll bet anything Sister Mary was on that flight.'

A week later she interrupted breakfast after pulling an all-nighter in the attic. 'I found it. The plane from Las Vegas operates out of a private airfield in Kansas. There are CCTV images of it outside a hangar four times in the past six months. If Sister Mary landed there, she can't be more than a couple of hours' drive away from the airfield.'

Little by little, the clues were building up, but Pandora felt a growing sense of frustration. While her companions were occupied in useful tasks, she herself had little to do and spent her days wandering aimlessly around the house or the grounds. For a while she busied herself assisting Holly with her scheme of redecorating Blackthorn. By now, Holly's plans had matured to a stage where she was comfortable showing her sketches to others, and Harfield admitted he was intrigued by her ideas. He authorized the purchase of a large quantity of art supplies from a list drawn up by Pandora, and then they began clearing the drawing room of all furniture. A painter's scaffold on caster wheels was erected on the wooden floor, and then Holly set to work.

The first task was the removal of the old wallpaper, a rococo monstrosity in an unpleasant shade of green. Pandora thought it must have been hideous when it was new, but now after more than a century it was tobacco-stained and peeling from the corners. Harfield protested that the wallpaper was historic. Holly didn't care. It was ugly and she tore it down with relish.

When the walls were clean and smooth, Holly painted a panoramic mural around the entire room. It was a forest scene rendered in an Arts and Crafts style which was in perfect sympathy with Blackthorn's architecture. Elegant, stylized trees formed the foreground, with gently rolling hills glimpsed in the distance, and a blue sky above. She maintained the room's masculine atmosphere by depicting majestic animals moving through the trees. Eagles and hawks soared through the skies or rested on branches, while game birds and peacocks moved through the understory. A life-size Rocky Mountain elk stood six feet tall at the shoulder, with broad antlers reaching all the way to the ceiling. A golden lion stalked between rose bushes beneath a fluttering banner inscribed with a motto in Gothic letters. Pandora had never in her life seen Holly use words in her art, and she was fascinated by the cryptic phrase her sister had written: *The wilderness shall blossom as the rose.*

Harfield solved the riddle for her during one of his daily inspections of Holly's progress. The phrase was from the book of Isaiah, a prophecy foretelling that the land which was destroyed long ago shall one day be restored. Pandora lay awake that night, wondering at the meaning of those words.

A week later, Holly completed the first stage of her scheme. The drawing room, previously a dark, grim space with a gloomy, depressing atmosphere, had been transformed into a bright and cheerful place. The ceiling was a clear blue sky with the sun's rays emanating from the central plaster rose. In the south west corner, where the room received the least natural light, a crescent moon rose above the cornice, accompanied by the first evening stars. Around the doors were twining branches of wisteria flowering in clusters of purple. The window frames were adorned with Boston ivy with leaves of red and orange. Harfield declared it was the most wonderful thing he had ever seen. He remained in the drawing room all day, drinking black coffee. Holly shifted her attention to the front parlor, where she had planned a garden trellis theme, and once again Pandora found herself with nothing to do.

She couldn't have said exactly when she made the decision to leave. It was a slow, dawning realization that formed in her mind over several weeks. She had observed the developing closeness between her sister and Fiona with an ache in her heart. Holly taught Fiona to play the piano on Blackthorn's magnificent walnut Steinway, and soon they were belting out duets of Pachelbel's Canon, The Can-Can, and Fly Me to the Moon in the music room. In turn, Fiona taught Holly a version of speedball using regular baseball equipment, although this resulted in a minor crisis when Holly hit a fast curveball and smashed Harfield's bedroom window. Holly had a panic attack and locked herself in the downstairs bathroom for hours, only emerging after Harfield spoke softly to her through the closed door, promising he could hold no grudge against Blackthorn's official artist-in-residence.

Holly and Fiona were safe and happy here at Blackthorn, and Pandora's continuing presence was a threat to that safety. Inevitably the agency would track her here, and when that happened there would be no more safe havens for any of them. However, she realized that by leaving she could preserve the safety of Blackthorn by diverting the agency's attention elsewhere. If she could travel far away and lead Agent Arnold on a wild goose chase across America, Blackthorn might remain forever hidden from his knowledge.

She finally made up her mind after Jackie and Fiona both delivered bad news on the same day. Fiona trudged down to breakfast after another late-night session in the attic. Normally an exuberant morning person, on this day she slouched in her chair moodily and poked at her food. Holly was alert to her feelings and nudged Pandora with her elbow.

'What's up, Fi?' Pandora asked. 'Bad night?'

'I know Sister Mary's still alive,' Fiona said, stirring her cereal miserably with a spoon. 'There are at least a dozen people like her who've vanished from all across America. I found their stories all over the Internet. It's always the same story. A person with disabilities is reported missing, and then a relative or carer is charged with their murder. But no body is ever found, and there's never a trial.'

'You'll find Sister Mary soon,' Pandora said, squeezing her hand. 'Just don't give up hope.'

'The prison's gotta be somewhere in Kansas. It's gotta be. But every time I feel like I'm getting close to finding it, the trail goes cold. It's like trying to squeeze a balloon full of water. Every time you think you've got a grip on it, the darn thing slips away.'

'You're working too hard,' Pandora said. 'You look exhausted. Take a break for a few days and come back to the job fresh.'

Fiona shook her head slowly. 'It won't do any good. That prison must be the most secret place on planet Earth. The agency knows that people with special gifts might try to break in, or break out, so they make an extra effort to hide themselves. I can work computers, but I can't read minds, or blink millions of miles. I don't think it's possible to find them just using a computer, and I don't have any other skills that might help us.'

Later that morning, Jackie returned in the Airstream. She had been absent for a week, cooped up in the UCLA law library, checking on clues she had uncovered in the thousands of documents subpoenaed from the agency. She entered the house with a sullen expression, turning away the happy hugs of her friends. Calling the travelers to a meeting on the veranda, she summarized the results of her research.

'The National Counter-Terrorism Agency is like no other organization in the history of the United States,' she said, tapping the stack of files on the table before her. 'Their public-facing image is that of a federal law-enforcement agency, just like the FBI, the ATF, or a dozen other government institutions. But the reality is that they operate like a covert organization, as if they were a foreign force operating within the United States but outside government authority. They have free rein to spy on American citizens without a warrant, and detain people indefinitely without charge. The only way they could possibly have gained this much power is if the government has developed a pathological delusion that there are lethally dangerous enemies operating at all levels of American society. The agency exists in a perpetual state of war, and the American people are its enemy. I honestly think the only reason they haven't arrested me yet is because they're hoping I'll lead them to you.' She shook her head regretfully. 'I haven't given up hope yet, but I can't promise any quick solution. I'm sorry, girls. I feel like I've let you down.'

That afternoon, it rained for the first time since they arrived at Blackthorn, the downpour heralding the end of a long and glorious summer. Holly and Fiona canceled their plans for horse riding and hung around in the drawing room doing jigsaw puzzles. Jackie went to her room to sleep, exhausted after her long drive.

Pandora sat on the porch alone and listened to the rain. Her mind wandered, and her thoughts kept returning to Ojai and the little house on Edgewood Avenue. She had grown up in that house, never knowing any other home. Every good memory in her life was in some way connected to that place. Now she admitted to herself that she would never see it again. She could never return to those simple and happy days in sunny Ojai, and instead her future promised only turmoil and strife. Either she would spend her life as a fugitive running from the agency, or she would be captured and end her days in dismal and unjust imprisonment.

She would never see Holly again. No matter what happened, after this day she and her sister would be parted forever. Her options had narrowed to a single dark tunnel with no light at the end. She must leave Blackthorn at once and accept her fate, driven by hope that Holly could continue to evade her pursuers with the help of Fiona and Jackie.

CHAPTER 49

After sundown she went to her room and wrote three letters. The first was to Holly, and in it she expressed as best she could her reasons for leaving, her sorrow at their parting, and her never-ending love and admiration for her sister. In a second letter to Fiona she lamented that they had so little time to get to know each other, and indicated her wish that she would think of Holly and Jackie as her adoptive parents. The third letter was for Jackie and entrusted to her a duty of care for Holly and Fiona. She suggested that Holly could continue to produce art professionally under a pseudonym, which would allow her to pursue her vocation and provide an income to support herself and Fiona. She thanked Jackie for her help, friendship, and loyalty, but requested that she not waste time searching for her, or fighting against the agency. She sealed the letters with kisses and left them on the dresser to be found the following day.

It was well after midnight when the rain finally let up. She put on her shoes and picked up the bag she had packed earlier in the day. Her plan was very simple. She would walk into Zenith, a journey that would take the rest of the night, and when morning came she would take the first bus to anywhere. The destination was not important, so long as it was far from here. When she reached a major city where homelessness was commonplace she would find a quiet place on the streets and stay there for a few days before moving on. She had none of the addictions to alcohol or drugs that afflicted many of the poor souls who dwelled in the streets, so she hoped to keep herself reasonably healthy and well-fed. If she was fortunate she might even have opportunity to help those in more need than herself. It would be a mistake to form friendships with the other homeless people, however. She recalled only too well the effect the promise of reward money had on Katrina, though Pandora no longer felt any ill-will towards the girl.

So she would continue her journey from city to city, and in this manner live out her days as long as she remained free. Eventually she expected to be recognized and apprehended, but by that time the trail leading back to Blackthorn would be cold, and her sister would be safe.

She shouldered her bag and went out into Blackthorn's upper hall. The hallway was lit day and night by low-wattage lamps and she had no trouble finding her way. After only a few paces a floorboard betrayed her with a long groan.

A door opened and Holly stood there in her nightdress. At a glance she took in Pandora's shoes, her coat, and the pack on her shoulders.

Pandora whispered. 'Sorry, Hol, did I wake you? I couldn't sleep so I'm going for a walk.'

Holly considered this and nodded. She reached inside the door, picked up her shoes and slipped them on.

'No, no, you can't go outside in your nightie, silly. It's still wet out there and you'll catch your death.'

A frown of suspicion darkened Holly's face. Pandora pushed her gently back into the room. 'I'm just going for a wander around the fields. I've got a picnic blanket in the bag so I can sit down on the grass without getting wet. Go on back to bed and I'll see you in the morning, okay?'

She pulled the door closed and lingered for a moment to be sure Holly wasn't going to follow. From inside she heard the *clump-clump* of Holly removing her shoes and dropping them to the floor. When she resumed her journey along the hall she walked briskly, ignoring the protests of the wooden floors beneath her feet. Moving furtively in an old house like this only drew attention to her clandestine departure and she wanted to be gone quickly before anyone else ventured outside their rooms.

Leaving the house via the kitchen door, she walked by the light of the moon peeking through the departing rain clouds. The road to Zenith was half a mile distant, and soon she was enveloped by the forest. She had a penlight in her pocket, and switched it on to guide her way. The rain had stopped, but the trees still showered a constant pitter-patter of droplets all around. The driveway was muddy from the downwash, and rivulets of water cascaded across the tarmac, reflecting silvery light from the torch.

She was halfway to the Zenith road when she heard splashes of footsteps behind. Turning the light on her pursuer, she saw Holly trotting down the path towards her.

'Holly, what are you doing? I told you to go back to bed.'

Her sister was fully dressed, wearing hiking boots and carrying a heavy pack on her shoulders. When she reached Pandora, she deposited the bag on a dry patch in the road. Opening the top flap, she revealed hurriedly packed clothes, toiletries, water bottles, and packaged snacks in the glow of the flashlight.

Pandora almost burst into tears at the sight of Holly's swift preparations after only a few minutes of her absence. She reminded herself what was at stake and choked back her sobs. 'No, you can't come with me. I'm sorry, Hol, but it's better this way. I'm putting you in danger by staying here. You and Fiona will only be safe when I'm gone. Maybe one day Jackie can find a way to get the agency off my back, and then we can be together again, but right now I'm too dangerous to be around.'

She was glad the remnant of rain falling from the trees hid the tears on her cheeks. Picking up the backpack, she placed it in Holly's arms. 'Go back to the house. I promise

I'll be okay.' She tried to turn her sister back towards Blackthorn, but she wouldn't budge.

'I'm not kidding.' A touch of anger in her voice. 'Get back to the house and stay there. This isn't a game. It's life or death.'

She pushed Holly towards Blackthorn. Holly staggered, but held her ground. She pushed again, and this time Holly pushed back. She lifted the backpack and threw it at Pandora. It struck her in the chest and fell to the floor, tipping clothes, cookies, and toiletries onto the path.

'Holly, stop this,' she snapped. 'Take your stuff and go back to the house.' She picked up the fallen things and pushed them back into the bag. Holly snatched it from her hands, tipped it upside down and emptied it onto the path. She grabbed up a handful of clothes and ripped them, threw them on the ground and stamped them into the mud. She tore open packets of cookies and ground them to powder in her fists. She picked up the toiletries bag and flung the contents at Pandora.

Pandora reached for her sister, saying soothing words to calm her down. Holly flailed with her fists, striking her sister in the head and the chest. Pandora lost her grip on the torch, which sailed into the undergrowth and vanished. Holly turned and ran off the path.

Pandora's heart skipped a beat when she saw the direction Holly was fleeing. 'Holly, wait! That's the ravine, you'll be hurt.'

Holly ignored her. Pandora cast around for the torch, but it was gone. She had no choice but to run blindly into the forest.

Beyond the path was a tapestry of shifting shadows and unknown sounds. Ferns swayed in the breeze, creating phantom figures in her peripheral vision. Animals moved unseen along the ground, and water fell in fat droplets, making deceptive sounds on all sides. She cried out Holly's name, twisting this way and that, peering into the dark. The ground was uneven and treacherous, and over and over she fell into the sludge of mud and pine needles.

When she reached the blackthorn bushes, she knew the ravine was near. The rainfall had swelled the stream into a raging torrent. Even at this distance she could hear the roar of the water on the rocks.

'Holly please, come back,' her voice was swallowed by the night.

She pushed through the blackthorns, heedless of the scratches to her face and her arms. The ravine yawned before her without warning and she grasped the vicious thorns to prevent herself falling.

'Oh my God.' She gazed into the chasm. The narrow creek had transformed into a lethal flood of violent cataracts tumbling over the rocks. If she had fallen in, she would be dead. 'Holly? Holly, where are you?' She strained her voice against the thundering waters.

Movement to her left. Holly was walking along the edge of the abyss, clambering around trees that leaned drunkenly over the precipice. When she saw Pandora, she turned and walked the other way.

'No, please come back,' Pandora scrambled towards her. 'Oh God, Holly, please don't fall.'

She had to move fast to catch up. The blackthorns formed an angry phalanx of needles at the brink of the ravine, leaving only the narrowest of ledges. Thorns pressed her towards the crevasse, and the raging water drove her into the thorns. At last she was near enough to grab Holly's coat. Holly saw her coming and pounded her with her fists, yelling in inarticulate fury.

'I'm sorry, I'm sorry,' was all Pandora could say. She held on tight to her sister, refusing to let go. Without warning, the muddy ground moved and she lost her balance. The world turned sideways, and her last vision was a pandemonium of water and rocks as she tumbled into the ravine.

CHAPTER 50

She woke up coughing. Her chest was painful and her lungs felt heavy, like she was breathing through a wet sponge. Her surroundings were unfamiliar. Sunlight shone through an oval window onto a circular room with a domed roof. She lay on a contoured platform that was neither a bed nor a couch, but it was soft and changed shape to match her body when she moved. On the other side of the room, Holly lay on a similar bed-couch-thing.

'Holly?'

She sat up and instantly regretted it. Nausea churned in her stomach and fluid shifted in her lungs, bringing on another fit of coughing. When she recovered, she got to her feet unsteadily.

Holly was apparently asleep, but she did not wake when Pandora squeezed her hand and spoke her name. She was wearing a kind of medical smock made of a light blue material, and her feet were bare. Pandora looked down at herself and saw she wore a similar getup.

Between the beds stood a bulky box-like device on wheels. Several long manipulator arms extended from its body, each terminating in a mechanical tool. A graphical display on the front of the box depicted clusters of three-dimensional shapes that shifted, merged, and morphed in complex ways. She could make no sense of it. Crossing to the window, she saw a pleasant lawn bordered by shrubs and trees. Spheres, conical towers, and dome-shaped buildings could be seen in the distance. Astari architecture.

'Ah, you're awake. I'm glad.' An unfamiliar voice.

She swung around and saw a man in an open doorway. He was about thirty-five, handsome, with wavy dark hair worn long on his shoulders. He had an intellectual air and a kind smile.

'Where am I?' she asked.

'This is my home,' he replied, stepping into the room. He wore long black robes that shimmered slightly as he moved. 'My name is Aiden. I'm a researcher here at Aurora Station, which some call the Garden of Entara.'

Entara. So that confirmed Holly had blinked them away from the ravine before they could be killed by the flood. Her memories of those events were fragmentary and confused. She remembered plunging into the maelstrom. Her whole world was consumed by pounding water and deafening noise. Then everything went white, and the waters became still. She knew at once what had happened. Holly had leapt into the ravine and found her in the churning rapids. She had blinked them to Entara, and they had escaped the deadly torrent only to arrive in yet another body of water, less chaotic but no less dangerous.

'What's wrong with Holly?' Pandora said. 'She won't wake up.'

'We found you both unconscious yesterday morning on the bank of the river. Each of you had substantial quantities of water in your lungs, but your companion – Holly, did you say? – suffered a wound to her head. Her body needs rest for a full recovery.'

Pandora remembered a little more. She had thrashed about in the black waters, crying out Holly's name. She found her sister face down, limp and lifeless, a nasty gash pouring blood down her face. She fought to keep Holly afloat and struggled towards the shore, visible only as a silhouette of treetops drifting against the night sky. The river was almost a mile wide, and the current kept sweeping her back to deeper waters. No matter how hard she kicked with her legs, those trees never seemed to get any closer. Before long her strength began to give out.

'I fell in the water,' Pandora said. 'Holly must have jumped in after me and hit her head on the rocks. God, I'm such an idiot. I tried to keep her afloat and swim to shore, but it was all I could do to keep my own head above the water.'

'The river is sluggish, but with treacherous currents,' Aiden said. 'You would have to be an expert swimmer to cross it, especially while supporting your friend. I'd say you saved her life.'

That made her feel worse. She had left Blackthorn to ensure Holly's safety, and instead she became responsible for smashing her sister's skull against a rock. She brushed Holly's hair aside to examine her wound, but frowned in consternation when she could not find it.

'The wound has been healed,' Aiden indicated the boxy device beside the bed. 'This is a medical computer, equipped to perform a great many healing functions. The medicomp has nursed you both back to health, but it has determined that your friend needs a little more time before she can safely awaken. Rest assured that within a few hours she will be as right as rain.'

There was no sign Holly had been hurt at all. Evidently the medicomp was more technologically advanced than anything they had yet seen on Entara. That brought to mind the high-tech buildings she had seen through the window, and her curiosity was piqued. 'What did you say this place was?'

Aiden smiled. 'All in good time. First, you must dress. You can't walk around in that sack all day. You will find your clothes washed and dried in a cabinet over there. When you are ready, you can find me outside.'

CHAPTER 51

Pandora took her time getting dressed, hoping Holly would wake up while she dawdled. She felt guilty about the prospect of leaving her alone in this strange place, but was eager to explore their new surroundings. She studied the 3D readout on the medicomp, trying to interpret the endlessly morphing shapes. It was all nonsense to her. Reluctantly, she entrusted Holly to the care of the machine and went outside.

Aiden's home was a cluster of domes connected by cylindrical hallways. It was set in its own grounds linked to the other Astari buildings by pathways laid discreetly between the trees. Aiden led her along shaded avenues and across sunny plazas, pointing out features and places of interest. The settlement was arranged like a college campus, with buildings grouped by function. There was a data collection center in a group of spheres of different sizes, a library in a triad of mushroom-like structures, laboratories installed in a row of interconnected cylinders.

'The entire facility is a vast research center,' Aiden explained as they walked across a pentagonal lawn surrounded by egg-shaped constructions. 'The Astari didn't build villages or towns as we understand them. Their outposts on Entara were purely scientific in nature.'

'It's amazing,' Pandora said. 'Are you all by yourself

here? This place is huge, but I haven't seen any other people.'

'Aurora Station has been abandoned for many centuries, but I live here with Sirella, my assistant. You will have an opportunity to meet her later today.'

'This is the first time I've seen Astari buildings that aren't in ruins. I've heard the Old Kingdom was destroyed in some kind of war. How come this place is so perfectly preserved?'

'A very perceptive question,' Aiden said. 'Actually, Aurora Station is protected by tremendous energies emanating from the artifact tower at its center. The garden was shielded from the devastation of the final war, and it remains exactly as it was on the day the Astari departed this world.'

'The artifact?'

Aiden pointed to another structure of startling design and appearance that rose high above everything else. It was a shard of dark gray rising from a wide expanse of lawn. As tall as a skyscraper, it was the focal point of the garden, and all the paths terminated at its base.

'The artifact was the Astari's highest scientific achievement,' Aiden said. 'The culmination of a million years of study and research. It is fitting your journey should end here. This is the place all travelers are searching for, whether they know it or not. You see, the artifact emits subtle psychic vibrations that draw people subconsciously from all across Entara. People journey for many years to reach this place, facing untold perils and dangers, without ever knowing why they feel compelled to complete their quest. When they arrive at the garden, they finally understand why their voyage was so important to them. The artifact is the end of all adventures, the source of all wonder and mystery, the fulfillment of mankind's deepest desires.'

A fly was buzzing in the air nearby. It landed on Aiden's cheek, scuttled across his nose and came to rest beneath his left eye. Pandora found this repellent, and the fact that Aiden seemed not to notice it made her uneasy.

'Come along,' Aiden said, emerging from his reverie. 'I'll show you to a place where you can rest during your stay with us.'

They walked along a meandering path flanked by fruit trees and came to a dome set in its own patch of lawn. A door glided open at their approach, and Aiden led her inside. The dome was fitted out like a residence, with two bedrooms, a living area, and a work area. At the rear was a glazed extension like a greenhouse where long trestle tables were covered with potted plants.

Pandora was fascinated by everything she saw. Every object in every room was distractingly beautiful, no matter how mundane its function. She felt like she had wandered into a gallery displaying the finest works of the Bauhaus School, Frank Lloyd Wright, and Charles Eames.

Aiden noted her interest with approval. 'The Astari were artists of extraordinary achievement, were they not? Nothing they made was ordinary, and everything was as beautiful as possible. Their philosophy was that aesthetics has a practical function, and form and purpose flow from it. Look, let me show you another wonder.' He led her to a niche in the wall with another three-dimensional graphical display. Aiden tapped it with his finger as if it was a keyboard, and a blue glow illuminated the niche. A tray materialized out of thin air, holding two mugs of steaming liquid. Aiden picked one up and presented it to Pandora with a flourish. 'Careful, it's hot.'

It was hot chocolate. Pandora sipped it gratefully, but Aiden frowned as if she had broken some rule of etiquette. 'I thought you had never seen Astari technology before?' he said with a trace of suspicion.

Pandora realized he expected her to be shocked and startled by the sudden appearance of the hot drink from nowhere. In truth she had been impressed, but she had also seen Star Trek, and nothing so mundane as a matter replicator could amaze her at this stage in her adventure. In fact, it dawned on her that Aiden's whole spiel had been intended to dazzle her with the marvels of the Old Kingdom: The healing of Holly's wound, the guided tour of the garden, the panegyric about the artifact, and now the luxurious dome with its magic food dispenser. Her failure to gasp in wonder at each new revelation had become a source of disquiet for him.

She decided she didn't like Aiden very much, despite his good looks and charming manner.

'Oh, well, Holly and I have traveled a long way to be here. We've seen many miracles and wonders on our journey. Just last week, we went to a Starbucks drive-thru in Ventura and had the most amazing mocha frappuccinos.' *Let him figure that one out*, she thought.

The outer door slid open, and a woman entered the dome. She was young, and might have been very beautiful except that her skin was pallid and her eyes sunken as if she was suffering from an ailment. Like Aiden, she wore long shimmering robes, though hers were white, and she walked with a smooth metal cane. 'So here you both are. I was beginning to think you two had eloped.'

Aiden went to her side and offered his arm for support. 'Pandora, this is Sirella, my assistant. She was the one who found you and Holly at the river.'

'I always go for a walk along the river in the morning,' Sirella said. 'I find the water very peaceful. When I found you lying there unconscious, I had the fright of my life.'

'It looks like you saved our lives,' Pandora said. 'Thank you.'

Sirella took a wheezing breath and leaned against Aiden. He examined the pallor of her cheeks with concern. 'Sirella, you should be resting. You can socialize with our guests tomorrow.'

She dismissed him affectionately with a wave of her hand. 'Aiden coddles me like I'm an invalid. I've been sickly since I was very young, but I don't let it slow me down. I love having visitors here in the garden, and I insist on being the one to show newcomers our accommodations. Aiden here is stealing my thunder by bringing you to the residential dome.'

Aiden sighed indulgently. 'I shall consider myself properly reprimanded. Sirella has taken on the role of unofficial hostess here at Aurora Station. When guests are in residence she is queen of all she surveys, and I am relegated to the role of mere butler.'

Pandora was charmed at the intimacy between her two hosts, but she couldn't quite figure out the relationship between them. She didn't think they were romantically involved, but neither were they simply friends or colleagues.

'I want to hear all about your journey to reach us,' Sirella said. 'All the pilgrims who arrive at the garden have been through such trials and hardships. You are all so brave and determined. I find your stories very inspiring.'

'Well, I'm not sure we're exactly like your normal guests,' Pandora said. 'We didn't follow any call from the artifact. We only left our home because we were escaping persecution. My sister Holly has a neurodevelopmental disorder that makes her stand out as unusual where we come from. In our community, those kinds of differences aren't tolerated, and we had to run away. We arrived here totally by accident.' It wasn't the complete truth, but it was close enough.

Sirella smiled in understanding. 'The artifact calls to people in many different ways. It may not have been a conscious choice, but it brought you here nevertheless.'

'I guess that could be true,' Pandora said doubtfully. 'But I still don't understand what this artifact is supposed to be. How can we be searching for something we've never heard of?'

Aiden held up his hand to forestall further discussion. 'I think we should wait until your companion has woken up before we start delving into the deeper mysteries of Aurora Station. Why don't we head back to my house and see how she's doing?'

Holly was still asleep when they arrived, but Aiden examined the readout on the medicomp and expressed satisfaction with her progress. 'Holly will be good as new by the end of the day,' he promised.

Sirella was looking faint so Aiden led her away to another part of the garden where she had lodgings, leaving Pandora alone with Holly. She sat with her sister awhile and talked with her in the way one sometimes does with sick relatives, telling her deeply-held feelings she would never usually admit, half-hoping Holly might hear her words and half-hoping she would not.

After a time, she became restless and decided Holly would be in no danger if she went for a walk. The sunshine outside was glorious, and the garden was in full bloom. She found the river and walked for a while along its banks, idly wondering exactly where Sirella had found them. Aurora Station occupied a large area bordered on one side by a wide loop of the river, and on the other side by a curved wall of white stone. The riverside was elegantly landscaped and scattered with abstract sculptures formed of sweeping arcs of metal and stone that made her think of the flight of birds or the leaping of gazelles. The wall was broken at intervals by arched gateways through which smooth roads led into the garden. She took a detour through one of these arches to explore the outside world, but the land beyond was a stony waste.

She had the unnerving sensation that someone was following her. At one point she even doubled back along a path, certain someone had ducked out of sight behind a tree when she looked around. There was no one there, and she walked on warily.

Her meanderings led her towards the artifact which loomed high over everything, prominently visible from every point in the garden. The shard-like tower was not quite perpendicular and leaned slightly to one side as if it was a titanic javelin hurled aloft by some vanished god to land here where divine will had caused a garden to flourish at its base.

The scale of the artifact only became apparent as she got closer. It must have been a mile high, and two hundred feet across at its base. There were no doors, windows or external features of any kind. It was constructed of a dark, glassy substance which was cloudy and gray in color. Up close, the material revealed itself to be semi-transparent, and strange shadowy shapes shifted and churned within as if driven by unfathomable convection currents. Straining her neck upwards, she saw that the air at the pinnacle of the shard shimmered faintly as if electrical energy was being dispersed into the atmosphere.

She thought about the mysterious claims Aiden and Sirella had made about the tower. They each evinced an almost religious fervor for this structure, as if it was a sacred object of great spiritual significance, worthy of reverence if not actual worship. Could it really have called to Holly and herself from across entire galaxies to bring them here? It did not seem likely. Now she was standing beside the artifact Pandora felt no more drawn to it than she had an hour ago. If Aiden had not pointed it out to her during his tour she would not have found it particularly remarkable except for its extraordinary height.

It reminded her of booklets she had seen at the convent in Las Vegas. In the lobby and in their room there were pamphlets advertising pilgrimages to the sacred grottoes at Fatima and Lourdes, inviting the faithful to visit sites where apparitions of the Virgin Mary had performed miracles. Perhaps the artifact served a similar function for the people of Entara. Like the Shroud of Turin, or the Spear of Longinus, it was a relic of a lost golden age whose inhabitants were remembered only vaguely as great heroes of saintly virtue. The historical reality could have become distorted and magnified by the passing of centuries until it became a holy place where people journeyed many miles to receive blessings.

She made a full circuit of the artifact's base and saw she was wrong. There was a door after all. Or at least, she thought it was a door. There was a rectangle in the center of one wall at ground level, ten feet high and five feet wide. Unlike the swirling gray walls, it was solid black and seemed designed to slide open. She pushed, tapped, knocked and kicked at the presumptive opening, but it responded to her not at all.

The sun was past its zenith, and she decided it was time to check on Holly. On her way back to Aiden's house she was dogged by the buzzing of a fly that droned around her head, provoking an irritated side-swipe with her hand. The fly landed on her arm and she stared at it with disbelief and disgust. This was no ordinary housefly. It was something weird. Something alien. It was a fat, bloated creature with a chitinous body of glass bottle green. Its four wings buzzed and twitched nastily, and its too-long legs writhed like worms against her flesh. Worst of all was its eye. A single, bulbous red protrusion in the center of its furry black head like a drop of crimson blood. Serrated pincers stretched out in front of its body, flanking a proboscis that pulsated and probed the skin of her arm.

It bit her. She yelped in pain and swatted it away. Already her skin was swelling into a bump crowned by a spot of blood that looked horribly as if the fly-thing had left its eye behind as a parting gift.

CHAPTER 52

Holly was awake. With no one attendance and left to her own devices she had discovered the food synthesizer and was eating a small bowl of ice cream on the couch.

'Oh Holly, thank God you're okay,' Pandora said, wrapping her arms around her sister in a hug. Holly twisted away and grunted in annoyance, a rare vocalization that made Pandora draw back in surprise. 'Okay, I'm still in the doghouse, am I?'

Holly turned aside and continued her snack, studiously ignoring her. She was still wearing the shapeless medical smock, so Pandora went to the bedroom and retrieved her clothes.

'This house belongs to a man called Aiden. He's some kind of historian of Astari gadgets. His friend Sirella found us next to the river and rescued us. Look, they've cleaned your clothes for you, isn't that nice? You should get dressed before they come back.'

Holly casually swatted the clothes onto the floor. She scraped the ice cream bowl clean and crossed to the food niche. Apparently the synthesizer would not produce portions big enough to satisfy her appetite because there were already three empty bowls inside. She ordered another, and walked out of the house.

Pandora groaned inwardly. It was tempting to interpret

Holly's behavior as childish or petulant, but without the power to communicate this was the only way she could express her severe displeasure.

She collected the clothes from the floor and went outside. She found Holly a short distance away in a sunny glade, perched on the lip of a stone fountain and swirling the water with her fingers.

Pandora sat beside her. 'Holly, listen, about what happened at Blackthorn. I'm really sorry I upset you. You must feel like I was betraying you and Fiona, but I was only trying to do what I thought was best. Do you understand?'

No response, but at least Holly didn't walk away. At that moment Aiden and Sirella appeared, strolling along a path towards the house. Sirella waved and crossed the lawn as fast as her cane would allow. 'Hello Holly, I'm so glad you're awake. My name is Sirella, and this is Aiden. How are you feeling?'

Holly studied the newcomers each in turn as if memorizing their features for future reference, then resumed her snack. Sirella and Aiden shared a look of concern, and Pandora intervened. 'Don't worry, this is normal for Holly. She doesn't talk, but sometimes she draws pictures.'

Sirella was relieved. 'Oh yes, I remember you mentioning a neurodevelopmental condition. Well, Holly, it's good to see you up and about anyway.'

Holly acknowledged Pandora's presence long enough to hand her the empty ice cream bowl. She stood and walked briskly away in the direction of Aiden's house.

Pandora was left holding the clothes and the bowl, and felt rather stupid. 'I'm sorry, she's not normally like this. Holly's very friendly, really. She enjoys meeting new people, but I'm afraid I've upset her and she's taking it out on me.'

'No need to apologize,' Aiden said. 'Your sister's mental aberration is only a symptom of a world that has fallen into darkness. People come to the garden for healing from every kind of sickness imaginable, and every one of them leaves here in perfect health.'

Pandora bristled at that. 'Holly does not have an aberration of any kind.'

Aiden was taken aback. 'I'm sorry, I didn't mean to cause offense. I only meant that you must have faith that Holly will be made whole again by the artifact.'

Pandora shook her head in confusion. 'Made whole? What are you talking about?'

Sirella took her hands and squeezed them earnestly. 'Holly will be healed. She will speak and be understood. Isn't that wonderful? Isn't that the miracle you have come here to witness?'

Pandora didn't know how to reply. She pulled free of Sirella's hands and turned away. 'I, uh... I'd better go and see where Holly's got to before she eats her own weight in ice cream.'

They found Holly lying outstretched on the lawn outside Aiden's house, sunning herself. Pandora decided to leave her there and give her a chance to get over herself. Sirella invited her to sit with them under the shade of a sycamore, where there was garden furniture that gave a good view of the house and of Holly. She sat with Sirella while Aiden went inside to get refreshments. Conversation was stilted. She didn't really want to talk to these people who, though friendly and welcoming, were also strange and creepy in a way she couldn't quite identify.

'Have you had a chance to enjoy the garden at all?' Sirella said when Aiden returned with cold drinks.

'I went for a walk, yes,' Pandora said, keeping her replies short.

An unspoken communication passed between her hosts, and Aiden picked up on her brevity. 'Pandora, I feel I must apologize for our behavior since you have arrived. Although our primary role here is research, as the years have passed we have become a kind of welcome committee for pilgrims who have spent years searching for the artifact. When they arrive, the pilgrims are often overawed by Aurora Station, which for them represents all the power and majesty of the Old Kingdom before the final war. As a result, we feel obliged to fulfill people's expectations and give them a warm welcome that makes their long journey feel worthwhile. I'm afraid that in your case, that welcome has backfired and we have unwittingly caused offense. We are so accustomed to our visitors being overwhelmed by their surroundings that we were prejudiced against you and Holly. We have treated you like tourists and acted in a way which is both patronizing and arrogant. For that we are truly sorry.'

'I must admit, you did come on a little strong,' Pandora said. 'But I appreciate the apology, thank you.'

'We should have known straight away that you weren't simple pilgrims.' Sirella said. 'When I took your clothing to be cleaned, I noticed it was made of synthetic materials that could only have been produced in an advanced culture.'

'We come from a very distant land that doesn't have much communication with the outside world,' Pandora said. 'Like I said before, we had to leave because Holly was being mistreated. Our home is high-tech, but not always kind.'

Aiden shook his head sadly. 'Science and morality are seldom developed at an equal rate. It is a story the Astari themselves would have understood well.'

Sirella squeezed her hand. 'Whatever your reasons for traveling, we want you to know this is a safe place and we are happy to have you here.'

'That's good to know, thank you,' Pandora said.

'Honestly, it gets a little lonely in the garden, just me and Aiden. We're glad to have you both as company, however long you choose to stay.'

That made Pandora think of the figure that had followed her earlier in the day. 'That reminds me, I think you might have another visitor lurking about the place. When I went for a walk, I saw a man following me. I tried to chase after him, but he slipped out of my sight.'

Aiden and Sirella looked at each other in alarm. 'You saw a man in the garden?' Aiden said. 'What did he look like?'

Pandora shrugged. 'I don't know. I only caught a glimpse of him. Why? What's wrong? I just thought it might be another pilgrim.'

'Pilgrims arrive through the gates in the outer wall,' Aiden said. 'There are proximity sensors that alert us to their arrival. We have received no such notifications for months.'

'Okay, but me and Holly came down the river. You didn't know we were here until you found us lying on the riverbank, right? Maybe this guy came in a boat or something.'

'There is a man who lives in the wilderness outside the garden,' Sirella said. 'A hermit. Sometimes he climbs over the wall and harasses the pilgrims. We thought that we had driven him off years ago, but perhaps he has returned.'

'Is he dangerous?' Pandora said. 'Should I be worried?'

Aiden considered this for a moment and shook his head. 'No, I'm sure he won't cause you any problems. Just stay away from him if you see him again.'

Holly got up off the lawn. She took a glass of orange juice from the table and drained it in one long gulp.

'Would you like to join us?' Sirella said, drawing out a chair. Holly ignored her and picked up the stack of her clothes. Without acknowledging anyone, she stomped into the house and was gone from sight.

'Holly is an expert at this sort of treatment,' Pandora said ruefully. 'She could teach a snowman a thing or two about giving the cold shoulder.'

'I hope we're not making things worse by monopolizing your attention,' Sirella said. 'Perhaps it would be better if we left you two alone to make amends.'

Pandora thought that was a good idea. When Holly emerged from the house fully dressed, she bid goodbye to their hosts and led her sister to the residential dome. Holly made a tour of the dome's rooms, examining the alien furniture and fittings with great curiosity.

Pandora followed close behind and decided it was time to swallow her pride. 'Holly, I'm sorry I abandoned you at Blackthorn. It was wrong of me to run away like that. We're stronger as a team and we should stick together from now on. Will you forgive me?'

Holly turned to her. Their eyes met, and for an instant Pandora sensed the turmoil of emotion churning within her sister. There was accusation, pain, sorrow, and love, all mixed together on Holly's face. The transient moment of understanding passed, and Holly looked away.

She went to the glasshouse at the rear of the dome and walked between the tables, examining the potted plants. The plants were of no species Pandora could identify, and appeared native to Entara. An automated watering system kept the plants nourished, but they were too big for their pots and leaned crazily this way and that. Some had fallen over and rolled onto the ground, smashing their pots. Holly picked one up and examined the roots overflowing the tiny pot and growing out of the drainage holes.

'This looks like a nursery,' Pandora said. 'But no one's been looking after the seedlings. They've all outgrown their pots. I wonder who planted them, and where they've gone?'

A metal tool cabinet stood against the far wall. Holly opened it, and two shovels and a hoe fell out with a clatter.

'I guess we could make ourselves useful for a while. Maybe take the seedlings out into the garden and find somewhere to plant them. What do you think?' She placed her arm gently around Holly's shoulder. 'Can we be friends again and do some planting together?'

Holly didn't look at her, but she didn't shrug her off either. It was a start.

They spent the rest of the day working outside. The dome was set in its own little mini-enclosure separated from the wider garden by a low hedge bordered by flower beds and shrubberies. Without knowing what the plants in the nursery were, it was difficult to know where to plant them. Holly had an intuition about such things and chose a shaded area beneath a grove of magnolias. They found a wooden compost bin behind the glasshouse and cleared a patch of turf for the seedlings.

While they worked, Pandora's thoughts kept returning to the extraordinary claims Aiden and Sirella had made about the artifact. She did not share the religious zeal their hosts felt about the tower, but the Astari clearly had access to technology far more advanced than anything on Earth.

She put down her trowel and crawled to her sister. 'Holly, there's something I've got to tell you. You know the big tower at the center of the garden? It's some kind of device built by the Astari thousands of years ago. Aiden and Sirella think it's a holy relic, but it's probably just a very advanced machine. Hol, people come here because they want to be healed. Maybe the Astari had some way of scanning the human body and fixing anything wrong with it. When Sirella found us, you had a really bad cut on your head, but now it's healed completely. What if there's something even more powerful inside the tower? What if there's something inside there that can heal you?'

Holly put down her tools and looked at her.

'Holly, what if... what if you could talk?' Pandora said. This time it was impossible to intuit her sister's thoughts, though she felt an agonizing need to understand her feelings. 'I won't make you do anything you don't want to, but maybe we should find out what this artifact really is. What do you think?'

Holly picked up her trowel and continued digging.

In the early evening Sirella visited for a short time to check the sisters were settling in, and to invite them for dinner at Aiden's residence. Pandora declined politely. Holly was still treating her like the enemy, and she preferred to take some quiet time alone rather than spend the evening socializing with strangers while Holly ignored her. She ate by herself in the garden, leaning her back against a tree while Holly stayed in the dome and played with the food synthesizer.

When night fell she learned why this place was called Aurora Station. As the sunlight faded, the shimmering light at the peak of the artifact turned into a riot of swirling color that reached high up into the stratosphere, bathing the garden in a glow of gold, red, emerald and blue. The aurora must have been visible for hundreds of miles in every direction. No wonder people traveled long distances to find out what it was.

At some point during the evening Holly discovered that the matter synthesizer could produce things other than food, and Pandora returned to find the dome cluttered with oddities. There were dozens of glass tubes, spheres, pyramids and cubes, balls of yarn in many colors, a set of animal figurines cast in a substance like amber, and a metallic sphere two feet in diameter that was so heavy it had left a crater in the floor where it had rolled out of the machine.

Holly had already retired to bed. Pandora opened her door to say goodnight, but got only the sight of her sister's back and a long-suffering sigh in response.

When she went to her own room, she found a set of pajamas neatly folded on her bed along with a teddy bear. She doubted Aiden or Sirella had supplied these thoughtful gifts, so Holly must have manufactured them somehow using the matter synthesizer. Perhaps there was hope for reconciliation after all.

CHAPTER 53

The next morning she got up early and pottered around the dome tidying up the mess. It was time to start thinking about returning to Earth, and she wanted to be a responsible guest and make sure the dome was neat and tidy for the next group of pilgrims who stayed here in this alien holiday home.

When everything was spick and span, she turned her attention to breakfast, which on this day had a dual role as both meal and peace offering. Before she could broach the subject of returning to Earth, she needed to be on friendly terms with her sister again. Knowing that the way to Holly's heart was ultimately through her digestive system, she planned a breakfast fit for a king, including all of Holly's favorite morning foods.

During her time alone the previous evening, Pandora worried about a lot of things, but mainly Fiona and Jackie. By now they would have discovered her farewell letters, but with Holly also missing they would know something had gone terribly wrong. In all likelihood they believed the sisters had been captured by the agency in a stealth operation during the night.

She needed to make Holly understand the importance of returning to Earth, but she also needed to reassure her that she would never abandon her again. Regaining Holly's trust would not be easy. She was stubborn and heedful of grudges, and if she suspected Pandora might sneak away again, she would keep them on Entara indefinitely. To remedy this, Pandora had returned to the living area late last night and taught herself to use the matter synthesizer. After some trial and error she created a pair of matching friendship necklaces from a mysterious midnight-blue crystal with flecks of gold that shone like tiny stars. Holly was fundamentally soft-hearted and susceptible to gifts. Pandora hoped she would accept this present as a promise that they would never be parted again.

The breakfast spread was also carefully devised to appeal to Holly's heart as well as her stomach. Pandora went to some lengths to reproduce the blue check kitchen cloth from their house in Ojai, along with a fair imitation of their mother's antique floral breakfast set. She filled every inch of table space with croissants, waffles, strawberries, bacon, eggs, and cereal. She even had a try at manufacturing Pop-Tarts with moderate success.

When everything looked just right she synthesized a small silver bell and shook it energetically outside Holly's door. 'Come on, wake up sleepyhead. Come and see what's cooking for breakfast.'

Holly stirred beneath a mound of sheets. Pandora hurried back to the table to brew tea in a facsimile of their mother's floral teapot.

A fly had found its way into the room and buzzed around the table, hovering over the plates and crawling on the foodstuffs. After all her hard work and planning, the sight of the fly made her angry, and she swatted it away in irritation. The fly darted out of reach easily and returned to the food almost at once with little regard for her scowl of disgust.

Holly emerged from her room, wearing her synthesized pajamas. Pandora chased the fly away from the table again and called her sister inside. 'Good morning. Come and sit down. I was going to put some music on, but the synthesizer doesn't know any Ozzy Osbourne.'

Holly made a low moaning sound. The moan turned into an unpleasant gurgle, and blood erupted from Holly's nose and gushed down her face onto her pajamas. She touched her fingers to the blood and stared at her soiled hand with a blank expression that made Pandora's soul shrivel in fear. Then her legs gave way and she collapsed onto the floor.

'Oh God, Holly? Holly, what's wrong?' Pandora ran to her sister. Holly's eyes were rolled back in their sockets, and she began to shake uncontrollably. Her feet kicked out, toppling an end table and sending ornaments flying. Pandora held her down, trying in vain to limit the thrashing of her limbs.

Gradually, Holly's convulsions reduced to mere tremors, but she remained unresponsive and her heartbeat was erratic. Pandora fled the dome and returned accompanied by Aiden pushing the medicomp. They lifted Holly onto the couch, and Aiden operated the computer for several minutes, his expression set in an inscrutable frown.

Pandora paced the room in agitation. 'What's wrong with her?' she said, shocked to hear the tearful shakiness of her voice. 'Holly was absolutely fine yesterday,'

'Pandora, please sit down,' Aiden said gently.

'I don't want to sit down. What have you found out?'

Aiden hesitated, and Pandora scoffed at his prevarication. She picked up a napkin from the table, wetted it in a water jug and cleaned the blood from Holly's face.

'You have to understand I'm not an expert at using this machine,' Aiden said feebly. 'I was never trained as a doctor, and I've learned to operate the computer out of necessity.'

'You healed her wound yesterday, didn't you? Why can't you heal her again now?'

'It's not that simple. I think Holly's brain injury may be significantly worse than we suspected.'

Pandora stopped and stared at him. 'Brain injury? You never said anything about a brain injury. Holly had a cut on her head, that's all.'

Aiden held up his hands helplessly. 'I'm sorry, I'm doing the best I can. My interpretation of the computer's initial diagnosis was that Holly's head wound was purely superficial.'

'So what does it say now?' She pointed at the squiggles on the 3D display.

'It seems there was a deeper injury that the computer did not detect. There is damaged tissue in Holly's frontal lobe which has caused a slow brain bleed.'

'Oh my God.' Pandora felt like her world was falling apart. She sank into a chair. 'Will she be okay?'

'I don't know. The computer has treated the damaged tissue, but I have no way of knowing what the result will be. I think the only thing we can do is wait.'

So they waited. Holly remained still, and the flow of blood from her nostrils ceased. Her eyes were closed, and she seemed to be merely sleeping. Aiden hovered over her, fidgeting and adjusting the computer. Pandora found his presence intrusive and she sent him away after demanding a crash course in how to interpret the medicomp's three-dimensional display.

Hours passed. To occupy herself, Pandora cleared away the uneaten breakfast. When that brief task was complete she resumed her fretful pacing around the room.

The fly returned and made endless buzzing circuits of the living area as if in mockery of her faithful vigil. She synthesized a fly swatter and chased the hateful creature around the dome. Every time she was certain she had killed it the buzzing recommenced from another part of the room. She recalled the bite she had received yesterday and examined the bump on her arm. It had swelled into a nasty welt that she had been unconsciously scratching so it weeped pus that had dried into a disgusting yellow scab. A horrible thought occurred to her that Holly had also been bitten and was suffering an allergic reaction that had caused her comatose state. She searched her sister's body for evidence of such a bite, but found nothing.

When her feet were tired from endless pacing she sat beside Holly and stared at the swirling images on the medicomp screen, representing her sister's respiration, heart rate and brain activity. All were distressingly weak. A nightmare scenario formed in Pandora's mind, whispering unthinkable things. Holly was going to die, and she would be left alone in a strange world with no friends and no way home.

Some time mid-afternoon the door opened and Sirella hovered at the threshold. 'May I come in?' Pandora didn't feel like company right now, but she beckoned with her hand and Sirella entered. 'I would have visited earlier, but Aiden suggested you might want some time alone. How is Holly?'

'She's just fading away,' Pandora said bleakly, choking back a sob that had been building within her for hours. 'I just can't believe this is happening. Holly hit her head trying to save my life, and now she's like this. It's just not fair.'

Sirella drew up a chair beside Holly. 'Head injuries are very unpredictable. It could be that Holly just needs a little extra recovery time.'

Pandora knew that Sirella was trying to be kind, but one glance at the medicomp readout told the whole story. Holly's life signs were barely registering. Her skin was cold, and her fingers were blue.

'Back home we had a neighbor, Derek, who got a brick dropped on his head while he was building an extension on his house,' Pandora said. 'He seemed fine, and he wouldn't even go to the hospital to get checked out. A week later he dropped dead in the supermarket checkout line. Just like that. One moment he was chatting to Angie, his wife, about where they were going to go on vacation, and the next he was dead. Angie said it was just like God reached into his head and switched off the light. That's what's happening to Holly, isn't it? She's just going to slip away and we won't even have a chance to say goodbye to each other.'

Sirella rubbed Pandora's arm. 'Don't give up hope.

Aurora Station is a special place where impossible things sometimes happen.'

'You mean a miracle cure?' Pandora said. 'Sirella, I'm sorry, but I don't believe in miracles. Sure, the Astari had some fancy tech, but this damn computer couldn't even figure out Holly had brain damage until it was too late.'

'The medicomp is only an emergency device. Essentially, it's an ancient first aid kit, intended for use only when no other assistance was available. Aurora Station has other facilities of far greater power. You should keep an open mind and consider all the options before you give in to despair.'

'You're talking about the artifact, aren't you? Yesterday I found a door in the side of the tower. I tried to open it, but it wouldn't budge. What the hell is inside that thing?'

Sirella hesitated. 'It's very difficult to explain. It would be easier if you would come and see for yourself. We can prepare a stretcher for Holly and—'

'No, I don't want Holly going anywhere near that thing. Not until I've seen it for myself and judged whether or not it's safe.'

When Pandora had reassured herself that Holly's condition was stable for the time being, they left the dome and found Aiden waiting outside. He led them to the artifact, and when they reached the door he opened it with a wave of his hand.

It was dark inside, and at first Pandora could see little. Aiden ushered them into a huge chamber constructed of the same shifting slate gray material as the rest of the tower. Massive buttresses held up the walls, and the lofty ceiling was vaulted, giving the place a cathedral-like feel. There were no furnishings, decorations, or adornments of any kind. The only object was a ring of stone hovering upright at the center of the chamber with no apparent means of support. It was around twenty feet in diameter and revolved slowly on its horizontal axis like a cog in some vast invisible machine. The spinning ring was filled with an amorphous fog that swirled within like a whirlpool and spilled out across the floor, creating a blanket of cloud that hid their feet as they approached.

Pandora's eyes adapted to the gloom and she saw symbols etched into the stone circle. Each runic emblem was imbued with symbolic meaning that tickled her consciousness with vague recognition. During her journey across Entara she had seen many strange things, but this was the first time she felt like she was in the presence of true Power. That was how she imagined the word, with a capital letter, as if the ring was a divine treasure placed here by God for safekeeping until the hour of mankind's greatest need. Her skin rose in goosebumps, and her hair stood on the back of her neck.

'This is the real artifact, isn't it?' Pandora said in a hushed voice. 'The tower is just a place to put it.'

'This is the object the Astari traveled the universe to find,' Aiden said. 'It is the fulfillment of their billion-year quest to find meaning and purpose in the universe. As it was for the Astari, so it is for us all: The end of all journeys.'

Pandora didn't have to ask what it was. She already knew. Somehow she had known ever since she arrived in this place. The ring had been calling to her, speaking in a voice she had never heard but had always known. 'It's a portal,' she said in awe. 'A gateway to… to another place.'

'The final act of the Astari in this universe was to step through the portal,' Aiden continued. 'It was the realization of their ultimate dream to achieve a new kind of existence beyond all space and time.'

Pandora felt afraid. The atmosphere of the tower was oppressive. The air was cold and a chill shook her body. 'Why have you brought me here? What does any of this have to do with Holly?'

'On the other side of the portal is a place of healing,' Sirella said, urging her forward. 'Just take a look, and you will see.'

Stone steps led up to the lip of the portal. Pandora

climbed them cautiously. The mist faded away and revealed a familiar scene. Through the ring, she saw the little house on Edgewood Avenue. The sun was shining, and a breeze rustled the branches in San Antonio Creek. Tied to the porch rail was a trio of helium balloons bobbing in the wind. Two of them said *Happy Birthday!* and the third had the number twelve emblazoned in numbers shaped like cartoon dinosaurs.

Pandora remembered this day. It was Holly's twelfth birthday. In less than three weeks, the sisters would blink to Entara for the first time, beginning an adventure that would change their lives.

Aiden joined her on the step. 'Whatever you are seeing is only a symbolic representation. The world beyond the portal transcends human understanding. You are perceiving it in a way which is comprehensible to your mind. The reality will be so much more.'

She understood. The memories that formed this vision represented an idealized moment of love, happiness and comfort. It was a day she remembered with great fondness, captured in family photographs framed on the living room wall. However, she knew that heartbreak and sorrow would follow soon after the happy events of this day. Not long after the sisters' discovery of Entara, their mother would die suddenly and painfully from cancer. Only a few short years later, their father would be killed during a routine traffic stop by a drunk driver with a gun under his seat. Pandora and Holly found themselves orphaned as young adults, and the house had become a place of sadness for a long while. It had taken many years of mutual support and love to achieve the happiness they had found before their return to Entara.

The portal offered a different possibility. The world she now glimpsed through the spinning ring was a place where those painful memories would be wiped away. If she stepped through the portal, she could return to those golden days, but this time things would be different. This time their mother would not be diagnosed with cancer. This time their father would not be shot six times in the chest. This time there would be only eternities of adventure in worlds beyond imagination, surrounded by the love of family and friends.

She descended the steps and turned to Aiden and Sirella. 'I need time to think this over.'

'Of course,' Aiden said, smiling benevolently. 'Take as long as you need.'

CHAPTER 54

She returned to the dome by herself. Holly lay motionless on the couch, her skin waxy and grey. For an awful instant Pandora thought she was dead, but the medicomp registered feeble evidence of respiration. Holly's chest rose and fell almost imperceptibly.

She picked up her sister's cold hands and rubbed life back into them. 'Don't you give up, Holly. Don't leave me alone here. We've still got so many things to do together. When all this is over we'll take that long cruise around South America we've been talking about, how does that sound? Three whole months of all-inclusive bars, beaches, museums, galleries. We can go scuba diving in the Gulf of Mexico, and jet-skiing, take a boat tour up the Amazon. Did you know you can go hiking with llamas in Peru? Wouldn't it be fun to walk a llama all the way up to those lovely old Inca ruins and camp out under the stars?'

She rambled and blubbered incoherently for a long time. Eventually she told Holly what she had seen through the portal. 'Do you think it could be true, Hol?' she said, almost in a whisper. 'We've seen so many amazing things these past few days. I mean, anything could be possible, right? Maybe there really is a better world waiting for us over there. All we have to do is make the choice to go through the portal and you won't be sick any more. I hope so, I really hope so, because oh God Holly I don't know what I'd do if I lost you.'

A shadow fell across Holly's body and she looked up, startled. A man stood at the window. His clothes were ragged, his hair and beard were long and tangled. Wild, staring eyes regarded her with hostility and suspicion.

Hadn't Sirella said something about a hermit who attacked pilgrims? She got up and crossed to the door, searching for some means of locking it. There was a small panel that opened the door in response to hand gestures, but she could see no method of securing it against intruders.

The door opened. The man stepped inside. Pandora retreated across the room, casting about for a weapon. With little to choose from she picked up a dining chair and held it like a shield.

'Don't come any closer,' she said. 'I don't want any trouble.'

'Who are you?' he demanded in a rasping voice.

'If it's food you're after, there's a synthesizer in the corner. Take whatever you want and get out of here.'

He stepped around the room, staring at her. 'I know you. I know your face.'

'That's because you were following me yesterday. Please, just go away. Leave us alone.'

His attention shifted to Holly's unconscious form. He moved towards her, but Pandora blocked his path.

'Hey! You leave her alone,' she said.

'What's wrong with her?'

'Nothing. She's just dying, that's all. Why won't you just leave us in peace?'

'Dying? Of what?' He took another step, and Pandora jabbed the chair at him in a warning maneuver. He sidestepped the blow and grabbed the medicomp, turning its screen to face him.

'What are you doing? Leave that alone.' She wanted to sound fierce and protective of her sister, but her voice was edged with uncertainty. Something about this man unsettled her more than just his threatening manner. He looked desperate, hungry, dangerous, but he also looked very familiar.

He studied the computer readout and nodded with grim satisfaction. 'The miasma. What bullshit did Aiden tell you? That she's oppressed by evil spirits? That she's got an imbalance in her humors?'

'No, of course not,' Pandora said. 'Holly suffered a serious head injury that caused brain damage and a slow brain bleed.'

'Holly?' he looked shaken at the mention of her name. 'No, this can't be Holly.' He reached out to touch her face, but Pandora held him at bay with the chair.

'Stay back, I'm warning you,' she said.

'Pandora?' He stared at her in wonderment.

She was not impressed. 'You've been spying on us. I want you out of here, right now.'

He stepped back, gazing at the sisters in confusion. From his pocket he withdrew a crumpled piece of paper and held it towards her. She snatched it from his hand and what she saw made her drop the chair to the ground. It was a Polaroid photograph of herself and Holly as children. They stood on the bank of a river beside a small rowing boat painted in blue and white. In the bow of the boat were fishing rods, a picnic hamper, and a ukulele. Standing between the sisters with his arms around their shoulders was a boy wearing a Guns 'N' Roses t-shirt and a Yankees baseball cap.

'Jason,' Pandora breathed. The man standing before her was bearded and ragged, but there was no mistaking the features of the boy from a forgotten childhood only recalled in diaries recounting adventures in another world.

She shook her head and turned away. This was too much for her to deal with right now. Holly was dying right before her eyes and she had a hard decision to make. The sudden reappearance of this ghost from her childhood was unwelcome and unhelpful. The boy in the photograph was a stranger to her, and the man he had grown into frightened her.

'I want you to go away, please,' she said. 'I don't remember you. You're just a face from a photograph. My sister is dying and I don't have time for reunions right now.'

Something buzzed noisily at her ear. That damn fly was in the room again, droning around her head, getting tangled in her hair. She cried out in disgust and clawed at her head, batting the creature away. It flew at her face and landed on her cheek. She saw its bulbous form quivering at the corner of her eye and felt the awful slithering of its legs against her skin. She swore and smacked it across the room.

Jason watched her with curiosity. 'What are you doing?'

'It's that goddamn fly, or whatever it is,' she said testily. 'The disgusting thing bit me yesterday, look.' She held out her arm to display the swollen lump above her wrist. It was worse than ever, itched like crazy, and now it was surrounded by a spreading ring of puffy red skin that was hot and tender to the touch.

Jason looked at her arm blankly. 'How do you feel?'

'Honestly? Not good. I think the bite might be infected. I'm developing a fever.'

Jason looked grave. 'It will get worse. By this time tomorrow you'll feel like hell. The day after you'll be like an old woman, hobbling around with a walking stick.'

'What are you talking about? Do these flies carry some kind of disease? Like malaria, or something?'

Jason ignored her question and knelt beside Holly, felt the cold skin of her hands. 'She's very weak. It's possible she'll die.'

'No, she's not going to die,' Pandora said defiantly.

'We need to get her away from here as soon as possible.' He lifted Holly from the couch and she hung limp in his arms.

'What the hell are you doing? Put her down right now.' She put her arms around her sister and was prepared to have a fight to win her back.

Jason stood firm. 'Listen to me, there's something very wrong here at Aurora Station. I don't understand what it is, but there's something in the air here. It makes people sick.'

'That's not true. This is a place famous for healing. People come from all across Entara to be healed. I didn't understand that when we first arrived, but now I know how lucky we were to wash up here after Holly hit her head.'

'Lucky? So you plan to take her into the artifact?'

'What other choice do I have?' She pulled at her sister's body again.

Jason grunted in resignation and released his hold on Holly, lowering her gently onto the couch.

Pandora went to the door and opened it. 'I want you to leave.'

Jason pulled at his hair in frustration. 'Don't you think this is all a little convenient? You arrive here in a place renowned for healing, and within days Holly develops a life-threatening condition that only the artifact can cure.'

'You call that convenient?' she said, pointing to Holly. 'If I don't take her through the portal within the next few hours, she could be dead when I wake up tomorrow. Now please, just get out of here. I have to find Aiden and get Holly ready to leave.'

'No, I'm not leaving,' he said. 'I won't let you take Holly through the portal.'

'Oh my God, Sirella said this would happen. She said you come here and harass the pilgrims. Why? What do you want?'

'Someone has to show you the truth.'

'What truth?'

Jason pulled out the photograph again and held it up to her. 'There was a time when you trusted me. You trusted me enough to show me your secret world. For the sake of the girls in this picture, please trust me again. Just one more time.'

She looked at the children in the picture. Best friends. That's what they were. The kind of friends you only have once in your life. Pandora and Holly had been best friends a long time, but there had once been a third person who shared in their adventures. She looked across the dome to where Holly lay, barely breathing. 'If Holly was awake right now, would she trust you?'

He hesitated, uncertain. 'I don't know. Everything's so hazy. I don't know what she remembers. Probably she'd be afraid of me, like you are right now. I'm a lot different from the kid in the picture.'

She sagged her shoulders in resignation. 'Alright, what is it you want to show me?'

CHAPTER 55

She fussed over Holly for several minutes, plumping a pillow to put under her head, covering her in blankets to keep the warmth in her dying body. When she was satisfied that Holly would be okay without her, Jason led her across the garden through a district she had not visited before, characterized by rows of upright cylinders topped by complex arrays of antennae.

'I don't remember you,' Jason said as they walked. 'Just your faces. Your names. I've carried that Polaroid a long time. I spent half my life wondering who the girls in that picture were.'

'It was the same for us,' Pandora said. 'I didn't just forget you, I forgot this whole world.'

'Then how did you get back here?'

'A few days ago Holly and I were in an accident. A scaffold collapsed and Holly saved us by taking us to Candlewick. We met Catherine and she remembered who we were.'

'Catherine?' Jason turned to her in surprise. 'You've seen her? How is she?'

'She's well, but I'm afraid Galen died a few days ago.' She couldn't bring herself to say how.

He sighed. 'After all these years I assumed they'd both be dead.'

'She misses you. She gave me a letter to bring to you, but somehow in the craziness of everything that's happened I lost it. I'm sorry.'

'It's okay, I don't need the letter. I know what she wanted to say.'

The avenue of cylinders came to an end and they entered a wide plaza bordered by trees. At its center was a huge dome, the largest building Pandora had seen except for the artifact shard. Jason took them towards it, and a door opened automatically at their approach. They entered a network of tunnels that criss-crossed the dome's lower levels, reminding Pandora of the underground labyrinth that riddled the great Colosseum in Rome. Much of the maze was in darkness, though their passage was lit by a curious sourceless light that moved with them as they walked, as if the walls themselves knew people had returned after long eons of emptiness and glowed softly to guide their way. Arched portals led to many chambers shrouded in shadow. Pandora thought she could spend the rest of her life exploring the hidden places of the Astari and never exhaust their mystery.

Jason seemed to know his way around. He took them to a cylindrical elevator which rose swiftly to a high level. The cylinder opened on a balcony overlooking a large open space.

'It's a theater,' Pandora said, leaning against the rail and looking down. Thousands of seats were arranged in rising tiers facing a broad stage on the far side of the dome. Spotlights cast brilliant beams on the stage as if some great drama of the Old Kingdom was about to be re-enacted there.

'I think this was once a teaching hall,' Jason said. 'The Astari scientists wanted to share what they had learned about the universe with other people. There are recording disks in here that would blow your mind, but that's not what we're here to see. Come on.'

At the mid-point of the balcony was a control booth with a panoramic view of the theater. Beneath the viewing window was a console set with many buttons, switches, screens and levers. Jason seated himself and manipulated several controls. The lights dimmed, casting the dome into dramatic shadow. Moments later another light illuminated the wall behind the stage. It was a projector, and the moving image showed a recording of an event that had taken place within the auditorium itself.

The camera panned across the dome revealing thousands of people packed into every seat. Most wore simple homespun clothing, though there were more outlandish outfits to be seen in the crowd. Everyone was on their feet, applauding, but the film was without sound. The camera turned to the stage, on which was arrayed colossal pieces of scientific apparatus: Electrical coils, oscillators, plasma globes, and many other instruments Pandora couldn't identify. Some of the machines were the size of apartment blocks, and all crackled with energy that arced across the stage, sometimes whiting out the camera completely.

'This recording was made here about twelve years ago,' Jason said.

'So these people are all pilgrims?' Pandora said. 'I never knew there were so many. Why is there no sound?'

'I'm not sure. The machines on the stage emit some kind of radiation that interferes with the recording.'

A man walked onto the stage. The camera zoomed in on the impressive figure as he stood regarding the crowd, nodding in solemn approval of their adulation.

'Oh my God,' Pandora said miserably. 'It's the wizard. It's Flak.'

'You've seen him before?'

'Let's just say his face is familiar. What the hell was he doing here?'

Jason frowned. 'You mean you don't know? This is where Flak brought the people from Candlewick, and from other places across Entara. This was his goddamn promised land.'

The camera angle changed again to display the rapture

on the faces of the ordinary people of Entara. Their wild, exultant expressions reminded her of footage of the Beatles touring America, when young women screamed without ceasing until their throats bled and they passed out from exhaustion. Flak inspired even greater passion in his audience. Some seemed to be suffering religious ecstasies at his appearance.

Flak approached the lectern and launched into a passionate tirade. Even though the film was silent, it was clear he was the most gifted public speaker who ever lived. No dictator had ever looked so intense, no televangelist had ever looked so fervent as he harangued the crowd, leaning over the lectern with his arms raised, pushing his whole body into emphasizing a word or phrase. When the camera cut to the crowd their exaltation was redoubled and they screamed in joyful delirium.

Pandora was grateful she could not hear Flak's words. She had an intuition that to hear his voice, even electronically recorded, would be to fall under his spell, to be influenced by him and allow his thought patterns to enter her mind. Nevertheless, she was curious. 'What on earth is he saying? What could get people riled up like that?'

'Most of the people in the audience are from simple farming communities,' Jason said. 'To them, Aurora Station was like Eden, a living relic of the Old Kingdom. Flak was their savior who'd brought them out of the wilderness into paradise. They loved him.'

'Were you here to witness this?'

'No, I didn't arrive until later.'

Flak raised his hands for silence and the audience fell into their seats as if knocked back by the force of his command. He turned aside and a small figure walked onto the stage. The audience leaned forward in anticipation as she walked to the lectern.

'That's Sirella,' Pandora said in amazement.

'She was only sixteen at the time,' Jason said. 'Sirella was from a remote village in the vale of Candlewick. She was born with a twisted spine and was bedridden all her life. When Flak arrived he healed her in a public display. He built a machine and placed it in the square. A thousand people saw Sirella go into the machine a twisted mess and come out perfectly healed. After that she became his student. They spent months together in the wilderness while he tutored her.'

Pandora recognized a strained tone in Jason's voice. 'She was your friend, wasn't she? No, more than your friend.'

Jason looked away. 'I met her in Candlewick during the summer fayre. Her family brought her on the back of a wagon and her brother Hector carried her around strapped to his back so she could enjoy the games, the singing and the dancing. The fayre was on the green beside the river, and she wanted to swim in the water. Hector couldn't swim, so I offered to take her instead. I carried her out into the river and she asked me to let go. She'd been very quiet and withdrawn up until that point, but when she was floating in the water she started laughing. She said being in the water made her forget her twisted body and made her feel free.

'The fayre lasted a week and we saw each other every day. On the day she left, I asked her father for permission to marry her. People get married young in the vale, you know. He said yes, and that made our parting all the more difficult because her village was two days away by road. I built a wheelchair in the barn and walked all the way across the vale to give it to her. For the first time in her life she could move around under her own power. She needed weeks of exercise to build up the strength to go any distance but before long she made the trip to Candlewick with me.'

Jason's voice trailed off, and Pandora prompted him. 'Then Flak arrived and changed everything.'

'When she was healed, Flak ordered the wheelchair burned as a symbol of her renewed life. After that I barely saw her. She was totally in his power.'

'That must have been very hard.' Pandora said.

'I was furious, but what could I do? Everyone adored Flak. When he led everyone away from the vale I begged her to stay. I'll never forget the look on her face. She said she pitied me for my lack of faith. Can you believe that?'

'Catherine said you didn't follow the rest of the villagers. Had you given up on Sirella?'

'She made her choice,' Jason said. 'I'm convinced of that. The wizard is a master of deception, but ultimately people have to want to be deceived. I went back to the farm and tried to make the best of things, but it was hard. With everyone gone the vale was a different place. The wizard had destroyed our future. Catherine tried to convince me to look for a better life elsewhere, but all the communities we knew were deserted. There was nothing left. Eventually I decided to find out where Flak had taken the people. I thought I could convince them to come back if I could make the wizard show his true colors. By the time I arrived at Aurora Station it was too late.'

Pandora shook her head. 'But that's the thing I don't understand. Where is everyone? Where are the thousands of people in this recording? They didn't go back to Candlewick. God, it's that damn fly again.' The fly was back. It bounced madly off the window and made two circuits of the room before landing on the control console. Pandora brought her hand down hard and felt the sickening crunch of its hideous body beneath her palm. 'Finally. Got you, you bastard.'

Jason took her shoulders firmly. 'Pandora, listen to me. There is no fly. You've been waving your arms around like a lunatic, but there's nothing there.'

'What are you talking about? Look, it's—' She gestured at the console but the dead fly was gone. She looked at her hand. Her palm was clean. 'What the hell? What's happening?'

'This is what I've been trying to tell you. There is something poisoning the air at Aurora Station, a miasma. It makes people believe they are sick, but it's not real. Look at your arm.'

Pandora searched for the suppurating welt where the fly had bitten her. It was gone. 'There's nothing there. I've been feeling worse and worse ever since that damn thing bit me. I was convinced it had laid eggs inside me. I had nightmares about worms growing under my skin, feeding off my organs. Are you saying it was a hallucination?'

'I don't know,' Jason said. 'All I know is that anyone who comes to Aurora Station gets sick. Within days they develop horrific symptoms with no apparent cause.'

On the screen Sirella concluded her speech, which she delivered quietly but with rapt attention from the audience. Flak guided her away from the podium and the audience cheered like she was a beloved queen. The film flickered, and came to an end.

'The wizard left Aurora Station shortly after this film was made,' Jason continued. 'He said he had to search the world for more lost people so he could bring them to paradise. That was when people started to get sick. Their illnesses were varied. There was no pattern. Some got debilitating headaches, or went suddenly and inexplicably blind. Some got hideous growths on their faces, or their extremities began to rot and fall off. There was a panic. Without their savior to guide them they looked to Sirella as his protege. She told them to wait for a sign, and that's when Aiden came out of the wilderness. He carried the key that unlocked the artifact tower. As soon as the portal was revealed people went through in their thousands, including all the people from Candlewick.'

'Of course,' Pandora said, understanding at last. 'They believed it was the only way they could be healed. What the hell is on the other side of that portal?'

'I don't know, but I'm sure it isn't what Aiden and Sirella say it is. When I arrived they were the only people here, waiting for more stragglers to arrive so they could trick them into walking through the portal. I got sick just like everyone else, but I didn't buy what Sirella was selling. I left Aurora Station and I got better after only a few hours. That's when I realized what was happening and I knew I had to stop any more pilgrims going through that damn ring.'

'So that's why you've been living outside the garden, only coming inside to speak with pilgrims?'

'Exactly. I'm never here for more than a few hours. I try to warn people, but of course they never listen.'

Pandora suddenly realized what was happening to Holly. 'Oh God, Holly's not really sick, is she? It's just this miasma, or whatever it is. If we can get her away from this place she'll be okay. We need to get back to the dome right away.'

CHAPTER 56

They raced through the garden, where the peaceful paths and quiet avenues had taken on a sinister aspect in Pandora's mind. Everything her hosts had told her was a lie. There were never any pilgrims at Aurora Station, only innocent victims of Flak's evil schemes. Driven from their homes by plagues, famines, and disasters, they were manipulated into following the very man who caused their misery on arduous treks across the wilderness to this place where he planned a final brutal betrayal.

Well, Pandora was sick of it. She would take her sister beyond the walls of the garden straight away, carrying Holly with her own two arms if necessary. If what Jason said was true she would show signs of improvement almost immediately. If they were lucky they might be able to blink back to Earth before Aiden and Sirella even knew they were gone.

The residential dome came into view and they hurried inside. Holly was gone.

'Oh-no-no-no,' Pandora shook her head in panic. 'Holly? Holly, are you here?' She searched the bedrooms and the atrium. There was no sign of her anywhere. 'She must have woken up and wandered off. We have to find her before Aiden and Sirella do.'

'I think they already found her,' Jason said. 'The

medical computer is gone.'

The boxy contraption was nowhere to be seen. It was unlikely Holly had taken it with her.

'Oh God, they've taken her,' Pandora said. 'They've sent her into the portal without me.'

They sprinted across the garden towards the looming shadow of the artifact. The obsidian door stood open, revealing shadows and mist within. The first thing she saw was a wheeled gurney in the middle of the floor amid the swirling vapors. The padded bed was empty and Pandora's heart contracted in agony, believing Holly had already been taken into the ring. Then she saw Aiden at the steps of the portal, holding Holly's limp form in his arms.

'Get away from her you asshole,' she thundered, her voice echoing around the chamber.

Beside Aiden, Sirella smiled with pure compassion. 'Pandora, it's going to be all right, you'll see. In just a few moments you and your sister will be together in eternal bliss.'

'Fuck you!' Pandora dashed across the open space, her feet throwing up currents of thick fog in her wake. She flung herself at Aiden but something struck her knee with incredible force and knocked her to the ground where she writhed in excruciating pain.

Sirella stood over her, wielding her cane like a club. Her frail, weak form had looked almost insubstantial in her voluminous robes, but this was revealed to be just another fraud. She glared at Pandora, her face twisted in a scowl of fury. 'Why would you oppose us? Why would you turn away the beautiful gift we are offering?'

Jason reached Aiden and wrestled Holly from his arms. Aiden proved stronger than his bookish appearance suggested. He took Holly back and threw her aside like a rag doll to be lost in the mist. He launched himself at Jason, pounding him with blows that forced him to retreat across the chamber.

Sirella held aloft the walking stick like a woodcutter's axe. She brought it down hard, but Pandora rolled aside and seized Sirella's robe. The long flapping cloth got caught up in their thrashing limbs and Sirella tumbled on top of her.

Pandora fought to her feet, tearing Sirella's robes away in the process. Beneath, she wore a plain white shift that exposed arms and legs which were covered in running sores that leaked blood and pus over her body. So she was not immune to the miasma that sickened the residents of the garden, but nor was she weakened by it.

With a scream of hate Sirella threw herself at Pandora and put her hands around her throat. Her windpipe closed tight under the fierce pressure from Sirella's thumbs. She choked in panic. Sirella took advantage of her surprise and dragged her towards the portal. She pushed her face into Pandora's and grimaced. 'I'm going to show you things beyond your wildest dreams.'

In her peripheral vision she saw Jason pull a knife from his belt. He slashed at Aiden, cutting his face, his chest and his arms. Pink foam spewed forth from his wounds, hissing noisily in the air as Aiden backed off, screaming expletives. He was not human. Why was Pandora not surprised?

Jason's victory was too far away to improve Pandora's situation. Sirella maintained a crushing grip on her throat and pulled her up the steps to the portal. Still she spat into Pandora's face. 'This is what eternity looks like, cunt. This is what you deserve.'

For an instant they teetered on the brink. Pandora had time to notice that the mist inside the portal had cleared and showed another idyllic scene. This time it was the living room on Edgewood Avenue. The season had changed to midwinter and the Christmas tree was luminous with festive splendor. Two stacks of neatly wrapped presents were under the tree, and the choir of King's College, Cambridge, was singing Hark the Herald Angels Sing on the CD player.

Sirella shifted her weight and kicked Pandora's feet out from under her. Locked together in a fatal embrace they fell into the portal.

The vision of the house in Ojai vanished. Another cruel illusion dispelled. The reality of the far side of the ring was darkness. Utter darkness. Utter silence. She could no longer feel Sirella's hands at her throat. She could no longer feel anything. There was no sensation in her hands, her feet. She tried to draw breath into her tortured lungs but she had no lungs with which to breathe. She tried to cry out in fear but she had no mouth. She tried to run back towards the ring but she had no legs. This was a realm without matter and form.

It was not without time, however. She was aware of the passage of one moment to the next, and that allowed the possibility of change. She told herself this formless feeling was just another trick, another deception by the wizard to make her believe she had been stripped of her body and cast into the limitless darkness beyond the universe. Any minute now the lights would go up and she would see the wizard's gloating face, mocking her. Any minute now.

Time passed. The void was silent but it was not peaceful. Pandora had experienced sensory deprivation tanks that made her feel like she was floating in an astral plane of calm, but here in the true void there was no calm. Instead there was chaos that churned endlessly inside her mind. Starved of input, her consciousness began consuming itself, replaying thoughts and memories that tormented her with blame, resentment, misery and fear.

It had been too long now. Much too long. With never an instant of relief in the unrelenting screaming darkness she tried to bring her thoughts under control by counting slowly. She counted to a hundred. A thousand. Many thousands and tens of thousands. She lost count and started again. And again. And again.

Time extended to infinity and Pandora went mad.

CHAPTER 57

Light. Brilliant, unbelievable light, blinding her, scouring her flesh with ecstatic burning sensation. She screamed, terrified at the sudden and unexpected return of body, form, matter and feeling. Her leg was an agony of pain and her throat felt so tight she could barely gasp for breath.

A figure stood over her, indistinct, blocking out the light. The wizard had finally arrived to inflict further torment and laugh at her suffering. She struck out with her fists and her feet. 'Get away from me. Get away!'

Her eyes focused and she saw it was only Jason. 'Whoa, whoa, calm down,' he said. 'You're okay now.'

She sat up and looked around. The light that blinded her was just the daylight through the open doorway of the artifact tower. She lay on the steps of the spinning ring, struggling to suck air into her lungs. 'How long? How long was I in there?'

Jason shrugged. 'How long? I don't know. A few seconds. I saw you fall through and ran over to pull you out.'

She glared at him. Did he think that was funny? What a sick joke to play on her. Yet there was evidence to support his words. The scene around her had not changed since the fight that had taken place in this chamber all that time ago. The gurney still sat in the middle of the room, and beside it was the medicomp. Aiden's broken body lay twitching on the floor, his head almost decapitated by Jason's knife. Pink gunge oozed out onto the floor and frothed nastily.

Holly was barely visible through the mist, lying in a heap. Jason checked her pulse. 'She's still alive. Just.'

Pandora stood shakily, trying to process the sensory overload crowding her mind. Everything looked exactly as it had before Sirella cast them through the portal. But that was years ago. Many years.

Jason picked Holly up and placed her on the gurney. 'Come on,' he said. 'We have to get out of this place before it kills us all.'

She followed Jason outside in a daze. He guided them towards one of the arched gates in the outer wall. Her legs felt strange, like prosthetic attachments that had replaced her real limbs. It was a conscious effort to put one foot in front of the other. After a hundred yards she stopped and fell to her knees.

'What's wrong?' Jason knelt at her side.

Her lips were dry. She had forgotten the sensation. She wetted them with her tongue and almost wept at the feeling. 'This isn't another trick, is it?' she said, fearing the worst. 'Is this a delusion, or a hallucination?'

She vomited onto the path. Jason held her upright to prevent her falling into the sickly puddle. 'Pandora, what happened to you? What was on the other side of the portal?'

'Nothing!' Her voice had a hysterical edge to it. In the void she had had no voice and she no longer knew how to moderate her tone. 'There was nothing there. It was just... it was just eternity in nothingness. Alone. Forever. Please, please tell me it's over. This isn't just a fantasy, is it?'

He held her tight. 'It's over. You're alright now. Holly will be alright, too. We just have to get you both away from here.'

He helped her to her feet. She walked unsteadily to Holly, unconscious on the gurney. She was so beautiful it made her cry. They continued on their way, Pandora pushing the gurney because holding onto it gave her support, both physical and emotional.

Beyond the garden the landscape was bleak. The ground was dusty and hard, with only a few outcroppings of rock and straggly trees to break the monotony. A mile from the gate was a patch of scrub bushes, in the midst of which was a broken-down vehicle of some kind. It was about the size of a school bus and had short stubby wings. It had crashed here a long time ago, and its metal frame was stained with corrosion and lichen. A hatch was open, leading to a cabin which had been converted into a simple home.

'Not much of a bachelor pad, I'll admit,' Jason said as he carried Holly inside and placed her on the bed.

Actually, the den was quite homey. Jason had spent most of his life living in a simple community, and he knew well how to provide comfort in primitive surroundings. The bed was a frame of bamboo poles supporting a mattress of foam that looked like insulation from the craft itself. A table had been constructed from metal sheets, and two chairs had been salvaged from the cockpit. There was a makeshift galley with a water tank and a stove improvised from high-tech engine components.

Pandora stood in the entryway and waited to be told what to do. She had forgotten what it was like to be a human being with a will of her own and agency to act in the world. Jason guided her to a chair beside the bed where she could see Holly and touch her.

'I have to return to the garden now,' Jason spoke slowly as if explaining to a child. 'I've spent the past few years figuring out some of this old tech, and I think I've built an effective bomb out of some fuel cells. I'm going to place it inside the artifact tower and blow it to hell.'

It was like listening to a radio broadcast from a faraway country. Pandora could hear his words and understand them, but what did it have to do with her? 'All those people on the other side,' she mumbled.

'I don't think there's any way back for them,' he said. 'I

grabbed you because you were only in there for an instant. I couldn't even pull Sirella out. She was just gone.'

'Just gone.' What terrible words.

Jason spent a few minutes making preparations and then departed, carrying a heavy pack on his back. Pandora remained inside the cabin, staring at a blank patch of wall. She knew that she had become insane. While imprisoned in the void she had spent long ages fantasizing about ways of ending her existence, to bring an end to the pain and misery. A thousand scenarios for suicide had been her comfort and recreation. Now that she was incarnate once more she could see a dozen methods of killing herself within this very room.

Not yet.

There was a knife on the table, fashioned from a strip of metal sharpened to a wicked edge. She could slice open her throat and let the hot arterial blood spray across the room. She could stab herself in the eye and force the blade through her brain.

Wait.

On the other hand, she had prepared many other methods that required no tools at all. Using only her teeth she could tear into the flesh of her wrists, chewing through her skin, sinew and muscle until she found a vein and ripped it out of her arm. She looked at her wrist and studied the vein.

Please wait.

'I'm not listening to you,' she said aloud. The void had been filled with voices that existed only in her mind. She had long ago accepted them as her only companions and friends. The voices spoke constantly, shouting accusations, whispering hatred, arguing, suggesting novel torments to each other. But there had been one voice that was different. Quieter than the others, often drowned out, it was audible only in rare moments when Pandora was able to distract the others into arguing among themselves.

Wait just a little while longer.

'Why should I? I don't need you any more. Get lost.'

Something wondrous is going to happen.

'Fuck off.'

Holly opened her eyes and sat up. She coughed, farted, scratched herself, and looked at Pandora expectantly.

'Hi Hol,' Pandora said flatly. 'Glad you're okay.'

Holly, ever alert to the feelings of others, knew something was wrong. She rearranged herself on the bed so she could put an arm around her sister and rub her shoulder.

'I'm not well, Hol. Don't think I'll ever be well again, to be honest. Something happened to me while you were unconscious. I went on a little jaunt. A long jaunt, actually. Longer than you think.'

Holly squeezed her hand and kissed her cheek. Pandora found the physical sensation overwhelming and she began to sob uncontrollably, a gibbering wreck reduced to the emotional level of an infant. Holly held her and rocked her gently.

A long while later Jason returned. Pandora was curled up on the bed, incapable of making introductions. Holly stared at the newcomer warily and then her face lit up with recognition. She threw herself at Jason, wrapping her legs around his middle and showering his face with kisses. The vehicle was really too cramped for this kind of behavior and the cabin rattled as knick-knacks flew off shelves and clattered to the metal floor.

'Wow, it's good to see you too,' Jason laughed, gently peeling Holly off his body. Once the fuselage stopped rocking from side to side, his expression became serious. 'Listen, both of you, I've made all the preparations to destroy the artifact. If you want to see some fireworks you should come outside now.'

Pandora had no interest in the activities of these ghosts and specters who had materialized around her after so much time alone, but Holly prodded her into an upright position and pushed her out of the door.

The day had grown old and the sun was setting in the west. The artifact tower was a dramatic spike rising from the flat land, visible for many miles in every direction. In the fading daylight the aurora at its pinnacle painted the sky in shades of red and green. Above the perimeter wall, lesser buildings were visible, forming a complex skyline of curves, pyramids, spirals and spires.

Jason held a remote control device in his hands. 'I hope I haven't overcooked this. If the power cells from this old craft release too much energy we could have a nuclear explosion on our hands.'

Death by atomic incineration. Pandora looked forward to it.

He lifted the device and hesitated. 'Pandora, I need your advice. If I blow up the portal, those people on the other side will never be able to return. They'll be dead.'

'Blow it up,' she said. 'You'll be releasing them from hell.'

Jason activated a switch and the garden was engulfed in flame. The ground rumbled and a peal of thunder shook the air. Smoke rose from the base of the tower, and the entire structure toppled like some vast prehistoric tree.

Then a strange thing happened. The air around the garden shimmered like a mirage, and Aurora Station vanished. The perimeter wall disappeared, along with all the Astari domes, towers, and spheres. The long avenues of trees and lush flower beds were also gone. Only the gray wasteland remained around the fallen ruins of the tower.

'The whole thing was an illusion,' Jason said. 'Only the tower was real.'

There wasn't much to be said after that. They returned to the crashed aircraft where Jason cooked a simple broth. Pandora had difficulty coordinating her limbs to guide the food into her mouth and made a mess on herself, the table, the floor. Depressed with her failure at this simple task she pushed the bowl aside miserably. Thereafter, Holly fed her with a spoon.

When night came the sisters slept on the bed together while Jason took the floor. Holly wrapped Pandora up in hugs that she found smothering and claustrophobic, but her sister would not let go. She surrendered herself to Holly's suffocating love, and soon found something like peace. Sleep was longer in coming. She had forgotten sleep as a concept and for hours she lay in Holly's embrace with her eyes open, staring into the dark.

CHAPTER 58

When morning came she felt different. She was no longer obsessed with the urge to destroy herself. Instead her thoughts kept returning to a strange dream she had had when sleep finally overtook her weary body. The dream had something to do with the garden, and when her companions were awake she insisted on returning there to search for its meaning.

Jason watched her guardedly as they wandered aimlessly around the ruins of the tower. Her insanity was as plain to him as to herself, and she knew he had agreed to this exploration only as a way of humoring the deranged woman who had emerged from the artifact after enduring indescribable torments in a realm beyond comprehension. Holly, too, looked at her with concern and with pity. But something had changed within her. Hidden somewhere in this blasted land was a secret neither Sirella nor Aiden had known. Something wondrous.

That there had once been an outpost of the Old Kingdom here was obvious, though its ruined structures were almost hidden beneath the scrub. A fragment of wall here, or a patch of roadway there, was all that remained of a fine city that had been destroyed in the distant past. Only the auditorium was largely intact, though its dome was cracked and open to the sky.

She led them between crumbling walls and along overgrown avenues, searching, trying to recall the elusive details of her dream. Using the base of the tower as a reference they located the residential dome where they had lived since arriving at Aurora Station. With the illusion of the garden stripped away it was revealed as a hovel of rough wooden poles covered with rotting canvas. Within, the elegant Astari furniture had transformed into shapeless heaps of wood. The soft comfortable beds had become stinking animal skins lying in the dirt. Where the food synthesizer had been was only a wooden box filled with unspeakable things none of them wanted to investigate too closely. The pleasant patch of lawn where she and Holly had planted seedlings was just dust and weeds. On an impulse Pandora kicked around inside the hovel searching for the friendship necklaces she had made. There was nothing but filth and rubbish.

They continued onward. Pandora knew her companions' patience was wearing thin, but she remained determined and single-minded. It was almost midday when she finally saw it.

'There! Look, that's it,' she said. 'That's the place from my dream.'

Rounding a tangle of gorse sprouting from a ruined dome, they came to a building that was wholly intact. It was a cupola of spotless white stone supported by tall fluted columns, enclosing an area around thirty feet across. It resembled an ancient Greek temple, though its marble blocks were perfectly smooth and white as though masons had completed its construction only yesterday.

'This wasn't here before,' she said, pointing insistently at the building. 'I remember this place. There was a big pyramid-shaped building here. Aiden said it was a data processing center.'

Jason nodded patiently. 'Okay. I recognize this building. It's called a sending circle.'

'A sending circle? What's that?'

'Sending circles were a communication device used by

the Old Kingdom. I don't remember seeing one here at Aurora Station, but they're common all across Entara. I must have seen half a dozen during my journey here.'

'A communication device?' Pandora said. 'Who does it communicate with?'

'Don't get excited. All the sending circles are broken. They just repeat an emergency message that was sent at the end of the last war.'

'How does it work?'

Jason gestured with his hand. 'Just step inside the circle and you'll see.'

They mounted the steps and walked under the shade of the dome. As soon as Pandora's feet touched the inner circle, a soft chime filled the air. Particles of light gathered at the center of the structure, forming into the shape of a beautiful young woman. The image was holographic, faintly transparent, and glowed with ethereal light. The woman wore a long cloak of dark material covered with silver stars that shimmered and sparkled as if whole galaxies were woven into the fabric. Addressing an invisible audience, the woman began to speak.

'Friends, it is my sad duty to bring you news that our enemy is victorious, and our once-beautiful kingdom lies defeated and in ruins. The evacuation has begun, and now all Knights of Entara must hasten to the last fortress still standing against the powers of darkness, the Crystal Spire. There we shall make our final stand.

'It pains me deeply to leave so many of you behind. A shadow has fallen across our land, and the darkness will rule for many long years to come. But you must not despair, for although these dark times may be hard and filled with sadness, they will not last forever. You must trust and have faith that some day, in a distant future, heroes shall return to Entara and lift the curse that lies on our beloved land. Then we may meet again, with joy and with love, and we shall be together until the end of days.' The chime sounded a second time, and the woman faded into nothingness.

Pandora watched in astonishment. 'Who is she?'

'No one knows her name,' Jason said. 'People call her the Starlight Queen, because of her robes. The folklore is that she was the last ruler of the Old Kingdom before it was destroyed.'

'So what happened to her?'

Jason shrugged. 'Who knows? That message was sent ten thousand years ago, to an army that had already been defeated. Presumably she died along with all the other Astari.'

'No, she's not dead. I know that woman. I've seen her before.'

'Pandora, that's not possible.'

She grunted in frustration. She knew she was right. How could she explain what she had learned? Late last night, the Starlight Queen had appeared to her in a dream. No, a *vision*. It was a strange dream filled with symbolism and hidden meaning.

The queen had met her here in the sending circle, a lone building amid the ruins. When Pandora climbed the steps beneath the cupola, the queen lifted a crystal bottle and presented it to her. Pandora took it and removed the stopper, understanding its purpose without needing to be told.

Then a very disturbing thing happened. Something stirred within Pandora's chest and erupted out through her throat. A black cloud spewed forth from her mouth, twisting through the air like a serpent made of smoke. The cloud expanded to incredible size and became a storm that blackened the sky; a vortex of incredible power that tore trees from the ground and toppled the ancient walls of the Astari.

When it seemed the storm must consume the entire world, the queen spoke a single word in a language Pandora did not know. The word vibrated through the air, growing larger and larger until it encircled the storm. Writhing like a living thing, the storm fought against the word, but it had no power to resist. The storm was forced inside the crystal bottle until it was filled to the brim.

Pandora replaced the stopper. The air became still, sunlight filled the sky, and suddenly the wasteland was gone. The garden had returned, along with the trees, the flowers and all the beautiful buildings of the Old Kingdom. Birds sang lullabies to each other, and the air was filled with sweet scents.

The queen surveyed the transformed landscape with satisfaction. 'Pandora, I have freed you from the storm, and now you may enjoy the garden as it was intended to be, many long eons ago. I will keep this special place for you alone so you may visit it during sleep and replenish yourself for the long journey ahead. You have suffered dreadfully on account of me, and that is something I cannot bear to witness. The wizard cannot reach me where I am, and this drives him into a frenzy of rage and madness. For the sake of hatred of me, he inflicts pain on those I have called to be my servants.'

She took the crystal bottle from Pandora's hands. Inside its glass prison the storm continued to twist and writhe. The queen continued. 'I have taken away your pain, but I must warn you that it is only a temporary reprieve. One day, you must open this bottle again and face the full power of the storm within. Only if you are true to your quest will you have the strength to overcome it.'

'What quest?' Pandora said. 'I don't understand.'

'You will. Now awaken, and receive another gift as a token of my love.'

She came out of her reverie and faced Jason. 'Elaine. Her name is Elaine.'

Jason shook his head. 'You can't possibly know that. Pandora, this message is ancient history. We don't even know if that's what the Astari really looked like. This could be a recreation that somebody made thousands of years later, as a teaching tool, or a storytelling device.'

Pandora dismissed him with an impatient wave. 'That's ridiculous. And there's something else. I just figured out what this whole charade has been about. The artifact, the garden, the pilgrims. This place, I mean the sending circle, has been here all along but Flak hid it behind one of his illusions.'

'Why would he do that?' Jason said. 'I told you, sending circles are all over the place in the wilderness. The message here is the same as all the others.'

'Exactly, that's why he needed to hide it. Don't you see? Flak built the artifact to make people think *this* was the place the Astari went after they were defeated. He wanted to trick them into thinking the Astari traveled through the portal. The pilgrims believed they were going to meet the Starlight Queen.'

Jason grudgingly acceded her logic. 'Okay, that makes sense.'

'Of course it makes sense,' Pandora said. 'But instead of finding an eternity of happiness on the other side, there's just a never-ending void. The wizard altered time over there somehow. One second here is many years on the other side. I was only in the void for a few moments but I experienced years alone. If the people of Candlewick went through the portal twelve years ago, they must have suffered subjectively for millions of years. Oh God, Jason, it's a good thing you blew up that portal, believe me.'

'All right, I believe you. It must have been a horrific experience.'

She sighed. 'Jason, I'm okay. Last night I dreamed about Elaine. I met her here and she healed me.'

'She healed you?' Incredulity.

'How can I make you understand? I'm not crazy, okay? I was crazy before, but I'm not crazy now. I know it sounds crazy, but I'm not crazy. Does that make sense?'

Jason looked doubtful. She turned to Holly for support. 'Holly, back home in your studio, you painted a portrait of a beautiful queen. Do you remember? That was the Starlight Queen, wasn't it? It looked exactly like her. That means you've seen her too, right? Was it in a dream? Did you blink somewhere else and meet her?'

Holly was meandering around the circle in her airy

way. She spotted something glittering on the floor and picked it up.

'What is it, Hol?' Pandora said. 'What have you found?'

Holly held out two golden necklaces, each with a heart-shaped pendant of midnight-blue crystal with flecks of gold.

'What is it?' Jason said, looming over them.

'Oh my God, it's the friendship necklaces,' Pandora said. 'Holly, I made two necklaces using the matter synthesizer because I wanted to say how sorry I am for abandoning you at Blackthorn. They vanished when the artifact was destroyed.'

'Then how did they end up here?' Jason said.

Holly looked pleased. She placed one of the gold chains around Pandora's neck, and handed her sister the other so she could reciprocate.

'She left them here for us,' Pandora said while Holly held her hair aside to receive the necklace. 'Holly, this is my promise that I'll never leave you again. No matter what happens, we face our troubles together. Agreed?'

Jason was nonplussed. 'Wait a minute, who left them for you?'

Pandora laughed and shook her head. It was too difficult to explain. She felt good. Elated. The demons had fled her mind and the voices were silent at last. The memories of what she had suffered in the void were still with her, but it was as if a veil had been thrown over those experiences so she perceived them only dimly.

She felt empowered. Brave. Ready for anything. After all, what could the wizard do to her now that was worse than what she had already suffered? Nothing, that's what. Now there was only one thing to do: Return to Earth and start kicking some serious ass.

'It doesn't matter,' she said. 'All that matters right now is we have to get back to Earth as soon as possible. Holly, are you ready?'

Holly stood to attention and gave her best Captain

Invincible salute.

Jason was alarmed by this sudden development. 'You're leaving?'

'Yes. We have a lot of things to deal with back home. You could come with us. I have a feeling Holly's power brought us to you for a reason.'

'Back to Earth? I'd never even thought about it before. It didn't seem possible.'

Holly held out her hand. He stared at it uncomprehendingly.

Pandora gestured at the wasteland. 'There's not much for you here any more. Are you going to live alone in that crashed plane forever?'

Jason scratched his head. 'I guess not. Hey, maybe we should talk this over first.'

Holly grabbed his hand.

'Remember to blink,' Pandora said.

'Remember to what?'

CHAPTER 59

They materialized in a public park. Pandora assessed their situation and judged that they had arrived in a safe place. A few people were dazzled by the momentary flash of light, but they were looking up at the sky for an explanation and took no notice of the travelers. She guided her companions out of the park and onto a commercial street that looked like the downtown area of a small town somewhere in the Mountain West.

'I have absolutely no idea where we are,' she said. 'We must be miles away from Blackthorn.'

Jason was rubbing his eyes vigorously. 'Can't see a damn thing. Couldn't you have given me some warning?'

'I gave you ample warning. Hey look, all these cars have Colorado plates. So at least we're still in the right state.'

'Colorado? I thought we were going back to California. I was just beginning to remember it.'

'No, we had to run away from California to escape the police. I probably should have mentioned it sooner, but I'm being chased by federal agents for committing terrorist acts, blowing up shopping malls, mass poisonings, acid attacks, murder, and probably some other stuff I can't remember right now.'

'Good to know,' Jason said. 'Are these activities purely

recreational or are you on the global terrorism payroll?'

'Oh, I didn't actually do any of that stuff, obviously. Some people found out about Holly's power, and they want to capture her and study her. They're framing me for a whole load of crimes to make it hard for us to evade them.'

'I see. Remind me why we came back to this planet, exactly?'

'We're in Wayfield, Colorado.' She pointed to a sign outside a public library. 'Never heard of it. Damn. We're staying with some friends in a place called Blackthorn. We have to find a way to contact them without alerting the police. Blackthorn doesn't have a telephone, but maybe I can call the post office in Zenith and have them deliver a message. Still, that would take at least a day to arrive, and we don't have anywhere to go in the meantime.'

Jason had recovered his eyesight and stood staring at passing traffic and pedestrians. He was transfixed by the pickup trucks, neon bar signs, and the women with short skirts. A trio of Harley-Davidsons thundered past, and he covered his ears at the noise.

'I never thought I'd see any of this again,' he said. 'I don't belong here any more.'

'Don't worry, we'll trim that beard, get you some Levi's and a flannel shirt. You'll be an American again before you know it.'

Actually, Pandora was concerned about Jason's appearance. He was ragged and hairy, wearing homespun clothing and, now that she thought about it, no shoes. He looked like a Neanderthal, and he was attracting attention. That was the last thing they needed right now.

Down the street, the Harleys abruptly stopped in traffic. The three riders turned in their saddles to stare at the travelers. A brief conference took place and they made a rapid U-turn that left long arcs of rubber on the tarmac. They reached the travelers and surrounded them, mounting the sidewalk and revving their engines. The bikers wore grim chapter badges of a winged skull on a gothic cross with the motto *Hell Riders*. All of the riders were women.

One of them removed a pair of aviators and spat onto the ground. 'Is your name Pandora Castell?'

Pandora's heart was racing. No doubt her face still featured on every damn front page in America. How much was the reward for her arrest now? A quarter of a million dollars? That would buy a lot of shiny chrome fittings for a vigilante biker. She stepped towards Holly, ready to shield her from harm until they could blink back to Entara again, only moments after arriving on Earth.

The bikers glanced at each other. 'It's okay, we're here to help,' the lead biker said. 'Sister Mary sent us.'

Pandora gaped in disbelief. 'Sister Mary? What do you know about Sister Mary?'

An old Dodge van pulled up at the curb alongside the bikes. It was a custom wagon with gleaming chrome wheels, flaming arches, and spectacular fantasy artwork on its flanks depicting an angel and a demon locked in combat. Another leather-clad woman was at the wheel, and in the passenger seat was a familiar face.

'Mother Abigail,' Pandora exclaimed as the passenger door opened and Abigail climbed out. Instead of her gray habit and headscarf she wore secular clothes, blue jeans and a cream blouse.

'I'm so glad to see you both,' she said as Holly wrapped her up in a bear hug. 'Your friends at Blackthorn have been beside themselves with worry.'

'How is this possible?' Pandora said, joining Holly in the embrace. 'I thought you'd been arrested. How did you know we were here?'

'Explanations will have to wait. We have to get you off the street right away before anyone recognizes you.'

'You'll get no argument from me,' she turned to indicate Jason. 'Mother Abigail, this is Jason. He's our friend and he needs to come with us.'

Abigail nodded. 'Very well. Now come along, all of you, we have to get moving.'

The back of the Dodge was a velvet wonderland with

padded purple walls, a double bed, leopard-skin cushions, a fridge, a TV, and a PlayStation. Pandora and Jason perched awkwardly on the bed while Holly sat cross-legged on the thick pile rug and investigated the contents of the fridge.

No sooner were the doors closed than the van lurched into motion, accompanied by the roar of motorbike engines. The van's driver picked up a curious circular device covered in flashing lights and buttons. Operating a switch with her thumb she spoke into the gadget. 'Control, this is Ghost Leader. We have the eggs in the basket and are returning to the nest. Over.'

An excitable girlish voice buzzed from the device in response. 'Roger, Ghost Leader. That's the news we've been dying to hear.'

Pandora lunged forward and seized the handset. 'Fiona? Is that you?'

'Pandora! Yes, it's me. Oh well, so much for code names. But this is, like, a totally secure channel. I made these radio-things using quantum frequencies so no one can listen in on us.'

'You're a genius,' Pandora said.

'Is Holly there?'

'Yes, she can hear you.'

'Holly, I missed you so much. I was so worried about you. Are you okay?'

Holly cast about her for some method of reply. There was a minibar beside the fridge and she grabbed a glass and a spoon, tapping a rapid tattoo into the radio.

'Can you hear that?' Pandora said. 'I think it means she's okay.'

'Yes, I can hear. Thanks, Hol. Listen, I gotta go. I'm monitoring your progress by satellite and I have to make sure no one's following you. I'll see you guys back at Blackthorn.'

The Dodge sped out of Wayfield, Colorado, with their escort of bikers. Once they were on Route 160 headed west, Abigail turned in her seat to address the travelers.

'It's about a four hour drive back to Blackthorn. That should be plenty of time for us to catch up and compare notes. First, allow me to introduce Ruby Reardon, who has been kind enough to organize our transport for today.'

'Hi guys,' Ruby grinned over her shoulder.

'Ruby is the director of a society of lay-sisters under the authority of the Sisters of the Sacred Heart,' Abigail continued. 'Many of our former residents maintain close contact with the convent and take vows as secular members of our community. As you can see, they are also keen bikers.'

Ruby rolled up the sleeve of her leather jacket to reveal a tattoo of a winged skull on a gothic cross, identical to the bikers' patches. Beneath the skull were the words *RIP Ruby Rox*. 'I lived at the convent for six months. I was into some bad stuff in Vegas. Always in and out of jail, hospital ICUs, homeless hostels. Ruby Rox could make a thousand dollars a night and blow it all on drugs and casinos the next day. Mother Abigail saved my life. I'd be dead if it wasn't for her.'

'Same here,' Pandora said.

'I got this tattoo to mark the end of my old life and the beginning of a new one. Some of the other girls did the same, and before long it became our symbol. The Hell Riders, we called ourselves; the ghosts who rode out of Hell. When we heard about the convent fire, we rode straight to Vegas to see if we could help. It was chaos there, what with Mother Abigail in jail and Sister Mary missing. We all knew the accusations against Mother Abigail were false, but the police wouldn't talk to us, neither would the press.'

Pandora interjected. 'I was so shocked to hear what happened. The agency punishes anyone who tries to help us. I'm so sorry we've brought this down upon you. But how did you escape from prison?'

Abigail chuckled. 'Thankfully, escape wasn't necessary. I owe your friend Jackie a great debt of gratitude. She contacted me in her capacity as an attorney and got me released from jail without any stain on my record.'

'That's amazing,' Pandora said. 'Jackie's the best.'

'She spirited me away to your stronghold at Blackthorn, and it is from there that we set out to meet you today.'

'But I still don't understand how you found us so fast. We'd only been back on Earth for a few minutes before you arrived.'

'That is a little more difficult to explain,' Abigail said. 'Ever since the convent fire, I have experienced vivid dreams about Sister Mary. At first, I thought they were just my own subconscious dealing with the trauma of the fire and my wrongful arrest. But the dreams had a strange quality of realism to them. I dreamed that Sister Mary was imprisoned in a dark place, with no windows, surrounded by people who had been specially trained to resist her gift of natural prophecy. There were other detainees in that place, each of them gifted in different ways. I came to believe that Sister Mary was using her gift to reach out to me for help, but I was powerless to do anything for her.

'Then last night I saw Sister Mary in a dream once again, and this time she was greatly excited. She told me she had succeeded in psychically contacting Holly, who had sent her a single vivid image: A street sign in Wayfield, Colorado.'

Pandora stroked Holly's hair. 'You knew where we were going before we were even ready to leave.'

'As soon as I woke up, I recognized the significance of that dream and I asked Ruby to bring us here as soon as possible. It's a wonder she didn't think I was crazy.'

'We all know about Sister Mary's gift,' Ruby added. 'She's real, real bad at keeping it a secret. As soon as Mother Abigail said she'd dreamed about her, I knew it was the real deal so we fueled up and got ready to ride.'

'Well, I think that about brings us up to date,' Abigail said. 'But what about you? Where have your adventures taken you since we last met? And what about your friend, Jason? How do you fit in with all this?'

'I don't think I fit in anywhere,' Jason said, sucking thoughtfully on a Coke from the fridge. 'I've been away for fifteen years and I'm a little out of the loop. Actually, I want to hear more about this group that kidnaps people with gifts.'

Pandora began her story as the convoy turned north onto Route 550, the same winding mountain road Jackie had used to smuggle them to Blackthorn weeks earlier. The journey north was a long one, and Pandora had plenty of time to recount all the events that had transpired since she and Holly had rediscovered Entara. It was a revelatory experience for Mother Abigail, and especially for Ruby, who punctuated the story with cries of amazement and disbelief. Jason listened in silence without commenting at all. When she was finished with her tale he lay back on the bed and closed his eyes as if contemplating all he had heard.

Afterwards it was quiet in the van for a long time until Ruby put a tape on the stereo, and Creedence Clearwater Revival blared through the open windows for many miles.

They arrived at Blackthorn in the early evening just as the sun was disappearing behind the jagged peaks. To Pandora's surprise, the mountain prairie was a hive of activity. A dozen pickup trucks were parked in a field west of the house, along with several large RVs and many motorbikes. Ruby and her biker escort maneuvered through the open gate and parked in a row of other customized vehicles. Camping chairs were arranged around beer coolers, and music blared from stereos. Smoke rose from barbecues, and the air was filled with the scent of cooking meat. The sigil of the winged skull and gothic cross was prominent everywhere, on leather jackets, motorcycle gas tanks, tattooed on exposed flesh and flying from pennants.

Ruby and her fellow bikers were greeted raucously by a throng of black-clad women at the nearest barbecue. From another direction, a smaller figure darted through the crowd and flew at Holly.

'Holly-Holly-Holly!' Fiona shouted. Holly picked her up and spun her around and around until they both collapsed onto the grass in a dizzy heap of happy hugs.

Jackie arrived at a slightly more decorous pace and entangled Pandora in her arms. 'Oh God, we thought you were dead.'

'Jackie, we're okay,' Pandora said.

'We found a rucksack of belongings strewn about the path, and footprints in the mud leading to the ravine. We thought you had been confronted by the agency and fled into the woods, then fell into the water and drowned.'

'It's all my fault,' Pandora said. 'I tried to sneak away during the night but Holly followed me. We had an argument and fell into the ravine, but Holly blinked us to Entara. We would have come back sooner, but you know how these intergalactic journeys are.'

'Well, you're safe now, that's all that matters.'

'Jackie, what on Earth is happening here? Where did all these people come from?'

Jackie gestured to take in the whole field. 'Take a look around. Don't you recognize them?'

Pandora turned a full three-sixty and took a close look at the bikers for the first time. Most were strangers, but she was startled to see several familiar faces. 'Oh my God, it's the sisters from the convent.'

There was no doubt in her mind that several of the nearby bikers had been present at the convent in Las Vegas. Shorn of their sober gray habits and clad in black leather, denim and boots, these were the Sisters of the Sacred Heart.

Abigail came to join them. 'Our order is homeless now. The residents have each found good homes in other refuges, but our sisters are living vagrant without a vocation to pursue. Jackie's father has generously agreed to give us lodging here at Blackthorn.'

'Generosity had nothing to do with it,' Harfield emerged from the crowd carrying a six-pack of beer that he distributed to the new arrivals. 'I awoke Tuesday morning to the sound of thunder and found the Sisters of Our Lady of Motorcycles making themselves at home in the west paddock. Only when I tracked down my daughter did she explain just how generous I was about to be.'

Abigail cracked open her beer. 'Harfield has kindly donated the stables to be converted into a new convent. The building is perfect for the role. Solid oak frame, tiled floors, electricity and plumbing already installed. The staff quarters make ideal cells for the sisters, and the stalls can be easily turned into rooms for guests.'

Pandora gazed around at the biker-sisters in wonder. Sister Gabriela was nearby, sitting astride a custom Softail and adjusting the carburetor. 'Back at the convent they all looked so quiet and gentle. Now they look... badass.'

Abigail laughed. 'Most members of our order are former prostitutes and gang members. They may have taken vows of poverty, chastity and obedience, but they are certainly not shrinking violets.'

'Okay, but isn't Blackthorn a little remote for your needs?' Pandora said. 'There can't be much call for a women's refuge all the way up here in the mountains. We must be eighty miles from a major city. Where will your guests come from?'

Jackie interrupted. 'Ah, and on that note, I think we should all retire indoors. We have many things to discuss together about our future plans.'

CHAPTER 60

A group assembled in Fiona's attic around a broad table cluttered with computer printouts, satellite photographs, maps, and newspaper reports. A dozen computer workstations surrounded them, tucked between rafters or shoved under the eaves. Screens shone everywhere, displaying 24-hour news channels, flight tracking data, multi-spectrum EM analyzers, and orbital uplink streams. Fiona's alien computer code controlled everything, scrolling in incomprehensible never-ending streams of symbols, letters and numbers on green-screen CRT terminals.

Pandora sat between Holly and Fiona while Jackie, Abigail and Ruby sat opposite. Jason refused a seat at the table, instead occupying a distant corner where he watched the gathering from the shadows.

Jackie called the meeting to order and began by welcoming the travelers back to Blackthorn.

'Pandora, Holly, this time yesterday I expected to be planning a funeral. After we followed your trail to the ravine I was certain your bodies would be found washed up by the roadside miles downstream. I believed you had died fleeing the NCA, who had murdered you by their senseless pursuit just as surely as if they had shot you dead. The thought that you had died so needlessly filled us all with a great sadness we never thought we would recover from.

'But now you are here with us again and our mood has turned from sorrow to celebration. You are our dear friends, but you are also more than that. You are travelers on a strange journey that has come to involve all of us on some level. We have become a part of your adventure in different ways and for different reasons, and that gives us a bond closer than friendship.

'You have suffered unimaginable hardships as a consequence of evil people who despise the real magic and wonder embodied in this beautiful young woman, Holly. We are inspired by your courage, resilience and fortitude in the face of seemingly unbeatable odds. As fellow travelers on your journey, we here in this room are resolved to help ensure that this power does not fall into the hands of those who would manipulate it for their own ends. And I suppose all of that is just to say: Welcome back, girls. We've missed you.'

Fiona broke into spontaneous applause and whoops of joy. More beers were passed around, and Jackie had to bang her fist on the table to regain silence.

'Now then, glad though we are to have you returned to the fold, we still have a job of work to do. In your absence we have gained the friendship of the Sisters of the Sacred Heart, together with the Hell Riders, and I count these as powerful allies in our cause. Mother Abigail's supernatural communications with Sister Mary have confirmed the existence of a detainment facility where people with special gifts are imprisoned against their will. The question now is what to do about it. My own work pursuing a legal solution has unfortunately failed. The NCA operates above the law in an invisible stratosphere of secret black budget organizations which have the power to seize property, abduct citizens, and even murder them with impunity. With no recourse to law, we must now consider other approaches. Does anybody have any ideas?'

Ruby spoke up. 'I say we bust Sister Mary out of that

place. Camped outside, you've got upwards of fifty women who've got more experience of dangerous situations than an army platoon. We've got the manpower, the vehicles, and the weapons to get Sister Mary back. Just point us in the right direction and we're ready to ride at dawn.'

Mother Abigail spoke next. 'Although I am loath to endorse violence, I believe we must consider a more direct approach. In our work at the convent we were sometimes obliged to take extreme measures to protect our residents. On several occasions gangs broke into the convent to abduct women who planned to give evidence against them in court. Our sisters are thoroughly trained in the art of self-defense as a means to protect our wards, and several have received state awards for bravery in recognition of their commitment to defending justice. I consider our present situation merely an escalation of our ordinary business. A member of our community is threatened by thugs who wish her harm, and we intend to bring the hammer of justice down upon them.'

'Then it's agreed,' Jackie said. 'We're going to take the battle to the enemy. Mother Abigail, what information has Sister Mary given you about her situation?'

Abigail shook her head. 'Very little that might help us, I'm afraid. Sister Mary is being kept in a place that seems to her like an underground version of the convent. There is a large common room where detainees are free to socialize, and there are small bedrooms where they rest at night. There are no windows, which is probably what leads her to believe she is underground. There are guards who are present at all times, and it seems they have been specially trained to block attempts at psychic contact. She has been unable to recover any useful information from their minds. Her fellow detainees are all people with special gifts of an astonishing variety, though none are anywhere near as powerful as our dear Holly.'

'Does she have any idea where the facility is?' Jackie said.

'No, she doesn't.'

Jackie sighed. 'That is unfortunate. In that case, we must depend upon Fiona and her computer skills. Fi, what can you tell us?'

'Not much,' Fiona shrugged helplessly. 'For a while I was making progress, but now it's like I've hit a brick wall. I've had false leads, dead ends, crazy labyrinths of information that go around and around in circles. It's as if the agency knows I'm looking for them and they're blocking me at every turn.'

Abigail reached out and took her hand. 'Fiona, when the agency raided the convent they found a lot of strange equipment in your room. Agent Arnold was particularly interested, and he confiscated all of it before the convent burned down.'

'That must be it,' Fiona said. 'The machines I left in that room were all for diverting unwanted surveillance. They've reverse-engineered my technology and they're using it against me. God, I hate that guy.'

Pandora put her arm around Fiona. 'You've done amazing things to help us. Don't feel bad because he cheated you. He cheated us all.'

'Well, there are a couple of things I have been able to find out,' Fiona said. 'The NCA has its headquarters in Washington, DC, but the detainment facility is somewhere in Kansas. I've been able to track agency aircraft, purchases of drugs, chemicals, requisitioning of medical supplies. All of it points to Kansas, but that's all I know. Kansas is a big place. The agency could be hiding Sister Mary anywhere in an eighty-thousand-square-mile area.'

The table fell silent. No one knew what to say.

'I know where your friend is.' All eyes turned to Jason. He had not said a word since their arrival at Blackthorn and now he spoke from the shadows. 'I know where the agency keeps its prisoners.'

CHAPTER 61

The journey began two nights later. At midnight a long cavalcade set out from Blackthorn in an exodus that shook the mountains with the rumble of engines. Four dozen motorbikes, monster trucks, muscle cars, and lowriders tore across Colorado throughout the hours of darkness. They descended from the mountains and thundered east along I-70 with no regard for stealth or secrecy. Only when the sun was peeking over the horizon did they rest for a couple of hours at a truck stop on the border of Kansas.

From there, the convoy separated into two groups. The bikers continued east along the interstate while the larger vehicles traveled south to enter Kansas on a county road.

One vehicle remained behind at the truck stop, a Ford Galaxy rented by Fiona using an online pseudonym. Inside the car, nursing half-eaten McDonald's breakfasts, Pandora, Holly and Jason sat in silence and waited. Jason's appearance had been transformed since his return to Earth. His beard was gone and his hair had been neatly shorn and styled by one of the Hell Riders who ran a chain of hair salons in Arizona. He wore gray slacks and a blue polo shirt with a sports coat. At a glance he looked like a handsome young professional, perhaps a junior executive at a tech firm on his day off. Pandora had had her image similarly spruced up and wore dark pants and a yellow blouse to complement Jason's outfit. Her hair had been restyled to make her less recognizable and she wore horn-rimmed glasses, giving her a clerical appearance. Holly dressed more casually in a long flowery skirt and a voluminous knitted sweater. At frequent intervals she reached out to stroke Jason's newly shaven cheek, smiling as if perpetually delighted by its smoothness.

Jason had said little since the meeting in Fiona's attic. During that session he had stunned all present with a long and detailed description of a secret underground research facility hidden beneath a veterans' nursing home on the High Plains of Kansas. He did not know its precise location, but he knew its name: Beech Tree Lodge. Fiona worked at her computer and found it quickly, bringing up a satellite image on a projector screen.

For the next two hours the assembled group listened closely while Jason deconstructed the image, presenting them with intimate knowledge of the building's layout. Fiona used infrared and radar imaging from orbital platforms she had hijacked to reveal the internal structure of the building, confirming all that Jason had said. He added fresh detail to her images, describing guard stations, power generators, and most importantly, a classified laboratory positioned in an annex attached to the main structure.

He warned them that his information depended on faded memories from long ago, and that the detainees were being kept in a chamber deep underground where Fiona's sensors could not confirm his recollections.

The conclave had many questions, which Jason did his best to answer. He would not, however, be drawn on how he came by this information. He said only that he had once spent a lot of time there, many years ago.

Pandora sat in the driver's seat of the Ford MPV and watched the digital clock tick slowly towards their departure time. The Hell Riders had further to travel along rougher roads, while the three in the MPV had to arrive at their destination seeming calm and collected. Therefore they waited.

'I've been remembering more about when we were kids,' Pandora said after a long silence. 'After Holly first took us to Entara, we went back every chance we got. There was a whole new world to explore, and we wanted to go on an adventure every day. I'd cook up any excuse to get us out of the house for a few hours. We joined every after-school club and never turned up to any of them. We got junior memberships at the sports center, bought tennis rackets and swimsuits, but we never set foot in the place again. It was like leading a double life. I lied about us going out to the Arcade for sodas or ice creams, visiting the library, visiting friends or relatives. It's a wonder we never got caught out.

'I think our parents knew something was up, but they never mentioned it. Ever since I can remember, Holly and me have been in a world of our own, so to speak. Because Holly can't talk, we developed our own way of communicating that no one else could understand. It drove us away from other kids, and we spent all our time with each other. I guess Mom and Dad were just kind've used to us disappearing for hours, but they must have known we were lying about all those long absences from the house. God, we used to climb out our bedroom windows in the middle of the night and sneak over to the creek and blink to Entara, just so we could lie on the ground and look at the strange stars. Looking back, there's no way Mom and Dad didn't know we were gone. For some reason they never confronted us about it. They let us have our own space, and I really love them for that.

'Then one day everything was different. Every time we went to Entara you were already there, waiting for us. We were always excited to see you because you had all day every day to explore, and you always had new things to show us.

'It's all so blurry in my head. Catherine tried to tell us how it happened, but she only knew that we'd taken you to Entara because your life was in danger somehow. Jason, it has something to do with the agency, doesn't it? You were running away from them, weren't you?'

Jason stared out of the window at the early morning traffic. 'Do you remember on the day we met, I pointed a gun at you?'

'Yeah, you called us the snooping sisters,' Pandora said. 'I guess we were being pretty nosy, but that was quite an overreaction.'

'But that's not why I had the gun, remember?'

'Oh, I remember now. You said you were waiting for your dad because you were going to blow his head off. I was really shocked at that. My dad was a hero to me, and I never thought anyone could want to shoot their own father.'

'If you'd ever met my dad, you'd understand,' Jason said. 'The reason my mom and I were living in that abandoned trailer with no electricity and no running water is because we were running away from him. He was a psychopathic, murdering maniac, and we ran away because we feared for our lives.'

'That's awful, I'm so sorry. Was it alcohol, or drugs, or domestic violence?'

He laughed bitterly. 'None of those things. My dad never drank. He thought drugs were for losers.'

He fell silent and Pandora hesitated to ask more. 'I'm sorry, this is all very private for you, isn't it?'

'No, it's not that. It's just that… I didn't *remember* these things until a few hours ago. Every time I think about those days my head fills up with images so fast I can't make sense of them. It's disorienting, like a movie that's playing triple speed with all the scenes jumbled together.'

'I know how you feel,' Pandora said. 'When we first went back to Entara I felt like someone was rewriting my whole life right before my eyes. When we went to Catherine's house I damn near fainted. Even now I'm still processing everything that's happened.'

Jason took a moment to collect his thoughts. 'My dad was a psychologist, Doctor Henry Wyatt. He worked for the Army, studying soldiers who'd suffered psychological trauma in warzones. He was very good at his job. His studies demonstrated the importance of providing psychiatric care to soldiers before, during, and after their tours of duty. He conducted trials on Special Forces troops operating in Iraq. Under his care, combat-related stress declined eighty percent, depression declined sixty percent, and post-traumatic stress disorder was almost eliminated.

'The top brass were impressed and they gave him a grant to develop a broader psychological training program. He used the money to found a research facility, the Lethean Institute. The focus of his research was the changing nature of warfare in the modern era. He argued that war had become fundamentally psychological in nature, and troops needed to be trained accordingly. Modern warfare would be unrecognizable to a professional soldier from only a few decades ago. In the past, war was stunningly simple: Two armies met on opposing sides of a field and marched towards each other until one side or the other was victorious. Today's soldiers have to deal with improvised explosive devices hidden in roads, children with suicide bombs strapped to their chests, pregnant women with hand grenades in their purses. In a modern war, you'll never see the person who kills you. The future holds even more unexpected dangers, like intelligent killing machines, slow-acting poisons in food and water supplies, radiation beamed from satellites that cooks your brain inside your skull.

'My dad said that after the fall of the Berlin Wall, America's enemies could never again threaten us with jet planes, warships, or missiles. Instead, our enemies would use new, unpredictable tactics to shock us into submission. Asymmetric warfare is the technical term.

'9/11 was the big confirmation of his theories. No conventional army could predict or prevent attacks committed by ordinary people using jumbo jets as weapons. The brass panicked, and my dad's funding tripled. He published a report predicting a cascading emergency in the near future. Radical ideologies would spread across the Internet with unbelievable speed. Large numbers of people would fall prey to enemy propaganda. Our own people would become the enemy. Every doctor, artist, housewife and schoolchild would be a potential enemy agent. It would be the perfect terrorist organization, totally decentralized, with no hierarchy, no leaders, no soldiers, no weapons caches. Deadly new weapons could be developed and produced by a dispersed population with no direct links to each other. The situation would make it impossible for conventional troops to maintain order. The only possibility was total societal collapse within just a few years.'

Pandora felt a creeping sense of dread. 'That all sounds very familiar.'

'I thought it might,' Jason said. 'The report contained one important recommendation: A new federal agency was needed which could operate in the shadows, beyond any laws and without government oversight.'

'So your father founded the NCA,' Pandora said.

'That's right. And it gets worse. About the same time as the report came out, the Army asked my dad to study a woman named Delphine. She'd been captured during a Special Forces raid on a terrorist hideout in Somalia. According to reports, she had unusual psychic abilities that enabled her to stop a man's heart from a hundred yards away, see into people's minds, or teleport into locked vaults and steal the contents.

'My dad thought it was just superstitious nonsense. But he had his orders, so he agreed to examine her. At first he made no progress. Delphine had been severely abused by the Somalian warlord and his men, and she was in a catatonic state. The brass were demanding results and my dad got frustrated, so he tried more vigorous interrogation methods. I don't know exactly what happened next, but there was an explosion at the lab, and she escaped.

'After that, my dad wrote a second report that remained classified. In it, he stated that the most serious threat to civilization was what he called Delphinian Catastrophe. He theorized that psychic powers were present in a small fraction of the population, and each represented a serious threat to the stability of society. Those people, the Delphinians, could never be adequately controlled by any conventional means. No army could be trained to resist mind-control on a large scale. No weapons could defend against psychokinesis or teleportation. By definition, Delphinians existed outside the law because no conceivable law could be enforced against them. A single, powerful Delphinian could bring down governments, destroy economies, or bring about natural disasters. He decided that the only safe way to deal with Delphinians was to lock them all away.'

'Born secret,' Pandora said. 'That's what Agent Arnold said about Holly's power. He said she was so dangerous that her very existence was a threat to the world.'

'Right out of my dad's handbook. I was proud of my dad, can you believe that? He was an important man, making a difference in the world. He took me to the facility at Beech Tree Lodge and told me all about his work. I thought the people locked up there in underground rooms were monsters. Who wouldn't be frightened by someone who can control fire, or electricity, or change their shape? I was glad my dad had caught them and locked them away.'

Pandora was beginning to understand. 'Your mom didn't feel that way, though, did she?'

'Mom was completely devoted to my dad. She was in awe of him, really. She'd grown up dirt poor in the Ozarks, and he'd raised her up out of poverty to become the wife of a prominent doctor and scientist. She changed her whole persona to meet his expectations of a good wife. Changed her accent, changed her clothes, changed her tastes in music, art, movies. Everything.'

'I wrote in my diary about the day we met your mom,' Pandora said. 'I remember really wanting to make a good impression because we liked you and we wanted to be friends. But it was like she hated us on sight. She told us to get lost and never come back. I was really upset about that.'

'Your dad was a police officer,' Jason said. 'My dad controls the police. She was terrified you'd tell your dad about us and the information would get back to the agency.'

Pandora frowned as she remembered more. 'But there was something else weird as well. I planned to just ignore what your mom said and come back to visit you anyway. But every time I had an idea to ride out to your trailer, I got this awful feeling of guilt, like I was about to do something terribly wrong. I kept remembering that she had grabbed my hand and told me not to come again, and I couldn't bear to disobey.'

'Ironic, isn't it?' Jason said. 'Mom had totally subsumed her personality to obey my father, but she could make anybody else do anything she wanted.'

'Your mom had a gift, didn't she?' Pandora said. 'She was one of these Delphinians.'

'She avoided using her power because she hated coercing people. Her gift worked through touch, and she could plant an instruction in a person's mind. She kept it hidden from my father, but when she learned about the detainment facility, she tried to influence him. She worked subtly, implanting suggestions to persuade him to relax his rules and release the prisoners. Unfortunately, he was already developing sophisticated techniques for resisting mind-control, and he knew what she was doing straight away. He was furious, but also conflicted. If he ordered the agency to arrest her, it would be embarrassing for him, so he planned to murder her in secret. When she realized what was going to happen, we fled during the night.'

'So you had to live on the run,' Pandora said. 'Pursued by a government agency that could deny you access to housing, bank accounts, and legal aid.'

'We lived like that for over a year. We'd hole up in some abandoned place for a few weeks and then move on.

The trailer in Ojai was remote and comfortable, and we stayed there longer than anywhere else. We let our guard down, and that's when he found us. A dozen vehicles turned up in the dead of night, and NCA agents smashed down the door. They caught my mom, but I escaped out of a window. As I ran down the hillside, I could see they had set the trailer alight.'

'I remember now,' Pandora said. 'Dad got a callout in the middle of the night because of a fire in the hills. Mom went to the station as well to help with dispatch. We could see the fire from Holly's window, and we knew it was your trailer. Then I saw a shadow in the backyard. At first I thought it was a raccoon climbing over the fence from the creek, but it was you. You ran into the kitchen, covered in mud and blood.'

'I didn't know where else to go,' Jason said. 'I didn't have any friends, any relatives. Holly had left her backpack at our house, and it had your address sewn on the inside. It was the first place I thought of.'

'And then we took you to the one place your father could never follow.'

'After that, everything gets hazy. My mom was dead, so I had no reason to go back to Earth. You guys visited me in Candlewick almost every day for six months, but then one day you just never arrived. My memories faded quickly after that. A year later, I didn't remember anything at all.'

'I think I've figured out why we never came back.' Pandora said. 'Our mom died of cancer very suddenly a few months after we took you to Candlewick. Holly was very shaken by that. We both were, but Holly became totally withdrawn. I think maybe she lost her power temporarily because we never went back to Entara, and just like you, we forgot about it.'

'Holly didn't forget,' Jason turned to her, and she reached out to stroke his cheek. 'She was just waiting for the right moment to come back.'

Pandora glanced at the digital clock. 'It's time.'

CHAPTER 62

They crossed into Kansas and drove for a long time along a seemingly endless straight road. Traffic was mostly big rigs hauling the agricultural produce of the Sunflower State to the wider world. After a lifetime in the beautiful Ojai Valley, Kansas struck Pandora as being a very boring place, with nothing to break the flat monotony of the landscape except the occasional grain silo looming like a concrete titan.

An hour after they set out from the truck stop, Scott City appeared out of nowhere. With its charming clapboard farmhouses, quaint cottages and redbrick public buildings, the town felt like it was stuck in another age when the world was a lot bigger and life was simpler. Pandora envied the residents with their pretty houses, leafy avenues, and boring scenery. This was not a place for terror, secrets, and danger. They passed through swiftly, and Scott City vanished in their rear-view mirror just as quickly as it had arrived.

Thirty minutes later a patch of trees appeared in the flat fields, a small hummock of forest on the endless plain.

'That's the place,' Jason said, pointing through the window. 'The turnoff is coming up on the right.'

A granite sign stood beside the road, nestled in rose bushes. *Beech Tree Lodge, Nursing Home for Veterans*. As soon as they turned off the highway, they were halted at a sturdy iron gate. A portly guard in military uniform emerged from a concrete security hut. He carried a clipboard, and his utility belt was laden with a nightstick, a sidearm, and a radio. A second guard remained at the gate, an assault rifle at his side.

'Help you folks?' the guard said as Pandora rolled down her window.

Pandora prepared her most winning smile. 'Hello, we're the Carver family. We've booked a viewing for eleven am?'

The guard referred to the clipboard. 'Debra and Benjamin Carver. There's three of you in the car, but I only got two names on the list.'

Jason leaned across. 'No, you got that wrong. We called and asked for my sister Lisa to be added. Her minder canceled at the last minute and we had to bring her with us.'

'Her minder?' The guard bent down to peer into the rear window at Holly.

'My sister's mentally disabled,' Jason said. 'Can't leave her alone or she'll eat dirt and slugs right out of the yard.'

Holly rolled down her window and offered the guard a paper bag filled with candies. Sweetness and innocence personified.

'No thank you, little lady,' the guard patted his protuberant belly. 'No candies for me, I'm sweet enough already.'

'She can come in with us, right?' Pandora said, concern etched into her expression.

'Yeah, I guess. I'll call ahead and have them prepare an extra visitor pass.'

'Thanks so much. There sure is a lot of security here just for a veterans' home, isn't there?'

'The home's just a part of the facility, ma'am,' the guard said. 'There's also a military research hospital in an annex. That means a lot of security, even if it's just old folks and doctors around.'

The guard returned to his hut, and the gate rattled open slowly on tracks. Pandora waved her thanks and drove through onto a private road, smoother and wider than the state highway. The driveway led in sweeping arcs through shady stands of beech trees for almost a mile. The view widened out and they entered a landscaped park. The nursing home was a modern white building with two wings forming an 'H' with four stories and myriad windows. Arrayed along its broad frontage were flags representing every branch of the armed forces: The Army, Marine Corps, Navy, Air Force, Space Force, and the Coast Guard.

There was a staff parking area filled with vehicles, and a much smaller visitor area, which was empty. Pandora halted the car, and they got out. She turned slowly on the spot, pretending to admire the grounds. There was a lake with a boathouse, a picnic area, tennis courts, a children's play park for visiting grandchildren. There was nobody in sight.

'Looks nice, but where are all the old folks?' Pandora said. 'On a day like this, I'd have thought people would be enjoying the sunshine.'

'This is a place designed to look good in brochures,' Jason said. 'The reality is quite different.'

Beyond the lake a tall security fence marked the boundary of the home's grounds. On the far side was undeveloped range land with a large, windowless structure like an aircraft hangar. 'What's that place over there?' Pandora asked.

'That's the NCA storage facility. Everything the agency confiscates from its victims ends up stored there.'

'I wonder if any of our stuff ended up in there.'

'Anything of value is sold to fund the agency's activities. They're only interested in holding onto objects they deem dangerous to society.'

She turned back to the nursing home. 'Where's the annex?'

'It's around the back. You can't see it from here. Come on, we look suspicious just standing around.'

They entered the foyer through sliding glass doors. The air was cool and dry from powerful air conditioning fans in the ceiling. A reception desk divided the lobby in two, where two women in civilian clothes were working at computers. In a booth, another armed guard was visible, his gaze fixed on a dozen security screens.

'Mr and Mrs Carver?' One of the receptionists stood to welcome them.

'Hello, yes,' Pandora said. 'We have an appointment for eleven. We're a little late, I'm sorry.'

The receptionist smiled sympathetically. 'Beech Tree Lodge is a long way from anywhere. It always takes longer to get here than people think.'

'It is kinda remote, isn't it?'

'We like the peace and quiet.' She handed them three plastic cards on lanyards. 'Here are your visitor passes. Please display them at all times. Take a seat, and Doctor Hendricks will be with you in just a moment.'

The seating area was comfortable but oddly sterile, bereft of old magazines and leaflets. The air conditioning was noisy and made Pandora's throat dry. She could have used a glass of water, but there was no facility for refreshments. In the booth, the security guard was watching them. She felt self-conscious under his gaze.

'This is pretty bold stuff,' Jason said quietly. 'We're marching right into the lion's den. Any one of us could get recognized. If that happens this will be a real short trip.'

'The agency thinks we're in hiding,' Pandora said. 'They're spending all their resources searching homeless shelters and soup kitchens. The last thing they'll expect is for us to walk right in the front door.'

'I recognize the name Hendricks. He worked closely with my father. I met him once or twice.'

'That was when you were ten years old. There's no way he'd remember you.'

A door opened, and a man wearing a lab coat appeared. He was about sixty, tall, with a pinched face and too-prominent ears. He greeted the newcomers with a gravelly voice. 'Welcome, welcome. I'm Doctor Hendricks. You are the family of William Carver, yes?'

'My brother,' Jason said, shaking Hendricks' hand. 'Green Beret, weapons sergeant, served in Iraq, Afghanistan, bunch of other places. Got discharged about six years ago. Been living with us for four of those years after he lost his job at the auto parts warehouse. I love the guy, but he's getting harder and harder to deal with. It used to be okay, but now we're planning kids and I don't want crazy uncle Billy frightening them.'

'Of course, of course,' Hendricks said. 'Your brother wasn't able to join us today?'

'No, no, we uh, haven't mentioned this little trip to him just yet. We wanted to scout out the place and make sure this was the best place for him before we sign any papers.'

'Ah, I understand, I understand. Very wise, very wise. However, I assure you this is the world's premier treatment center for PTSD. Actually, I was hoping to take a look at your brother's medical file before you arrived, but apparently it hasn't been sent through yet.'

'I got a copy for you right here,' Jason reached into a leather messenger bag and handed Hendricks a thick manila file.

'Splendid, splendid,' Hendricks opened the file and stared at the page for a long time, a deep frown lining his forehead. Pandora and Jason shared an anxious glance. Fiona had forged the documents to create a fictitious brother for Jason using all her skills with computers, but her knowledge of Earth was still incomplete. There was a possibility she had made an error that would give away their duplicity.

Hendricks nodded to himself. 'Yes, yes, this is all sadly familiar. Your brother is a brave man and a patriot. It must be very distressing to witness these dramatic changes in personality.'

'Angry one minute, crying the next,' Jason said. 'It's all getting too much for us to handle, I'm afraid.'

'Quite so, quite so. Well, please, follow me. Let me

show you the facilities.'

The inner doors opened, and they entered the nursing home proper. Hendricks gave them some background on the facility as he led them through the public areas. Beech Tree Lodge had been founded in 2002 on a hundred acres of fallow crop land and range land, specially sited to provide a restful atmosphere far from the noise and chaos of any cities. The facility had eighty-five rooms for veterans suffering from all manner of psychological illnesses, mostly battlefield trauma, stress, and related secondary pathologies, including addictions and emotional control problems.

The home's public rooms were airy and spacious. There was a cafeteria, several lounges, a dining hall, a library, and a large conservatory overlooking the lake. Everything was modern, spotlessly clean, and so coldly clinical Pandora actually shivered. The cafe was fitted out with off-brand designer furniture set amid plastic ferns. The long stainless steel service counter was devoid of food, and the only sustenance on sale was from a vending machine stocked with pre-packaged snacks. The lounges were furnished with identical sets of couches with wipe-clean vinyl covers. A smattering of residents populated each area, standing or sitting widely separated from their fellows. Nobody spoke. Pandora was surprised how many of the residents were not elderly at all. There were a lot of younger men, some in wheelchairs, some with missing arms or legs, staring out of windows or at muted television screens.

The dull hum of the air conditioning was omnipresent, accompanied by a kind of old-fashioned easy listening exotica piped through speakers in every room. The sight of the silent, motionless veterans juxtaposed with the smoochy bachelor's den music was surreal and disturbing.

Holly made friends in every quarter. Concealed within her baggy sweater was a Polaroid camera she had found in Jackie's childhood belongings at Blackthorn. Armed with the camera and her paper bag of candies, she approached any resident who looked particularly lonely or unhappy – which was all of them – and offered them a treat from the bag. She then posed for a Polaroid selfie with her new acquaintance. There were a lot of veterans and only a few moments of time in each room, so she worked quickly. Each new friend got a treat, a hug, a picture, and then she was gone.

The effect on the residents was miraculous. Veterans trapped in an internal world of unhappy memory found themselves looking into the eyes of this pretty, silent blonde girl, grinning goofily with her bag of goodies. Everywhere she went, she left behind a trail of smiles, laughter, and murmurs of conversation.

Holly was doing more for the mental health of these veterans with a few caring gestures than all the doctors and nurses combined. She was also leaving behind dozens of photographs of her cheeky, smiling face scattered around the very facility which sought to imprison her. Pandora had to bite her lip to avoid laughing out loud at the irony.

Hendricks was entirely oblivious to all this and continued his tour with professional detachment as he led them into the residential wing. A long corridor was lined with doors opening on bland bedrooms which lacked any kind of personal adornment. Many of the rooms were occupied by veterans who lay asleep, catatonic or comatose in their beds. Holly's mission to befriend the entire population anticipated these sorry individuals, for whom she had procured a wide variety of greeting cards in Zenith. Each card had a cheery printed message like *Always in my heart*, or *Have a great day!*, accompanied by a pretty picture drawn by herself. She darted in and out of every room, leaving a card by the bedside for the sleeping veterans to find when they awoke.

Hendricks was saying something about the awards Beech Tree Lodge had won for cleanliness and hygiene when Jason interrupted. 'Doctor Hendricks, may I ask a question?'

The doctor looked startled, as if he had quite forgotten

he was addressing visitors at all. 'A question? Oh, I suppose so.'

'Is this a private nursing home, or is it military? I'm seeing a lot of uniformed personnel around the place.'

'Oh that. Well, you see, Beech Tree Lodge is a joint operation between private contractors, government agencies and the military. It is a pioneering approach that tears down the old barriers between public and private clinics that have hindered healthcare for so long.'

Pandora joined in. 'But why did you choose such a lonely place? If we put Billy here, I don't think we'd be able to visit more than once or twice a year.'

'Mrs Carver, peace and quiet is what our residents need. The patients at Beech Tree Lodge suffer from traumas few human beings ever recover from. Our therapies allow them to find inner calm. Our groundbreaking research ensures future generations of soldiers will never suffer as they have done. For this, we require isolation, and solitude.'

'You're talking about the Lethean Institute, aren't you?' Jason said. 'I read an article somewhere about the work you do training soldiers to survive battlefield trauma.'

'That's right,' Hendricks said. 'The Lethean Institute operates from an annex here at the home. Most of our work is classified, naturally, but I'm gratified that some news of our accomplishments filters through to the outside world.'

'Would Billy be eligible to contribute to those studies?' Jason said. 'If you look at his file, you'll see the nature of his trauma is quite unusual.'

Hendricks browsed through the medical file again. 'Well, I don't see anything here...'

'Not that file,' Jason said, reaching into the messenger bag again. 'This one.'

Jason handed him another file folder, this one much thinner. Hendricks opened it, and his eyes went wide. 'I see, I see. Your brother was dishonorably discharged for his role in an incident that resulted in the deaths of three children and their mother in Afghanistan.'

'His unit was stuck in traffic in Kabul,' Jason said. 'A woman and her children ran up to the truck to beg for food. He yelled at them to go away, as per protocol. Suicide bombers often pose as beggars. They wouldn't leave, and one of the kids reached into his pocket. Billy thought he was reaching for a detonator, and he shot him. The mother went crazy and pulled out a knife. He shot her, as well. The other two kids got hit by stray bullets.'

'And your brother's trauma developed as a result of this incident?' Hendricks said.

'Right. He murdered four innocent people. He's obsessed with it. He hears the mother's voice telling him he's going to burn in hell. He wakes up screaming in the middle of the night and ransacks the house because he's convinced the children's bodies are hidden somewhere. Doctor Hendricks, I'll be perfectly honest, all this is putting a serious strain on our marriage. The guy that came home from Afghanistan is not my brother.'

'We need to get him out of our house, for our own mental health,' Pandora added. 'And we had thought that, well, since the Army is responsible for his condition, maybe the Army should look after him.'

Hendricks inclined his head. 'I think I understand what you are saying. However, with a dishonorable discharge, your brother-in-law will be liable to pay full fees, which at Beech Tree Lodge are not cheap.'

'But if Billy enrolled in your Lethean Program, you'd waive those fees, right?' Jason said.

'Yes, that's right.' Hendricks studied the file again. 'As the perpetrator of a mass killing, your brother has a unique perspective on violence which is highly relevant to our studies. Most unusual, most unusual. Mr and Mrs Carver, I would like you to accompany me next door to the Lethean Institute, where we can continue this discussion in a more suitable environment.'

CHAPTER 63

Hendricks veered left and took them down a series of corridors. They left the residential wing and entered a backrooms area of storage and utility spaces. The lights here were dimmer and flickered from overhead fluorescents. Underfoot, carpets gave way to vinyl, causing their shoes to echo in the silence. They arrived in a windowless lobby where a guard sat at a metal desk. Ahead, the way was blocked by a plain, featureless door with a security panel set into the wall.

Hendricks asked them to sign a visitor sheet. The guard pointed at Holly's camera. 'Can't take that with you into the annex, ma'am. Classified area.'

Holly handed over the camera with a theatrical sigh. The guard rose from his seat and crossed to the door. He took a security card from his belt and passed it through the reader, then entered a five-digit code. A red light turned to green, there was a loud click of an electronic lock and the door swung open.

On the far side was another long corridor. The walls were bare concrete, unpainted, and the lights were naked bulbs dangling on cords. Closed doors lined both walls, all featureless, without even a handle or a keyhole. Beside each door was a security panel and a tiny plastic marker bearing a number.

Hendricks' lecture changed tone as he led them down the passage. Before, he had been tedious and pedantic. Now he spoke with passion. 'The Lethean Program is the most significant research project in psychological sciences ever undertaken. Here, we study the psychological effects of violence on the human mind. We want to understand why it is that one man can become a multiple murderer while another man faints at the sight of blood. What is it about violence that causes excitement in one person and revulsion in another? These are not merely academic questions. The United States military is in the business of violence, one way or another. So are the police, the FBI, basically anyone who carries a gun for a living. Do you know how much money is lost every year to PTSD? 42.7 billion in the armed forces alone, and 232 billion across the United States as a whole. It is vitally important, therefore, that we understand how to treat this condition and, more importantly, how to prevent it. In ancient Greek mythology, Lethe was the name of the river of forgetfulness. It flowed through the underworld, where the dead would drink its waters and forget their mortal lives. The founder of the Lethean Institute, Doctor Henry Wyatt, believed this was an excellent metaphor for the recovery from trauma.'

'Is Doctor Wyatt available for us to speak to?' Jason said. Pandora shot him a panicked look. This was not what they were here for.

'Not at present, I'm afraid.' Hendricks said.

Pandora changed the subject quickly. 'Doctor Hendricks, can you tell us a little more about how Billy would be treated here?'

'Well, in the case of your brother-in-law, his trauma is the result of guilt. He has performed deeds which his upbringing and social conditioning tell him are wrong and repugnant. This causes an existential crisis. He believes he cannot exist in a society whose most basic commandment he has broken: Thou shalt not kill. In these cases, the patient tells himself he is worthless, evil, and deserving of hell. Mr Carver, you mentioned your brother hears the voice of the murdered mother telling him precisely this. That hallucinatory voice is a manifestation of the superego passing judgment on the ego.'

'Sounds like a fancy description of conscience,' Pandora said.

'Conscience is a delusion, Mrs Carver,' Hendricks said. 'A pathological short-circuit of the rational pathways of the brain. When conscience overtakes reason, the human person suffers needlessly, as in the case of your brother-in-law. Our therapies will rid him of this unfortunate condition.'

Pandora could hardly contain her dismay. 'You're going to cure him of conscience? How?'

'Let me show you.' Hendricks used his security card to open a door, and they entered a small cinema. The room was in darkness, and a movie was playing to a group of five individuals seated in the front row, visible only as silhouettes against the screen. The film was a military training video featuring severely wounded children being treated by medics in a jungle clearing. It was a gruesome, vividly gory movie, and Pandora had difficulty looking at the screen without feeling nauseous.

Hendricks continued eagerly. 'Here we can see several young army volunteers undergoing a training session to inure them to a particular category of emotionally-laden images. In this instance, children injured in war. The subjects are in a deep trance state, induced by chemical and hypnotic techniques developed by our scientists. With many hours' repeated viewing, these images reprogram the mind to overcome the superego and place the ego firmly in charge. The rational mind is triumphant.'

'So these soldiers won't suffer mental anguish when they see dying children in real life?' Pandora said. 'Is that a good idea? I mean, maybe I'm crazy, but perhaps seeing a child cut in half by a landmine is just inherently shocking, right? Maybe soldiers are exactly the kind of people who should be shocked by that. Their moral compass needs a true north to govern their actions when they've got a gun in their hands. Without a deep revulsion at images like these, soldiers might commit even more atrocities.'

Hendricks' smile was grotesque in the flickering light of the maimed children. 'Mrs Carver, those archaic attitudes are rapidly going the way of the dinosaur. These young men are being liberated from thousands of years of irrational conditioning. We are setting their minds free. The human mind is incredibly malleable. If we wanted, we could program our subjects to find images such as these pleasing, even exciting. Of course, that is beyond the scope of our present research, but I assure you that in the near future the moral landscape of humanity will be radically different.'

'And that's a good thing?' Pandora said, aghast.

'Of course,' Hendricks said. 'The practical advantages of eliminating conscience should be obvious. Let me give you an example. For years, scientists have known that the only economical way to operate a public healthcare service is with mandatory organ harvesting. By operating a national lottery, the government can randomly select healthy individuals to be humanely terminated and their internal organs harvested for sick individuals. A single donor can save the lives of ten people. The benefits are overwhelmingly obvious, but at present this policy would meet with widespread public outrage. However, in just a few years it will be completely accepted, even applauded. Future generations will look back on the days of voluntary organ donation as a dark age of ignorance.'

'You're saying these methods are already being applied outside the military?' Pandora said.

'Most certainly. We live in an age of unprecedented apathy towards violence. People watch news reports of murder, war, and genocide while eating their dinner in front of the television. All of it is part of a wider plan, Mrs Carver. The world may seem a chaotic place, but I assure you that the right people are in charge where it matters.'

Pandora wanted to argue with him. This place sickened her to the core. Beech Tree Lodge was an insult to the veterans who had suffered in service to their country. It was a mockery of their sacrifice. She wanted to burn it to the ground.

She smiled at Hendricks through gritted teeth. 'I guess you're right.'

'So this is the program my brother Billy would partake in?' Jason said.

'As the perpetrator of a so-called atrocity, we are interested in his case, yes. If you are willing to sign the papers to volunteer him for study, Beech Tree Lodge would waive all fees.'

'Sounds intriguing. Where do we sign?' Pandora said, shielding her eyes from the screen to avoid retching.

Hendricks led them out of the cinema and through a labyrinth of ugly, dark corridors to an administrative area. Here, at least, someone had thought to paint the walls and provide windows for natural light. Several staff were at work in an open-plan office. Hendricks conferred with a woman in a nursing uniform who provided a sheaf of papers for them to sign.

'These are the documents,' Hendricks said. 'At this stage you are not committed to anything, but these consent forms give us authority to take custody of your brother and assess his suitability for our project.'

At that moment an explosion rocked the building. Glass shook in the window frames, and light fittings swung on cords. The nurse screamed and put her hands over her head instinctively.

'What in God's name was that?' Hendricks stared about him in confusion.

Right on time, Pandora thought.

CHAPTER 64

She crossed to the window and pointed outside. 'Hey, look over here. That big building next door is on fire.'

Everyone crowded the window to see the NCA storage building was ablaze. One corner of the structure had crumpled, and a plume of black smoke rose into the sky. The source of the explosion was clear. A large panel van had crashed into the wall at high speed, smashing through the outer cladding and igniting its fuel tank, resulting in a blazing inferno. Only Pandora and her companions knew that the van's cargo area had been crammed with 55-gallon drums of kerosene to add to the destructive force of the fire. The driver had jumped clear moments before the collision and could be seen running across the tarmac to her friends at the perimeter fence.

'God dammit,' Hendricks said. 'Fucking activists. Hippies. Terrorists.' He went to a desk and picked up a telephone. 'Hello? Security? Some maniac has driven a van straight through the security fence into unit two. The perimeter is open. I can see people running through now. Probably some crazy human rights group. Put the whole facility on high alert right away.'

The Hell Riders poured through the breach in the security perimeter. They had approached Beech Trees along minor roads and unmarked tracks across the High

Plains and range land. They wore ski masks and bullet-proof vests, and in their hands they carried the implements of mayhem: Bolt-cutters, smoke grenades, shotguns, batons and riot shields. In the lead was a tall, athletic woman, unmistakably Ruby Reardon. She reached an outer door in the hangar and set to work with bolt-cutters. Within moments she had cut through the lock and the Hell Riders vanished inside.

Hendricks barked orders into the phone and slammed the handset down. 'Mr and Mrs Carver, I'm very sorry but you'll have to excuse me while I attend to this disruption.'

'What's happening?' Pandora said. 'Is everything all right?'

'Please just remain here in this office. I'm sure everything will settle down in just a few minutes.'

Hendricks sped out of the room, shouting for a guard. A man in military uniform entered and took up station beside the door. Outside, more guards raced towards the blazing building. Black Humvees screeched across the tarmac. Alarms sounded in the distance.

Only the guard and the nurse remained in the office with the travelers. All the other staff had departed with Hendricks. Jason leaned towards Pandora and spoke softly. 'It's working. All the guards are going to fight off the Hell Riders.'

'God, I hope no one gets hurt,' Pandora said.

'Those girls know what they're doing,' Jason said. 'Now we've just got to deal with our babysitter here.'

Pandora pulled Holly close and whispered. 'Okay, Hol, things are going to get dangerous now. Your job is to blink us away from here if the plan fails. Can you do that?'

Holly's expression said everything. Her gaze was steely, and her jaw was set. She was ready.

Pandora turned to the guard. 'Excuse me, I have to use the restroom.'

'Remain where you are, ma'am.' The guard moved to block her path. He was armed with a nightstick and a sidearm, but he did not seem to consider her a threat. That changed quickly when Jason reached into his messenger bag and pulled out a sawn-off shotgun.

'The lady says she wants to use the restroom.' Jason pointed the gun at the guard's belly. 'I suggest you step aside.'

The guard reached for his sidearm, but thought better of it. He put his hands up and stepped aside. From the corner of her eye, Pandora saw the nurse reach under her desk, probably for a panic button. She grabbed the woman's arm and twisted it behind her back. 'Don't even think about it. Lie down on the floor.' She took cable ties from her handbag and bound the nurse's wrists and ankles. The guard submitted to the same treatment with a scowl of fury, and she took the security card clipped to his belt.

They left the office and moved quickly along the corridor. At an intersection, they paused while Jason considered their route. 'The detainees are locked in a sub-basement, deep underground,' he said. 'We passed an elevator outside the theater room.'

They retraced their steps swiftly. Sirens howled in the distance along with echoes of gunfire. Rounding a corner, they arrived at a security post. A guard was seated at the desk, but he did not stir as they approached. He sat slumped in his chair, snoring loudly.

Holly grabbed his shoulder and shook him roughly. He snorted and mumbled incoherently, but did not wake. She reached into her bag of candies and withdrew a smaller parcel of treats. This was a special batch of candies heavily laced with Rohypnol supplied by a Hell Rider with contacts in the drugs world. During her busy ministering to the veterans, Holly had not neglected to offer every guard a special something from her paper bag, subtly shifting the contents so the security staff would not know they were drawing from poisoned stock. Holly patted the guard on the head and dropped the candies in his lap.

'Well done, Holly,' Pandora said. 'That should keep them snoozing peacefully until we're long gone from here.'

'Here's the elevator,' Jason said, examining the electronic panel beside the double doors. 'Security's been upgraded since I was last here. We need a security code.'

'I'll see if Fiona can help.' Pandora reached into her handbag and pulled out one of the radio-things. 'Fi, how're we doing?'

'Whoa, it's crazy out there,' Fiona's excited voice buzzed from her command post at Blackthorn. 'The Hell Riders are attacking the hangar site from three directions. Agency guards are stretched across more than thirty acres, and the Hell Riders are using bikes to run rings around them. Radio chatter's hard to follow. It sounds like there are extra troops being called in from Scott City, but they won't be here for at least thirty minutes. How are you?'

'We've reached the elevator, but we can't open the doors,' Pandora said. 'We've got a swipe card, but no security code. Can you do anything?'

'I'll try. Hold the radio-thing up to the panel and swipe the card.'

They did as they were told. The radio-thing beeped and flashed in increasingly rapid patterns until a green light shone and the doors slid open.

'Did it work?' Fiona said.

'It worked,' Pandora replied. 'You're amazing.'

It was a cargo elevator, designed for transporting substantial pieces of equipment to the depths of the facility. Six levels of basement were accessible from the inner panel, and Jason's hand hovered over the buttons. 'Damn, I can't remember which level the detainees are on.'

'Should we search level by level?' Pandora said.

'No, it would take too long.' Jason punched B6. 'Remember, my dad thinks the Delphinians are the most dangerous threat to civilization the world has ever seen. He'll keep them on the lowest level.'

The elevator rattled and clattered slowly down. The door opened on another security post, and this time the guard was awake and alert. He rose from his desk and reached for his sidearm. Jason aimed the shotgun and unloaded the barrel at close range. The sound of the blast was deafening in the enclosed space. The guard was thrown hard against the wall. He slid down to the floor and became still.

Pandora was stunned by the noise and the sudden violence. Then she noticed the guard was not bleeding, and he was still breathing shallowly. She knelt and picked up a handful of blue pellets rolling about on the floor.

'Rubber bullets,' Jason said. 'Mother Abigail was very insistent that we use non-lethal rounds.'

Pandora was relieved that the Hell Riders were not as bloodthirsty as they appeared in their ski masks and combat gear. She thought back to the gunshots she had heard upstairs and doubted the agency guards would be as considerate in reply.

The guard was unconscious, but he would soon recover and summon aid. She took more cable ties from her bag and bound him tightly.

'We should keep moving,' she said when she was done. 'Which way do we go from here?'

In fact, there was only one path available. A single door opened onto a long tunnel. Jason led them through into a nightmare subterranean world. If Beech Tree Lodge was Purgatory, this place was truly Hell. The walls were concrete reinforced with steel, forming a cramped passage so narrow they had to walk single file. There was an aura of great antiquity to the place. Long ago, the structure had been painted green, but now the paint was faded and peeling and the metal had turned to rust. Exposed pipework cluttered the walls and ceiling, all crumbling with dereliction. It was like being in a submarine that had lain stricken on the ocean floor for decades.

'What in God's name is this place?' Pandora whispered.

'Back in the sixties, Kansas was one of the main locations for America's nuclear arsenal,' Jason said. 'These tunnels are part of the old Minuteman missile silos.'

The air was stale, metallic, and with a hint of something worse. Rotting flesh. Pandora reached up to a ventilation grill, but detected no breeze. It was unbelievable that anyone could live down here, and she feared for the condition of Sister Mary and the other prisoners.

'Everything's so old and broken-down,' she said. 'Didn't this place get restored when your father turned it into a laboratory?'

'I think you've misunderstood the nature of my dad's work,' Jason said. 'He wasn't interested in studying the Delphinians. He was only interested in locking them away.'

'This isn't a research facility at all, is it? It's a tomb.'

Jason took them through more claustrophobic chambers and tunnels that made Pandora feel like she was trapped in the innards of some vast, hideous machine. Her chest felt tight from fear and lack of air.

They passed a row of niches where modern desks and computers had been installed. Screens flickered with data, but no staff were present. Pandora recalled Jason's stories about being brought down here as a child to witness his father's work.

'Do you think your father is down here?' she asked.

'No, he's probably in DC at the NCA headquarters. We won't find him here.'

'But your dad brought you down here as a child, didn't he? Why would he do that?'

'It was all part of his program,' Jason said. 'He wanted to expose me at a young age to shocking scenes so I would become accustomed to them.'

'Accustomed? No one could be accustomed to this.'

'You'd be surprised. I used to play in these tunnels.'

They passed huge rusting machines from an era before miniaturized electronics. Posters decorated the walls with ancient political slogans. *Only a Strong America Can Prevent Atomic War*, *STOP Communism – It's Everybody's Job.* The entire place was a temple of paranoia. A shrine to perpetual war.

They turned a corner and entered yet another narrow tunnel. This one was lined with locked doors, each with a viewing hatch at eye level.

'These look like cells.' Pandora hurried into the passage and banged on the doors. 'Hello? Sister Mary? Are you here?'

She drew aside one of the sliding hatches and gasped in horror. Inside the cell was a narrow bed of 1960s military vintage, rusted and sagging beneath filthy sheets. On the stained mattress lay a corpse.

Whether the cadaver was male or female, she could not tell. The poor soul who had perished in this lonely place had died many years before, and now the body was merely a dry husk. She moved on to the next cell and opened the viewing hatch. Another dismal chamber. Another fossilized corpse.

'They're dead,' she said softly. 'They died in their cells and nobody came to take them away.'

'I remember this place,' Jason said. 'These Delphinians were considered too dangerous to interact with in any way. They were sealed in their cells and left to die.'

Pandora moved along the corridor, opening every hatch. She felt compelled to gaze upon every scene of tragic death, to show the spirits of these murdered souls they were not forgotten. At each door she whispered under her breath. 'Whoever you are, I'm so sorry. Please be at peace.'

The occupant of the last cell was not dead. Like the others it featured a rotten camp bed and bare walls stained with decades of mold and filth. The body that lay on the foul sheets was skeletally thin, but when Pandora muttered her mournful prayer the bones moved and the flesh stretched. A woman sat up and sucked in a long, rasping breath.

'Jesus, she's alive!' Pandora yelled and wrestled with the door handle. It was rusted solid and released a rain of red dust as she fought to turn it. Her companions had moved on to explore the next passage while she lingered with the dead. She turned and shouted after them. 'Jason, Holly! Help me with this door.'

The half-dead woman rose from the bed and staggered across the floor on pencil-thin legs. Her hair was like spiderwebs stretched across her skull-like face. Her arms were mere sticks of bone hanging from her rib cage. She had once been beautiful, this tortured woman. Even years of suffering could not erase that.

Then she *was* beautiful. The pale white wisps of hair became luxuriant golden locks flowing over her shoulders. The paper-thin flesh filled out to form voluptuous curves beneath her gown. Her face was that of an angel, smiling at Pandora through the hatch.

'Thank God you're okay,' Pandora breathed a sigh of relief. 'We're going to get this door open. We're going to get you out.'

Jason and Holly returned. 'What's going on? We heard you shouting.'

'Jason, she's still alive,' Pandora said. 'Help me get this door open.'

Holly looked through the hatch and cried out in a sharp scream of terror. She seized Pandora's arm and pulled her away.

'Holly, stop it,' she said. 'What are you doing? What's wrong?'

Jason looked into the cell. 'What the hell?'

Pandora yanked free of Holly's grip and returned to the door. The beautiful prisoner had reached the hatch and was gazing out at them. She opened her mouth wide, and continued opening it until her jaw cracked and snapped with the breaking of bone and sinew. There was something inside the woman's throat, a bulbous, red slimy thing that pulsated as it rose up from the depths of her body like a living tumor trying to escape its host. The fleshy mass burst open, freeing dozens of pink tendrils that writhed through the hatch, reaching for Pandora's face.

She swore and leapt backwards against the far wall. Holly clawed at her clothes, trying to drag her away, but

Pandora was too consumed with horrified curiosity. The woman-thing in the cell wheezed a long, agonized breath and collapsed out of sight, pulling the squirming mass of tentacles down with her. Pandora crept back to the door and peered inside.

Perhaps Doctor Henry Wyatt had been correct on one count. Some Delphinians were indeed monsters. This monster had been imprisoned for too long, however, and its weakened limbs could no longer support its weight. Returned to its true form, the living skeleton writhed on the floor, its flesh splitting open to reveal hundreds of twitching tendrils that reached feebly for the door. Unable to shift its dying bulk, the creature attempted one final and awful maneuver. Its head detached from its body, propelled by wriggling tentacles, and made one last leap at the door.

There was a thud that made Pandora jump backwards. She did not look through the hatch again.

CHAPTER 65

Jason urged them onward with renewed haste. There were no guards, but Pandora didn't know whether to find that reassuring or not. Surely their presence had by now been detected. No doubt plans were afoot to ambush them, or simply lock them down here to suffocate in this underworld of rusty metal.

They came to a dead end, blocked by an immense blast door secured with a hand wheel. Jason turned the handle, which spun reluctantly and with a screech of decaying iron. The door opened on groaning hinges to reveal a circular chamber in twilight. Dark shapes moved within and Jason raised the shotgun, prepared to fire a defensive shot.

A small figure raced out of the gloom and collided with Pandora. 'I knew you'd come!' Sister Mary beamed at her. She was wearing a Disneyland t-shirt and Hawaiian shorts, but seemed otherwise her normal self.

'Mary, it's so good to see you. Are you okay?' Pandora said, returning her embrace.

'Yes, we're all fine. A little hoarse, but otherwise okay. We've been shouting for you since we sensed you arrive, but I guess you didn't hear through the doors.'

'How many of you are there?'

'Twelve of us.'

Pandora stepped inside and looked around. The room was sparsely furnished with threadbare couches and tatty armchairs on a bare concrete floor. Battered tables were covered with half-finished board games. Narrow doorways led to closet-like bedrooms.

Standing or sitting around the room were the helpless, innocent victims Jason's father had called a threat to civilization. There were men, women, children, adults and old folks. They were thin and bedraggled in their ill-fitting clothes, with pale sallow skin from their long imprisonment underground. Many of the prisoners had obvious physical abnormalities or disabilities. Four of the detainees were wheelchair-bound. Others had missing eyes, limbs, twisted spines and tumorous growths.

A young woman approached Pandora. Her face was friendly, intelligent and kind, like everyone's favorite schoolteacher. From her left side a smaller, distorted version of the same face gazed at Pandora from a tiny, gnarled torso with claw-like arms.

'We're so glad you came,' the woman said, taking Pandora's hand. Her face was wet with tears. 'My name is Gina, this is my sister Ella. We've been in this place for three years.'

'Gina! Ella!' the tiny conjoined twin shouted joyfully.

One by one, the prisoners came forward and greeted the travelers. Holly made her rounds with the bag of candies, which were well-received.

Pandora was moved to tears by the gratitude of the prisoners, but the scale of the task ahead was daunting. She took Jason aside and spoke quietly. 'A lot of these people have limited mobility. This place wasn't exactly built with wheelchairs in mind.'

'Do you think Holly can blink everyone out of here?' Jason said.

She shook her head. 'I don't think so. I'm not sure how many people she can take at once, and we'd all have to be touching her. Besides, we're so far underground I'm not even sure her power will work at all.'

Gina tapped Pandora's shoulder. She spread her arm to indicate the gathered prisoners. 'We're ready to go when you are. Lead the way.'

The detainees, under the guidance of Sister Mary and Gina, had in the space of a few moments organized themselves into teams of walkers, pushers and carriers in ranks beside the open door. Those with better mobility had placed themselves behind wheelchairs, or stood beside the frail to support them.

'When Sister Mary told us you were coming, we started practicing our escape routine,' Gina explained. 'We made obstacle courses out of the furniture and spent hours speeding everyone around the room. We made a fun game of it, and it kept our spirits up.'

'Ella! Ella!' her sister exclaimed in agreement.

The travelers divided their efforts to assist the prisoners as they navigated the tunnels. Jason went first to lead the way while Holly took up the rear to ensure no stragglers got lost. Pandora moved up and down the line, helping where necessary if anyone got stuck.

It all seemed so easy. The tunnels were empty and silent as if no one had been down here for years. The prisoners had formed close bonds of friendship during their long captivity. They chatted brightly and encouraged each other with uplifting words as they clambered over broken machinery, exposed pipes and through bulkhead doors.

Pandora saw Agent Arnold before Holly did, but it was too late. Holly was helping a wheelchair user over a step in the floor when Arnold emerged from a side passage.

'Holly, look out!' Pandora warned.

Holly was slow to react. Arnold lunged forward and clapped handcuffs around Holly's wrist, and then his own, locking them together. He held a gun to her head and shouted into her ear. 'Go ahead, try it,' he gripped her cuffed hand so hard she winced at the pain. 'Just try that little magic trick of yours and I'll blow your goddamn head off.'

The passage was narrow, and there were six people

between Pandora and her sister. She raced back along the tunnel, barging the prisoners out of the way. Arnold saw her coming and retrained the gun at her face. Pandora didn't care. She would willingly take a bullet for her sister if only it gave her a chance to get away.

Holly took a deep breath, and blinked.

THE HELL WORLD

Heat struck Holly like a blow to the face and acidic air stung her eyes. Arnold closed his eyes at just the right moment, so he saw everything she did. The cracked and burning plain, the luminescent sky, the squat stone igloos.

He drew breath in surprise and immediately doubled over in a fit of coughing. Flecks of blood stained his pristine shirt.

'Take us back,' Arnold croaked. He grabbed her free hand and aimed the pistol into her palm. 'Take us back right now or I'll put a hole in your hand. You hear me?'

His tone was commanding but his expression was pure panic. His eyes darted around the landscape. Three suns were in the sky. A heat haze obscured everything except the immediate vicinity. Another bout of coughing caused him to stagger, leaning against an igloo's arched door. Holly was dragged helplessly along beside him as he drooled blood onto the sandy ground.

'What the fuck is this place?' he said when he recovered.

From within the igloo came a shuffling sound. Arnold jerked away and pointed the pistol into the dark opening.

'Is someone in there? Come on out, slowly, with your hands up.'

Something chittered in the shadows. The shadows

moved.

'I'm warning you. I'm armed and I mean business.'

A creature skittered out into the triple sunlight. It was about the size of a large dog, hairy, with eight shining green eyes on its bulbous head. It had eight long legs, segmented like a tapeworm that quivered and vibrated with barely restrained excitement at these fresh visitors. Three more igloos disgorged their inhabitants, and watched the newcomers with curiosity.

A soft jangling sound. Arnold did not notice Holly had taken the keys from his belt.

'*Spiders!*' Arnold's voice rose in a hysterical girlish shriek. He opened fire on the closest beast, emptying an entire clip into its face. The creature seemed not to notice. It reached out a long leg and seized Arnold around the shoulder. With a sound like wet rags tearing his arm came off and slithered into the creature's maw. '*Spiders! Spiders!*' Arnold continued his screeching cries as more legs wrapped around his body and pulled him apart.

RETURN

Pandora was startled by the flash of light in the confined space as her sister reappeared.

'Holly, oh God, are you alright? What happened?' She drew her sister into a hug, and recoiled with horror when she saw the severed human hand dangling from the handcuffs attached to her wrist.

Holly was equally surprised, and there was a flurry of frantic activity while she struggled to fit the tiny key into the lock. The cuffs clattered to the floor with their grisly load.

The prisoners had moved out of sight, and the sisters were trailing behind the group. Fearing becoming lost in this foul place, Pandora grabbed Holly's arm and ran to catch up. 'Come on, we have to keep moving.'

They arrived at the elevator to find Jason herding everyone inside. There was just enough space for them all, wheelchairs included. Once the doors were closed the elevator rattled slowly upwards and Pandora spoke into the radio-thing. 'Fi, we've got Sister Mary and all her friends. We're on our way out. Is the coast clear?'

'Hi guys,' Fiona said. 'It's pretty hectic outside, but all the fighting is far away from Beech Trees. You should be clear to get back to the main gate.'

'Okay, but the guards at the gate didn't take any of Holly's candies. Are they still there?'

'Yeah, 'fraid so, but I might still have a trick or two up

my sleeve. Call me back when you get within sight of the gate.'

The elevator doors opened. The drugged guard slept soundly at his desk while the travelers led their charges through the dim corridors of the annex. They met no resistance as they passed more snoozing security staff on their way back through Beech Tree Lodge. The veterans observed their passage passively, and Pandora wished she could take them all with her.

In the lobby they found Hendricks blocking their way. He had a pistol taken from an unconscious guard, and brandished it at the group. 'I can't let you leave. What you're doing is wrong.'

Something snapped inside Pandora at those words. 'What the hell do you know about right and wrong? Aren't those just archaic attitudes? Irrational conditioning? Where's your triumphant ego now, Doctor Hendricks?'

'Don't you understand these people are a menace? If they get out they could wreak all kinds of havoc. They're monsters. Aberrations. They're... *unnatural*.' Hendricks' voice was plaintive as if he was desperate for her to see things from his perspective. His hand was shaking and his hold on the gun was unsteady. Pandora realized he was actually frightened of the prisoners. To him they were creatures from a nightmare come to torment him with their incomprehensible powers that defied his rational mind. She plucked the gun from his hand and pushed him aside. He retreated into a corner and whimpered pathetically while Jason filed the prisoners out of Beech Tree Lodge.

Outside was like a warzone. Around the storage hangar the fighting between the Hell Riders and the agency guards was intense. The hangar itself was entirely engulfed in flames. The roof had collapsed, and a vast pillar of black smoke darkened the sky. The Hell Riders were visible as tiny black dots in the distance, crouching behind vehicles or hiding behind trees. They had the agency guards with their backs against the blazing hangar, fighting a losing battle.

The visitor parking lot was deserted except for the Ford Galaxy that the travelers had arrived in. Fiona had rented the largest vehicle that would not arouse suspicion, but it had only eight seats and with twelve refugees from the agency dungeon, that meant a crowded journey lay ahead. They abandoned the wheelchairs and crammed the prisoners in like sardines.

Pandora got behind the wheel and started the engine. Beside her, Holly sat in Jason's lap with her head pressed into the roof. Somewhere in the crowded seats behind her, Sister Mary called out. 'I hope everyone remembered to go before we got in the car.'

Everyone laughed. The courage of these people in the face of adversity was remarkable, and Pandora felt tears in her eyes again. She blinked them away and gunned the engine, which protested against the unusual load.

It was almost a mile back to the public highway, and Pandora's nerve almost broke when the main gate came into view. Two black Humvees blocked the path. Positioned behind them were six guards with assault rifles. From open hatches in the Humvees' roofs two more guards manned machine guns on tripods. All eight guns took aim at the Galaxy's windshield.

Pandora grabbed the radio-thing and shouted into it. 'Fi, this is bad. Lots of guns pointed at us. Whatever it is you're about to do, do it now.'

Fiona replied immediately. 'Okay, okay. Don't slow down. Just keep driving. Gosh, I hope this works.'

The Humvees exploded. First one vehicle and then the other detonated in orange fireballs that sent the heavy trucks spiraling through the air. At first, Pandora couldn't tell what had happened. When the third blast came she saw a crimson beam of light shining down from the sky. It struck the guard hut and blew it apart, sending fragments of broken concrete in every direction.

The guards fled, tossing their weapons aside and covering their heads to avoid the destruction raining down from the sky upon them. A fourth crimson beam struck the gates, turning the iron into white-hot rods that disintegrated into a shower of sparks.

Pandora put her foot on the gas. The Ford responded sluggishly, but sheer inertia carried them through the melting gates and out into the road. All four tires burst simultaneously from the superheated iron spreading across the tarmac. The car lurched across the highway into a ditch, toppled onto its roof and came to a rest in a patch of long grass.

'Is everyone okay?' Pandora called out. There were mutterings and mumbles from all sides, but no screams of pain or fright, so she assumed the best.

She climbed out of the car and surveyed the damage. The Galaxy's wheels were smoking lumps of scrap metal. Even if they could get the vehicle upright, they were going nowhere.

Jason and Holly extricated themselves from the passenger side and opened the rear doors. The prisoners spilled out onto the grassy verge in undignified ways, but seemed none the worse for the crash.

The highway was deserted. Across the road, the main gate had been obliterated. Trees were ablaze on both sides of the private driveway, and the concrete guard hut was reduced to rubble. Of the gates there was no sign except charred stumps of iron.

Fiona's voice buzzed from the radio-thing somewhere inside the car. 'Hello? Pandora? Did it work? Are you okay?'

Pandora reached into the car and found the gadget under the steering wheel. 'Fi, we're okay. What the hell was that thing?'

'It worked? Oh cool-cool-cool. I found a secret military satellite drifting around in orbit. It's got a whole ton of awesome stuff on board, but I figured the laser cannon would be the most effective.'

'Well, you were right,' Pandora said. 'Listen, we're free but we're immobile. The car's a wreck and we're miles from anywhere.'

'Don't worry, I'm sending some transport your way right now. Take a look to the west.'

Pandora looked down the road and saw the welcome sight of the vast silver Airstream gliding down the highway. The RV came to a halt and Jackie leaned out of the window. 'Hello all. Fiona said you folks might need a ride.'

CHAPTER 66

The prisoners helped each other into the Airstream where Sister Mary began raiding the galley for snacks and refreshments. Fiona radioed back with news that she had used the satellite laser cannon to destroy the public highway ten miles to the west, preventing the agency reinforcements from arriving. Jackie would need to take a longer route to return to Blackthorn, but the chances of hostile pursuit were minimal. Ruby reported via Fiona that she had withdrawn the Hell Riders from the hangar site and they had scattered into the Great Plains. The agency guards were not pursuing.

While the last of the former prisoners got comfy in the RV, Pandora took Holly aside to stand on the grassy verge. 'We did it, Hol. We showed those bastards they can't push us around unless they expect some serious pushback. But this is just the beginning, okay? We've got our freedom, but there's still a long way to go. We're not going to rest until we've got back our house and our lives. We've got friends and allies now, and most important, we've got each other. This moment, right here, this is the turning of the tide.'

From out of nowhere a fist struck Pandora in the mouth, knocking her to the ground.

'Forgot about me, didn't you, bitch?' Agent Tina Slade

stood over her. She wore SWAT gear filthy with mud and charred from laser cannon fire. Pandora guessed she had been one of the guards at the gate.

Slade pulled her upright and thrust a gun into her mouth. 'Stand back,' she yelled at Holly. 'I swear I will blow this whore's brains out the back of her skull if you so much as breathe.'

Jason emerged from the RV, drawn by the sound of raised voices. Slade pushed the gun deeper into Pandora's mouth. 'Don't come any closer. I'll kill her and then I'll kill you.'

Jason backed off, his hands raised. 'Okay, okay. What do you want?'

'Get back in the RV,' Slade said. 'I don't want you. I want these two bitches.'

Jason did as he was ordered. Slade called to Jackie in the driver's seat. 'Drive away. Put your foot down and don't look back, do you hear me?'

Jackie looked stricken, but there was nothing she could do. The Airstream jerked into motion and drove down the empty highway, leaving only Slade and the sisters behind.

Slade grabbed Pandora by her hair and hauled her towards the burning gatehouse. With the barrel of the gun pressing against the back of her throat, she was helpless to do anything but gag.

'You walk in front,' Slade shouted at Holly. 'I want you where I can see you. I'm going to make you regret the day you ever fucked with me.'

Holly collapsed onto the ground. Her body convulsed violently, eyes rolled back into her head. Spittle flew from her mouth, and she gurgled horribly. The head injury Holly had suffered in Entara must have been more serious than they thought. Maybe.

Slade did not know about that, but she did think Holly was a feeble-minded simpleton. 'What's wrong with the retard?' Slade spat at Pandora and withdrew the gun from her mouth.

'She's susceptible to fits,' Pandora lied, gasping for

breath. ‘Please, let me go to her before she swallows her tongue.’

Slade laughed. ‘You must think I’m a moron.’ She stood over Holly and kicked her in the stomach. ‘Get up, freak. I said up, or I’ll put a bullet through your sister’s eye socket.’

Holly flailed. With one arm she grabbed Slade’s ankle. With the other she grabbed Pandora.

Pandora knew when to blink. Slade did not.

THE WASTELAND

They blinked onto a rocky slope. The ground was unstable, and as soon as they arrived a rockslide began. Slade was disoriented and off balance, giving Pandora the chance to knock the gun from her hand as all three of them tumbled down the steep incline.

Slade kept a firm grip on Pandora's hair, and she felt her scalp tear with excruciating pain as they toppled head over heels down the slope. Dust filled the air, choking her lungs and scratching her eyes.

The rockslide intensified as they fell. Fist-sized stones clattered around her head and heavier boulders thudded ominously on all sides.

At last they came to a rest. Slade's grip loosened, and Pandora blinked the dust from her eyes.

She couldn't move her legs. The rockslide had buried her up to the waist and she was pinned in place by a boulder above her knees.

Agent Slade was motionless beside her. Her head was at a strange angle, her face distorted and slack. With a start, Pandora realized her head had been crushed by a falling rock. Her skull was flattened on one side, and her face was slowly collapsing into the concavity.

She struggled to free her legs, but it was no use. Contorting her upper body, she saw Holly further down the slope, uninjured and fully recovered from her feigned seizure. They had blinked into a dusty desert land with a dirt road at the base of a ridge. Stunted trees struggled out of the ground. There were no other signs of life.

'Holly, I need your help,' Pandora said. 'I'm stuck.'

Holly seemed not to hear.

'Hol? Are you listening?' She twisted around to see what Holly was looking at. Further up the road, a cloud of dust rose from the wheels of an approaching vehicle.

Holly wandered away and stood beside the road. Pandora called her back. She didn't listen.

The vehicle was a horse-drawn carriage. It clattered to a halt fifty yards from where Pandora lay trapped in the dirt. The driver was a cloaked figure with a hood drawn over his face to hide his features.

Holly approached the carriage, craning her neck to see inside. Pandora wriggled painfully on the ground to get a better look.

The carriage door opened. A passenger emerged. He was an older man wearing the clothing of an old-fashioned gentleman. He was handsome, with a lean, craggy face and intelligent eyes.

'*Holly!*' Pandora shrieked so hard her voice cracked at the effort. 'It's him, it's the wizard.'

Hieronymus Flak spoke quietly. He took Holly's hand and kissed it.

'Don't you touch her, you bastard.' Pandora fought to move her legs. She clawed at the rocks, but only loosed another layer of dirt that covered her again.

The wizard lifted Holly's chin so she looked into his eyes.

'No, don't look at him. Don't listen.' She seized a rock and hurled it, but missed by a good ten yards. Slade had a gun. Where was it? She grabbed the dead woman and turned her over, pawing at her corpse. The gun was gone, buried under tons of rubble.

Flak stroked her cheek. Touched her hair. Holly smiled shyly.

'It's a trick,' she screamed. 'Don't look at him.'

The wizard glanced in her direction. A sly smile spread across his lips. He whispered in Holly's ear.

Holly looked at her. Pandora's blood ran cold. There was no recognition in her eyes.

'Holly, please! Please, don't listen to him.'

Flak snapped his fingers to draw her attention. He spoke a brief command. Holly climbed into the carriage.

'No! No, please. Please-please-please no!' Pandora blubbered and sobbed.

Flak put a foot on the carriage steps. He looked back at her, laughed, and disappeared inside.

The driver snapped the reins and turned the carriage around. He spurred the horses into a gallop, and the carriage was away.

For a long time Pandora lay in the dirt, screaming. When the carriage was no more than a speck on the horizon there was a flash like distant lightning. The carriage was gone.

BLINK is the first installment in the Crystal Spire saga.

Visit
www.thecrystalspire.com
for updates on future releases.

Printed in Dunstable, United Kingdom

78988496R00265